Great Short Stories by African-American Writers

EDITED BY
CHRISTINE RUDISEL
AND
BOB BLAISDELL

❧

DOVER PUBLICATIONS, INC.
Mineola, New York

DOVER THRIFT EDITIONS

GENERAL EDITOR: MARY CAROLYN WALDREP
EDITOR OF THIS VOLUME: JANET B. KOPITO

Bibliographical Note

Great Short Stories by African-American Writers, first published by Dover Publications, Inc., in 2015, is a new anthology of stories reprinted from standard editions. Please see the Acknowledgments for additional publication information. An Introduction, a Bibliography, and Biographical Notes have been provided specially for this edition by Christine Rudisel and Bob Blaisdell.

International Standard Book Number

ISBN-13: 978-0-486-47139-6
ISBN-10: 0-486-47139-X

Manufactured in the United States by Courier Corporation
47139X01   2015
www.doverpublications.com

Contents

Introduction

These twenty-six great stories by famous, overlooked, and unknown authors are marvelously various: from the experimental to what might be thought of as traditional, from novelistic to impressionistic, from comic sketches to ponderous moments-of-truth. That they are all written by men and women of African descent does not limit their variety in mood, manner, or topic. As we travel through time with the stories, from Alice Ruth Moore (Dunbar-Nelson's) and Charles W. Chesnutt's to Kia Penso's and Edwidge Danticat's, we see characters struggling with themselves and with their relationships, with death and responsibility, and with identity and color. We sympathize as we watch hope and desire conflict with disappointment and frustration, Northern ways with Southern ways, truth with stereotype, and black with white. These stories also reveal how youth and innocence clash with age and experience, how religious beliefs wrestle with impulses and inclinations, and how street-smarts bump against formal education. More often than not, these stories remind us that reality and chaos shake up the peace and harmony we strive for in our lives.

We repeatedly encounter the fabled North, its nineteenth- and early twentieth-century promises of beauty, heavenliness, and freedom, in the mind and experiences for instance of Chesnutt's likable and distractible protagonist Uncle Wellington: "Giving full rein to his fancy, he saw in the North a land flowing with milk and honey,—a land peopled by noble men and beautiful women, among whom colored men and women moved with the ease and grace of acknowledged right." We also meet the North's real allure and dangers in several stories. In Rudolph Fisher's "The City of

Refuge," a hustler preys on "a baby jess in from the land o' cotton and so dumb he thinks ante-bellum's an old woman." In Zora Neale Hurston's "Muttsy," a young Southern migrant must rely on a shady character upon her arrival in Harlem: " 'Come on upstairs to yo' room—thass all right 'bout the price—we'll come to some 'greement tomorrow. Jes' go up an take off yo' things.'

"Pinkie put back the little rosy leather purse of another generation and followed Ma. She didn't like Ma—her smile resembled the smile of the Wolf in Red Riding Hood. Anyway back in Eatonville, Florida, 'ladies,' especially old ones, didn't put powder and paint on the face."

What are we to make of the anxiety coursing through several stories? Consider, for example, Breena Clarke's description of the neverending, timeless anxiety of motherhood in "The Drill": "She can feel the brush of the bird's wing—the bird who brushes his wing against the mountaintop and in an eternity will have worn it to a pebble. This tiny bird of worry who brushes his wing against the soul of a mother, and thus shortens her life by minutes, hours, days." Consider, too, in "Condemned House," Lucille Boehm's identification of the dangers, real and imagined, of living in an environment that threatens to come tumbling down: "You walked as far as your own stoop, down toward the end of the street. Across the way were the condemned houses. Half a block of them. They stood there sagging against each other like tired women in a subway jam—ready to collapse. Some of the windows were gaping black holes, where the boards had been chopped away for fire wood. An iron girder held two of the walls apart over a dark alleyway that looked like a missing tooth in the long row. In the end house was a big, jagged opening where the stoop used to be."

There are issues and moments certainly exclusive to the African-American experience, side-by-side with universal conditions, feelings, and situations. In "Mary Elizabeth," Jessie Fauset shows the life-altering effects of slavery on her heroine. In "Mammy," Dorothy West looks at the way racism causes a woman to remain silent about her identity. In the rueful "The Woman in the Window," Ramona Lowe sympathetically describes a mother who must explain to her children why she has taken a racially offensive, demeaning job and who must teach them how to respond to their peers: " '. . . 'N' if your little fren's asks questions, you tell'm, that's your mama all right. She's got t'work for a livin'.' She paused.

"N', son, doan you never let me see you run no more when a body say nigger. You turn roun' 'n' give'm such a thrashin' they woan never forget. Unnerstan'?'" In "Becky," a famous episode from *Cane,* Jean Toomer examines the consequences of intra- and inter-racial censure: "Becky was the white woman who had two Negro sons. She's dead; they've gone away. The pines whisper to Jesus. The Bible flaps its leaves with an aimless rustle on her mound."

All of the stories in part or in whole are necessarily about human conditions, such as Gertrude H. Dorsey Browne's "An Equation," in which the narrator declares that the "power of loving is not variable." Time versus timelessness is also a subject—how much America has changed and how little—revealed very well in such gems as Ralph Ellison's "Afternoon," wherein two boys rediscover their own neighborhood on a lazy summer day and casually remark on what we would call today "the white flight": "They walked over to the fence and looked into the yard. The earth beneath the trees was bare and moist. Up near the house the grass was short and neat. Flagstones leading out of the garage made a pattern in the grass.

"'White folks live here?'

"'Naw, colored. White folks moved out when we moved in the block,' Buster said."

It should be said that the historical literary background for many of the stories is the Harlem Renaissance, which took place, primarily, during the 1920s. Although scholars and cultural critics have debated about this era for years, questioning, for example, the terms *Harlem* and *Renaissance,* contesting the period's dates (anywhere from the first decade of the 1900s to the late 1930s), and even disputing the actuality of the period, most would not only acknowledge that the Harlem Renaissance existed, but would also define it as a time during which people of African descent produced a remarkable body of racially expressive art and letters. Many of these writers believed, as did the period's leadership, that their texts would help change the way black people were perceived and improve race relations. In *The New Negro* (1925), Alain Locke's definitive text of the period, it was posited that the creative production of New Negro artists would force a reappraisal of blacks by the entire society. To this end, a significant number of the period's writers published their work in *Opportunity: A Journal of Negro Life* and *The Crisis: A Record of the Darker Races,* the chief magazines of New Negro cultural, social, and political thought. *Opportunity*, organ of the National Urban League and edited by Charles S. Johnson, focused primarily on black culture. *The Crisis*, organ of the National Association for the Advancement of Colored People and edited by W. E. B. Du Bois, focused on black politics. Both magazines reached national and interracial audiences and introduced their readers to emerging black writers through well-publicized literary contests.

In addition to *Opportunity* and *The Crisis*, the period's writers published their work in *The Messenger*, founded by A. Phillip Randolph and Chandler Owen. Although *The Messenger* initially ranked politics and socialism over literature, it later devoted many of its pages to poems, short stories, plays and essays authored by black writers. A few of the period's writers published their work in radical and/or left wing periodicals aimed mainly at white audiences. Jean Toomer and Claude McKay, for example, were published in Max Eastman's *The Liberator*, a magazine that "st[ood] for very definite progressive principles in politics and labor unionism as well as freedom in art and literature."[1] Equally important to the writers of the Harlem Renaissance were black literary journals such as *The Saturday Evening Quill*, an annual magazine published by the members of Boston's Saturday Evening Quill Club and the short-lived *Fire!!*, a magazine "devoted to the younger, Negro artists"[2] and produced solely to celebrate black artistry. Well-known writers such as Zora Neale Hurston and Langston Hughes saw *Fire!!* as their declaration of freedom from propaganda and the influence of civil rights organizations. These progressive, revolutionary, and/or race-centered periodicals played important roles in spotlighting the evolution of black cultural production across the country, which is evidenced by the number of stories in this collection that were originally published in their pages.

This anthology's stories are arranged chronologically by the date of their publication. Some of the fine writers of the first two decades of the twentieth century, particularly women, who published stories in the African-American magazines of their time have slipped into obscurity. Unfortunately, all knowledge of these authors beyond the fact of their having written those stories has

---

1. From "Three Ways You Can Help *The Liberator* Become a Better Magazine," Advertisement, *Liberator* April 1923: 35.
2. From the front cover of *Fire!!* November 1926.

disappeared. The short biographical notes in the back of this anthology and the bibliography will, we hope, lead the curious to further reading and investigation of the authors and the captivating genre of short fiction.

Christine M. Rudisel and Bob Blaisdell
Kingsborough Community College
The City University of New York

Acknowledgments

Great Short Stories by African-American Writers

A CARNIVAL JANGLE

Alice Ruth Moore (Dunbar-Nelson)

(from *Violets and Other Tales*, 1895)

THERE IS A merry jangle of bells in the air, an all-pervading sense of jester's noise, and the flaunting vividness of royal colors; the streets swarm with humanity,—humanity in all shapes, manners, forms,—laughing, pushing, jostling, crowding, a mass of men and women and children, as varied and as assorted in their several individual peculiarities as ever a crowd that gathered in one locality since the days of Babel.

It is Carnival in New Orleans; a brilliant Tuesday in February, when the very air effervesces an ozone intensely exhilarating—of a nature half spring, half winter—to make one long to cut capers. The buildings are a blazing mass of royal purple and golden yellow, and national flags, bunting and decorations that laugh in the glint of the Midas sun. The streets a crush of jesters and maskers, Jim Crows and clowns, ballet girls and Mephistos, Indians and monkeys; of wild and sudden flashes of music, of glittering pageants and comic ones, of befeathered and belled horses. A madding dream of color and melody and fantasy gone wild in an effervescent bubble of beauty that shifts and changes and passes kaleidoscope-like before the bewildered eye.

A bevy of bright-eyed girls and boys of that uncertainty of age that hovers between childhood and maturity, were moving down Canal Street when there was a sudden jostle with another crowd meeting them. For a minute there was a deafening clamor of laughter, cracking of whips, which all maskers carry, jingle and clatter of carnival bells, and the masked and unmasked extricated

1

themselves and moved from each other's paths. But in the confusion a tall Prince of Darkness had whispered to one of the girls in the unmasked crowd: "You'd better come with us, Flo, you're wasting time in that tame gang. Slip off, they'll never miss you; we'll get you a rig, and show you what life is."

And so it happened that when a half hour passed, and the bright-eyed bevy missed Flo and couldn't find her, wisely giving up the search at last, that she, the quietest and most bashful of the lot, was being initiated into the mysteries of "what life is."

Down Bourbon Street and on Toulouse and St. Peter Streets[1] there are quaint little old-world places, where one may be disguised effectually for a tiny consideration. Thither guided by the shapely Mephisto, and guarded by the team of jockeys and ballet girls, tripped Flo. Into one of the lowest-ceiled, dingiest and most ancient-looking of these disguise shops they stopped.

"A disguise for this demoiselle," announced Mephisto to the woman who met them. She was small and wizened and old, with yellow, flabby jaws and neck like the throat of an alligator, and straight, white hair that stood from her head uncannily stiff.

"But the demoiselle wishes to appear a boy, *un petit garçon*?"[2] she inquired, gazing eagerly at Flo's long, slender frame. Her voice was old and thin, like the high quavering of an imperfect tuning fork, and her eyes were sharp as talons in their grasping glance.

"Mademoiselle does not wish such a costume," gruffly responded Mephisto.

"*Ma foi,*[3] there is no other," said the ancient, shrugging her shoulders. "But one is left now, mademoiselle would make a fine troubadour."

"Flo," said Mephisto, "it's a daredevil scheme, try it; no one will ever know it but us, and we'll die before we tell. Besides, we must; it's late, and you couldn't find your crowd."

And that was why you might have seen a Mephisto and a slender troubadour of lovely form, with mandolin flung across his shoulder, followed by a bevy of jockeys and ballet girls, laughing and singing as they swept down Rampart Street.

When the flash and glare and brilliancy of Canal Street have palled upon the tired eye, and it is yet too soon to go home, and

---

1. Bourbon Street and on Toulouse and St. Peter Streets: Famous streets in the French Quarter of New Orleans.

2. *un petit garçon*; French: a little boy.

3. *Ma foi*: A French exclamation: My faith; indeed.

to such a prosaic thing as dinner, and one still wishes for novelty, then it is wise to go in the lower districts. Fantasy and fancy and grotesqueness in the costuming and behavior of the maskers run wild. Such dances and whoops and leaps as these hideous Indians and devils do indulge in; such wild curvetings and great walks. And in the open squares, where whole groups do congregate, it is wonderfully amusing. Then, too, there is a ball in every available hall, a delirious ball, where one may dance all day for ten cents; dance and grow mad for joy, and never know who were your companions, and be yourself unknown. And in the exhilaration of the day, one walks miles and miles, and dances and curvets, and the fatigue is never felt.

In Washington Square, away down where Royal Street empties its stream of children and men into the broad channel of Elysian Fields Avenue, there was a perfect Indian dance. With a little imagination one might have willed away the vision of the surrounding houses and fancied one's self again in the forest, where the natives were holding a sacred riot. The square was filled with spectators, masked and unmasked. It was amusing to watch these mimic Redmen, they seemed so fierce and earnest.

Suddenly one chief touched another on the elbow. "See that Mephisto and troubadour over there?" he whispered huskily.

"Yes, who are they?"

"I don't know the devil," responded the other quietly, "but I'd know that other form anywhere. It's Leon, see? I know those white hands like a woman's and that restless head. Ha!"

"But there may be a mistake."

"No. I'd know that one anywhere; I feel it's him. I'll pay him now. Ah, sweetheart, you've waited long, but you shall feast now!" He was caressing something long, and lithe, and glittering beneath his blanket.

In a masked dance it is easy to give a death-blow between the shoulders. Two crowds meet and laugh and shout and mingle almost inextricably, and if a shriek of pain should arise, it is not noticed in the din, and when they part, if one should stagger and fall bleeding to the ground, who can tell who has given the blow? There is naught but an unknown stiletto on the ground, the crowd has dispersed, and masks tell no tales anyway. There is murder, but by whom? for what? *Quien sabe?*[4]

---

4. *Quien sabe?*: Spanish: Who knows?

And that is how it happened on Carnival night, in the last mad moments of Rex's reign, a broken-hearted woman sat gazing wide-eyed and mute at a horrible something that lay across the bed. Outside the long sweet march music of many bands floated in in mockery, and the flash of rockets and Bengal lights illumined the dead, white face of the girl troubadour.

UNCLE WELLINGTON'S WIVES

Charles W. Chesnutt

(from *The Wife of His Youth and Other Stories of the Color Line,* 1899)

I.

UNCLE WELLINGTON BRABOY was so deeply absorbed in thought as he walked slowly homeward from the weekly meeting of the Union League, that he let his pipe go out, a fact of which he remained oblivious until he had reached the little frame house in the suburbs of Patesville, where he lived with aunt Milly, his wife. On this particular occasion the club had been addressed by a visiting brother from the North, Professor Patterson, a tall, well-formed mulatto, who wore a perfectly fitting suit of broadcloth, a shiny silk hat, and linen of dazzling whiteness,—in short, a gentleman of such distinguished appearance that the doors and windows of the offices and stores on Front Street were filled with curious observers as he passed through that thoroughfare in the early part of the day. This polished stranger was a traveling organizer of Masonic lodges, but he also claimed to be a high officer in the Union League, and had been invited to lecture before the local chapter of that organization at Patesville.

The lecture had been largely attended, and uncle Wellington Braboy had occupied a seat just in front of the platform. The subject of the lecture was "The Mental, Moral, Physical, Political, Social, and Financial Improvement of the Negro Race in America," a theme much dwelt upon, with slight variations, by colored orators. For to this struggling people, then as now, the problem of their

uncertain present and their doubtful future was the chief concern of
life. The period was the hopeful one. The Federal Government
retained some vestige of authority in the South, and the newly
emancipated race cherished the delusion that under the Constitution,
that enduring rock on which our liberties are founded, and under
the equal laws it purported to guarantee, they would enter upon the
era of freedom and opportunity which their Northern friends had
inaugurated with such solemn sanctions. The speaker pictured in
eloquent language the state of ideal equality and happiness enjoyed
by colored people at the North: how they sent their children to
school with the white children; how they sat by white people in the
churches and theatres, ate with them in the public restaurants, and
buried their dead in the same cemeteries. The professor waxed eloquent with the development of his theme, and, as a finishing touch
to an alluring picture, assured the excited audience that the inter-
marriage of the races was common, and that he himself had espoused
a white woman.

Uncle Wellington Braboy was a deeply interested listener. He
had heard something of these facts before, but his information had
always come in such vague and questionable shape that he had paid
little attention to it. He knew that the Yankees had freed the
slaves, and that runaway negroes had always gone to the North to
seek liberty; any such equality, however, as the visiting brother had
depicted, was more than uncle Wellington had ever conceived as
actually existing anywhere in the world. At first he felt inclined to
doubt the truth of the speaker's statements; but the cut of his
clothes, the eloquence of his language, and the flowing length of
his whiskers, were so far superior to anything uncle Wellington
had ever met among the colored people of his native State, that he
felt irresistibly impelled to the conviction that nothing less than the
advantages claimed for the North by the visiting brother could
have produced such an exquisite flower of civilization. Any lingering doubts uncle Wellington may have felt were entirely dispelled
by the courtly bow and cordial grasp of the hand with which the
visiting brother acknowledged the congratulations showered upon
him by the audience at the close of his address.

The more uncle Wellington's mind dwelt upon the professor's
speech, the more attractive seemed the picture of Northern life
presented. Uncle Wellington possessed in large measure the imaginative faculty so freely bestowed by nature upon the race from
which the darker half of his blood was drawn. He had indulged in

occasional day-dreams of an ideal state of social equality, but his wildest flights of fancy had never located it nearer than heaven, and he had felt some misgivings about its practical working even there. Its desirability he had never doubted, and the speech of the evening before had given a local habitation and a name to the forms his imagination had bodied forth. Giving full rein to his fancy, he saw in the North a land flowing with milk and honey,—a land peopled by noble men and beautiful women, among whom colored men and women moved with the ease and grace of acknowledged right. Then he placed himself in the foreground of the picture. What a fine figure he would have made in the world if he had been born at the free North! He imagined himself dressed like the professor, and passing the contribution-box in a white church; and most pleasant of his dreams, and the hardest to realize as possible, was that of the gracious white lady he might have called wife. Uncle Wellington was a mulatto, and his features were those of his white father, though tinged with the hue of his mother's race; and as he lifted the kerosene lamp at evening, and took a long look at his image in the little mirror over the mantelpiece, he said to himself that he was a very good-looking man, and could have adorned a much higher sphere in life than that in which the accident of birth had placed him. He fell asleep and dreamed that he lived in a two-story brick house, with a spacious flower garden in front, the whole inclosed by a high iron fence; that he kept a carriage and servants, and never did a stroke of work. This was the highest style of living in Patesville, and he could conceive of nothing finer.

Uncle Wellington slept later than usual the next morning, and the sunlight was pouring in at the open window of the bedroom, when his dreams were interrupted by the voice of his wife, in tones meant to be harsh, but which no ordinary degree of passion could rob of their native unctuousness.

"Git up f'm dere, you lazy, good-fuh-nuffin' nigger! Is you gwine ter sleep all de mawnin'? I's ti'ed er dis yer runnin' 'roun' all night an' den sleepin' all day. You won't git dat tater patch hoed ovuh ter-day 'less'n you git up f'm dere an' git at it."

Uncle Wellington rolled over, yawned cavernously, stretched himself, and with a muttered protest got out of bed and put on his clothes. Aunt Milly had prepared a smoking breakfast of hominy and fried bacon, the odor of which was very grateful to his nostrils.

"Is breakfus' done ready?" he inquired, tentatively, as he came into the kitchen and glanced at the table.

"No, it ain't ready, an' 't ain't gwine ter be ready 'tel you tote dat wood an' water in," replied aunt Milly severely, as she poured two teacups of boiling water on two tablespoonfuls of ground coffee.

Uncle Wellington went down to the spring and got a pail of water, after which he brought in some oak logs for the fire place and some lightwood for kindling. Then he drew a chair towards the table and started to sit down.

"Wonduh what's de matter wid you dis mawnin' anyhow," remarked aunt Milly. "You must 'a' be'n up ter some devilment las' night, fer yo' recommemb'ance is so po' dat you fus' fergit ter git up, an' den fergit ter wash yo' face an' hands fo' you set down ter de table. I don' 'low nobody ter eat at my table dat a-way."

"I don' see no use 'n washin' 'em so much," replied Wellington wearily. "Dey gits dirty ag'in right off, an' den you got ter wash 'em ovuh ag'in; it's jes' pilin' up wuk what don' fetch in nuffin'. De dirt don' show nohow, 'n' I don' see no advantage in bein' black, ef you got to keep on washin' yo' face 'n' han's jes' lack w'ite folks." He nevertheless performed his ablutions in a perfunctory way, and resumed his seat at the breakfast-table.

"Ole 'oman," he asked, after the edge of his appetite had been taken off, "how would you lack ter live at de Norf?"

"I dunno nuffin' 'bout de Norf," replied aunt Milly. "It's hard 'nuff ter git erlong heah, whar we knows all erbout it."

"De brother what 'dressed de meetin' las' night say dat de wages at de Norf is twicet ez big ez dey is heah."

"You could make a sight mo' wages heah ef you'd 'ten' ter yo' wuk better," replied aunt Milly.

Uncle Wellington ignored this personality, and continued, "An' he say de cullud folks got all de privileges er de w'ite folks,—dat dey chillen goes ter school tergedder, dat dey sets on same seats in chu'ch, an' sarves on jury, 'n' rides on de kyars an' steamboats wid de w'ite folks, an' eats at de fus' table."

"Dat 'u'd suit you," chuckled aunt Milly, "an' you 'd stay dere fer de secon' table, too. How dis man know 'bout all dis yer foo-lis'ness?" she asked incredulously.

"He come f'm de Norf," said uncle Wellington, "an' he 'speu-nced it all hisse'f."

"Well, he can't make me b'lieve it," she rejoined, with a shake of her head.

"An' you would n' lack ter go up dere an' 'joy all dese privileges?" asked uncle Wellington, with some degree of earnestness.

The old woman laughed until her sides shook. "Who gwine ter take me up dere?" she inquired.

"You got de money yo'se'f."

"I ain' got no money fer ter was'e," she replied shortly, becoming serious at once; and with that the subject was dropped.

Uncle Wellington pulled a hoe from under the house, and took his way wearily to the potato patch. He did not feel like working, but aunt Milly was the undisputed head of the establishment, and he did not dare to openly neglect his work.

In fact, he regarded work at any time as a disagreeable necessity to be avoided as much as possible.

His wife was cast in a different mould. Externally she would have impressed the casual observer as a neat, well-preserved, and good-looking black woman, of middle age, every curve of whose ample figure—and her figure was all curves—was suggestive of repose. So far from being indolent, or even deliberate in her movements, she was the most active and energetic woman in the town. She went through the physical exercises of a prayer-meeting with astonishing vigor. It was exhilarating to see her wash a shirt, and a study to watch her do it up. A quick jerk shook out the dampened garment; one pass of her ample palm spread it over the ironing-board, and a few well-directed strokes with the iron accomplished what would have occupied the ordinary laundress for half an hour.

To this uncommon, and in uncle Wellington's opinion unnecessary and unnatural activity, his own habits were a steady protest. If aunt Milly had been willing to support him in idleness, he would have acquiesced without a murmur in her habits of industry. This she would not do, and, moreover, insisted on his working at least half the time. If she had invested the proceeds of her labor in rich food and fine clothing, he might have endured it better; but to her passion for work was added a most detestable thrift. She absolutely refused to pay for Wellington's clothes, and required him to furnish a certain proportion of the family supplies. Her savings were carefully put by, and with them she had bought and paid for the modest cottage which she and her husband occupied. Under her careful hand it was always neat and clean; in summer the little yard was gay with bright-colored flowers, and woe to the heedless pickaninny who should stray into her yard and pluck a rose or a verbena! In a stout oaken chest under her bed she kept a capacious stocking, into which flowed a steady stream of fractional currency. She carried the key to this chest in her pocket, a proceeding regarded by uncle Wellington with no little disfavor. He was of the opinion—an opinion he would not have dared to assert in her presence—that his wife's earnings were his own property; and he looked upon this stocking as a drunkard's wife might regard the saloon which absorbed her husband's wages.

Uncle Wellington hurried over the potato patch on the morning of the conversation above recorded, and as soon as he saw aunt Milly go away with a basket of clothes on her head, returned to the house, put on his coat, and went uptown.

He directed his steps to a small frame building fronting on the main street of the village, at a point where the street was intersected by one of the several creeks meandering through the town, cooling the air, providing numerous swimming-holes for the amphibious small boy, and furnishing water-power for grist-mills and saw-mills. The rear of the building rested on long brick pillars, built up from the bottom of the steep bank of the creek, while the front was level with the street. This was the office of Mr. Matthew Wright, the sole representative of the colored race at the bar of Chinquapin County. Mr. Wright came of an "old issue" free colored family, in which, though the Negro blood was present in an attenuated strain, a line of free ancestry could be traced beyond the Revolutionary War. He had enjoyed exceptional opportunities, and enjoyed the distinction of being the first, and for a long time the only colored lawyer in North Carolina. His services were frequently called into requisition by impecunious people of his own race; when they had money they went to white lawyers, who, they shrewdly conjectured, would have more influence with judge or jury than a colored lawyer, however able.

Uncle Wellington found Mr. Wright in his office. Having inquired after the health of the lawyer's family and all his relations in detail, uncle Wellington asked for a professional opinion.

"Mistah Wright, ef a man's wife got money, whose money is dat befo' de law—his'n er her'n?"

The lawyer put on his professional air, and replied:——

"Under the common law, which in default of special legislative enactment is the law of North Carolina, the personal property of the wife belongs to her husband."

"But dat don' jes' tech de p'int, suh. I wuz axin' 'bout money."

"You see, uncle Wellington, your education has not rendered you familiar with legal phraseology. The term 'personal property' or 'estate' embraces, according to Blackstone, all property other than land, and therefore includes money. Any money a man's wife has is his, constructively, and will be recognized as his actually, as soon as he can secure possession of it."

"Dat is ter say, suh—my eddication don' quite 'low me ter understan' dat—dat is ter say"—

"That is to say, it's yours when you get it. It isn't yours so that the law will help you get it; but on the other hand, when you once lay your hands on it, it is yours so that the law won't take it away from you."

Uncle Wellington nodded to express his full comprehension of the law as expounded by Mr. Wright, but scratched his head in a way that expressed some disappointment. The law seemed to wobble. Instead of enabling him to stand up fearlessly and demand his own, it threw him back upon his own efforts; and the prospect of his being able to overpower or outwit aunt Milly by any ordinary means was very poor.

He did not leave the office, but hung around awhile as though there were something further he wished to speak about. Finally, after some discursive remarks about the crops and politics, he asked, in an offhand, disinterested manner, as though the thought had just occurred to him:——

"Mistah Wright, w'ile's we're talkin' 'bout law matters, what do it cos' ter git a defoce?"

"That depends upon circumstances. It isn't altogether a matter of expense. Have you and aunt Milly been having trouble?"

"Oh no, suh; I was jes' a-wond'rin'."

"You see," continued the lawyer, who was fond of talking, and had nothing else to do for the moment, "a divorce is not an easy thing to get in this State under any circumstances. It used to be the law that divorce could be granted only by special act of the legislature; and it is but recently that the subject has been relegated to the jurisdiction of the courts."

Uncle Wellington understood a part of this, but the answer had not been exactly to the point in his mind.

"S'pos'n', den, jes' fer de argyment, me an' my ole 'oman sh'd fall out en wanter separate, how could I git a defoce?"

"That would depend on what you quarreled about. It's pretty hard work to answer general questions in a particular way. If you merely wished to separate, it wouldn't be necessary to get a divorce; but if you should want to marry again, you would have to be divorced, or else you would be guilty of bigamy, and could be sent to the penitentiary. But, by the way, uncle Wellington, when were you married?"

"I got married 'fo' de wah, when I was livin' down on Rockfish Creek."

"When you were in slavery?"

"Yas, suh."

"Did you have your marriage registered after the surrender?"

"No, suh; never knowed nuffin' 'bout dat."

After the war, in North Carolina and other States, the freed people who had sustained to each other the relation of husband and wife as it existed among slaves, were required by law to register their consent to continue in the marriage relation. By this simple expedient their former marriages of convenience received the sanction of law, and their children the seal of legitimacy. In many cases, however, where the parties lived in districts remote from the larger towns, the ceremony was neglected, or never heard of by the freedmen.

"Well," said the lawyer, "if that is the case, and you and aunt Milly should disagree, it wouldn't be necessary for you to get a divorce, even if you should want to marry again. You were never legally married."

"So Milly ain't my lawful wife, den?"

"She may be your wife in one sense of the word, but not in such a sense as to render you liable to punishment for bigamy if you should marry another woman. But I hope you will never want to do anything of the kind, for you have a very good wife now."

Uncle Wellington went away thoughtfully, but with a feeling of unaccustomed lightness and freedom. He had not felt so free since the memorable day when he had first heard of the Emancipation Proclamation. On leaving the lawyer's office, he called at the workshop of one of his friends, Peter Williams, a shoemaker by trade, who had a brother living in Ohio.

"Is you hearn f'm Sam lately?" uncle Wellington inquired, after the conversation had drifted through the usual generalities.

"His mammy got er letter f'm 'im las' week; he's livin' in de town er Groveland now."

"How's he gittin' on?"

"He says he gittin' on monst'us well. He 'low ez how he make five dollars a day w'ite-washin', an' have all he kin do."

The shoemaker related various details of his brother's prosperity, and uncle Wellington returned home in a very thoughtful mood, revolving in his mind a plan of future action. This plan had been vaguely assuming form ever since the professor's lecture, and the events of the morning had brought out the detail in bold relief.

Two days after the conversation with the shoemaker, aunt Milly went, in the afternoon, to visit a sister of hers who lived several miles out in the country. During her absence, which lasted until nightfall, uncle Wellington went uptown and purchased a cheap oilcloth valise from a shrewd son of Israel, who had penetrated to this locality with a stock of notions and cheap clothing. Uncle Wellington had his purchase done up in brown paper, and took the parcel under his arm. Arrived at home he unwrapped the valise, and thrust into its capacious jaws his best suit of clothes, some underwear, and a few other small articles for personal use and adornment. Then he carried the valise out into the yard, and, first looking cautiously around to see if there was any one in sight, concealed it in a clump of bushes in a corner of the yard.

It may be inferred from this proceeding that uncle Wellington was preparing for a step of some consequence. In fact, he had fully made up his mind to go to the North; but he still lacked the most important requisite for traveling with comfort, namely, the money to pay his expenses. The idea of tramping the distance which separated him from the promised land of liberty and equality had never occurred to him. When a slave, he had several times been importuned by fellow servants to join them in the attempt to escape from bondage, but he had never wanted his freedom badly enough to walk a thousand miles for it; if he could have gone to Canada by stage-coach, or by rail, or on horseback, with stops for regular meals, he would probably have undertaken the trip. The funds he now needed for his journey were in aunt Milly's chest. He had thought a great deal about his right to this money. It was his wife's savings, and he had never dared to dispute, openly, her right to exercise exclusive control over what she earned; but the lawyer had assured him of his right to the money, of which he was already constructively in possession, and he had therefore determined to possess himself actually of the coveted stocking. It was impracticable for him to get the key of the chest. Aunt Milly kept it in her pocket by day and under her pillow at night. She was a light sleeper, and, if not awakened by the abstraction of the key, would certainly have been disturbed by the unlocking of the chest.

But one alternative remained, and that was to break open the chest in her absence.

There was a revival in progress at the colored Methodist church. Aunt Milly was as energetic in her religion as in other respects, and had not missed a single one of the meetings. She returned at nightfall from her visit to the country and prepared a frugal supper. Uncle Wellington did not eat as heartily as usual. Aunt Milly perceived his want of appetite, and spoke of it. He explained it by saying that he did not feel very well.

"Is you gwine ter chu'ch ter-night?" inquired his wife.

"I reckon I'll stay home an' go ter bed," he replied. "I ain't be'n feelin' well dis evenin', an' I 'spec' I better git a good night's res'."

"Well, you kin stay ef you mineter. Good preachin' 'u'd make you feel better, but ef you ain't gwine, don' fergit ter tote in some wood an' lighterd 'fo' you go ter bed. De moon is shinin' bright, an' you can't have no 'scuse 'bout not bein' able ter see."

Uncle Wellington followed her out to the gate, and watched her receding form until it disappeared in the distance. Then he re-entered the house with a quick step, and taking a hatchet from a corner of the room, drew the chest from under the bed. As he applied the hatchet to the fastenings, a thought struck him, and by the flickering light of the pine-knot blazing on the hearth, a look of hesitation might have been seen to take the place of the determined expression his face had worn up to that time. He had argued himself into the belief that his present action was lawful and justifiable. Though this conviction had not prevented him from trembling in every limb, as though he were committing a mere vulgar theft, it had still nerved him to the deed. Now even his moral courage began to weaken. The lawyer had told him that his wife's property was his own; in taking it he was therefore only exercising his lawful right. But at the point of breaking open the chest, it occurred to him that he was taking this money in order to get away from aunt Milly, and that he justified his desertion of her by the lawyer's opinion that she was not his lawful wife. If she was not his wife, then he had no right to take the money; if she was his wife, he had no right to desert her, and would certainly have no right to marry another woman. His scheme was about to go to shipwreck on this rock, when another idea occurred to him.

"De lawyer say dat in one sense er de word de ole 'oman is my wife, an' in anudder sense er de word she ain't my wife. Ef I goes ter de Norf an' marry a w'ite 'oman, I ain't commit no brigamy, 'caze in dat sense er de word she ain't my wife; but ef I takes dis money, I ain't stealin' it, 'caze in dat sense er de word she is my wife. Dat 'splains all de trouble away."

Having reached this ingenious conclusion, uncle Wellington applied the hatchet vigorously, soon loosened the fastenings of the chest, and with trembling hands extracted from its depths a capacious blue cotton stocking. He emptied the stocking on the table. His first impulse was to take the whole, but again there arose in his mind a doubt—a very obtrusive, unreasonable doubt, but a doubt, nevertheless—of the absolute rectitude of his conduct; and after a moment's hesitation he hurriedly counted the money—it was in bills of small denominations—and found it to be about two hundred and fifty dollars. He then divided it into two piles of one hundred and twenty-five dollars each. He put one pile into his pocket, returned the remainder to the stocking, and replaced it where he had found it. He then closed the chest and shoved it under the bed. After having arranged the fire so that it could safely be left burning, he took a last look around the room, and went out into the moonlight, locking the door behind him, and hanging the key on a nail in the wall, where his wife would be likely to look for it. He then secured his valise from behind the bushes, and left the yard. As he passed by the wood-pile, he said to himself:——

"Well, I declar' ef I ain't done fergot ter tote in dat lighterd; I reckon de ole 'oman'll ha' ter fetch it in herse'f dis time."

He hastened through the quiet streets, avoiding the few people who were abroad at that hour, and soon reached the railroad station, from which a North-bound train left at nine o'clock. He went around to the dark side of the train, and climbed into a second-class car, where he shrank into the darkest corner and turned his face away from the dim light of the single dirty lamp. There were no passengers in the car except one or two sleepy negroes, who had got on at some other station, and a white man who had gone into the car to smoke, accompanied by a gigantic bloodhound.

Finally the train crept out of the station. From the window uncle Wellington looked out upon the familiar cabins and turpentine stills, the new barrel factory, the brickyard where he had once worked for some time; and as the train rattled through the outskirts of the town, he saw gleaming in the moonlight the white headstones of the colored cemetery where his only daughter had been buried several years before.

Presently the conductor came around. Uncle Wellington had not bought a ticket, and the conductor collected a cash fare. He was not acquainted with uncle Wellington, but had just had a drink at the saloon near the depot, and felt at peace with all mankind.

"Where are you going, uncle?" he inquired carelessly.

Uncle Wellington's face assumed the ashen hue which does duty for pallor in dusky countenances, and his knees began to tremble. Controlling his voice as well as he could, he replied that he was going up to Jonesboro, the terminus of the railroad, to work for a gentleman at that place. He felt immensely relieved when the conductor pocketed the fare, picked up his lantern, and moved away. It was very unphilosophical and very absurd that a man who was only doing right should feel like a thief, shrink from the sight of other people, and lie instinctively. Fine distinctions were not in uncle Wellington's line, but he was struck by the unreasonableness of his feelings, and still more by the discomfort they caused him. By and by, however, the motion of the train made him drowsy; his thoughts all ran together in confusion; and he fell asleep with his head on his valise, and one hand in his pocket, clasped tightly around the roll of money.

II.

The train from Pittsburgh drew into the Union Depot at Groveland, Ohio, one morning in the spring of 187–, with bell ringing and engine puffing; and from a smoking-car emerged the form of uncle Wellington Braboy, a little dusty and travel-stained, and with a sleepy look about his eyes. He mingled in the crowd, and, valise in hand, moved toward the main exit from the depot. There were several tracks to be crossed, and more than once a watchman snatched him out of the way of a baggage-truck, or a train backing into the depot. He at length reached the door, beyond which, and as near as the regulations would permit, stood a number of hackmen, vociferously soliciting patronage. One of them, a colored man, soon secured several passengers. As he closed the door after the last one he turned to uncle Wellington, who stood near him on the sidewalk, looking about irresolutely.

"Is you goin' uptown?" asked the hackman, as he prepared to mount the box.

"Yas, suh."

"I'll take you up fo' a quahtah, ef you want ter git up here an' ride on de box wid me."

Uncle Wellington accepted the offer and mounted the box. The hackman whipped up his horses, the carriage climbed the steep hill leading up to the town, and the passengers inside were soon deposited at their hotels.

"Whereabouts do you want to go?" asked the hackman of uncle Wellington, when the carriage was emptied of its last passengers.

"I want ter go ter Brer Sam Williams's," said Wellington.

"What's his street an' number?"

Uncle Wellington did not know the street and number, and the hackman had to explain to him the mystery of numbered houses, to which he was a total stranger.

"Where is he from?" asked the hackman, "and what is his business?"

"He is f'm Norf Ca'lina," replied uncle Wellington, "an' makes his livin' w'itewashin'."

"I reckon I knows de man," said the hackman. "I 'spec' he's changed his name. De man I knows is name' Johnson. He b'longs ter my chu'ch. I'm gwine out dat way ter git a passenger fer de ten o'clock train, an I'll take you by dere."

They followed one of the least handsome streets of the city for more than a mile, turned into a cross street, and drew up before a small frame house, from the front of which a sign, painted in white upon a black background, announced to the reading public, in letters inclined to each other at various angles, that whitewashing and kalsomining were "dun" there. A knock at the door brought out a slatternly looking colored woman. She had evidently been disturbed at her toilet, for she held a comb in one hand, and the hair on one side of her head stood out loosely, while on the other side it was braided close to her head. She called her husband, who proved to be the Patesville shoemaker's brother. The hackman introduced the traveler, whose name he had learned on the way out, collected his quarter, and drove away.

Mr. Johnson, the shoemaker's brother, welcomed uncle Wellington to Groveland, and listened with eager delight to the news of the old town, from which he himself had run away many years before, and followed the North Star to Groveland. He had changed his name from "Williams" to "Johnson," on account of the Fugitive Slave Law, which, at the time of his escape from bondage, had rendered it advisable for runaway slaves to court obscurity. After the war he had retained the adopted name. Mrs. Johnson prepared breakfast for her guest, who ate it with an appetite sharpened by his journey. After breakfast he went to bed, and slept until late in the afternoon.

After supper Mr. Johnson took uncle Wellington to visit some of the neighbors who had come from North Carolina before the war. They all expressed much pleasure at meeting "Mr. Braboy," a title which at first sounded a little odd to uncle Wellington. At home he had been "Wellin'ton," "Brer Wellin'ton," or "uncle Wellin'ton"; it was a novel experience to be called "Mister," and he set it down, with secret satisfaction, as one of the first fruits of Northern liberty.

"Would you lack ter look 'roun' de town a little?" asked Mr. Johnson at breakfast next morning. "I ain' got no job dis mawnin', an' I kin show you some er de sights."

Uncle Wellington acquiesced in this arrangement, and they walked up to the corner to the street-car line. In a few moments a car passed. Mr. Johnson jumped on the moving car, and uncle Wellington followed his example, at the risk of life or limb, as it was his first experience of street cars.

There was only one vacant seat in the car and that was between two white women in the forward end. Mr. Johnson motioned to the seat, but Wellington shrank from walking between those two rows of white people, to say nothing of sitting between the two women, so he remained standing in the rear part of the car. A moment later, as the car rounded a short curve, he was pitched sidewise into the lap of a stout woman magnificently attired in a ruffled blue calico gown. The lady colored up, and uncle Wellington, as he struggled to his feet amid the laughter of the passengers, was absolutely helpless with embarrassment, until the conductor came up behind him and pushed him toward the vacant place.

"Sit down, will you," he said; and before uncle Wellington could collect himself, he was seated between the two white women. Everybody in the car seemed to be looking at him. But he came to the conclusion, after he had pulled himself together and reflected a few moments, that he would find this method of locomotion pleasanter when he got used to it, and then he could score one more glorious privilege gained by his change of residence.

They got off at the public square, in the heart of the city, where there were flowers and statues, and fountains playing. Mr. Johnson pointed out the court-house, the post-office, the jail, and other public buildings fronting on the square. They visited the market near by, and from an elevated point, looked down upon the extensive lumber yards and factories that were the chief sources of the city's prosperity. Beyond these they could see the fleet of ships that lined the coal and iron ore docks of the harbor. Mr. Johnson, who was quite a fluent talker, enlarged upon the wealth and prosperity of the city; and Wellington, who had never before been in a town of more than three thousand inhabitants, manifested sufficient interest and wonder to satisfy the most exacting *cicerone*.[1] They called at the office of a colored lawyer and member of the legislature, formerly from North Carolina, who, scenting a new constituent and a possible client, greeted the stranger warmly, and in flowing speech pointed out the superior advantages of life at the North, citing himself as an illustration of the possibilities of life in a country really free. As they wended their way homeward to dinner uncle Wellington, with quickened pulse and rising hopes, felt that this was indeed the promised land, and that it must be flowing with milk and honey.

Uncle Wellington remained at the residence of Mr. Johnson for several weeks before making any effort to find employment. He spent this period in looking about the city. The most commonplace things possessed for him the charm of novelty, and he had come prepared to admire. Shortly after his arrival, he had offered to pay for his board, intimating at the same time that he had plenty of money. Mr. Johnson declined to accept anything from him for board, and expressed himself as being only too proud to have Mr. Braboy remain in the house on the footing of an honored guest, until he had settled himself. He lightened in some degree, however, the burden of obligation under which a prolonged stay on these terms would have placed his guest, by soliciting from the latter occasional small loans, until uncle Wellington's roll of money began to lose its plumpness, and with an empty pocket staring him in the face, he felt the necessity of finding something to do.

During his residence in the city he had met several times his first acquaintance, Mr. Peterson, the hackman, who from time to time inquired how he was getting along. On one of these occasions Wellington mentioned his willingness to accept employment. As good luck would have it, Mr. Peterson knew of a vacant situation.

---

1. *cicerone*: Italian: a guide.

He had formerly been coachman for a wealthy gentleman residing on Oakwood Avenue, but had resigned the situation to go into business for himself. His place had been filled by an Irishman, who had just been discharged for drunkenness, and the gentleman that very day had sent word to Mr. Peterson, asking him if he could recommend a competent and trustworthy coachman.

"Does you know anything erbout hosses?" asked Mr. Peterson.

"Yas, indeed, I does," said Wellington. "I wuz raise' 'mongs' hosses."

"I tol' my ole boss I'd look out fer a man, an' ef you reckon you kin fill de 'quirements er de situation, I'll take yo' roun' dere termorrer mornin'. You wants ter put on yo' bes' clothes an' slick up, fer dey're partic'lar people. Ef you git de place I'll expec' you ter pay me fer de time I lose in 'tendin' ter yo' business, fer time is money in dis country, an' folks don't do much fer nuthin'."

Next morning Wellington blacked his shoes carefully, put on a clean collar, and with the aid of Mrs. Johnson tied his cravat in a jaunty bow which gave him quite a sprightly air and a much younger look than his years warranted. Mr. Peterson called for him at eight o'clock. After traversing several cross streets they turned into Oakwood Avenue and walked along the finest part of it for about half a mile. The handsome houses of this famous avenue, the stately trees, the wide-spreading lawns, dotted with flower beds, fountains and statuary, made up a picture so far surpassing anything in Wellington's experience as to fill him with an almost oppressive sense of its beauty.

"Hit looks lack hebben," he said softly.

"It's a pootty fine street," rejoined his companion, with a judicial air, "but I don't like dem big lawns. It's too much trouble ter keep de grass down. One er dem lawns is big enough to pasture a couple er cows."

They went down a street running at right angles to the avenue, and turned into the rear of the corner lot. A large building of pressed brick, trimmed with stone, loomed up before them.

"Do de gemman lib in dis house?" asked Wellington, gazing with awe at the front of the building.

"No, dat's de barn," said Mr. Peterson with good-natured contempt; and leading the way past a clump of shrubbery to the dwelling-house, he went up the back steps and rang the door-bell.

The ring was answered by a buxom Irishwoman, of a natural freshness of complexion deepened to a fiery red by the heat of a kitchen range. Wellington thought he had seen her before, but his mind had received so many new impressions lately that it was a minute or two before he recognized in her the lady whose lap he had involuntarily occupied for a moment on his first day in Groveland.

"Faith," she exclaimed as she admitted them, "an' it's mighty glad I am to see ye ag'in, Misther Payterson! An' how hev ye be'n, Misther Payterson, sence I see ye lahst?"

"Middlin' well, Mis' Flannigan, middlin' well, 'ceptin' a tech er de rheumatiz. S'pose you be'n doin' well as usual?"

"Oh yis, as well as a dacent woman could do wid a drunken baste about the place like the lahst coachman. O Misther Payterson, it would make yer heart bleed to see the way the spalpeen cut up a-Saturday! But Misther Todd discharged 'im the same avenin', widout a characther, bad 'cess to 'im, an' we 've had no coachman sence at all, at all. An' it's sorry I am"——

The lady's flow of eloquence was interrupted at this point by the appearance of Mr. Todd himself, who had been informed of the men's arrival. He asked some questions in regard to Wellington's qualifications and former experience, and in view of his recent arrival in the city was willing to accept Mr. Peterson's recommendation instead of a reference. He said a few words about the nature of the work, and stated his willingness to pay Wellington the wages formerly allowed Mr. Peterson, thirty dollars a month and board and lodging.

This handsome offer was eagerly accepted, and it was agreed that Wellington's term of service should begin immediately. Mr. Peterson, being familiar with the work, and financially interested, conducted the new coachman through the stables and showed him what he would have to do. The silver-mounted harness, the variety of carriages, the names of which he learned for the first time, the arrangements for feeding and watering the horses,—these appointments of a rich man's stable impressed Wellington very much, and he wondered that so much luxury should be wasted on mere horses. The room assigned to him, in the second story of the barn, was a finer apartment than he had ever slept in; and the salary attached to the situation was greater than the combined monthly earnings of himself and aunt Milly in their Southern home. Surely, he thought, his lines had fallen in pleasant places.

Under the stimulus of new surroundings Wellington applied himself diligently to work, and, with the occasional advice of Mr.

Peterson, soon mastered the details of his employment. He found
the female servants, with whom he took his meals, very amiable
ladies. The cook, Mrs. Katie Flannigan, was a widow. Her husband, a sailor, had been lost at sea. She was a woman of many
words, and when she was not lamenting the late Flannigan's loss,—
according to her story he had been a model of all the virtues,—she
would turn the batteries of her tongue against the former coachman. This gentleman, as Wellington gathered from frequent
remarks dropped by Mrs. Flannigan, had paid her attentions clearly
susceptible of a serious construction. These attentions had not
borne their legitimate fruit, and she was still a widow unconsoled,—
hence Mrs. Flannigan's tears. The housemaid was a plump, good-
natured German girl, with a pronounced German accent. The
presence on washdays of a Bohemian laundress, of recent impor-
tation, added another to the variety of ways in which the English
tongue was mutilated in Mr. Todd's kitchen. Association with the
white women drew out all the native gallantry of the mulatto, and
Wellington developed quite a helpful turn. His politeness, his willingness to lend a hand in kitchen or laundry, and the fact that he
was the only male servant on the place, combined to make him a
prime favorite in the servants' quarters.

It was the general opinion among Wellington's acquaintances
that he was a single man. He had come to the city alone, had never
been heard to speak of a wife, and to personal questions bearing
upon the subject of matrimony had always returned evasive
answers. Though he had never questioned the correctness of the
lawyer's opinion in regard to his slave marriage, his conscience had
never been entirely at ease since his departure from the South, and
any positive denial of his married condition would have stuck in
his throat. The inference naturally drawn from his reticence in
regard to the past, coupled with his expressed intention of settling
permanently in Groveland, was that he belonged in the ranks of
the unmarried, and was therefore legitimate game for any widow
or old maid who could bring him down. As such game is bagged
easiest at short range, he received numerous invitations to tea-
parties, where he feasted on unlimited chicken and pound cake.
He used to compare these viands with the plain fare often served
by aunt Milly, and the result of the comparison was another item
to the credit of the North upon his mental ledger. Several of the
colored ladies who smiled upon him were blessed with good looks,

and uncle Wellington, naturally of a susceptible temperament, as people of lively imagination are apt to be, would probably have fallen a victim to the charms of some woman of his own race, had it not been for a strong counter-attraction in the person of Mrs. Flannigan. The attentions of the lately discharged coachman had lighted anew the smouldering fires of her widowed heart, and awakened longings which still remained unsatisfied. She was thirty-five years old, and felt the need of some one else to love. She was not a woman of lofty ideals; with her a man was a man——

"For a' that an' a' that;" and, aside from the accident of color, uncle Wellington was as personable a man as any of her acquaint-ance. Some people might have objected to his complexion; but then, Mrs. Flannigan argued, he was at least half white; and, this being the case, there was no good reason why he should be regarded as black.

Uncle Wellington was not slow to perceive Mrs. Flannigan's charms of person, and appreciated to the full the skill that prepared the choice tidbits reserved for his plate at dinner. The prospect of securing a white wife had been one of the principal inducements offered by a life at the North; but the awe of white people in which he had been reared was still too strong to permit his taking any active steps toward the object of his secret desire, had not the lady herself come to his assistance with a little of the native coquetry of her race.

"Ah, Misther Braboy," she said one evening when they sat at the supper table alone,—it was the second girl's afternoon off, and she had not come home to supper,—"it must be an awful lone-some life ye've been afther l'adin', as a single man, wid no one to cook fer ye, or look afther ye."

"It are a kind er lonesome life, Mis' Flannigan, an' dat's a fac'. But sence I had de privilege er eatin' yo' cookin' an' 'joyin' yo' society, I ain' felt a bit lonesome."

"Yer flatthrin' me, Misther Braboy. An' even if ye mane it"——

"I means eve'y word of it, Mis' Flannigan."

"An' even if ye mane it, Misther Braboy, the time is liable to come when things'll be different; for service is uncertain, Misther Braboy. An' then you'll wish you had some nice, clean woman, 'at knowed how to cook an' wash an' iron, ter look afther ye, an' make yer life comfortable."

Uncle Wellington sighed, and looked at her languishingly.

"It 'u'd all be well ernuff, Mis' Flannigan, ef I had n' met you; but I don' know whar I's ter fin' a colored lady w'at'll begin ter suit me after habbin' libbed in de same house wid you."

"Colored lady, indade! Why, Misther Braboy, ye don't nade ter demane yerself by marryin' a colored lady—not but they're as good as anybody else, so long as they behave themselves. There's many a white woman 'u'd be glad ter git as fine a lookin' man as ye are."

"Now *you're* flattrin' *me, Mis'* Flannigan," said Wellington. But he felt a sudden and substantial increase in courage when she had spoken, and it was with astonishing ease that he found himself saying:—

"Dey ain' but one lady, Mis' Flannigan, dat could injuce me ter want ter change de lonesomeness er my singleness fer de 'sponsibilities er matermony, an' I'm feared she'd say no ef I'd ax her."

"Ye'd better ax her, Misther Braboy, an' not be wastin' time a-wond'rin'. Do I know the lady?"

"You knows 'er better 'n anybody else, Mis' Flannigan. *You* is de only lady I'd be satisfied ter marry after knowin' you. Ef you casts me off I'll spen' de rest er my days in lonesomeness an' mis'ry."

Mrs. Flannigan affected much surprise and embarrassment at this bold declaration.

"Oh, Misther Braboy," she said, covering him with a coy glance, "an' it's rale 'shamed I am to hev b'en talkin' ter ye ez I hev. It looks as though I'd b'en doin' the coortin'. I didn't drame that I'd b'en able ter draw yer affections to mesilf."

"I's loved you ever sence I fell in yo' lap on de street car de fus' day I wuz in Groveland," he said, as he moved his chair up closer to hers.

One evening in the following week they went out after supper to the residence of Rev. Caesar Williams, pastor of the colored Baptist church, and, after the usual preliminaries, were pronounced man and wife.

III.

According to all his preconceived notions, this marriage ought to have been the acme of uncle Wellington's felicity. But he soon found that it was not without its drawbacks. On the following morning Mr. Todd was informed of the marriage. He had no special objection to it, or interest in it, except that he was opposed on principle to having husband and wife in his employment at the same time. As a consequence, Mrs. Braboy, whose place could be more easily filled than that of her husband, received notice that her services would not be required after the end of the month. Her husband was retained in his place as coachman.

Upon the loss of her situation Mrs. Braboy decided to exercise the married woman's prerogative of letting her husband support her. She rented the upper floor of a small house in an Irish neighborhood. The newly wedded pair furnished their rooms on the installment plan and began housekeeping.

There was one little circumstance, however, that interfered slightly with their enjoyment of that perfect freedom from care which ought to characterize a honeymoon. The people who owned the house and occupied the lower floor had rented the upper part to Mrs. Braboy in person, it never occurring to them that her husband could be other than a white man. When it became known that he was colored, the landlord, Mr. Dennis O'Flaherty, felt that he had been imposed upon, and, at the end of the first month, served notice upon his tenants to leave the premises. When Mrs. Braboy, with characteristic impetuosity, inquired the meaning of this proceeding, she was informed by Mr. O'Flaherty that he did not care to live in the same house "wid naygurs." Mrs. Braboy resented the epithet with more warmth than dignity, and for a brief space of time the air was green with choice specimens of brogue, the altercation barely ceasing before it had reached the point of blows.

It was quite clear that the Braboys could not longer live comfortably in Mr. O'Flaherty's house, and they soon vacated the premises, first letting the rent get a couple of weeks in arrears as a punishment to the too fastidious landlord. They moved to a small house on Hackman Street, a favorite locality with colored people.

For a while, affairs ran smoothly in the new home. The colored people seemed, at first, well enough disposed toward Mrs. Braboy, and she made quite a large acquaintance among them. It was difficult, however, for Mrs. Braboy to divest herself of the consciousness that she was white, and therefore superior to her neighbors. Occasional words and acts by which she manifested this feeling were noticed and resented by her keen-eyed and sensitive colored neighbors. The result was a slight coolness between them. That her few white neighbors did not visit her, she naturally and no doubt correctly imputed to disapproval of her matrimonial relations.

Under these circumstances, Mrs. Braboy was left a good deal to her own company. Owing to lack of opportunity in early life, she was not a woman of many resources, either mental or moral. It is therefore not strange that, in order to relieve her loneliness, she should occasionally have recourse to a glass of beer, and, as the habit grew upon her, to still stronger stimulants. Uncle Wellington himself was no tee-totaler, and did not interpose any objection so long as she kept her potations within reasonable limits, and was apparently none the worse for them; indeed, he sometimes joined her in a glass. On one of these occasions he drank a little too much, and, while driving the ladies of Mr. Todd's family to the opera, ran against a lamp-post and overturned the carriage, to the serious discomposure of the ladies' nerves, and at the cost of his situation.

A coachman discharged under such circumstances is not in the best position for procuring employment at his calling, and uncle Wellington, under the pressure of need, was obliged to seek some other means of livelihood. At the suggestion of his friend Mr. Johnson, he bought a whitewash brush, a peck of lime, a couple of pails, and a hand-cart, and began work as a whitewasher. His first efforts were very crude, and for a while he lost a customer in every person he worked for. He nevertheless managed to pick up a living during the spring and summer months, and to support his wife and himself in comparative comfort.

The approach of winter put an end to the whitewashing season, and left uncle Wellington dependent for support upon occasional jobs of unskilled labor. The income derived from these was very uncertain, and Mrs. Braboy was at length driven, by stress of circumstances, to the washtub, that last refuge of honest, able-bodied poverty, in all countries where the use of clothing is conventional.

The last state of uncle Wellington was now worse than the first. Under the soft firmness of aunt Milly's rule, he had not been required to do a great deal of work, prompt and cheerful obedience being chiefly what was expected of him. But matters were very different here. He had not only to bring in the coal and water, but to rub the clothes and turn the wringer, and to humiliate himself before the public by emptying the tubs and hanging out the wash in full view of the neighbors; and he had to deliver the clothes when laundered.

At times Wellington found himself wondering if his second marriage had been a wise one. Other circumstances combined to change in some degree his once rose-colored conception of life at the North. He had believed that all men were equal in this favored locality, but he discovered more degrees of inequality than he had ever perceived at the South. A colored man might be as good as a white man in theory, but neither of them was of any special consequence without money, or talent, or position. Uncle Wellington found a great many privileges open to him at the North, but he had not been educated to the point where he could appreciate them or take advantage of them; and the enjoyment of many of them was expensive, and, for that reason alone, as far beyond his reach as they had ever been. When he once began to admit even the possibility of a mistake on his part, these considerations presented themselves to his mind with increasing force. On occasions when Mrs. Braboy would require of him some unusual physical exertion, or when too frequent applications to the bottle had loosened her tongue, uncle Wellington's mind would revert, with a remorseful twinge of conscience, to the *dolce far niente*[2] of his Southern home; a film would come over his eyes and brain, and, instead of the red-faced Irishwoman opposite him, he could see the black but comely disk of aunt Milly's countenance bending over the washtub; the elegant brogue of Mrs. Braboy would deliquesce into the soft dialect of North Carolina; and he would only be aroused from this blissful reverie by a wet shirt or a handful of suds thrown into his face, with which gentle reminder his wife would recall his attention to the duties of the moment.

There came a time, one day in spring, when there was no longer any question about it: uncle Wellington was desperately homesick.

Liberty, equality, privileges,—all were but as dust in the balance when weighed against his longing for old scenes and faces. It was the natural reaction in the mind of a middle-aged man who had tried to force the current of a sluggish existence into a new and radically different channel. An active, industrious man, making the change in early life, while there was time to spare for the waste of adaptation, might have found in the new place more favorable conditions than in the old. In Wellington age and temperament combined to prevent the success of the experiment; the spirit of enterprise and ambition into which he had been temporarily

---

2. *dolce far niente*: An Italian phrase for "the sweetness of doing nothing."

galvanized could no longer prevail against the inertia of old habits of life and thought.

One day when he had been sent to deliver clothes he performed his errand quickly, and boarding a passing street car, paid one of his very few five-cent pieces to ride down to the office of the Hon. Mr. Brown, the colored lawyer whom he had visited when he first came to the city, and who was well known to him by sight and reputation.

"Mr. Brown," he said, "I ain' gitt'n' 'long very well wid my ole 'oman."

"What's the trouble?" asked the lawyer, with business-like curtness, for he did not scent much of a fee.

"Well, de main trouble is she doan treat me right. An' den she gits drunk, an' wuss'n dat, she lays vi'lent han's on me. I kyars de marks er dat 'oman on my face now."

He showed the lawyer a long scratch on the neck.

"Why don't you defend yourself?"

"You don' know Mis' Braboy, suh; you don' know dat 'oman," he replied, with a shake of the head. "Some er dese yer w'ite women is monst'us strong in de wris'."

"Well, Mr. Braboy, it's what you might have expected when you turned your back on your own people and married a white woman. You weren't content with being a slave to the white folks once, but you must try it again. Some people never know when they've got enough. I don't see that there's any help for you; unless," he added suggestively, "you had a good deal of money."

"'Pears ter me I heared somebody say sence I be'n up heah, dat it wuz 'gin de law fer w'ite folks an' colored folks ter marry."

"That was once the law, though it has always been a dead letter in Groveland. In fact, it was the law when you got married, and until I introduced a bill in the legislature last fall to repeal it. But even that law didn't hit cases like yours. It was unlawful to make such a marriage, but it was a good marriage when once made."

"I don'jes' git dat th'oo my head," said Wellington, scratching that member as though to make a hole for the idea to enter.

"It's quite plain, Mr. Braboy. It's unlawful to kill a man, but when he's killed he's just as dead as though the law permitted it. I'm afraid you haven't much of a case, but if you'll go to work and get twenty-five dollars together, I'll see what I can do for you. We may be able to pull a case through on the ground of extreme cruelty. I might even start the case if you brought in ten dollars."

Wellington went away sorrowfully. The laws of Ohio were very little more satisfactory than those of North Carolina. And as for the ten dollars,—the lawyer might as well have told him to bring in the moon, or a deed for the Public Square. He felt very, very low as he hurried back home to supper, which he would have to go without if he were not on hand at the usual supper-time.

But just when his spirits were lowest, and his outlook for the future most hopeless, a measure of relief was at hand. He noticed, when he reached home, that Mrs. Braboy was a little preoccupied, and did not abuse him as vigorously as he expected after so long an absence. He also perceived the smell of strange tobacco in the house, of a better grade than he could afford to use. He thought perhaps some one had come in to see about the washing; but he was too glad of a respite from Mrs. Braboy's rhetoric to imperil it by indiscreet questions.

Next morning she gave him fifty cents.

"Braboy," she said, "ye've be'n helpin' me nicely wid the washin', an' I 'm going ter give ye a holiday. Ye can take yer hook an' line an' go fishin' on the breakwater. I'll fix ye a lunch, an' ye needn't come back till night. An' there's half a dollar; ye can buy yerself a pipe er terbacky. But be careful an' don't waste it," she added, for fear she was overdoing the thing.

Uncle Wellington was overjoyed at this change of front on the part of Mrs. Braboy; if she would make it permanent he did not see why they might not live together very comfortably.

The day passed pleasantly down on the breakwater. The weather was agreeable, and the fish bit freely. Towards evening Wellington started home with a bunch of fish that no angler need have been ashamed of. He looked forward to a good warm supper; for even if something should have happened during the day to alter his wife's mood for the worse, any ordinary variation would be more than balanced by the substantial addition of food to their larder. His mouth watered at the thought of the finny beauties sputtering in the frying-pan.

He noted, as he approached the house, that there was no smoke coming from the chimney. This only disturbed him in connection with the matter of supper. When he entered the gate he observed further that the window-shades had been taken down.

" 'Spec' de ole 'oman's been house-cleanin'," he said to himself. "I wonder she didn' make me stay an' he'p 'er."

He went round to the rear of the house and tried the kitchen door. It was locked. This was somewhat of a surprise, and disturbed still further his expectations in regard to supper. When he had found the key and opened the door, the gravity of his next discovery drove away for the time being all thoughts of eating.

The kitchen was empty. Stove, table, chairs, wash-tubs, pots and pans, had vanished as if into thin air.

"Fo' de Lawd's sake!" he murmured in open-mouthed astonishment.

He passed into the other room,—they had only two,—which had served as bedroom and sitting-room. It was as bare as the first, except that in the middle of the floor were piled uncle Wellington's clothes. It was not a large pile, and on the top of it lay a folded piece of yellow wrapping-paper.

Wellington stood for a moment as if petrified. Then he rubbed his eyes and looked around him.

"W'at do dis mean?" he said. "Is I er-dreamin', er does I see w'at I 'pears ter see?" He glanced down at the bunch of fish which he still held. "Heah's de fish; heah's de house; heah I is; but whar 's de ole 'oman, an' whar's de fu'niture? *I* can't figure out w'at dis yer all means."

He picked up the piece of paper and unfolded it. It was written on one side. Here was the obvious solution of the mystery,—that is, it would have been obvious if he could have read it; but he could not, and so his fancy continued to play upon the subject. Perhaps the house had been robbed, or the furniture taken back by the seller, for it had not been entirely paid for.

Finally he went across the street and called to a boy in a neighbor's yard.

"Does you read writin', Johnnie?"

"Yes, sir, I'm in the seventh grade."

"Read dis yer paper fuh me."

The youngster took the note, and with much labor read the following:——

"Mr. Braboy:
    "In lavin' ye so suddint I have ter say that my first husban' has turned up unixpected, having been saved onbeknownst ter me from a wathry grave an' all the money wasted I spint fer masses fer ter rist

his sole an' I wish I had it back I feel it my dooty ter go an' live wid 'im again. I take the furnacher because I bought it yer close is yors I leave them and wishin' yer the best of luck I remane oncet yer wife but now agin

"Mrs. Katie Flannigan.

"N.B. I'm lavin' town terday so it won't be no use lookin' fer me."

On inquiry uncle Wellington learned from the boy that shortly after his departure in the morning a white man had appeared on the scene, followed a little later by a moving-van, into which the furniture had been loaded and carried away. Mrs. Braboy, clad in her best clothes, had locked the door, and gone away with the strange white man.

The news was soon noised about the street. Wellington swapped his fish for supper and a bed at a neighbor's, and during the evening learned from several sources that the strange white man had been at his house the afternoon of the day before. His neighbors intimated that they thought Mrs. Braboy's departure a good riddance of bad rubbish, and Wellington did not dispute the proposition.

Thus ended the second chapter of Wellington's matrimonial experiences. His wife's departure had been the one thing needful to convince him, beyond a doubt, that he had been a great fool. Remorse and homesickness forced him to the further conclusion that he had been knave as well as fool, and had treated aunt Milly shamefully. He was not altogether a bad old man, though very weak and erring, and his better nature now gained the ascendency. Of course his disappointment had a great deal to do with his remorse; most people do not perceive the hideousness of sin until they begin to reap its consequences. Instead of the beautiful Northern life he had dreamed of, he found himself stranded, penniless, in a strange land, among people whose sympathy he had forfeited, with no one to lean upon, and no refuge from the storms of life. His outlook was very dark, and there sprang up within him a wild longing to get back to North Carolina,—back to the little whitewashed cabin, shaded with china and mulberry trees; back to the woodpile and the garden; back to the old cronies with whom he had swapped lies and tobacco for so many years. He longed to kiss the rod of aunt Milly's domination. He had purchased his liberty at too great a price.

The next day he disappeared from Groveland. He had announced his departure only to Mr. Johnson, who sent his love to his relations in Patesville.

It would be painful to record in detail the return journey of uncle Wellington—Mr. Braboy no longer—to his native town; how many weary miles he walked; how many times he risked his life on railroad tracks and between freight cars; how he depended for sustenance on the grudging hand of back-door charity. Nor would it be profitable or delicate to mention any slight deviations from the path of rectitude, as judged by conventional standards, to which he may occasionally have been driven by a too insistent hunger; or to refer in the remotest degree to a compulsory sojourn of thirty days in a city where he had no references, and could show no visible means of support. True charity will let these purely personal matters remain locked in the bosom of him who suffered them.

IV.

Just fifteen months after the date when uncle Wellington had left North Carolina, a weather-beaten figure entered the town of Patesville after nightfall, following the railroad track from the north. Few would have recognized in the hungry-looking old brown tramp, clad in dusty rags and limping along with bare feet, the trim-looking middle-aged mulatto who so few months before had taken the train from Patesville for the distant North; so, if he had but known it, there was no necessity for him to avoid the main streets and sneak around by unfrequented paths to reach the old place on the other side of the town. He encountered nobody that he knew, and soon the familiar shape of the little cabin rose before him. It stood distinctly outlined against the sky, and the light streaming from the half-opened shutters showed it to be occupied. As he drew nearer, every familiar detail of the place appealed to his memory and to his affections, and his heart went out to the old home and the old wife. As he came nearer still, the odor of fried chicken floated out upon the air and set his mouth to watering, and awakened unspeakable longings in his half-starved stomach.

At this moment, however, a fearful thought struck him; suppose the old woman had taken legal advice and married again during his absence? Turn about would have been only fair play. He opened the gate softly, and with his heart in his mouth approached the window on tiptoe and looked in.

A cheerful fire was blazing on the hearth, in front of which sat the familiar form of aunt Milly—and another, at the sight of whom uncle Wellington's heart sank within him. He knew the other person very well; he had sat there more than once before uncle Wellington went away. It was the minister of the church to which his wife belonged. The preacher's former visits, however, had signified nothing more than pastoral courtesy, or appreciation of good eating. His presence now was of serious portent; for Wellington recalled, with acute alarm, that the elder's wife had died only a few weeks before his own departure for the North. What was the occasion of his presence this evening? Was it merely a pastoral call? or was he courting? or had aunt Milly taken legal advice and married the elder?

Wellington remembered a crack in the wall, at the back of the house, through which he could see and hear, and quietly stationed himself there.

"Dat chicken smells mighty good, Sis' Milly," the elder was saying; "I can't fer de life er me see why dat low-down husban' er yo'n could ever run away f'm a cook like you. It's one er de beatenis' things I ever heared. How he could lib wid you an' not 'preciate you *I* can't understan', no indeed I can't."

Aunt Milly sighed. "De trouble wid Wellin'ton wuz," she replied, "dat he didn' know when he wuz well off. He wuz alluz wishin' fer change, er studyin' 'bout somethin' new."

"Ez fer me," responded the elder earnestly, "I likes things what has be'n prove' an' tried an' has stood de tes', an' I can't 'magine how anybody could spec' ter fin' a better housekeeper er cook dan you is, Sis' Milly. I'm a gittin' mighty lonesome sence my wife died. De Good Book say it is not good fer man ter lib alone, en it 'pears ter me dat you an' me mought git erlong tergether monst'us well."

Wellington's heart stood still, while he listened with strained attention. Aunt Milly sighed.

"I ain't denyin', elder, but what I've be'n kinder lonesome myse'f fer quite a w'ile, an' I doan doubt dat w'at de Good Book say 'plies ter women as well as ter men."

"You kin be sho' it do," averred the elder, with professional authoritativeness; "yas'm, you kin be cert'n sho'."

"But, of co'se," aunt Milly went on, "havin' los' my ole man de way I did, it has tuk me some time fer ter git my feelin's straighten' out like dey oughter be."

"I kin 'magine yo' feelin's, Sis' Milly," chimed in the elder sympathetically, "w'en you come home dat night an' foun' yo' chist broke open, an' yo' money gone dat you had wukked an' slaved full f'm mawnin' 'tel night, year in an' year out, an' w'en you foun' dat no-'count nigger gone wid his clo's an' you lef' all alone in de worl' ter scuffle 'long by yo'self."

"Yas, elder," responded aunt Milly, "I wa'n't used right. An' den w'en I heared 'bout his goin' ter de lawyer ter fin' out 'bout a defoce, an' w'en I heared w'at de lawyer said 'bout my not bein' his wife 'less he wanted me, it made me so mad, I made up my min' dat ef he ever put his foot on my do'sill ag'in, I'd shet de do' in his face an' tell 'im ter go back whar he come f'm."

To Wellington, on the outside, the cabin had never seemed so comfortable, aunt Milly never so desirable, chicken never so appetizing, as at this moment when they seemed slipping away from his grasp forever.

"Yo' feelin's does you credit, Sis' Milly," said the elder, taking her hand, which for a moment she did not withdraw. "An' de way fer you ter close yo' do' tightes' ag'inst 'im is ter take me in his place. He ain' got no claim on you no mo'. He tuk his ch'ice 'cordin' ter w'at de lawyer tol' 'im, an' 'termine' dat he wa'n't yo' husban'. Ef he wa'n't yo' husban', he had no right ter take yo' money, an' ef he comes back here ag'in you kin hab 'im tuck up an' sent ter de penitenchy fer stealin' it."

Uncle Wellington's knees, already weak from fasting, trembled violently beneath him. The worst that he had feared was now likely to happen. His only hope of safety lay in flight, and yet the scene within so fascinated him that he could not move a step.

"It 'u'd serve him right," exclaimed aunt Milly indignantly, "ef he wuz sent ter de penitenchy fer life! Dey ain't nuthin' too mean ter be done ter 'im. What did I ever do dat he should use me like he did?"

The recital of her wrongs had wrought upon aunt Milly's feelings so that her voice broke, and she wiped her eyes with her apron.

The elder looked serenely confident, and moved his chair nearer hers in order the better to play the role of comforter. Wellington, on the outside, felt so mean that the darkness of the night was scarcely sufficient to hide him; it would be no more than right if the earth were to open and swallow him up.

"An' yet aftuh all, elder," said Milly with a sob, "though I knows you is a better man, an' would treat me right, I wuz so use' ter dat ole nigger, an' libbed wid 'im so long, dat ef he'd open dat do' dis minute an' walk in, I'm feared I'd be foolish ernuff an' weak ernuff to forgive 'im an' take 'im back ag'in."

With a bound, uncle Wellington was away from the crack in the wall. As he ran round the house he passed the wood-pile and snatched up an armful of pieces. A moment later he threw open the door.

"Ole 'oman," he exclaimed, "here's dat wood you tol' me ter fetch in! Why, elder," he said to the preacher, who had started from his seat with surprise, "w'at's yo' hurry? Won't you stay an' hab some supper wid us?"

AN EQUATION

Gertrude H. Dorsey [Browne]

(from *Colored American Magazine* 5, August 1902)

MISS SARAH GAUDY sat at the desk in the college office examining the past month's records, and filling out the report blanks which were to be forwarded to the parents of each student.

Jessie Kirkland, the A Monitor, had told me confidentially that Miss Gaudy was especially constituted for "office work," and there was some legend abroad that she never stopped work at noon, but simply sucked the ink off the pen, and thereby derived sufficient nourishment to satisfy her hunger until dinner. This may, or may not, be true, but it is a fact, nevertheless, that she was poring over records when I entered the office to report for misbehavior.

"Well, Miss Grace, what can I do for you?" she said pleasantly.

"The assistant, Miss Maloney, sent me to report to you for misbehavior and for having this in my possession"; as I spoke I thrust forward a small piece of folded paper and stood defiantly awaiting results. She took it mechanically and opened it; then moved by a better impulse, she refolded and returned it to me. "Miss Grace, can you, a senior, justify yourself in sending or passing a note during class recitation when you know it is against the rules and must be recorded in this book? What does this note say?" I replied with some spirit: "I did not pass the note and I don't know anything about it, for it fell out of Viola's rhetoric and I picked it up, just as Miss Maloney called the class, and she did not wait for an explanation, but sent me to you. I'm sorry to have troubled you about so small a matter, but I couldn't help it."

Poor little Miss Gaudy looked helplessly at the note and at me, and then we both smiled, and she said simply, "Read it." I was surprised and a little embarrassed to read in my own handwriting: "The product of the sum and difference of two quantities is equal to the difference of their squares," and this rather odd revelation was further endorsed by my name.

"My dear Miss Grace, what possible connection has the sum and difference of two quantities with your misconduct? You are studying trigonometry now, are you not?" she asked with a puzzled look. "Yes," I said. "I study trigonometry, but my room mate studies algebra and occasionally I help her in preparing her lessons, and in some unaccountable way that theorem has gotten into bad company. I like to go over those old principles and theorems." "Very well, you may return to the recitation room and tell Miss Maloney it was all a mistake," and Miss Gaudy resumed her interrupted task.

That day and that incident was the turning point in my school life, for, ever since, I have been prone to speak of events as happening before or since the day I was sent to the office to report.

After luncheon that same afternoon I received a note from Miss Gaudy asking if I could spend a few hours with her that afternoon and evening in correcting the algebra papers of the Sophomores. What girl of nineteen would not appreciate such a compliment, coming, as it did, from the gentlest and most winning of women? So as soon as I was excused from the music room, I went to the Office, where I spent a very busy hour, flattering myself all the while that if it had not been for me, those papers would never have been finished by the next day for the school inspector to examine.

And how very delightful it was, to be sure, to be allowed to talk whenever I pleased without the cruel formality of the recitation room staring me in the face like an evil genius.

Miss Gaudy, too, was so entertaining and talked freely of her anticipated visit from the inspector—Mr. Turner, whom she had never seen, but who she supposed was learned in all the wisdom of the Egyptians and was mighty in word and in deed.

Gradually even I entered into her enthusiasm, and more than once I found myself making computations on what Mr. Turner would be worth by the pound or cubic inch, but he always came out the Unknown Quantity.

After we had finished our task we went to the Principal's private sitting room and fared sumptuously on mustard sardines, Welsh rarebit, wafers, sweet pickles and chocolate.

Then it was, that I became skeptical on the subject of her lunching off the ink on her pen. Before I left she told me that the Board had promised her the aid of an assistant, after the next term, and she wondered if I would care for such a position. As I wished to continue my studies in music and German I was only too glad of the chance and thanked her for planning such an agreeable arrangement.

The next morning forty-three girls were in a flutter of excitement, and many and wild were the speculations on the Unknown Quantity, Mr. Turner. "He'll be sure to gaze on us very much as he would a spoiled copy book," declared Viola my chum. "Yes, and I know he's just full of ah's and big words, for they always are," came from another quarter.

"Of course, he'll wear nose glasses and will tell us how clever he was—'when he was a boy'—forty years ago, and did not begin to have the many advantages we enjoy, etc.," and thus they chatted until the A Monitor rang the bell and we went to chapel for worship.

If Mr. Turner had arrived, we saw nothing of him that morning, but as we were passing into the music-room, we heard laughing in the office, which certainly could not come from Miss Gaudy, "who had never been known to smile above a whisper," Viola said. At two o'clock the principal laid aside her "office" long enough to bring the visitor into the parlor to inspect us. We quite forgot our good manners when we beheld a young man, not a day over twenty-six (according to the A Monitor), "whose chin was but enriched with one appearing hair" and whose big brown eyes seemed to challenge laughing.

Well, he gave us a very jolly little talk about our work and he did not say "Ah" once, and moreover, he omitted the offending phrase, "when I was a boy." In fact, he addressed us very much on the "fellow-citizen" plan, and Jessie Kirkland proposed at the next class meeting to confer a degree upon him at once.

While we girls were discussing the inspector a half hour later and wondering if we could not find some excuse for reporting at the office, Miss Gaudy sent for me to come to her room. She met me at the door with "Oh, Miss Grace, it's so strange, Mr. Turner is an old, old pupil of my brother Thomas, and we are almost old friends, for I have often heard Thomas speak of Raymond Turner as one of the brightest boys in college, but I never dreamed of his being the inspector. However, this is his first year, and his first trip here. But what I want to tell you, is of an embarrassing mistake you have made in correcting those papers," and she handed me a paper whereon I had made the correction "$X = \frac{1}{4}$ the head of the Turner." "Oh, did he see it?" I asked. "Why certainly Miss Grace, he called my attention to it and laughed so heartily, I feared you all could hear him in the music room. After dinner you are to come to the office as he wishes to see you, and now I will not detain you longer," and she busied herself about the desk while I went to find Viola.

An hour later and (would you believe it?) I was sitting comfortably in the office talking to the inspector quite as much at my ease as I was when talking to Viola or a Freshman.

Commencement was near at hand and after that evening I had but little time to assist Miss Gaudy, although we met occasionally and she always had a smile or pleasant inquiry concerning my final, and for the ninety-ninth time she would offer me the use of her private library, or the benefit of her council.

After commencement, at which time, by the way, I received an appointment as regular assistant in the office, I spent a very delightful two weeks visit with Miss Gaudy and her brother at their home in Lexington. Mr. Turner was also a guest at the same time, and we each had the opportunity for becoming better acquainted.

Miss Gaudy never tired of telling the rest of the party about our calling Mr. Turner the Unknown Quantity, and even the quiet professor took delight in joking about it. One afternoon as we returned from an excursion to the woods for geological specimens I remarked that I was hungry, and was seconded by the others, so the professor started on a foraging expedition and returned soon, followed by a servant bearing a tray upon which were fresh rolls, milk and fruit. As he passed the fruit to the inspector and myself he solemnly repeated, "The same quantity may be added to both members of an equation without destroying the equality."

When my vacation was over, I returned to the college and began my work, which although in time it became monotonous, was yet interesting and I enjoyed it. The suggestions and advice which Miss Gaudy, from a long experience, was able to give me were so helpful, and I began to appreciate the quiet, wise little principal and to bless the mistakes which had been the means of drawing us together into such a warm and sympathetic friendship, as such friendships are really few.

The first term passed without incident, and we were nearing the close of the second, when one morning we were informed that the inspector would soon visit us and to have everything in readiness. Papers must be corrected, averages made out and report blanks filled, besides our other work must not be neglected, so we were very busy for a few days. However, the third term was almost at an end before he came.

Miss Gaudy received him with frank cordiality, and while he treated us with all respect, yet he was quite anxious to complete his task so that he might go, and addressed us all in the most perfunctory way. I was annoyed when I discovered how much I really cared whether he addressed me or not, so I assumed an indifference (which I did not feel) whenever his name was mentioned.

Vacation had come again and with my old enemy, Miss Maloney, and Miss Gaudy I attended the National Teachers' Association at Washington, D.C. We were sitting one morning in the large auditorium listening to a lecture by that wonderful man, Professor De Mott, when by a sly pinch on the arm and a little nod in the direction of the door, Miss Gaudy drew my attention to a group of ladies who had just entered. I had no trouble in recognizing the tall slender one as Viola Culver and the queenly beauty at her side as Jessie Kirkland.

The lecture did me no more good, and until I had managed by frantic and idiotic signs to attract the attention of three ushers and half the audience, I was as one deaf and dumb to all else. An usher made his way to me and I handed him my card with our hotel address, with the request that he would hand it to the persons who had just entered the hall. I then subsided into the depths of my program and remained an interested listener until the close of the session. As we passed out, we were accosted by Viola's friendly "Hello, Grace; what are you doing here? Oh, Miss Gaudy and Miss Maloney, how glad we are to see you, and just to think we have just been having no end of fun at your expense," and she passed her arm through mine and with Jessie and the rest bringing up the rear joined us in our walk to the car.

"Oh, Grace," she said, as soon as we were to ourselves, "I have made such a startling discovery, thanks to the stupid old policeman who misdirected us. You noticed we were late this morning. Well we just arrived last night and, of course, we had to be directed this morning which car to take for the hall, and the stupid fellow put us 'on the wrong car, which we did not know until we reached the government building, and as the crowd got off there, we did likewise, and I'm going again this afternoon and show you what I found. You little rogue, you keep your secrets as you do your seeds cakes, strictly to yourself. Why didn't you tell me about him and all the nice things he has said?" "About whom, Viola? What did you find? What secret have I kept from you?" I asked in bewilderment.

"O never mind, I have found out, and now you must give me your card so we can talk it out, in the good old way, in the privacy of a sitting room or chamber," she remarked, as the rest of the folks came to us. "I sent my card to you at the hall, by the usher, did you not get it?" I exclaimed. "Mercy, no, I'm sure I did not know you were here until I met you as we were coming out. Don't mind, Grace, I dare say you have more cards left, and one is quite as acceptable as another. Good bye, here comes our car; be ready by 2:30 and I'll come after you to show you one of the sights my investigating genius has discovered," and Viola and Jessie were soon seated in the car, and we walked a square further to the Pennsylvania Avenue line.

To Miss Gaudy I confided that part of Viola's conversation which mystified me and upon which I had placed grave fears of her sanity, but the little woman only smiled and remarked that Miss Viola had ranked first in our class, and was even then conducting a department in one of our best colleges.

We were discussing this subject in our room about two o'clock that afternoon when Miss Maloney entered, and gravely handed me a card with the words, "He's waiting in the parlor on the second floor." Why the card of Raymond Turner should be sent to me at that particular time I could not comprehend, so I hastily left the room and sought the second floor parlor.

He was alone, and as I entered he came forward with a pleased, expectant smile, which changed, as it encountered the look of annoyance and surprise on my face. "I was somewhat surprised to receive your card; the usher handed it to me as I entered the lecture hall this morning, and of course I am able to put but one construction on the case. You certainly meant that I should call, and you certainly know what such a summons means to me." He held out his hand as he spoke and in my astonishment, I forgot to take it, and simply stared at him, or perhaps glared would be the better word.

When I found my tongue, he was standing near the door, hat in hand, and was regarding me with an expression which might have been contempt and might have been pity. "There has been some mistake. I did not send my card to you and I know of no reason why your calling here would be of any special significance to either of us. Miss Gaudy would be glad to see you I do not doubt, but you really must excuse me as I have an engagement at 2:30 and it is nearly that now." With this rude speech, I returned to our room and soon afterwards Viola was admitted.

A half hour later and we were climbing the steps of a large building, and Viola with the confidence of a person "to the manor born" led the way to a gallery on the second floor, where in a glass case were exposed some thousands of written documents. Then she turned triumphantly to me and said, "This case of dead letters and rings and other valuables, was at the Exposition at—never mind where,—and has just been returned. You remember the day we girls went through the Government Building at the Chicago Exposition.[1] Well, there was just such a case there and we read no end of queer letters to mothers, sons, sweethearts, Santa Claus, and every conceivable person or organization of persons. But this is much more interesting, as I'm sure you'll agree after reading the portion of this letter that is exposed," and she pointed to a sheet of legal cap, six inches of whose length was uncovered. I read: "and now Miss Moorman (I hope soon to enjoy the right of calling you Grace) I have attempted to convince you of the similarity that exists in our tastes, inclinations, etc, and to one in your position it is hardly necessary to quote, as authority, 'Only similar quantities can be united in one term.' I have told you all, and shall expect your reply not later than Thursday next. Until then, and always, I am,

Yours to command
Raymond Turner.

Sept. 18, 19—."

"There now, I knew you had been cheating me. If I am not very much mistaken, I met the self same gentleman, Raymond Turner, as I entered the vestibule going to your room. One of his many avowals has been misdirected or is free from guilt of ever

---

1. Chicago Exposition: The World's Columbian Exposition, also known as the Chicago World's Fair, celebrated the 400th anniversary of Christopher Columbus's arrival in the new world. It was held in Chicago in 1893.

having been directed, but what is one letter among a hundred, perhaps? Of course, you have been so absorbed in him that you could not give a thought to your poor old chum," she exclaimed mockingly, as I suddenly espied an envelope hanging just above the legal cap, upon which was written in the same handwriting "Grace Darling."

"Well, I'm afraid, Viola, if I stay here much longer, I'll find myself a central figure in one of your scatter-brain modern novels, so let's go at once. Who knows, there may be a round dozen of Grace Moormans and as many Raymond Turners as there are changes of the moon," and although this brave speech of mine was received with a contemptuous "Bah" by my companion, we each felt a delicacy about discussing the affair.

I turned the matter over in my mind and out of the confused mass of materials, I built the following theory: Mr. Turner had written me (there was no doubt in my mind of the identity of the person referred to in the letter at the Dead Letter Office) some time in September, and being absentminded—poor fellow—had addressed Grace Darling instead of Grace Moorman, and there was nothing left to do but to send the letter to the Dead Letter Office, and as there was no possible chance for its identity to be learned, of course, it could be used along with thousands of others to help fill up space in Uncle Sam's cabinet of unclaimed or misdirected letters. I did not receive a second letter for the reason that Raymond is sensitive and did not care to presume upon an uncertainty. Certainly I shall call him Raymond. Who has a better right? As I was saying, he is sensitive, and hence his apparent indifference last May.

Who but Viola would have discovered that missing link? Viola has sharp, observant eyes, and I really believe I admired them more then than I ever did before. Wonder why? After a time, I suppose he thought I had reconsidered things, and sent my card to him in token of the same, and he had come, and alas,—he had gone. What could I do? Would I see him again? I was abruptly recalled to my surroundings by the information from Viola that she would now take the cable car, and would see me again after I had recovered from the shock she had been able to afford me.

I continued my walk alone to the hotel and with a guilty self-consciousness, I sought Miss Gaudy and told her all there was to tell. She listened very attentively to the entire story and then disappointed me at its close, by simply remarking: "While you were gone, I bought tickets for the concert for the three of us, and I hope you will be ready to go by seven." "She isn't a bit sympathetic, after all," I growled. "I would have found more consolation in telling my troubles to Miss Maloney."

I have never known just how it happened, but some few hours later as I sat in the concert hall, conversing in a low tone to— Raymond (it would have been rude to speak out loud, although several were doing it) it suddenly occurred to me that Miss Gaudy is sympathetic as well as diplomatic, for who else could have contrived to bring us together so soon after my discovery.

It must have sounded silly to those who sat near me to hear "him" say at the close of the program, "I insist, Grace, upon going to the Dead Letter Office now and you must accompany me." "The office has been closed since six o'clock, you 'Positive Quantity,' so you will have to wait awhile longer for an answer to the letter," and Miss Gaudy looked suspiciously at me, but I was waving my hand in the direction of some black plums, which I recognized as the property of Viola.

"But Grace, you must not take too many things for granted. How are you sure that his power of loving is not variable?" and Viola winked at Jessie who sat opposite me. "Why, don't you know, dear valedictorian, that 'All powers of a positive quantity are positive'?" I replied.

THE SCAPEGOAT

Paul Laurence Dunbar

(from *The Heart of Happy Hollow,* 1904)

I.

THE LAW IS usually supposed to be a stern mistress, not to be lightly wooed, and yielding only to the most ardent pursuit. But even law, like love, sits more easily on some natures than on others. This was the case with Mr. Robinson Asbury. Mr. Asbury had started life as a bootblack in the growing town of Cadgers. From this he had risen one step and become porter and messenger in a barber-shop. This rise fired his ambition, and he was not content until he had learned to use the shears and the razor and had a chair of his own. From this, in a man of Robinson's temperament, it was only a step to a shop of his own, and he placed it where it would do the most good.

Fully one-half of the population of Cadgers was composed of Negroes, and with their usual tendency to colonise, a tendency encouraged, and in fact compelled, by circumstances, they had gathered into one part of the town. Here in alleys, and streets as dirty and hardly wider, they thronged like ants.

It was in this place that Mr. Asbury set up his shop, and he won the hearts of his prospective customers by putting up the significant sign, "Equal Rights Barber-Shop." This legend was quite unnecessary, because there was only one race about, to patronise the place. But it was a delicate sop to the people's vanity, and it served its purpose.

Asbury came to be known as a clever fellow, and his business grew. The shop really became a sort of club, and, on Saturday nights especially, was the gathering-place of the men of the whole Negro quarter. He kept the illustrated and race journals there, and those who cared neither to talk nor listen to someone else might see pictured the doings of high society in very short skirts or read in the Negro papers how Miss Boston had entertained Miss Blueford to tea on such and such an afternoon. Also, he kept the policy returns, which was wise, if not moral.

It was his wisdom rather more than his morality that made the party managers after a while cast their glances toward him as a man who might be useful to their interests. It would be well to have a man—a shrewd, powerful man—down in that part of the town who could carry his people's vote in his vest pocket, and who at any time its delivery might be needed, could hand it over without hesitation. Asbury seemed that man, and they settled upon him. They gave him money, and they gave him power and patronage. He took it all silently and he carried out his bargain faithfully. His hands and his lips alike closed tightly when there was anything within them. It was not long before he found himself the big Negro of the district and, of necessity, of the town. The time came when, at a critical moment, the managers saw that they had not reckoned without their host in choosing this barber of the black district as the leader of his people.

Now, so much success must have satisfied any other man. But in many ways Mr. Asbury was unique. For a long time he himself had done very little shaving—except of notes, to keep his hand in. His time had been otherwise employed. In the evening hours he had been wooing the coquettish Dame Law, and, wonderful to say, she had yielded easily to his advances.

It was against the advice of his friends that he asked for admission to the bar. They felt that he could do more good in the place where he was.

"You see, Robinson," said old Judge Davis, "it's just like this: If you're not admitted, it'll hurt you with the people; if you are admitted, you'll move uptown to an office and get out of touch with them."

Asbury smiled an inscrutable smile. Then he whispered something into the judge's ear that made the old man wrinkle from his neck up with appreciative smiles.

"Asbury," he said, "you are—you are—well, you ought to be white, that's all. When we find a black man like you we send him to State's prison. If you were white, you'd go to the Senate."

The Negro laughed confidently.

He was admitted to the bar soon after, whether by merit or by connivance is not to be told.

"Now he will move uptown," said the black community. "Well, that's the way with a coloured man when he gets a start."

But they did not know Asbury Robinson yet. He was a man of surprises, and they were destined to disappointment. He did not move uptown. He built an office in a small open space next his shop, and there hung out his shingle.

"I will never desert the people who have done so much to elevate me," said Mr. Asbury.

"I will live among them and I will die among them."

This was a strong card for the barber-lawyer. The people seized upon the statement as expressing a nobility of an altogether unique brand.

They held a mass meeting and indorsed him. They made resolutions that extolled him, and the Negro band came around and serenaded him, playing various things in varied time.

All this was very sweet to Mr. Asbury, and the party managers chuckled with satisfaction and said, "That Asbury, that Asbury!"

Now there is a fable extant of a man who tried to please everybody, and his failure is a matter of record. Robinson Asbury was not more successful. But be it said that his ill success was due to no fault or shortcoming of his.

For a long time his growing power had been looked upon with disfavour by the coloured law firm of Bingo & Latchett. Both Mr. Bingo and Mr. Latchett themselves aspired to be Negro leaders in Cadgers, and they were delivering Emancipation Day orations and riding at the head of processions when Mr. Asbury was blacking boots. Is it any wonder, then, that they viewed with alarm his sudden rise? They kept their counsel, however, and treated with him, for it was best. They allowed him his scope without open revolt until the day upon which he hung out his shingle. This was the last straw. They could stand no more. Asbury had stolen their other chances from them, and now he was poaching upon the last of their preserves. So Mr. Bingo and Mr. Latchett put their heads together to plan the downfall of their common enemy.

The plot was deep and embraced the formation of an opposing faction made up of the best Negroes of the town. It would have looked too much like what it was for the gentlemen to show themselves in the matter, and so they took into their confidence Mr. Isaac Morton, the principal of the coloured school, and it was under his ostensible leadership that the new faction finally came into being.

Mr. Morton was really an innocent young man, and he had ideals which should never have been exposed to the air. When the wily confederates came to him with their plan he believed that his worth had been recognised, and at last he was to be what Nature destined him for—a leader.

The better class of Negroes—by that is meant those who were particularly envious of Asbury's success—flocked to the new man's standard. But whether the race be white or black, political virtue is always in a minority, so Asbury could afford to smile at the force arrayed against him.

The new faction met together and resolved. They resolved, among other things, that Mr. Asbury was an enemy to his race and a menace to civilisation. They decided that he should be abolished; but, as they couldn't get out an injunction against him, and as he had the whole undignified but still voting black belt behind him, he went serenely on his way.

"They're after you hot and heavy, Asbury," said one of his friends to him.

"Oh, yes," was the reply, "they're after me, but after a while I'll get so far away that they'll be running in front."

"It's all the best people, they say."

"Yes. Well, it's good to be one of the best people, but your vote only counts one just the same."

The time came, however, when Mr. Asbury's theory was put to the test. The Cadgerites celebrated the first of January as Emancipation Day. On this day there was a large procession, with speechmaking in the afternoon and fireworks at night. It was the custom to concede the leadership of the coloured people of the town to the man who managed to lead the procession. For two years past this honour had fallen, of course, to Robinson Asbury, and there had been no disposition on the part of anybody to try conclusions with him.

Mr. Morton's faction changed all this. When Asbury went to work to solicit contributions for the celebration, he suddenly became aware that he had a fight upon his hands. All the better-class Negroes were staying out of it. The next thing he knew was that plans were on foot for a rival demonstration.

"Oh," he said to himself, "that's it, is it? Well, if they want a fight they can have it."

He had a talk with the party managers, and he had another with Judge Davis.

"All I want is a little lift, judge," he said, "and I'll make 'em think the sky has turned loose and is vomiting niggers."

The judge believed that he could do it. So did the party managers. Asbury got his lift. Emancipation Day came.

There were two parades. At least, there was one parade and the shadow of another. Asbury's, however, was not the shadow. There was a great deal of substance about it—substance made up of many people, many banners, and numerous bands. He did not have the best people. Indeed, among his cohorts there were a good many of the pronounced rag-tag and bobtail. But he had noise and numbers. In such cases, nothing more is needed. The success of Asbury's side of the affair did everything to confirm his friends in their good opinion of him.

When he found himself defeated, Mr. Silas Bingo saw that it would be policy to placate his rival's just anger against him. He called upon him at his office the day after the celebration.

"Well, Asbury," he said, "you beat us, didn't you?"

"It wasn't a question of beating," said the other calmly. "It was only an inquiry as to who were the people—the few or the many."

"Well, it was well done, and you've shown that you are a manager. I confess that I haven't always thought that you were doing the wisest thing in living down here and catering to this class of people when you might, with your ability, to be much more to the better class."

"What do they base their claims of being better on?"

"Oh, there ain't any use discussing that. We can't get along without you, we see that. So I, for one, have decided to work with you for harmony."

"Harmony. Yes, that's what we want."

"If I can do anything to help you at any time, why you have only to command me."

"I am glad to find such a friend in you. Be sure, if I ever need you, Bingo, I'll call on you."

"And I'll be ready to serve you."

Asbury smiled when his visitor was gone. He smiled, and knitted his brow. "I wonder what Bingo's got up his sleeve," he said. "He'll bear watching."

It may have been pride at his triumph, it may have been gratitude at his helpers, but Asbury went into the ensuing campaign with reckless enthusiasm. He did the most daring things for the party's sake. Bingo, true to his promise, was ever at his side ready to serve him. Finally, association and immunity made danger less fearsome; the rival no longer appeared a menace.

With the generosity born of obstacles overcome, Asbury determined to forgive Bingo and give him a chance. He let him in on a deal, and from that time they worked amicably together until the election came and passed.

It was a close election and many things had had to be done, but there were men there ready and waiting to do them. They were successful, and then the first cry of the defeated party was, as usual, "Fraud! Fraud!" The cry was taken up by the jealous, the disgruntled, and the virtuous.

Someone remembered how two years ago the registration books had been stolen. It was known upon good authority that money had been freely used. Men held up their hands in horror at the suggestion that the Negro vote had been juggled with, as if that were a new thing. From their pulpits ministers denounced the machine and bade their hearers rise and throw off the yoke of a corrupt municipal government. One of those sudden fevers of reform had taken possession of the town and threatened to destroy the successful party.

They began to look around them. They must purify themselves. They must give the people some tangible evidence of their own yearnings after purity. They looked around them for a sacrifice to lay upon the altar of municipal reform. Their eyes fell upon Mr. Bingo. No, he was not big enough. His blood was too scant to wash away the political stains. Then they looked into each other's eyes and turned their gaze away to let it fall upon Mr. Asbury. They really hated to do it. But there must be a scapegoat. The god from the Machine commanded them to slay him.

Robinson Asbury was charged with many crimes—with all that he had committed and some that he had not. When Mr. Bingo saw what was afoot he threw himself heart and soul into the work of his old rival's enemies. He was of incalculable use to them.

Judge Davis refused to have anything to do with the matter. But in spite of his disapproval it went on. Asbury was indicted and tried. The evidence was all against him, and no one gave more damaging testimony than his friend, Mr. Bingo. The judge's charge was favourable to the defendant, but the current of popular opinion could not be entirely stemmed. The jury brought in a verdict of guilty.

"Before I am sentenced, judge, I have a statement to make to the court. It will take less than ten minutes."

"Go on, Robinson," said the judge kindly.

Asbury started, in a monotonous tone, a recital that brought the prosecuting attorney to his feet in a minute. The judge waved him down, and sat transfixed by a sort of fascinated horror as the convicted man went on. The before-mentioned attorney drew a knife and started for the prisoner's dock. With difficulty he was restrained. A dozen faces in the court-room were red and pale by turns.

"He ought to be killed," whispered Mr. Bingo audibly.

Robinson Asbury looked at him and smiled, and then he told a few things of him. He gave the ins and outs of some of the misdemeanours of which he stood accused. He showed who were the men behind the throne. And still, pale and transfixed, Judge Davis waited for his own sentence.

Never were ten minutes so well taken up. It was a tale of rottenness and corruption in high places told simply and with the stamp of truth upon it.

He did not mention the judge's name. But he had torn the mask from the face of every other man who had been concerned in his downfall. They had shorn him of his strength, but they had forgotten that he was yet able to bring the roof and pillars tumbling about their heads.

The judge's voice shook as he pronounced sentence upon his old ally—a year in State's prison.

Some people said it was too light, but the judge knew what it was to wait for the sentence of doom, and he was grateful and sympathetic.

When the sheriff led Asbury away the judge hastened to have a short talk with him.

"I'm sorry, Robinson," he said, "and I want to tell you that you were no more guilty than the rest of us. But why did you spare me?"

"Because I knew you were my friend," answered the convict.

"I tried to be, but you were the first man that I've ever known since I've been in politics who ever gave me any decent return for friendship."

"I reckon you're about right, judge."

In politics, party reform usually lies in making a scapegoat of someone who is only as criminal as the rest, but a little weaker. Asbury's friends and enemies had succeeded in making him bear the burden of all the party's crimes, but their reform was hardly a success, and their protestations of a change of heart were received with doubt. Already there were those who began to pity the victim and to say that he had been hardly dealt with.

Mr. Bingo was not of these; but he found, strange to say, that his opposition to the idea went but a little way, and that even with Asbury out of his path he was a smaller man than he was before. Fate was strong against him. His poor, prosperous humanity could not enter the lists against a martyr. Robinson Asbury was now a martyr.

II.

A year is not a long time. It was short enough to prevent people from forgetting Robinson, and yet long enough for their pity to grow strong as they remembered. Indeed, he was not gone a year. Good behaviour cut two months off the time of his sentence, and by the time people had come around to the notion that he was really the greatest and smartest man in Cadgers he was at home again.

He came back with no flourish of trumpets, but quietly, humbly. He went back again into the heart of the black district. His business had deteriorated during his absence, but he put new blood and new life into it. He did not go to work in the shop himself, but, taking down the shingle that had swung idly before his office door during his imprisonment, he opened the little room as a news- and cigar-stand.

Here anxious, pitying custom came to him and he prospered again. He was very quiet. Uptown hardly knew that he was again in Cadgers, and it knew nothing whatever of his doings.

"I wonder why Asbury is so quiet," they said to one another. "It isn't like him to be quiet." And they felt vaguely uneasy about him.

So many people had begun to say, "Well, he was a mighty good fellow after all."

Mr. Bingo expressed the opinion that Asbury was quiet because he was crushed, but others expressed doubt as to this. There are calms and calms, some after and some before the storm. Which was this?

They waited a while, and, as no storm came, concluded that this must be the after-quiet. Bingo, reassured, volunteered to go and seek confirmation of this conclusion.

He went, and Asbury received him with an indifferent, not to say, impolite, demeanour.

"Well, we're glad to see you back, Asbury," said Bingo patronisingly. He had variously demonstrated his inability to lead during his rival's absence and was proud of it. "What are you going to do?"

"I'm going to work."

"That's right. I reckon you'll stay out of politics."

"What could I do even if I went in?"

"Nothing now, of course; but I didn't know—"

He did not see the gleam in Asbury's half shut eyes. He only marked his humility, and he went back swelling with the news.

"Completely crushed—all the run taken out of him," was his report.

The black district believed this, too, and a sullen, smouldering anger took possession of them. Here was a good man ruined. Some of the people whom he had helped in his former days—some of the rude, coarse people of the low quarter who were still sufficiently unenlightened to be grateful—talked among themselves and offered to get up a demonstration for him. But he denied them. No, he wanted nothing of the kind. It would only bring him into unfavourable notice. All he wanted was that they would always be his friends and would stick by him.

They would to the death.

There were again two factions in Cadgers. The school-master could not forget how once on a time he had been made a tool of by Mr. Bingo. So he revolted against his rule and set himself up as the leader of an opposing clique. The fight had been long and strong, but had ended with odds slightly in Bingo's favour.

But Mr. Morton did not despair. As the first of January and Emancipation Day approached, he arrayed his hosts, and the fight for supremacy became fiercer than ever. The school-teacher brought the school-children in for chorus singing, secured an able orator, and the best essayist in town. With all this, he was formidable.

Mr. Bingo knew that he had the fight of his life on his hands, and he entered with fear as well as zest. He, too, found an orator, but he was not sure that he was as good as Morton's. There was no doubt but that his essayist was not. He secured a band, but still he felt unsatisfied. He had hardly done enough, and for the schoolmaster to beat him now meant his political destruction.

It was in this state of mind that he was surprised to receive a visit from Mr. Asbury.

"I reckon you're surprised to see me here," said Asbury, smiling.

"I am pleased, I know." Bingo was astute.

"Well, I just dropped in on business."

"To be sure, to be sure, Asbury. What can I do for you?"

"It's more what I can do for you that I came to talk about," was the reply.

"I don't believe I understand you."

"Well, it's plain enough. They say that the school-teacher is giving you a pretty hard fight."

"Oh, not so hard."

"No man can be too sure of winning, though. Mr. Morton once did me a mean turn when he started the faction against me."

Bingo's heart gave a great leap, and then stopped for the fraction of a second.

"You were in it, of course," pursued Asbury, "but I can look over your part in it in order to get even with the man who started it."

It was true, then, thought Bingo gladly. He did not know. He wanted revenge for his wrongs and upon the wrong man. How well the schemer had covered his tracks! Asbury should have his revenge and Morton would be the sufferer.

"Of course, Asbury, you know what I did I did innocently."

"Oh, yes, in politics we are all lambs and the wolves are only to be found in the other party. We'll pass that, though. What I want to say is that I can help you to make your celebration an overwhelming success. I still have some influence down in my district."

"Certainly, and very justly, too. Why, I should be delighted with your aid. I could give you a prominent place in the procession."

"I don't want it; I don't want to appear in this at all. All I want is revenge. You can have all the credit, but let me down my enemy."

Bingo was perfectly willing, and, with their heads close together, they had a long and close consultation. When Asbury was gone, Mr. Bingo lay back in his chair and laughed. "I'm a slick duck," he said.

From that hour Mr. Bingo's cause began to take on the appearance of something very like a boom. More bands were hired. The interior of the State was called upon and a more eloquent orator secured. The crowd hastened to array itself on the growing side.

With surprised eyes, the school-master beheld the wonder of it, but he kept to his own purpose with dogged insistence, even when he saw that he could not turn aside the overwhelming defeat that threatened him. But in spite of his obstinacy, his hours were dark and bitter. Asbury worked like a mole, all underground, but he was indefatigable. Two days before the celebration time everything was perfected for the biggest demonstration that Cadgers had ever known. All the next day and night he was busy among his allies.

On the morning of the great day, Mr. Bingo, wonderfully caparisoned, rode down to the hall where the parade was to form. He was early. No one had yet come. In an hour a score of men all told had collected. Another hour passed, and no more had come. Then there smote upon his ear the sound of music. They were coming at last. Bringing his sword to his shoulder, he rode forward to the middle of the street. Ah, there they were. But—but—could he believe his eyes? They were going in another direction, and at their head rode—Morton! He gnashed his teeth in fury. He had been led into a trap and betrayed. The procession passing had been his—all his. He heard them cheering, and then, oh! climax of infidelity, he saw his own orator go past in a carriage, bowing and smiling to the crowd.

There was no doubting who had done this thing. The hand of Asbury was apparent in it. He must have known the truth all along, thought Bingo. His allies left him one by one for the other hall, and he rode home in a humiliation deeper than he had ever known before.

Asbury did not appear at the celebration. He was at his little news-stand all day.

In a day or two the defeated aspirant had further cause to curse his false friend. He found that not only had the people defected from him, but that the thing had been so adroitly managed that he appeared to be in fault, and three-fourths of those who knew him were angry at some supposed grievance. His cup of bitterness was full when his partner, a quietly ambitious man, suggested that they dissolve their relations.

His ruin was complete.

The lawyer was not alone in seeing Asbury's hand in his downfall. The party managers saw it too, and they met together to discuss the dangerous factor which, while it appeared to slumber, was so terribly awake. They decided that he must be appeased, and they visited him.

He was still busy at his news-stand. They talked to him adroitly, while he sorted papers and kept an impassive face. When they were all done, he looked up for a moment and replied, "You know, gentlemen, as an ex-convict I am not in politics."

Some of them had the grace to flush.

"But you can use your influence," they said.

"I am not in politics," was his only reply.

And the spring elections were coming on. Well, they worked hard, and he showed no sign. He treated with neither one party nor the other. "Perhaps," thought the managers, "he is out of politics," and they grew more confident.

It was nearing eleven o'clock on the morning of election when a cloud no bigger than a man's hand appeared upon the horizon. It came from the direction of the black district. It grew, and the managers of the party in power looked at it, fascinated by an ominous dread. Finally it began to rain Negro voters, and as one man they voted against their former candidates. Their organisation was perfect. They simply came, voted, and left, but they overwhelmed everything. Not one of the party that had damned Robinson Asbury was left in power save old Judge Davis. His majority was overwhelming.

The generalship that had engineered the thing was perfect. There were loud threats against the newsdealer. But no one bothered him except a reporter. The reporter called to see just how it was done. He found Asbury very busy sorting papers. To the newspaper man's questions he had only this reply, "I am not in politics, sir." But Cadgers had learned its lesson.

POLLY'S HACK RIDE

Emma E. Butler

(from *The Crisis* 12, June 1916)

POLLY GRAY HAD lived six and one-half years without ever having enjoyed the luxury of a hack ride.

The little shanty, merely an apology for a house, in which she lived with her parents, sat in a hollow on the main road in the village, at least fifteen feet below the road; and when Polly sat or stood at the front window upstairs, she watched with envy the finely dressed ladies and gentlemen riding by on their way to the big red brick building on the hill.

On several occasions her secret longing got the best of her, and she mustered all the self control of which her nature boasted to keep from stealing a ride on behind, as she had seen her brothers do on the ice wagon, but the memory of the warm reception usually awaiting the little male Grays, accompanied by predictions of broken necks, arms, legs, etc., caused her little frame to shiver.

Who then could say that Polly was wanting in sisterly love when she exulted in the fact that she was going to a funeral? What did it matter if Ma Gray was heart-broken, and Pa Gray couldn't eat but six biscuits for his supper when he came home and found the long white fringed sash floating from the cracked door knob?

Polly reviewed the events leading up to her present stage of ecstasy: Ma Gray had sent in hot haste for Aunt Betty Williams, who came with question marks stamped on her face, and when she found Ella, the two-year-old pet of the family in the throes of death she was by far too discreet to say so but advised Ma Gray to put her down. Polly had then become afraid and had run down stairs. She felt it—yes, sir—she felt it 'way down in her "stummik!" Something was going to happen, so when Ma Gray appeared at the head of the stairs with eyes swollen, and still a-swellin', and told her in a shaky voice to go to school for the children, she knew it had happened.

She started off at break-neck speed but, undecided just as to the proper gait for one bearing a message of such grave importance, she walked mournfully along for a while, then as the vision of a hack and two white horses arose, she skipped and finally ran again until she reached the school-house.

The afternoon session had just begun, as she timidly knocked on the door of the class-room where the two elder Grays were "gettin' their schoolin'"; and when the teacher opened the door, she beheld a very dirty little girl blubbering, "Ella's dead; Mamma's cryin'. Kin Bobby and Sally cum home?"

Master Bobby and Miss Sally were dismissed with the reverence due the dignity of their bereavement, and on their way home they proceeded to extract such bits of information as they deemed suitable for the occasion: "Were her eyes open or shut? Had she turned black yet? Did Aunt Betty cry too? Did Mamma fall across the bed as the breath was leaving her body?" Whereupon Miss Polly, being a young lady of a rather keen imagination upon which she drew, and drew heavily in times of need, gave them quite a sensational version of the affair, and by the time they reached home they were fully prepared to grieve with a capital "G." Sally ran to Ma Gray and with a shriek, threw both arms around her neck, while Bobby fell on his knees by the deceased Ella, imploring her to come back and be his baby sister once more.

Aunt Betty told her next door neighbor afterwards that she had her hands full and her heart full too, trying to quiet them. And if the smell of fried liver and onions had not reminded Bobby that it was near dinner time, she really couldn't tell how she should have managed them.

As plateful after plateful of liver, onions and mashed potatoes disappeared, the raging storm of grief subsided in the hearts of the young Grays, and by the time dinner was over Bobby was kept busy unpuckering his lips to suppress a whistle, and Sally had tried several bows of black ribbon on her hair to see which one looked best.

After the dishes were cleared away, and Ma Gray was scouring the floor in a solution of concentrated lye, water and tears, Uncle

Bangaway, a retired deacon in the Baptist church, stepped in to pay his respects.

Uncle Bangaway was considered a fine singer in his younger days and was quite proud of the accusation, so he proceeded to express his sympathy for Ma Gray in the words of his favorite hymn, kept in reserve for such occasions:

> "Wasn't my Lord mighty good and kind?
> O Yeah!
> "Wasn't my Lord mighty good and kind?
> O Yeah!
> "Wasn't my Lord mighty good and kind
> "To take away the child and leave the mother behind?
> "O Yeah! O Yeah! O Yeah!"

When he finished singing Ma Gray stopped crying to smile on him. It seemed that the hymn brought to her mind certain facts that were well worth considering.

On the morning of the day appointed for the funeral, a dark cloud hung over the village when Polly awoke, and her heart sank within her. Oh! If it should rain! Every hack she had ever seen on a rainy day had the curtains down, and there was no use riding in a hack if you had to have the curtains down. Anyhow, she began to dress, and before she was half through the sun began to peep through the clouds, and finally it shone brightly; and so did Miss Polly's face.

Who, then, could not pardon the cheerful face she brought down stairs where the funeral party was gathered? Dressed in a new black dress, new shoes, new hair ribbon, even new gloves, and a hack ride scheduled for the next two hours, was enough to make her very soul shine.

She hardly heard the minister as he dwelt at length on the innocence of childhood; nor his reference to Him who suffered the little ones to come unto Him; but the closing strains of "Nearer My God To Thee"[1] seemed to awaken her from pleasant dreams.

When the funeral procession started out Polly felt very sad, but the tears wouldn't come and, of course, "you can't make 'em come, if you ain't got no raw onions."

---

1. "Nearer My God To Thee": a Christian hymn written in the 19th century and based on Genesis 28: 11-19 (the story of Jacob's dream).

Now, it fell to her lot to sit in the hack with her great uncle, "Uncle Billings" Ma Gray called him, but Polly often wondered why Pa Gray spoke of him as "Uncle Rummy."

One of the many reasons for Polly's aversion to Uncle Billings was because of his prompt appearance before dinner every Sunday, when he would call her mother's attention every time she, Polly, took another doughnut or cookie. So you may be sure her spirits fell when she realized the state of affairs.

On the way to the cemetery neither found much to say to the other, but when they started home Uncle Billings began to lecture Polly concerning her apparent indifference to the family bereavement; during which discourse Polly sat without hearing one word, as her mind was otherwise engaged. She was trying to think of some manner in which to attract the attention of the Higdon girls as she passed the pump; she knew they would be there.

Before her plans were matured, however, the red bonnet of Cecie Higdon loomed up at the corner, and standing right behind her were Bessie and Georgia Higdon and Lucy Matthews.

Now was her chance! Now or never! So she sprang from her seat, leaned far out of the window, and gave one loud "Whee!" to the girls, waving her black-bordered handkerchief meanwhile.

Uncle Billings had just dropped off in a doze, and Polly's whoop brought him out of it so suddenly that he could find nothing more appropriate to say than, "Hush your noise, gal!" when with a sudden jerk the hack stopped and they were home.

As Polly alighted from the hack, she began to realize how, as a mourner, she had lowered her dignity by yelling from the window like a joy-rider, and she was not a little uneasy as to how Ma Gray would consider the matter should old Rummy inform her. So during supper she cautiously avoided meeting his eye, and as soon as she had finished eating she ran upstairs to change her clothes.

Here her mother found her later, with her head resting on the open Bible, and when she tried to awaken her she said, "Yes'm, just tell him not to drive quite so fast."

MAMMY: A STORY

Adeline F. Ries

(from *The Crisis* 13, January 1917)

MAMMY'S HEART FELT heavy indeed when (the time was now two years past) marriage had borne Shiela, her "white baby," away from the Governor's plantation to the coast. But as the months passed, the old colored nurse became accustomed to the change, until the great joy brought by the news that Shiela had a son, made her reconciliation complete. Besides, had there not always been Lucy, Mammy's own "black baby," to comfort her?

Yes, up to that day there had always been Lucy; but on that very day the young Negress had been sold—sold like common household ware!—and (the irony of it chilled poor Mammy's leaden heart)—she had been sold to Shiela as nurse to the baby whose birth, but four days earlier had caused Mammy so much rejoicing. The poor slave could not believe that it was true, and as she buried her head deeper into the pillows, she prayed that she might wake to find it all a dream.

But a reality it proved and a reality which she dared not attempt to change. For despite the Governor's customary kindness, she knew from experience, that any interference on her part would but result in serious floggings. One morning each week she would go to his study and he would tell her the news from the coast and then with a kindly smile dismiss her.

So for about a year, Mammy feasted her hungering soul with these meagre scraps of news, until one morning, contrary to his wont, the Governor rose as she entered the room, and he bade her

61

sit in a chair close to his own. Placing one of his white hands over
her knotted brown ones, he read aloud the letter he held in his
other hand:

"Dear Father:—

"I can hardly write the sad news and can, therefore, fully appreciate
how difficult it will be for you to deliver it verbally. Lucy was found
lying on the nursery floor yesterday, dead. The physician whom I
immediately summoned pronounced her death a case of heart-
failure. Break it gently to my dear old mammy, father, and tell her
too, that the coach, should she wish to come here before the burial,
is at her disposal.

> "Your daughter,
> "SHIELA."

While he read, the Governor unconsciously nerved himself to a
violent outburst of grief, but none came. Instead, as he finished,
Mammy rose, curtsied, and made as if to withdraw. At the door
she turned back and requested the coach, "if it weren't asking too
much," and then left the room. She did not return to her cabin;
simply stood at the edge of the road until the coach with its horses
and driver drew up and then she entered. From that time and until
nightfall she did not once change the upright position she had
assumed, nor did her eyelids once droop over her staring eyes.
"They took her from me an' she died"—"They took her from me
an' she died"—over and over she repeated the same sentence.

When early the next morning Mammy reached Shiela's home,
Shiela herself came down the road to meet her, ready with words
of comfort and love. But as in years gone by, it was Mammy who
took the golden head on her breast, and patted it, and bade the girl
to dry her tears. As of old, too, it was Mammy who first spoke of
other things; she asked to be shown the baby, and Shiela only too
willingly led the way to the nursery where in his crib the child lay
cooing to itself. Mammy took up the little body and again and
again tossed it up into the air with the old cry, "Up she goes,
Shiela," till he laughed aloud.

Suddenly she stopped, and clasping the child close she took a
hurried step towards the open window. At a short distance from
the house rolled the sea and Mammy gazed upon it as if fascinated.
And as she stared, over and over the words formed themselves:

"They took her from me an' she died,"—"They took her from me an' she died."

From below came the sound of voices, "They're waiting for you, Mammy,"—it was Shiela's soft voice that spoke—"to take Lucy—you understand, dear."

Mammy's eyes remained fixed upon the waves,—"I can't go—go foh me, chile, won't you?" And Shiela thought that she understood the poor woman's feelings and without even pausing to kiss her child she left the room and joined the waiting slaves.

Mammy heard the scraping as of a heavy box upon the gravel below; heard the tramp of departing footsteps as they grew fainter and fainter until they died away. Then and only then, did she turn her eyes from the wild waters and looking down at the child in her arms, she laughed a low, peculiar laugh. She smoothed back the golden ringlets from his forehead, straightened out the little white dress, and then, choosing a light covering for his head, she descended the stairs and passed quietly out of the house.

A short walk brought Mammy and her burden to the lonely beach; at the water's edge she stood still. Then she shifted the child's position until she supported his weight in her hands and with a shrill cry of "Up she goes, Shiela," she lifted him above her head. Suddenly she flung her arms forward, at the same time releasing her hold of his little body. A large breaker caught him in its foam, swept him a few feet towards the shore and retreating, carried him out into the sea—

A few hours later, two slaves in frantic search for the missing child found Mammy on the beach tossing handfuls of sand into the air and uttering loud, incoherent cries. And as they came close, she pointed towards the sea and with the laugh of a mad-woman shouted: "They took her from me an' she died!"

MARY ELIZABETH

Jessie Fauset

(from *The Crisis* 19, December 1919)

MARY ELIZABETH WAS late that morning. As a direct result, Roger left for work without telling me good-bye, and I spent most of the day fighting the headache which always comes if I cry.

For I cannot get a breakfast. I can manage a dinner,—one just puts the roast in the oven and takes it out again. And I really excel in getting lunch. There is a good delicatessen near us, and with dainty service and flowers, I get along very nicely. But breakfast! In the first place, it's a meal I neither like nor need. And I never, if I live a thousand years, shall learn to like coffee. I suppose that is why I cannot make it.

"Roger," I faltered, when the awful truth burst upon me and I began to realize that Mary Elizabeth wasn't coming, "Roger, couldn't you get breakfast downtown this morning? You know last time you weren't so satisfied with my coffee."

Roger was hostile. I think he had just cut himself, shaving. Anyway, he was horrid.

"No, I can't get my breakfast downtown!" He actually snapped at me. "Really, Sally, I don't believe there's another woman in the world who would send her husband out on a morning like this on an empty stomach. I don't see how you can be so unfeeling."

Well, it wasn't "a morning like this," for it was just the beginning of November. And I had only proposed his doing what I knew he would have to do eventually.

I didn't say anything more, but started on that breakfast. I don't know why I thought I had to have hot cakes! The breakfast really was awful! The cakes were tough and gummy and got cold one second, exactly, after I took them off the stove. And the coffee boiled, or stewed, or scorched, or did whatever the particular thing is that coffee shouldn't do. Roger sawed at one cake, took one mouthful of the dreadful brew, and pushed away his cup.

"It seems to me you might learn to make a decent cup of coffee," he said icily. Then he picked up his hat and flung out of the house.

I think it is stupid of me, too, not to learn how to make coffee. But, really, I'm no worse than Roger is about lots of things. Take "Five Hundred." Roger knows I love cards, and with the Cheltons right around the corner from us and as fond of it as I am, we could spend many a pleasant evening. But Roger will not learn. Only the night before, after I had gone through a whole hand with him, with hearts as trumps, I dealt the cards around again to imaginary opponents and we started playing. Clubs were trumps, and spades led. Roger, having no spades, played triumphantly a Jack of Hearts and proceeded to take the trick.

"But, Roger," I protested, "you threw off."

"Well," he said, deeply injured, "didn't you say hearts were trumps when you were playing before?"

And when I tried to explain, he threw down the cards and wanted to know what difference it made; he'd rather play casino, anyway! I didn't go out and slam the door.

But I couldn't help from crying this particular morning. I not only value Roger's good opinion, but I hate to be considered stupid.

Mary Elizabeth came in about eleven o'clock. She is a small, weazened woman, very dark, somewhat wrinkled, and a model of self-possession. I wish I could make you see her, or that I could reproduce her accent, not that it is especially colored,—Roger's and mine are much more so—but her pronunciation, her way of drawing out her vowels, is so distinctively Mary Elizabethan!

I was ashamed of my red eyes and tried to cover up my embarrassment with sternness.

"Mary Elizabeth," said I, "you are late!" Just as though she didn't know it.

"Yas'm, Mis' Pierson," she said, composedly, taking off her coat. She didn't remove her hat,—she never does until she has been in the house some two or three hours. I can't imagine why. It is a small, black, dusty affair, trimmed with black ribbon, some dingy white roses and a sheaf of wheat. I give Mary Elizabeth a dress and hat now and then, but, although I recognize the dress from time to time, I never see any change in the hat. I don't know what she does with my ex-millinery.

"Yas'm," she said again, and looked comprehensively at the untouched breakfast dishes and the awful viands, which were still where Roger had left them.

"Looks as though you'd had to git breakfast yoreself," she observed brightly. And went out in the kitchen and ate all those cakes and drank that unspeakable coffee! Really she did, and she didn't warm them up either.

I watched her miserably, unable to decide whether Roger was too finicky or Mary Elizabeth a natural-born diplomat.

"Mr. Gales led me an awful chase last night," she explained. "When I got home yistiddy evenin', my cousin whut keeps house fer me (!) tole me Mr. Gales went out in the mornin' en hadn't come back."

"Mr. Gales," let me explain, is Mary Elizabeth's second husband, an octogenarian, and the most original person, I am convinced, in existence.

"Yas'm," she went on, eating a final cold hot-cake, "en I went to look fer 'im, en had the whole perlice station out all night huntin' 'im. Look like they wusn't never goin' to find 'im. But I ses, 'Jes' let me look fer enough en long enough en I'll find 'im,' I ses, en I did. Way out Georgy Avenue, with the hat on ole Mis' give 'im. Sent it to 'im all the way fum Chicaga. He's had it fifteen years,—high silk beaver. I knowed he wusn't goin' too fer with that hat on.

"I went up to 'im, settin' by a fence all muddy, holdin' his hat on with both hands. En I ses, 'Look here, man, you come erlong home with me, en let me put you to bed.' En he come jest as meek! No-o-me, I knowed he wusn't goin' fer with ole Mis' hat on."

"Who was old 'Mis,' Mary Elizabeth?" I asked her.

"Lady I used to work fer in Noo York," she informed me. "Me en Rosy, the cook, lived with her fer years. Old Mis' was turrible fond of me, though her en Rosy used to querrel all the time. Jes' seemed like they couldn't git erlong. 'Member once Rosy run after her one Sunday with a knife, en I kep 'em apart. Reckon Rosy musta bin right put out with ole Mis' that day. By en by her en Rosy move to Chicaga, en when I married Mr. Gales, she sent 'im that hat. That old white woman shore did like me. It's so late, reckon I'd better put off sweepin' tel termorrer, ma'am."

I acquiesced, following her about from room to room. This was partly to get away from my own doleful thoughts—Roger really had hurt my feelings—but just as much to hear her talk. At first I used not to believe all she said, but after I investigated once and found her truthful in one amazing statement, I capitulated.

She had been telling me some remarkable tale of her first husband and I was listening with the stupefied attention, to which she always reduces me. Remember she was speaking of her first husband.

"En I ses to 'im, I ses, 'Mr. Gale,—'"

"Wait a moment, Mary Elizabeth," I interrupted, meanly delighted to have caught her for once. "You mean your first husband, don't you?"

"Yas'm," she replied. "En I ses to 'im, 'Mr. Gale! I ses—'"

"But, Mary Elizabeth," I persisted, "that's your second husband, isn't it,—Mr. Gale?"

She gave me her long-drawn "No-o-me! My first husband was Mr. Gale and my second is Mr. *Gales*. He spells his name with a Z, I reckon. I ain't never see it writ. Ez I wus sayin', I ses to Mr. Gale—"

And it was true! Since then I have never doubted Mary Elizabeth.

She was loquacious that afternoon. She told me about her sister, "where's got a home in the country and where's got eight children." I used to read Lucy Pratt's stories about little Ephraim or Ezekiel, I forget his name, who always said "where's" instead of "who's," but I never believed it really till I heard Mary Elizabeth use it. For some reason or other she never mentions her sister without mentioning the home, too. "My sister where's got a home in the country" is her unvarying phrase.

"Mary Elizabeth," I asked her once, "does your sister live in the country, or does she simply own a house there?"

"Yas'm," she told me.

She is fond of her sister. "If Mr. Gales wus to die," she told me complacently, "I'd go to live with her."

"If he should die," I asked her idly, "would you marry again?"

"Oh, no-o-me!" She was emphatic. "Though I don't know why I shouldn't, I'd come by it hones'. My father wus married four times."

That shocked me out of my headache. "Four times, Mary Elizabeth, and you had all those stepmothers!" My mind refused to take it in.

"Oh, no-o-me! I always lived with mamma. She was his first wife."

I hadn't thought of people in the state in which I had instinctively placed Mary Elizabeth's father and mother as indulging in divorce, but as Roger says slangily, "I wouldn't know."

Mary Elizabeth took off the dingy hat. "You see, papa and mamma—" the ineffable pathos of hearing this woman of sixty-four, with a husband of eighty, use the old childish terms!

"Papa and mamma wus slaves, you know, Mis' Pierson, and so of course they wusn't exackly married. White folks wouldn't let 'em. But they wus awf'ly in love with each other. Heard mamma tell erbout it lots of times, and how papa wus the han'somest man! Reckon she wus long erbout sixteen or seventeen then. So they jumped over a broomstick, en they wus jes as happy! But not long after I come erlong, they sold papa down South, and mamma never see him no mo' fer years and years. Thought he was dead. So she married again."

"And he came back to her, Mary Elizabeth?" I was overwhelmed with the woefulness of it.

"Yas'm. After twenty-six years. Me and my sister where's got a home in the country—she's really my half-sister, see Mis' Pierson,—her en mamma en my step-father en me wus all down in Bumpus, Virginia, workin' fer some white folks, and we used to live in a little cabin, had a front stoop to it. En one day an ole cullud man come by, had a lot o' whiskers. I'd saw him lots of times there in Bumpus, lookin' and peerin' into every cullud woman's face. En jes' then my sister she call out, 'Come here, you Ma'y Elizabeth,' en that old man stopped, en he looked at me en he looked at me, en he ses to me, 'Chile, is yo' name Ma'y Elizabeth?'

"You know, Mis' Pierson, I thought he wus jes' bein' fresh, en I ain't paid no 'tention to 'im. I ain't sed nuthin' ontel he spoke to me three or four times, en then I ses to 'im, 'Go 'way fum here, man, you ain't got no call to be fresh with me. I'm a decent woman. You'd oughta be ashamed of yoreself, an ole man like you.'"

Mary Elizabeth stopped and looked hard at the back of her poor wrinkled hands.

"En he says to me, 'Daughter,' he ses, jes' like that, 'daughter,' he ses, 'hones' I ain't bein' fresh. Is yo' name shore enough Ma'y Elizabeth?'

"En I tole him, 'Yas'r.'

"'Chile,' he ses, 'whar is yo' daddy?'

"'Ain't got no daddy,' I tole him peart-like. 'They done tuk 'im away fum me twenty-six years ago, I wusn't but a mite of a baby. Sol' 'im down the river. My mother often talks about it.' And, oh, Mis' Pierson, you shoulda see the glory come into his face!

"'Yore mother!' he ses, kinda out of breath, 'yore mother! Ma'y Elizabeth, whar is your mother?'

"'Back thar on the stoop,' I tole 'im. 'Why, did you know my daddy?'

"But he didn't pay no 'tention to me, jes' turned and walked up the stoop whar mamma wus settin'! She was feelin' sorta porely that day. En you oughta see me steppin' erlong after 'im.

"He walked right up to her and giv' her one look. 'Oh, Maggie,' he shout out, 'oh, Maggie! Ain't you know me? Maggie, ain't you know me?'

"Mamma look at 'im and riz up outa her cheer. 'Who're you?' she ses kinda trimbly, 'callin' me Maggie thata way? Who're you?'

"He went up real close to her, then, 'Maggie,' he ses jes' like that, kinda sad 'n tender, 'Maggie!' And hel' out his arms.

"She walked right into them. 'Oh,' she ses, 'it's Cassius! It's Cassius! It's my husban' come back to me! It's Cassius!' They wus like two mad people.

"My sister Minnie and me, we jes' stood and gawped at 'em. There they wus, holding on to each other like two pitiful childrun, en he tuk her hands and kissed 'em.

"'Maggie,' he ses, 'you'll come away with me, won't you? You gona take me back, Maggie? We'll go away, you en Ma'y Elizabeth en me. Won't we, Maggie?'

"Reckon my mother clean fergot my stepfather. 'Yes, Cassius,' she ses, 'we'll go away.' And then she sees Minnie, en it all comes back to her. 'Oh, Cassius,' she ses, 'I cain't go with you, I'm married again, en this time fer real. This here gal's mine and three boys, too, and another chile comin' in November!'"

"But she went with him, Mary Elizabeth," I pleaded. "Surely she went with him after all those years. He really was her husband."

I don't know whether Mary Elizabeth meant to be sarcastic or not. "Oh, no-o-me, mamma couldn't a done that. She wus a good woman. Her ole master, whut done sol' my father down river, brung her up too religious fer that, en anyways, papa was married again, too. Had his fourth wife there in Bumpus with 'im."

The unspeakable tragedy of it!

I left her and went up to my room, and hunted out my dark-blue serge dress which I had meant to wear again that winter. But I had to give Mary Elizabeth something, so I took the dress down to her.

She was delighted with it. I could tell she was, because she used her rare and untranslatable expletive.

"Haytian!" she said. "My sister where's got a home in the country, got a dress looks somethin' like this, but it ain't as good. No-o-me. She got hers to wear at a friend's weddin',—gal she was riz up with. Thet gal married well, too, lemme tell you; her husband's a Sunday School sup'rintender."

I told her she needn't wait for Mr. Pierson, I would put dinner on the table. So off she went in the gathering dusk, trudging bravely back to her Mr. Gales and his high silk hat.

I watched her from the window till she was out of sight. It had been such a long time since I had thought of slavery. I was born in Pennsylvania, and neither my parents nor grandparents had been slaves; otherwise I might have had the same tale to tell as Mary Elizabeth, or worse yet, Roger and I might have lived in those black days and loved and lost each other and futilely, damnably, met again like Cassius and Maggie.

Whereas it was now, and I had Roger and Roger had me.

How I loved him as I sat there in the hazy dusk. I thought of his dear, bronze perfection, his habit of swearing softly in excitement, his blessed stupidity. Just the same I didn't meet him at the door as usual, but pretended to be busy. He came rushing to me with the *Saturday Evening Post,* which is more to me than rubies. I thanked him warmly, but aloofly, if you can get that combination.

We ate dinner almost in silence for my part. But he praised everything,—the cooking, the table, my appearance.

After dinner we went up to the little sitting-room. He hoped I wasn't tired,—couldn't he fix the pillows for me? So!

I opened the magazine and the first thing I saw was a picture of a woman gazing in stony despair at the figure of a man disappearing around the bend of the road. It was too much. Suppose that were Roger and I! I'm afraid I sniffled. He was at my side in a moment.

"Dear loveliest! Don't cry. It was all my fault. You aren't any worse about coffee than I am about cards! And anyway, I needn't have slammed the door! Forgive me, Sally. I always told you I was hard to get along with. I've had a horrible day,—don't stay cross with me, dearest."

I held him to me and sobbed outright on his shoulder. "It isn't you, Roger," I told him, "I'm crying about Mary Elizabeth."

I regret to say he let me go then, so great was his dismay. Roger will never be half the diplomat that Mary Elizabeth is.

"Holy smokes!" he groaned. "She isn't going to leave us for good, is she?"

So then I told him about Maggie and Cassius. "And oh, Roger," I ended futilely, "to think that they had to separate after all those years, when he had come back, old and with whiskers!" I didn't mean to be so banal, but I was crying too hard to be coherent.

Roger had got up and was walking the floor, but he stopped then aghast.

"Whiskers!" he moaned. "My hat! Isn't that just like a woman?" He had to clear his throat once or twice before he could go on, and I think he wiped his eyes.

"Wasn't it the——" I really can't say what Roger said here,— "wasn't it the darndest hard luck that when he did find her again, she should be married? She might have waited."

I stared at him astounded. "But, Roger," I reminded him, "he had married three other times, he didn't wait."

"Oh——!" said Roger, unquotably, "married three fiddlesticks! He only did that to try to forget her."

Then he came over and knelt beside me again. "Darling, I do think it is a sensible thing for a poor woman to learn how to cook, but I don't care as long as you love me and we are together. Dear loveliest, if I had been Cassius,"—he caught my hands so tight that he hurt them, "—and I had married fifty times and had come back and found you married to someone else, I'd have killed you, killed you."

Well, he wasn't logical, but he was certainly convincing.

So thus, and not otherwise, Mary Elizabeth healed the breach.

JESUS CHRIST IN TEXAS

W. E. B. Du Bois

(from *Darkwater: Voices from Within the Veil*, 1920)

IT WAS IN WACO, Texas.

The convict guard laughed. "I don't know," he said, "I hadn't thought of that." He hesitated and looked at the stranger curiously. In the solemn twilight he got an impression of unusual height and soft, dark eyes. "Curious sort of acquaintance for the colonel," he thought; then he continued aloud: "But that nigger there is bad, a born thief, and ought to be sent up for life; got ten years last time——"

Here the voice of the promoter, talking within, broke in; he was bending over his figures, sitting by the colonel. He was slight, with a sharp nose.

"The convicts," he said, "would cost us $96 a year and board. Well, we can squeeze this so that it won't be over $125 apiece. Now if these fellows are driven, they can build this line within twelve months. It will be running by next April. Freights will fall fifty per cent. Why, man, you'll be a millionaire in less than ten years."

The colonel started. He was a thick, short man, with a clean-shaven face and a certain air of breeding about the lines of his countenance; the word millionaire sounded well to his ears. He thought—he thought a great deal; he almost heard the puff of the fearfully costly automobile that was coming up the road, and he said:

"I suppose we might as well hire them."

"Of course," answered the promoter.

The voice of the tall stranger in the corner broke in here:

"It will be a good thing for them?" he said, half in question.

The colonel moved. "The guard makes strange friends," he thought to himself. "What's this man doing here, anyway?" He looked at him, or rather looked at his eyes, and then somehow he felt a warming toward him. He said:

"Well, at least, it can't harm them; they're beyond that."

"It will do them good, then," said the stranger again.

The promoter shrugged his shoulders. "It will do us good," he said.

But the colonel shook his head impatiently. He felt a desire to justify himself before those eyes, and he answered: "Yes, it will do them good; or at any rate it won't make them any worse than they are." Then he started to say something else, but here sure enough the sound of the automobile breathing at the gate stopped him and they all arose.

"It is settled, then," said the promoter.

"Yes," said the colonel, turning toward the stranger again. "Are you going into town?" he asked with the Southern courtesy of white men to white men in a country town. The stranger said he was. "Then come along in my machine. I want to talk with you about this."

They went out to the car. The stranger as he went turned again to look back at the convict. He was a tall, powerfully built black fellow. His face was sullen, with a low forehead, thick, hanging lips, and bitter eyes. There was revolt written about his mouth despite the hangdog expression. He stood bending over his pile of stones, pounding listlessly. Beside him stood a boy of twelve,—yellow, with a hunted, crafty look. The convict raised his eyes and they met the eyes of the stranger. The hammer fell from his hands.

The stranger turned slowly toward the automobile and the colonel introduced him. He had not exactly caught his name, but he mumbled something as he presented him to his wife and little girl, who were waiting.

As they whirled away the colonel started to talk, but the stranger had taken the little girl into his lap and together they conversed in low tones all the way home.

In some way, they did not exactly know how, they got the impression that the man was a teacher and, of course, he must be a foreigner. The long, cloak-like coat told this. They rode in the twilight through the lighted town and at last drew up before the colonel's mansion, with its ghost-like pillars.

The lady in the back seat was thinking of the guests she had invited to dinner and was wondering if she ought not to ask this man to stay. He seemed cultured and she supposed he was some acquaintance of the colonel's. It would be rather interesting to have him there, with the judge's wife and daughter and the rector. She spoke almost before she thought:

"You will enter and rest awhile?"

The colonel and the little girl insisted. For a moment the stranger seemed about to refuse. He said he had some business for his father, about town. Then for the child's sake he consented.

Up the steps they went and into the dark parlor where they sat and talked a long time. It was a curious conversation. Afterwards they did not remember exactly what was said and yet they all remembered a certain strange satisfaction in that long, low talk.

Finally the nurse came for the reluctant child and the hostess bethought herself:

"We will have a cup of tea; you will be dry and tired."

She rang and switched on a blaze of light. With one accord they all looked at the stranger, for they had hardly seen him well in the glooming twilight. The woman started in amazement and the colonel half rose in anger. Why, the man was a mulatto, surely; even if he did not own the Negro blood, their practised eyes knew it. He was tall and straight and the coat looked like a Jewish gabardine. His hair hung in close curls far down the sides of his face and his face was olive, even yellow.

A peremptory order rose to the colonel's lips and froze there as he caught the stranger's eyes. Those eyes,—where had he seen those eyes before? He remembered them long years ago. The soft, tear-filled eyes of a brown girl. He remembered many things, and his face grew drawn and white. Those eyes kept burning into him, even when they were turned half away toward the staircase, where the white figure of the child hovered with her nurse and waved good-night. The lady sank into her chair and thought: "What will the judge's wife say? How did the colonel come to invite this man here? How shall we be rid of him?" She looked at the colonel in reproachful consternation.

Just then the door opened and the old butler came in. He was an ancient black man, with tufted white hair, and he held before him a large, silver tray filled with a china tea service. The stranger rose slowly and stretched forth his hands as if to bless the viands. The old man paused in bewilderment, tottered, and then with sudden gladness in his eyes dropped to his knees, and the tray crashed to the floor.

"My Lord and my God!" he whispered; but the woman screamed: "Mother's china!"

The doorbell rang.

"Heavens! here is the dinner party!" exclaimed the lady. She turned toward the door, but there in the hall, clad in her night clothes, was the little girl. She had stolen down the stairs to see the stranger again, and the nurse above was calling in vain. The woman felt hysterical and scolded at the nurse, but the stranger had stretched out his arms and with a glad cry the child nestled in them. They caught some words about the "Kingdom of Heaven" as he slowly mounted the stairs with his little, white burden.

The mother was glad of anything to get rid of the interloper, even for a moment. The bell rang again and she hastened toward the door, which the loitering black maid was just opening. She did not notice the shadow of the stranger as he came slowly down the stairs and paused by the newel post, dark and silent.

The judge's wife came in. She was an old woman, frilled and powdered into a semblance of youth, and gorgeously gowned. She came forward, smiling with extended hands, but when she was opposite the stranger, somewhere a chill seemed to strike her and she shuddered and cried:

"What a draft!" as she drew a silken shawl about her and shook hands cordially; she forgot to ask who the stranger was. The judge strode in unseeing, thinking of a puzzling case of theft.

"Eh? What? Oh—er—yes,—good evening," he said, "good evening." Behind them came a young woman in the glory of youth, and daintily silked, beautiful in face and form, with diamonds around her fair neck. She came in lightly, but stopped with a little gasp; then she laughed gaily and said:

"Why, I beg your pardon. Was it not curious? I thought I saw there behind your man"—she hesitated, but he must be a servant, she argued—"the shadow of great, white wings. It was but the light on the drapery. What a turn it gave me." And she smiled again. With her came a tall, handsome, young naval officer. Hearing his lady refer to the servant, he hardly looked at him, but held his gilded cap carelessly toward him, and the stranger placed it carefully on the rack.

Last came the rector, a man of forty, and well-clothed. He started to pass the stranger, stopped, and looked at him inquiringly.

"I beg your pardon," he said. "I beg your pardon,—I think I have met you?"

The stranger made no answer, and the hostess nervously hurried the guests on. But the rector lingered and looked perplexed.

"Surely, I know you. I have met you somewhere," he said, putting his hand vaguely to his head. "You—you remember me, do you not?"

The stranger quietly swept his cloak aside, and to the hostess' unspeakable relief passed out of the door.

"I never knew you," he said in low tones as he went.

The lady murmured some vain excuse about intruders, but the rector stood with annoyance written on his face.

"I beg a thousand pardons," he said to the hostess absently. "It is a great pleasure to be here,—somehow I thought I knew that man. I am sure I knew him once."

The stranger had passed down the steps, and as he passed, the nurse, lingering at the top of the staircase, flew down after him, caught his cloak, trembled, hesitated, and then kneeled in the dust.

He touched her lightly with his hand and said: "Go, and sin no more!"

With a glad cry the maid left the house, with its open door, and turned north, running. The stranger turned eastward into the night. As they parted a long, low howl rose tremulously and reverberated through the night. The colonel's wife within shuddered.

"The bloodhounds!" she said.

The rector answered carelessly:

"Another one of those convicts escaped, I suppose. Really, they need severer measures." Then he stopped. He was trying to remember that stranger's name.

The judge's wife looked about for the draft and arranged her shawl. The girl glanced at the white drapery in the hall, but the young officer was bending over her and the fires of life burned in her veins.

Howl after howl rose in the night, swelled, and died away. The stranger strode rapidly along the highway and out into the deep forest. There he paused and stood waiting, tall and still.

A mile up the road behind a man was running, tall and powerful and black, with crime-stained face and convicts' stripes upon him, and shackles on his legs. He ran and jumped, in little, short steps, and his chains rang. He fell and rose again, while the howl of the hounds rang louder behind him.

Into the forest he leapt and crept and jumped and ran, streaming with sweat; seeing the tall form rise before him, he stopped suddenly, dropped his hands in sullen impotence, and sank panting to the earth. A greyhound shot out of the woods behind him, howled, whined, and fawned before the stranger's feet. Hound after hound bayed, leapt, and lay there; then silently, one by one, and with bowed heads, they crept backward toward the town.

The stranger made a cup of his hands and gave the man water to drink, bathed his hot head, and gently took the chains and irons from his feet. By and by the convict stood up. Day was dawning above the treetops. He looked into the stranger's face, and for a moment a gladness swept over the stains of his face.

"Why, you are a nigger, too," he said.

Then the convict seemed anxious to justify himself.

"I never had no chance," he said furtively.

"Thou shalt not steal," said the stranger.

The man bridled.

"But how about them? Can they steal? Didn't they steal a whole year's work, and then when I stole to keep from starving——" He glanced at the stranger.

"No, I didn't steal just to keep from starving. I stole to be stealing. I can't seem to keep from stealing. Seems like when I see things, I just must—but, yes, I'll try!"

The convict looked down at his striped clothes, but the stranger had taken off his long coat; he had put it around him and the stripes disappeared.

In the opening morning the black man started toward the low, log farmhouse in the distance, while the stranger stood watching him. There was a new glory in the day. The black man's face cleared up, and the farmer was glad to get him. All day the black man worked as he had never worked before. The farmer gave him some cold food.

"You can sleep in the barn," he said, and turned away.

"How much do I git a day?" asked the black man.

The farmer scowled.

"Now see here," said he. "If you'll sign a contract for the season, I'll give you ten dollars a month."

"I won't sign no contract," said the black man doggedly.

"Yes, you will," said the farmer, threateningly, "or I'll call the convict guard." And he grinned.

The convict shrank and slouched to the barn. As night fell he looked out and saw the farmer leave the place. Slowly he crept out and sneaked toward the house. He looked through the kitchen door. No one was there, but the supper was spread as if the mistress had laid it and gone out. He ate ravenously. Then he looked into the front room and listened. He could hear low voices on the porch. On the table lay a gold watch. He gazed at it, and in a moment he was beside it,—his hands were on it! Quickly he slipped out of the house and slouched toward the field. He saw his employer coming along the highway. He fled back in terror and around to the front of the house, when suddenly he stopped. He felt the great, dark eyes of the stranger and saw the same dark, cloak-like coat where the stranger sat on the doorstep talking with the mistress of the house. Slowly, guiltily, he turned back, entered the kitchen, and laid the watch stealthily where he had found it; then he rushed wildly back toward the stranger, with arms outstretched.

The woman had laid supper for her husband, and going down from the house had walked out toward a neighbor's. She was gone but a little while, and when she came back she started to see a dark figure on the doorsteps under the tall, red oak. She thought it was the new Negro until he said in a soft voice:

"Will you give me bread?"

Reassured at the voice of a white man, she answered quickly in her soft, Southern tones:

"Why, certainly."

She was a little woman, and once had been pretty; but now her face was drawn with work and care. She was nervous and always thinking, wishing, wanting for something. She went in and got him some corn-bread and a glass of cool, rich buttermilk; then she came out and sat down beside him. She began, quite unconsciously, to tell him about herself,—the things she had done and had not done and the things she had wished for. She told him of her husband and this new farm they were trying to buy. She said it was hard to get niggers to work. She said they ought all to be in the chain-gang and made to work. Even then some ran away. Only yesterday one had escaped, and another the day before.

At last she gossiped of her neighbors, how good they were and how bad.

"And do you like them all?" asked the stranger.

She hesitated.

"Most of them," she said; and then, looking up into his face and putting her hand into his, as though he were her father, she said:

"There are none I hate; no, none at all."

He looked away, holding her hand in his, and said dreamily:

"You love your neighbor as yourself?"

She hesitated.

"I try——" she began, and then looked the way he was looking; down under the hill where lay a little, half-ruined cabin.

"They are niggers," she said briefly.

He looked at her. Suddenly a confusion came over her and she insisted, she knew not why.

"But they are niggers!"

With a sudden impulse she arose and hurriedly lighted the lamp that stood just within the door, and held it above her head. She saw his dark face and curly hair. She shrieked in angry terror and rushed down the path, and just as she rushed down, the black convict came running up with hands outstretched. They met in mid-path, and before he could stop he had run against her and she fell heavily to earth and lay white and still. Her husband came rushing around the house with a cry and an oath.

"I knew it," he said. "It's that runaway nigger." He held the black man struggling to the earth and raised his voice to a yell. Down the highway came the convict guard, with hound and mob and gun. They paused across the fields. The farmer motioned to them.

"He—attacked—my wife," he gasped.

The mob snarled and worked silently. Right to the limb of the red oak they hoisted the struggling, writhing black man, while others lifted the dazed woman. Right and left, as she tottered to the house, she searched for the stranger with a yearning, but the stranger was gone. And she told none of her guests.

"No—no, I want nothing," she insisted, until they left her, as they thought, asleep. For a time she lay still, listening to the departure of the mob. Then she rose. She shuddered as she heard the creaking of the limb where the body hung. But resolutely she crawled to the window and peered out into the moonlight; she saw the dead man writhe. He stretched his arms out like a cross, looking upward. She gasped and clung to the window sill. Behind the swaying body, and down where the little, half-ruined cabin lay, a single flame flashed up amid the far-off shout and cry of the mob. A fierce joy sobbed up through the terror in her soul and then sank abashed as she watched the flame rise. Suddenly whirling into one great crimson column it shot to the top of the sky and threw great arms athwart the gloom until above the world and behind the roped and swaying form below hung quivering and burning a great crimson cross.

She hid her dizzy, aching head in an agony of tears, and dared not look, for she knew. Her dry lips moved:

"Despised and rejected of men."

She knew, and the very horror of it lifted her dull and shrinking eyelids. There, heaven-tall, earth-wide, hung the stranger on the crimson cross, riven and bloodstained, with thorn-crowned head and piercèd hands. She stretched her arms and shrieked.

He did not hear. He did not see. His calm dark eyes, all sorrowful, were fastened on the writhing, twisting body of the thief, and a voice came out of the winds of the night, saying:

"This day thou shalt be with me in Paradise!"

BECKY

Jean Toomer

(from *Cane*, 1923)

Becky was the white woman who had two Negro sons. She's dead; they've gone away. The pines whisper to Jesus. The Bible flaps its leaves with an aimless rustle on her mound.

BECKY HAD ONE Negro son. Who gave it to her? Damn buck nigger, said the white folks' mouths. She wouldnt tell. Common, God-forsaken, insane white shameless wench, said the white folks' mouths. Her eyes were sunken, her neck stringy, her breasts fallen, till then. Taking their words, they filled her, like a bubble rising—then she broke. Mouth setting in a twist that held her eyes, harsh, vacant, staring . . . Who gave it to her? Low-down nigger with no self-respect, said the black folks' mouths. She wouldnt tell. Poor Catholic poor-white crazy woman, said the black folks' mouths. White folks and black folks built her cabin, fed her and her growing baby, prayed secretly to God who'd put His cross upon her and cast her out.

When the first was born, the white folks said they'd have no more to do with her. And black folks, they too joined hands to cast her out . . . The pines whispered to Jesus . . . The railroad boss said not to say he said it, but she could live, if she wanted to, on the narrow strip of land between the railroad and the road. John Stone, who owned the lumber and the bricks, would have shot the man who told he gave the stuff to Lonnie Deacon, who stole out there at night and built the cabin. A single room held down to earth . . . O fly away to Jesus . . . by a leaning chimney . . .

* ★ *

Six trains each day rumbled past and shook the ground under her
cabin. Fords, and horse- and mule-drawn buggies went back and
forth along the road. No one ever saw her. Trainmen, and passengers who'd heard about her, threw out papers and food. Threw
out little crumpled slips of paper scribbled with prayers, as they
passed her eye-shaped piece of sandy ground. Ground islandized
between the road and railroad track. Pushed up where a blue-
sheen God with listless eyes could look at it. Folks from the town
took turns, unknown, of course, to each other, in bringing corn
and meat and sweet potatoes. Even sometimes snuff . . . O thank y
Jesus . . . Old David Georgia, grinding cane and boiling syrup,
never went her way without some sugar sap. No one ever saw her.
The boy grew up and ran around. When he was five years old as
folks reckoned it, Hugh Jourdon saw him carrying a baby. "Becky
has another son," was what the whole town knew. But nothing
was said, for the part of man that says things to the likes of that had
told itself that if there was a Becky, that Becky now was dead.

The two boys grew. Sullen and cunning . . . O pines, whisper to
Jesus; tell Him to come and press sweet Jesus-lips against their lips
and eyes . . . It seemed as though with those two big fellows there,
there could be no room for Becky. The part that prayed wondered
if perhaps she'd really died, and they had buried her. No one dared
ask. They'd beat and cut a man who meant nothing at all in mentioning that they lived along the road. White or colored? No one
knew, and least of all themselves. They drifted around from job to
job. We, who had cast out their mother because of them, could
we take them in? They answered black and white folks by shooting up two men and leaving town. "Godam the white folks;
godam the niggers," they shouted as they left town. Becky? Smoke
curled up from her chimney; she must be there. Trains passing
shook the ground. The ground shook the leaning chimney.
Nobody noticed it. A creepy feeling came over all who saw that
thin wraith of smoke and felt the trembling of the ground. Folks
began to take her food again. They quit it soon because they had
a fear. Becky if dead might be a hant, and if alive—it took some
nerve even to mention it . . . O pines, whisper to Jesus . . .

It was Sunday. Our congregation had been visiting at Pulverton, and were coming home. There was no wind. The autumn sun, the bell from Ebenezer Church, listless and heavy. Even the pines were stale, sticky, like the smell of food that makes you sick. Before we turned the bend of the road that would show us the Becky cabin, the horses stopped stock-still, pushed back their ears, and nervously whinnied. We urged, then whipped them on. Quarter of a mile away thin smoke curled up from the leaning chimney . . . O pines, whisper to Jesus . . . Goose-flesh came on my skin though there still was neither chill nor wind. Eyes left their sockets for the cabin. Ears burned and throbbed. Uncanny eclipse! fear closed my mind. We were just about to pass . . . Pines shout to Jesus! . . . the ground trembled as a ghost train rumbled by. The chimney fell into the cabin. Its thud was like a hollow report, ages having passed since it went off. Barlo and I were pulled out of our seats. Dragged to the door that had swung open. Through the dust we saw the bricks in a mound upon the floor. Becky, if she was there, lay under them. I thought I heard a groan. Barlo, mumbling something, threw his Bible on the pile. (No one has ever touched it.) Somehow we got away. My buggy was still on the road. The last thing that I remember was whipping old Dan like fury; I remember nothing after that—that is, until I reached town and folks crowded round to get the true word of it.

Becky was the white woman who had two Negro sons. She's dead; they've gone away. The pines whisper to Jesus. The Bible flaps its leaves with an aimless rustle on her mound.

THE CITY OF REFUGE

Rudolph Fisher

(from *Atlantic Monthly,* February 1925)

I.

CONFRONTED SUDDENLY BY daylight, King Solomon Gillis stood dazed and blinking. The railroad station, the long, white-walled corridor, the impassable slot-machine, the terrifying subway train—he felt as if he had been caught up in the jaws of a steam-shovel, jammed together with other helpless lumps of dirt, swept blindly along for a time, and at last abruptly dumped.

There had been strange and terrible sounds: "New York! Penn Terminal—all change!" "Pohter, hyer, pohter, suh?" Shuffle of a thousand soles, clatter of a thousand heels, innumerable echoes. Cracking rifle-shots—no, snapping turnstiles. "Put a nickel in!" "Harlem? Sure. This side—next train." Distant thunder, nearing. The screeching onslaught of the fiery hosts of hell, headlong, breathtaking. Car doors rattling, sliding, banging open. "Say, wha' d'ye think this is, a baggage car?" Heat, oppression, suffocation—eternity—"Hundred 'n turdy-fif' next!" More turnstiles. Jonah emerging from the whale.

Clean air, blue sky, bright sunlight.

Gillis set down his tan-cardboard extension-case and wiped his black, shining brow. Then slowly, spreadingly, he grinned at what he saw: Negroes at every turn; up and down Lenox Avenue, up and down One Hundred and Thirty-fifth Street; big, lanky Negroes, short, squat Negroes; black ones, brown ones, yellow ones; men standing idle on the curb, women, bundle-laden,

84

trudging reluctantly homeward, children rattle-trapping about the sidewalks; here and there a white face drifting along, but Negroes predominantly, overwhelmingly everywhere. There was assuredly no doubt of his whereabouts. This was Negro Harlem.

Back in North Carolina Gillis had shot a white man and, with the aid of prayer and an automobile, probably escaped a lynching. Carefully avoiding the railroads, he had reached Washington in safety. For his car a Southwest bootlegger had given him a hundred dollars and directions to Harlem; and so he had come to Harlem.

Ever since a traveling preacher had first told him of the place, King Solomon Gillis had longed to come to Harlem. The Uggams were always talking about it; one of their boys had gone to France in the draft and, returning, had never got any nearer home than Harlem. And there were occasional "colored" newspapers from New York: newspapers that mentioned Negroes without comment, but always spoke of a white person as "So-and-so, white." That was the point. In Harlem, black was white. You had rights that could not be denied you; you had privileges, protected by law. And you had money. Everybody in Harlem had money. It was a land of plenty. Why, had not Mouse Uggam sent back as much as fifty dollars at a time to his people in Waxhaw?

The shooting, therefore, simply catalyzed whatever sluggish mental reaction had been already directing King Solomon's fortunes toward Harlem. The land of plenty was more than that now: it was also the city of refuge.

Casting about for direction, the tall newcomer's glance caught inevitably on the most conspicuous thing in sight, a magnificent figure in blue that stood in the middle of the crossing and blew a whistle and waved great white-gloved hands. The Southern Negro's eyes opened wide; his mouth opened wider. If the inside of New York had mystified him, the outside was amazing him. For there stood a handsome, brass-buttoned giant directing the heaviest traffic Gillis had ever seen; halting unnumbered tons of automobiles and trucks and wagons and pushcarts and street-cars; holding them at bay with one hand while he swept similar tons peremptorily on with the other; ruling the wide crossing with supreme self-assurance; and he, too, was a Negro!

Yet most of the vehicles that leaped or crouched at his bidding carried white passengers. One of these overdrove bounds a few feet and Gillis heard the officer's shrill whistle and gruff reproof, saw the driver's face turn red and his car draw back like a threatened pup. It was beyond belief—impossible. Black might be white, but it couldn't be that white!

"Done died an' woke up in Heaven," thought King Solomon, watching, fascinated; and after a while, as if the wonder of it were too great to believe simply by seeing, "Cullud policemans!" he said, half aloud; then repeated over and over, with greater and greater conviction, "Even got cullud policemans—even got cullud—"

"Where y' want to go, big boy?"

Gillis turned. A little, sharp-faced yellow man was addressing him.

"Saw you was a stranger. Thought maybe I could help y' out."

King Solomon located and gratefully extended a slip of paper. "Wha' dis hyeh at, please, suh?"

The other studied it a moment, pushing back his hat and scratching his head. The hat was a tall-crowned, unindented brown felt; the head was brown patent-leather, its glistening brush-back flawless save for a suspicious crimpiness near the clean-grazed edges.

"See that second corner? Turn to the left when you get there. Number forty-five's about halfway [down] the block."

"Thank y', suh."

"You from—Massachusetts?"

"No, suh, Nawth Ca'lina."

"Is 'at so? You look like a Northerner. Be with us long?"

"Till I die," grinned the flattered King Solomon.

"Stoppin' there?"

"Reckon I is. Man in Washin'ton 'lowed I'd find lodgin' at dis ad-dress."

"Good enough. If y' don't, maybe I can fix y' up. Harlem's pretty crowded. This is me." He proffered a card.

"Thank y', suh," said Gillis, and put the card in his pocket.

The little yellow man watched him plod flat-footedly on down the street, long awkward legs never quite straightened, shouldered extension-case bending him sidewise, wonder upon wonder halting or turning him about. Presently, as he proceeded, a pair of bright green stockings caught and held his attention. Tony, the storekeeper, was crossing the sidewalk with a bushel basket of apples. There was a collision; the apples rolled; Tony exploded; King Solomon apologized. The little yellow man laughed shortly, took out a notebook, and put down the address he had seen on King Solomon's slip of paper.

"Guess you're the shine I been waitin' for," he surmised.

As Gillis, approaching his destination, stopped to rest, a haunting notion grew into an insistent idea. "Dat li'l yaller nigger was a sho' 'nuff gen'man to show me de road. Seem lak I knowed him befo'—" He pondered. That receding brow, that sharp-ridged, spreading nose, that tight upper lip over the two big front teeth, that chinless jaw—He fumbled hurriedly for the card he had not looked at and eagerly made out the name.

"Mouse Uggam, sho' 'nuff! Well, dog-gone!"

II.

Uggam sought out Tom Edwards, once a Pullman porter, now prosperous proprietor of a cabaret, and told him:—

"Chief, I got him: a baby jess in from the land o' cotton and so dumb he thinks ante-bellum's an old woman."

"Where'd you find him?"

"Where you find all the jay birds when they first hit Harlem—at the subway entrance. This one come up the stairs, batted his eyes once or twice, an' froze to the spot—with his mouth wide open. Sure sign he's from 'way down behind the sun an' ripe f' the pluckin'."

Edwards grinned a gold-studded, fat-jowled grin. "Gave him the usual line, I suppose?"

"Didn't miss. An' he fell like a ton o' bricks. 'Course I've got him spotted, but damn 'f I know jess how to switch 'em on to him."

"Get him a job around a store somewhere. Make out you're befriendin' him. Get his confidence."

"Sounds good. Ought to be easy. He's from my state. Maybe I know him or some of his people."

"Make out you do, anyhow. Then tell him some fairy tale that'll switch your trade to him. The cops'll follow the trade. We could even let Froggy flop into some dumb white cop's hands and 'confess' where he got it. See?"

"Chief, you got a head, no lie."

"Don't lose no time. And remember, hereafter, it's better to sacrifice a little than to get squealed on. Never refuse a customer. Give him a little credit. Humor him along till you can get rid of him safe. You don't know what that guy that died may have said; you don't know who's on to you now. And if they get you—I don't know you."

"They won't get *me*," said Uggam.

★ ★ ★

King Solomon Gillis sat meditating in a room half the size of his hencoop back home, with a single window opening into an airshaft.

An airshaft: cabbage and chitterlings cooking; liver and onions sizzling, sputtering; three player-pianos out-plunking each other; a man and woman calling each other vile things; a sick, neglected baby wailing; a phonograph broadcasting blues; dishes clacking; a girl crying heartbrokenly; waste noises, waste odors of a score of families, seeking issue through a common channel; pollution from bottom to top—a sewer of sounds and smells.

Contemplating this, King Solomon grinned and breathed, "Dog-gone!" A little later, still gazing into the sewer, he grinned again. "Green stockin's," he said; "loud green!" The sewer gradually grew darker. A window lighted up opposite, revealing a woman in camisole and petticoat, arranging her hair. King Solomon, staring vacantly, shook his head and grinned yet again. "Even got cullud policemans!" he mumbled softly.

III.

Uggam leaned out of the room's one window and spat maliciously into the dinginess of the airshaft. "Damn glad you got him," he commented, as Gillis finished his story. "They's a thousand shines in Harlem would change places with you in a minute jess f' the honor of killin' a cracker."

"But I didn't go to do it. 'T was a accident."

"That's the only part to keep secret."

"Know whut dey done? Dey killed five o' Mose Joplin's hawses 'fo he lef'. Put groun' glass in de feed-trough. Sam Cheevers come up on three of 'em one night pizenin' his well. Bleesom beat Crinshaw out o' sixty acres o' lan' an' a year's crops. Dass jess how 't is. Soon's a nigger make a li'l sump'n he better git to leavin'. An' 'fo long ev'ybody's goin' be lef'!"

"Hope to hell they don't all come here."

The doorbell of the apartment rang. A crescendo of footfalls in the hallway culminated in a sharp rap on Gillis's door. Gillis jumped. Nobody but a policeman would rap like that. Maybe the landlady had been listening and had called in the law. It came

again, loud, quick, angry. King Solomon prayed that the policeman would be a Negro.

Uggam stepped over and opened the door. King Solomon's
apprehensive eyes saw framed therein, instead of a gigantic officer,
calling for him, a little blot of a creature, quite black against even
the darkness of the hallway, except for a dirty, wide-striped silk
shirt, collarless, with the sleeves rolled up.

"Ah hahve bill fo' Mr. Gillis." A high, strongly accented
Jamaican voice, with its characteristic singsong intonation, interrupted King Solomon's sigh of relief.

"Bill? Bill fo' me? What kin' o' bill?"

"Wan bushel appels. T'ree seventy-fife."

"Apples? I ain' bought no apples." He took the paper and read
aloud, laboriously, "Antonio Gabrielli to K. S. Gillis, Doctor—"

"Mr. Gabrielli say, you not pays him, he send policemon."

"What I had to do wid 'is apples?"

"You bumps into him yesterday, no? Scatter appels everywhere—on de sidewalk, in de gutter. Kids pick up an' run away.
Others all spoil. So you pays."

Gillis appealed to Uggam. "How 'bout it, Mouse?"

"He's a damn liar. Tony picked up most of 'em; I seen him.
Lemme look at that bill—Tony never wrote this thing. This
baby's jess playin' you for a sucker."

"Ain' had no apples, ain' payin' fo' none," announced King
Solomon, thus prompted. "Didn't have to come to Harlem to git
cheated. Plenty o' dat right wha' I come fum."

But the West Indian warmly insisted. "You cahn't do daht,
mon. Whaht you t'ink, 'ey? Dis mon loose 'is appels an' 'is money
too?"

"What diff'ence it make to you, nigger?"

"Who you call nigger, mon? Ah hahve you understahn'—"

"Oh, well, white folks, den. What all you got t' do wid dis
hyeh, anyhow?"

"Mr. Gabrielli send me to collect bill!"

"How I know dat?"

"Do Ah not bring bill? You t'ink Ah steal t'ree dollar, 'ey?"

"Three dollars an' sebenty-fi' cent," corrected Gillis. "'Nuther
thing: wha' you ever see me befo'? How you know dis is me?"

"Ah see you, sure. Ah help Mr. Gabrielli in de store. When you
knocks down de baskette appels, Ah see. Ah follow you. Ah know
you comes in dis house."

"Oh, you does? An' how come you know my name an' flat an' room so good? How come dat?"

"Ah fin' out. Sometime Ah brings up here vegetables from de store."

"Humph! Mus' be workin' on shares."

"You pays, 'ey? You pays me or de policemon?"

"Wait a minute," broke in Uggam, who had been thoughtfully contemplating the bill. "Now listen, big shorty. You haul hips on back to Tony. We got your menu all right"—he waved the bill—"but we don't eat your kind o' cookin', see?"

The West Indian flared. "Whaht it is to you, 'ey? You can not mind your own business? Ah hahve not spik to you!"

"No, brother. But this is my friend, an' I'll be john-browned if there's a monkey-chaser in Harlem can gyp him if I know it, see? Bes' thing f' you to do is catch air, toot sweet."[1]

Sensing frustration, the little islander demanded the bill back. Uggam figured he could use the bill himself, maybe. The West Indian hotly persisted; he even menaced. Uggam pocketed the paper and invited him to take it. Wisely enough, the caller preferred to catch air.

When he had gone, King Solomon sought words of thanks.

"Bottle it," said Uggam. "The point is this: I figger you got a job."

"Job? No I ain't! Wha' at?"

"When you show Tony this bill, he'll hit the roof and fire that monk."

"What ef he do?"

"Then you up 'n ask f' the job. He'll be too grateful to refuse. I know Tony some, an' I'll be there to put in a good word. See?"

King Solomon considered this. "Sho' needs a job, but ain' after stealin' none."

"Stealin'? 'T wouldn't be stealin'. Stealin' 's what that damn monkey-chaser tried to do from you. This would be doin' Tony a favor an' gettin' y'self out o' the barrel. What's the hold-back?"

"What make you keep callin' him monkey-chaser?"

"West Indian. That's another thing. Any time y' can knife a monk, do it. They's too damn many of 'em here. They're an achin' pain."

"Jess de way white folks feels 'bout niggers."

"Damn that. How 'bout it? Y' want the job?"

---

1. toot sweet: this is an English version of the French phrase "tout de suite," which means "right away" or "immediately."

"Hm—well—I'd ruther be a policeman."

"Policeman?" Uggam gasped.

"M-hm. Dass all I wants to be, a policeman, so I kin police all de white folks right plumb in jail!"

Uggam said seriously, "Well, y' might work up to that. But it takes time. An' y've got to eat while y're waitin'." He paused to let this penetrate. "Now, how 'bout this job at Tony's in the meantime? I should think y'd jump at it."

King Solomon was persuaded.

"Hm—well—reckon I does," he said slowly.

"Now y're tootin'!" Uggam's two big front teeth popped out in a grin of genuine pleasure. "Come on. Let's go."

IV.

Spitting blood and crying with rage, the West Indian scrambled to his feet. For a moment he stood in front of the store gesticulating furiously and jabbering shrill threats and unintelligible curses. Then abruptly he stopped and took himself off.

King Solomon Gillis, mildly puzzled, watched him from Tony's doorway. "I jess give him a li'l shove," he said to himself, "an' he roll' clean 'cross de sidewalk." And a little later, disgustedly, "Monkey-chaser!" he grunted, and went back to his sweeping.

"Well, big boy, how y' comin' on?"

Gillis dropped his broom. "Hay-o, Mouse. Wha' you been las' two-three days?"

"Oh, around. Gettin' on all right here? Had any trouble?"

"Deed I ain't—'ceptin' jess now I had to throw 'at li'l jigger out."

"Who? The monk?"

"M-hm. He sho' Lawd doan like me in his job. Look like he think I stole it from him, stiddy him tryin' to steal from me. Had to push him down sho' 'nuff 'fo I could git rid of 'im. Den he run off talkin' Wes' Indi'man an' shakin' his fis' at me."

"Ferget it." Uggam glanced about. "Where's Tony?"

"Boss man? He be back direckly."

"Listen—like to make two or three bucks a day extra?"

"Huh?"

"Two or three dollars a day more 'n what you're gettin' already?"

"Ain' I near 'nuff in jail now?"

"Listen." King Solomon listened. Uggam hadn't been in France for nothing. Fact was, in France he'd learned about some valuable French medicine. He'd brought some back with him,—little white pills,—and while in Harlem had found a certain druggist who knew what they were and could supply all he could use. Now there were any number of people who would buy and pay well for as much of this French medicine as Uggam could get. It was good for what ailed them, and they didn't know how to get it except through him. But he had no store in which to set up an agency and hence no single place where his customers could go to get what they wanted. If he had, he could sell three or four times as much as he did.

King Solomon was in a position to help him now, same as he had helped King Solomon. He would leave a dozen packages of the medicine—just small envelopes that could all be carried in a coat pocket—with King Solomon every day. Then he could simply send his customers to King Solomon at Tony's store. They'd make some trifling purchase, slip him a certain coupon which Uggam had given them, and King Solomon would wrap the little envelope of medicine with their purchase. Mustn't let Tony catch on, because he might object, and then the whole scheme would go gaflooey. Of course it wouldn't really be hurting Tony any. Wouldn't it increase the number of his customers?

Finally, at the end of each day, Uggam would meet King Solomon some place and give him a quarter for each coupon he held. There'd be at least ten or twelve a day—two and a half or three dollars plumb extra! Eighteen or twenty dollars a week!

"Dog-gone!" breathed Gillis.

"Does Tony ever leave you here alone?"

"M-hm. Jess started dis mawnin'. Doan nobody much come 'round 'tween ten an' twelve, so he done took to doin' his buyin' right 'long 'bout dat time. Nobody hyeh but me fo' 'n hour or so."

"Good. I'll try to get my folks to come 'round here mostly while Tony's out, see?"

"I doan miss."

"Sure y' get the idea, now?" Uggam carefully explained it all again. By the time he had finished, King Solomon was wallowing in gratitude.

"Mouse, you sho' is been a friend to me. Why, 'f 't hadn't been fo' you—"

"Bottle it," said Uggam. "I'll be 'round to your room to-night with enough stuff for to-morrer, see? Be sure 'n be there."

"Won't be nowha' else."

"An' remember, this is all jess between you 'n me."

"Nobody else but," vowed King Solomon.

Uggam grinned to himself as he went on his way. "Dumb Oscar! Wonder how much can we make before the cops nab him? French medicine—Hmph!"

V.

Tony Gabrielli, an oblate Neapolitan of enormous equator, wabbled heavily out of his store and settled himself over a soap box.

Usually Tony enjoyed sitting out front thus in the evening, when his helper had gone home and his trade was slackest. He liked to watch the little Gabriellis playing over the sidewalk with the little Levys and Johnsons; the trios and quartettes of brightly dressed, dark-skinned girls merrily out for a stroll; the slovenly gaited, darker men, who eyed them up and down and commented to each other with an unsuppressed "Hot damn!" or "Oh no, now!"

But to-night Tony was troubled. Something was wrong in the store; something was different since the arrival of King Solomon Gillis. The new man had seemed to prove himself honest and trustworthy, it was true. Tony had tested him, as he always tested a new man, by apparently leaving him alone in charge for two or three mornings. As a matter of fact, the new man was never under more vigilant observation than during these two or three mornings. Tony's store was a modification of the front rooms of his flat and was in direct communication with it by way of a glass-windowed door in the rear. Tony always managed to get back into his flat via the side-street entrance and watch the new man through this unobtrusive glass-windowed door. If anything excited his suspicion, like unwarranted interest in the cash register, he walked unexpectedly out of this door to surprise the offender in the act. Thereafter he would have no more such trouble. But he had not succeeded in seeing King Solomon steal even an apple.

What he had observed, however, was that the number of customers that came into the store during the morning's slack hour had pronouncedly increased in the last few days. Before, there had been three or four. Now there were twelve or fifteen. The mysterious thing about it was that their purchases totaled little more than those of the original three or four.

Yesterday and to-day Tony had elected to be in the store at the time when, on other days, he had been out. But Gillis had not been overcharging or shortchanging; for when Tony waited on the

customers himself—strange faces all—he found that they bought
something like a yeast cake or a five-cent loaf of bread. It was puzzling. Why should strangers leave their own neighborhoods and
repeatedly come to him for a yeast cake or a loaf of bread? They
were not new neighbors. New neighbors would have bought more
variously and extensively and at different times of day. Living near
by, they would have come in, the men often in shirtsleeves and
slippers, the women in kimonos, with boudoir caps covering their
lumpy heads. They would have sent in strange children for things
like yeast cakes and loaves of bread. And why did not some of them
come in at night when the new helper was off duty?

As for accosting Gillis on suspicion, Tony was too wise for that.
Patronage had a queer way of shifting itself in Harlem. You lost
your temper and let slip a single "*nègre*." A week later you sold
your business.

Spread over his soap box, with his pudgy hands clasped on his
preposterous paunch, Tony sat and wondered. Two men came up,
conspicuous for no other reason than that they were white. They
displayed extreme nervousness, looking about as if afraid of being
seen; and when one of them spoke to Tony it was in a husky, tone-
less, blowing voice, like the sound of a dirty phonograph record.

"Are you Antonio Gabrielli?"

"Yes, sure." Strange behavior for such lusty-looking fellows. He
who had spoken unsmilingly winked first one eye then the other,
and indicated by a gesture of his head that they should enter the
store. His companion looked cautiously up and down the Avenue,
while Tony, wondering what ailed them, rolled to his feet and
puffingly led the way.

Inside, the spokesman snuffled, gave his shoulders a queer little
hunch, and asked, "Can you fix us up, buddy?" The other glanced
restlessly about the place as if he were constantly hearing unaccountable noises.

Tony thought he understood clearly now. "Booze, 'ey?" he
smiled. "Sorry—I no got."

"Booze? Hell, no!" The voice dwindled to a throaty whisper.
"Dope. Coke, milk, dice—anything. Name your price. Got to
have it."

"Dope?" Tony was entirely at a loss. "What's a dis, dope?"

"Aw, lay off, brother. We're in on this. Here." He handed
Tony a piece of paper. "Froggy gave us a coupon. Come on. You
can't go wrong."

"I no got," insisted the perplexed Tony; nor could he be budged on that point.

Quite suddenly the manner of both men changed. "All right," said the first angrily, in a voice as robust as his body. "All right, you're clever. You no got. Well, you will get. You'll get twenty years!"

"Twenty year? Whadda you talk?"

"Wait a minute, Mac," said the second caller. "Maybe the wop's on the level. Look here, Tony, we're officers, see? Policemen." He produced a badge. "A couple of weeks ago a guy was brought in dying for the want of a shot, see? Dope—he needed some dope—like this—in his arm. See? Well, we tried to make him tell us where he'd been getting it, but he was too weak. He croaked next day. Evidently he hadn't had money enough to buy any more.

"Well, this morning a little nigger that goes by the name of Froggy was brought into the precinct pretty well doped up. When he finally came to, he swore he got the stuff here at your store. Of course, we've just been trying to trick you into giving yourself away, but you don't bite. Now what's your game? Know anything about this?"

Tony understood. "I dunno," he said slowly; and then his own problem, whose contemplation his callers had interrupted occurred to him. "Sure!" he exclaimed. "Wait. Maybeso I know somet'ing."

"All right. Spill it."

"I got a new man, work-a for me." And he told them what he had noted since King Solomon Gillis came.

"Sounds interesting. Where is this guy?"

"Here in da store—all day."

"Be here to-morrow?"

"Sure. All day."

"All right. We'll drop in to-morrow and give him the eye. Maybe he's our man."

"Sure. Come ten o'clock. I show you," promised Tony.

VI.

Even the oldest and rattiest cabarets in Harlem have sense of shame enough to hide themselves under the ground—for instance, Edwards's. To get into Edwards's you casually enter a dimly lighted corner saloon, apparently—only apparently—a subdued memory of brighter days. What was once the family entrance is now a side entrance for ladies. Supporting yourself against close walls, you crouchingly descend a narrow, twisted staircase until, with a final turn, you find yourself in a glaring, long, low basement. In a moment your eyes become accustomed to the haze of tobacco smoke. You see men and women seated at wire-legged, white-topped tables, which are covered with half-empty bottles and glasses; you trace the slow-jazz accompaniment you heard as you came down the stairs to a pianist, a cornetist, and a drummer on a little platform at the far end of the room. There is a cleared space from the foot of the stairs, where you are standing, to the platform where this orchestra is mounted, and in it a tall brown girl is swaying from side to side and rhythmically proclaiming that she has the world in a jug and the stopper in her hand. Behind a counter at your left sits a fat, bald, tea-colored Negro, and you wonder if this is Edwards—Edwards, who stands in with the police, with the political bosses, with the importers of wines and worse. A white-vested waiter hustles you to a seat and takes your order. The song's tempo changes to a quicker [one]; the drum and the cornet rip out a fanfare, almost drowning the piano; the girl catches up her dress and begins to dance. . . .

Gillis's wondering eyes had been roaming about. They stopped.

"Look, Mouse!" he whispered. "Look a-yonder!"

"Look at what?"

"Dog-gone if it ain' de self-same gal!"

"Wha' d' ye mean, self-same girl?"

"Over yonder, wi' de green stockin's. Dass de gal made me knock over dem apples fust day I come to town. 'Member? Been wishin' I could see her ev'y sence."

"What for?" Uggam wondered.

King Solomon grew confidential. "Ain' but two things in dis world, Mouse, I really wants. One is to be a policeman. Been wantin' dat ev'y sence I seen dat cullud traffic-cop dat day. Other is to git myse'f a gal lak dat one over yonder!"

"You'll do it," laughed Uggam, "if you live long enough."

"Who dat wid her?"

"How 'n hell do I know?"

"He cullud?"

"Don't look like it. Why? What of it?"

"Hm—nuthin'—"

"How many coupons y' got to-night?"

"Ten." King Solomon handed them over.

"Y' ought to 've slipt 'em to me under the table, but it's all right now, long as we got this table to ourselves. Here's y' medicine for to-morrer."

"Wha'?"

"Reach under the table."

Gillis secured and pocketed the medicine.

"An' here's two-fifty for a good day's work." Uggam passed the money over. Perhaps he grew careless; certainly the passing this time was above the table, in plain sight.

"Thanks, Mouse."

Two white men had been watching Gillis and Uggam from a table near by. In the tumult of merriment that rewarded the entertainer's most recent and daring effort, one of these men, with a word to the other, came over and took the vacant chair beside Gillis.

"Is your name Gillis?"

"'T ain' nuthin' else."

Uggam's eyes narrowed.

The white man showed King Solomon a police officer's badge.

"You're wanted for dope-peddling. Will you come along without trouble?"

"Fo' what?"

"Violation of the narcotic law—dope-selling."

"Who—me?"

"Come on, now, lay off that stuff. I saw what happened just now myself." He addressed Uggam. "Do you know this fellow?"

"Nope. Never saw him before to-night."

"Didn't I just see him sell you something?"

"Guess you did. We happened to be sittin' here at the same table and got to talkin'. After a while I says I can't seem to sleep nights, so he offers me sump'n he says'll make me sleep, all right. I don't know what it is, but he says he uses it himself an' I offers to pay him what it cost him. That's how I come to take it. Guess he's got more in his pocket there now."

The detective reached deftly into the coat pocket of the dumbfounded King Solomon and withdrew a packet of envelopes. He tore off a corner of one, emptied a half-dozen tiny white tablets into his palm, and sneered triumphantly. "You'll make a good witness," he told Uggam.

The entertainer was issuing an ultimatum to all sweet mammas who dared to monkey 'round her loving man. Her audience was absorbed and delighted, with the exception of one couple—the girl with the green stockings and her escort. They sat directly in the line of vision of King Solomon's wide eyes, which, in the calamity that had descended upon him, for the moment saw nothing.

"Are you coming without trouble?"

Mouse Uggam, his friend. Harlem. Land of plenty. City of refuge—city of refuge. If you live long enough—

Consciousness of what was happening between the pair across the room suddenly broke through Gillis's daze like flame through smoke. The man was trying to kiss the girl and she was resisting. Gillis jumped up. The detective, taking the act for an attempt at escape, jumped with him and was quick enough to intercept him. The second officer came at once to his fellow's aid, blowing his whistle several times as he came.

People overturned chairs getting out of the way, but nobody ran for the door. It was an old crowd. A fight was a treat; and the tall Negro could fight.

"Judas Priest!"

"Did you see that?"

"Damn!"

White—both white. Five of Mose Joplin's horses. Poisoning a well. A year's crops. Green stockings—white—white—

"That's the time, papa!"

"Do it, big boy!"

"Good night!"

Uggam watched tensely, with one eye on the door. The second cop had blown for help—

Downing one of the detectives a third time and turning to grapple again with the other, Gillis found himself face to face with a uniformed black policeman.

He stopped as if stunned. For a moment he simply stared. Into his mind swept his own words like a forgotten song, suddenly recalled:—

"Cullud policemans!"

The officer stood ready, awaiting his rush.

"Even—got—cullud—policemans—"

Very slowly King Solomon's arms relaxed; very slowly he stood erect; and the grin that came over his features had something exultant about it.

MUTTSY

Zora Neale Hurston

(from *Opportunity: Journal of Negro Life,* 4.44, August 1926)

THE PIANO IN Ma Turner's back parlor stuttered and wailed. The pianist kept time with his heel and informed an imaginary deserter that "she might leave and go to Halimufack, but his slow-drag would bring her back," mournfully with a memory of tomtoms running rhythm through the plaint.

Fewclothes burst through the portieres, a brown chrysalis from a dingy red cocoon, and touched the player on the shoulder.

"Say, Muttsy," he stage whispered. "Ma's got a new lil' biddy in there—just come. And say—her foot would make all of dese Harlem babies a Sunday face."

"Whut she look like?" Muttsy drawled, trying to maintain his characteristic pose of indifference to the female.

"Brown skin, patent leather grass on her knob, kinder tallish. She's a lil' skinny," he added apologetically, "but ah'm willing to buy corn for that lil' chicken."

Muttsy lifted his six feet from the piano bench as slowly as his curiosity would let him and sauntered to the portieres for a peep:

The sight was as pleasing as Fewclothes had stated—only more so. He went on in the room which Ma always kept empty. It was her receiving room—her "front."

From Ma's manner it was evident that she was very glad to see the girl. She could see that the girl was not overjoyed in her presence, but attributed that to southern greenness.

"Who you say sentcher heah, dearie?" Ma asked, her face trying to beam, but looking harder and more forbidding.

"Uh-a-a man down at the boat landing where I got off—North River. I jus' come in on the boat."

Ma's husband from his corner spoke up. "Musta been Bluefront."

"Yeah, musta been him," Muttsy agreed.

"Oh, it's all right, honey, we New Yorkers likes to know who we'se takin' in, dearie. We has to be keerful. Whut did you say yo' name was?"

"Pinkie, yes, mam, Pinkie Jones."

Ma stared hard at the little old battered reticule that the girl carried for luggage—not many clothes if that was all—she reflected. But Pinkie had everything she needed in her face—many many trunks full. Several of them for Ma. She noticed the cold-reddened knuckles of her bare hands too.

"Come on upstairs to yo' room—thass all right 'bout the price—we'll come to some 'greement tomorrow. Jes' go up an take off yo' things."

Pinkie put back the little rosy leather purse of another generation and followed Ma. She didn't like Ma—her smile resembled the smile of the Wolf in Red Riding Hood. Anyway back in Eatonville, Florida, "ladies," especially old ones, didn't put powder and paint on the face.

"Forty-dollars-Kate sure landed a pippin' dis time," said Muttsy, sotto voce, to Fewclothes back at the piano. "If she ain't, then there ain't a hound dawk in Georgy. Ah'm goin' home an' dress."

No one else in the crowded back parlor let alone the house knew of Pinkie's coming. They danced on, played on, sang their "blues" and lived on hotly their intense lives. The two men who had seen her—no one counted ole man Turner—went on playing too, but kept an ear cocked for her coming.

She followed Ma downstairs and seated herself in the parlor with the old man. He sat in a big rocker before a copper-lined gas stove, indolence in every gesture.

"Ah'm Ma's husband," he announced by way of making conversation.

"Now you jus' shut up!" Ma commanded severely. "You gointer git yo' teeth knocked down yo' throat yit for runnin' yo' tongue. Lemme talk to dis gal—dis is *mah* house. You sets on the stool un do nothin' too much tuh have anything tuh talk over!"

"Oh, Lawd," groaned the old man feeling a knee that always pained him at the mention of work. "Oh, Lawd, will you sen' yo' fiery chariot an' take me 'way from heah?"

"Aw shet up!" the woman spit out. "Lawd don't wantcher—devil shouldn't have yuh." She peered into the girl's's face and leaned back satisfied.

"Well, girlie, you kin be a lotta help tuh me 'round dis house if you takes un intrus' in things—oh Lawd!" She leaped up from her seat. "That's mah bread ah smell burnin! . . .

No sooner had Ma's feet cleared the room than the old man came to life again. He peered furtively after the broad back of his wife.

"Know who she is," he asked Pinkie in an awed whisper. She shook her head. "You don't? Dat's Forty-dollars-Kate!"

"Forty-dollars-Kate?" Pinkie repeated open eyed. "Naw, I don't know nothin' 'bout her."

"Sh-h," cautioned the old man. "Course you don't. I fughits you ain't nothin' tall but a young 'un. Twenty-five years ago they all called her dat 'cause she *wuz* 'Forty-dollars-Kate.' She sho' wuz some p'uty 'oman—great big robu' lookin' gal. Men wuz glad 'nough to spend forty dollars on her if dey had it. She didn't lose no time wid dem dat didn't have it."

He grinned ingratiatingly at Pinkie and leaned nearer.

"But you'se better lookin' than she ever wuz, you might—taint no tellin' whut you might do ef you git some sense. I'm a gointer teach you, hear?"

"Yessuh," the girl managed to answer with an almost paralyzed tongue.

"Thass a good girl. You jus' lissen to me an' you'll pull thew alright."

He glanced at the girl sitting timidly upon the edge of the chair and scolded.

"Don't set dataway," he ejaculated. "Yo' back bone ain't no ram rod. Kinda scooch down on the for'ard edge uh de chear lak dis." (He demonstrated by "scooching" forward so far that he was almost sitting on his shoulder-blades.) The girl slumped a trifle.

"Is you got a job yit?"

"Nawsuh," she answered slowly, "but I reckon I'll have one soon. Ain't been in town a day yet."

"You looks kinda young—kinda little biddy. Is you been to school much?"

"Yessuh, went thew eight reader. I'm goin' again when I get a chance."

"Dat so? Well ah reckon ah kin talk some Latin tuh yuh den." He cleared his throat loudly. "Whut's you entitlum?"

"I don't know," said the girl in confusion.

"Well, den, whut's you entrimmins," he queried with a bit of braggadocio in his voice.

"I don't know," from the girl, after a long awkward pause.

"You chillun don't learn nothin' in school dese days. Is you got to 'goes into' yit?"

"You mean long division?"

"Ain't askin' 'bout de longness of it, dat don't make no difference," he retorted, "Sence you goin' to stay heah ah'll edgecate yuh—do yuh know how to eat a fish—uh nice brown fried fish?"

"Yessuh," she answered quickly, looking about for the fish.

"How?"

"Why, you jus' eat it with corn bread," she said, a bit disappointed at the non-appearance of the fish.

"Well, ah'll tell yuh," he patronized. "You starts at de tail an liffs de meat off de bones sorter gentle and eats him clear tuh de head on dat side; den you turn 'im ovah an' commence at de tail again an deat right up tuh de head; den you push *dem* bones way tuh one side an' takes another fish an' so on 'till de end—well, 'till der ain't no mo'!"

He mentally digested the fish and went on. "See," he pointed accusingly at her feet, "you don't even know how tuh warm yoself! You settin' dere wid yo' feet ev'y which a way. Dat ain't de way tuh git wahm. Now look at *mah* feet. Dass right put bofe big toes right togethah—now shove 'em close up tuh de fiah; now lean back so! Dass de way. Ah knows uh heap uh things tuh teach yuh sense you gointer live heah—ah learns all of 'em while de ole lady is paddlin' roun' out dere in de yard."

Ma appeared at the door an the old man withdrew so far into his rags that he all but disappeared. They went to supper where there was fried fish but forgot all rules for eating it and just ate heartily. She helped with the dishes and returned to the parlor. A little later some more men and women knocked and were admitted after the same furtive peering out through the nearest crack of the door. Ma carried them all back to the kitchen and Pinkie heard the clink of glasses and much loud laughter.

Women came in by ones and twos, some in shabby coats turned up about the ears, and with various cheap but showy hats crushed down over unkempt hair. More men, more women, more trips to the kitchen with loud laughter.

Pinkie grew uneasy. Both men and women stared at her. She kept strictly to her place. Ma came in and tried to make her join the others.

"Come on in, honey, a lil' toddy ain't gointer hurt nobody. Evebody know *me*, ah wouldn't touch a hair on yo' head. Come on in, dearie, all the' men wants tuh meethcer."

Pinkie smelt the liquor on Ma's breath and felt contaminated at her touch. She wished herself back home again even with the ill treatment and squalor. She thought of the three dollars she had secreted in her shoe—she had been warned against pickpockets—and flight but where? Nowhere. For there was no home to which *she* could return, nor any place else she knew of. But when she got a job, she'd scrape herself clear of people who took toddies.

A very black man sat on the piano stool playing as only a Negro can with hands, stamping with his feet and the rest of his body keeping time.

> *Ahm gointer make me a graveyard of mah own*
> *Ahm gointer make me a graveyard of mah own*
> *Carried me down on de smoky Road—*

Pinkie, weary of Ma's maudlin coaxing caught these lines as she was being pulled and coaxed into the kitchen. Everyone in there was shaking shimmies to music, rolling eyes heavenward as they picked imaginary grapes out of the air, or drinking. "Folkes," shouted Ma, "look a heah! Shut up dis racket! Ah wantcher tuh meet Pinkie Jones. She's de bes' frien' ah got." Ma flopped into a chair and began to cry into her whiskey glass.

"Mah comperments!" The men almost shouted. The women were less, much less enthusiastic.

"Dass de las' run uh shad," laughed a woman called Ada, pointing to Pinkie's slenderness.

"Jes' lak a bar uh soap aftah uh hard week's wash," Bertha chimed in and laughed uproariously. The men didn't help.

"Oh, Miss Pinkie," said Bluefront, removing his Stetson for the first time, "Ma'am, also Ma'am, ef you wuz tuh see me settin' straddle of ud Mud-cat leadin' a minner whut ud you think?"

"I—er, oh, I don't know, suh. I didn't know you-er anybody could ride uh fish."

"Stick uh roun' me, baby, an' you'll wear diamon's" Bluefront swaggered. "Lok heah, lil' Pigmeat, youse *some* sharp! If you didn't had but one eye ah'd hink you wuz a needle—thass how sharp you looks to me. Say, mah right foot is itchin'. Do dat mean ah'm gointer walk on some strange ground wid you?"

"Naw, indeedy," cut in Fewclothes. "It jes' means you feet needs to walk in some strange water—wid a lil' red seal lye thowed in."

But he was not to have a monopoly. Fewclothes and Shorty joined the chase and poor Pinkie found it impossible to retreat to her place beside the old man. She hung her head, embarrassed that she did not understand their mode of speech; she felt the unfriendly eyes of the women, and she loathed the smell of liquor that filled the house now. The piano still rumbled and wailed that same song—

> *Carried me down on de Smoky Road*
> *Brought me back on de coolin' board*
> *Ahm gointer make me a graveyard of mah own.*

A surge of cold, fresh air from the outside stirred the smoke and liquor fumes and Pinkie knew that the front door was open. She turned her eyes that way and thought of flight to the clean outside. The door stood wide open and a tall figure in an overcoat with a fur collar stood there.

"Good Gawd, Muttsy! Shet' at do'." cried Shorty. "Dass a pure razor blowing out dere tonight. Ah didn't know you wuz outa here nohow."

> *Carried me down on de Smoky Road*
> *Brought me back on de coolin' board*
> *Ahm gointer make me a graveyard of mah own,*

sang Muttsy, looking as if he sought someone and banged the door shut on the last words. He strode on in without removing hat or coat.

Pinkie saw in this short space that all the men deferred to him, that all the women sought his notice. She tried timidly to squeeze between two of the men and return to the quiet place beside old man Turner, thinking that Muttsy would hold the attention of her captors until she had escaped. But Muttsy spied her through the men about her and joined them. By this time her exasperation and embarrassment had her on the point of tears.

"Well, whadda yuh know about dis!" He exclaimed, "A real lil' pullet."

"Look out dere, Muttsy," drawled Dramsleg with objection, catching Pinkie by the arm and trying to draw her toward him. "Lemme tell dis lil' Pink Mama how crazy ah is 'bout her mahself. Ah ain't got no lady atall an'—"

"Aw, shut up Drams," Muttsy said sternly, "put yo' pocketbook where yo' mouf is, an' somebody will lissen. Ah'm a heavy-sugar papa. Ah eats fried chicken when the rest of you niggers is drinking rain water."

He thrust some of the others aside and stood squarely before her. With her downcast eyes, she saw his well polished shoes, creased trousers, gloved hands and at last timidly raised her eyes to his face.

"Look a heah!" he frowned, "you roughnecks done got dis baby ready tuh cry."

He put his forefinger under her chin and made her look at him. And for some reason he removed his hat.

"Come on in the sitten' room an' le's talk. Come on befo' some uh dese niggers sprinkle some salt on yuh and eat yuh clean up lak uh radish." Dramsleg looked after Muttsy and the girl as they swam through the smoke into the front room. He beckoned to Bluefront.

"Hey, Bluefront! Ain't you mah fren'?"

"Yep," answered Bluefront.

"Well, then why cain't you help me? Muttsy done done me dirt wid the lil' pigmeat—throw a louse on 'im."

Pinkie's hair was slipping down. She felt it, but her self-consciousness prevented her catching it and down it fell in a heavy roll that spread out and covered her nearly to the waist. She followed Muttsy into the front room and again sat shrinking in the corner. She did not wish to talk to Muttsy nor anyone else in the house, but there were fewer people in this room.

"Phew!" cried Bluefront, "dat baby sho got some righteous moss on her keg—dass reg'lar 'nearrow mah Lawd tuh thee' stuff." He made a lengthy gesture with his arms as if combing out long, silky hair.

"Shux," sneered Ada in a moist, alcoholic voice. "Dat ain't nothin.' Mah haih useter be so's ah could set on it."

There was general laughter from the men.

"Yas, ah know it's de truth!" shouted Shorty. "It's jus' ez close tuh yo' head *now* ez ninety-nine is tuh uh hund'ed."

"Ah'll call Muttsy tuh you," Ada threatened.

"Oh, 'oman, Muttsy ain't got you tuh study 'bout no mo' cause he's parkin' his heart wid dat lil' chicken wid white-folks' haih. Why, dat lil' chicken's foot would make you a Sunday face."

General laughter again. Ada dashed the whiskey glass upon the floor with the determined stalk of an angry tiger and arose and started forward.

"Muttsy Owens, uh nobody else ain't to gointer make no fool outer *me*. Dat lil' kack girl ain't gointer put *me* on de bricks—not much."

Perhaps Muttsy heard her, perhaps he saw her out of the corner of his eye and read her mood. But knowing the woman as he did he might have known what she would do under such circumstances. At any rate he got to his feet as she entered the room where he sat with Pinkie.

"Ah know you ain't lost yo' head sho' 'nuff, 'oman. 'Deed, Gawd knows you betah go 'way f'um me." He said this in a low, steady voice. The music stopped, the talking stopped and even the drinkers paused. Nothing happened, for Ada looked straight into Muttsy's eyes and went on outside.

"Miss Pinkie, Ah votes you g'wan tuh bed," Muttsy said suddenly to the girl.

"Yes-suh."

"An' don't you worry 'bout no job. Ah knows where you kin git a good one. Ah'll go see em first an' tell yuh tomorrow night."

She went off to bed upstairs. The rich baritone of the piano-player came up to her as did laughter and shouting. But she was tired and slept soundly.

Ma shuffled in after eight the next morning. "Darlin', ain't you got 'nuff sleep yit?"

Pinkie opened her eyes a trifle. "Ain't you the puttiest lil' trick! An' Muttsy done gone crazy 'bout yuh! Chile, he's lousy wid money an' diamon's an" everything—Yuh better grab him quick. Some folks has all de luck. Heah ah is—got uh man dat hates work lake de devil hates holy water. Ah gotta make dis house pay!"

Pinkie's eyes opened wide. "What does Mr. Muttsy do?"

"Mah Gawd, chile! He's de bes' gambler in three states, cards, craps un hawses. He could be a boss stevedore if he so wanted. The big boss down on de dock would give him a fat job—just begs him to take it cause he can manage the men. He's the biggest hero they got since Harry Wills left the waterfront. But he won't take it cause he makes so much wid the games."

"He's awful good-lookin'," Pinkie agreed, "An' he been mighty nice tuh me—but I like men to work. I wish he would. Gamlin' ain't nice."

"Yeah, 'tis, ef you makes money lak Muttsy. Maybe yo ain't noticed dat diamon' set in his tooth. He picks women up when he wants tuh an' puts 'em down when he choose."

Pinkie turned her face to the wall and shuddered. Ma paid no attention.

"You doan hafta git up till you git good an' ready, Muttsy says. Ah mean you kin stay roun' the house 'till you come to, sorter."

Another day passed. Its darkness woke up the land east of Lenox—all that land between the railroad tracks and the river. It was very ugly by day, and night kindly hid some of its sordid homeliness. Yes, nighttime gave it life.

The same women, or others just like them, came to Ma Turner's. The same men, or men just like them, came also and treated them to liquor or mistreated them with fists or cruel jibes. Ma got half drunk as usual and cried over everyone who would let her.

Muttsy came alone and went straight to Pinkie where she was trying to shrink into the wall. She had feared that he would not come.

"Howdy do, Miss Pinkie."

"How'do do, Mistah Owens," she actually achieved a smile. "Did you see bout m'job?"

"Well, yeah—but the lady says she won't needya fuh uh week yet. Doan' worry. Ma ain't gointer push yuh foh room rent. Mah wrist ain't got no cramps."

Pinkie half sobbed: "Ah wantsa job now!"

"Didn't ah say dass alright? Well, Muttsy doan lie. Shux! Ah might jes' es well tell yuh—ahm crazy 'bout yuh—money no objeck."

It was the girl herself who first mentioned "bed" this night. He suffered her to go without protest.

The next night she did not come into the sitting room. She went to bed as soon as the dinner things had been cleared. Ma begged and cried, but Pinkie pretended illness and kept to her bed. This she repeated the next night and the next. Every night Muttsy came and every night he added to his sartorial splendor; but each night he went away, disappointed, more evidently crestfallen than before.

But the insistence for escape from her strange surroundings grew on the girl. When Ma was busy elsewhere, she would take out the three one dollar bills from her shoe and reconsider her limitations. If that job would only come on! She felt shut in, imprisoned, walled in with these women who talked of nothing but men and the numbers and drink, and men who talked of nothing but the numbers and drink and women. And desperation took her.

One night she was still waiting for the job—Ma's alcoholic tears prevailed. Pinkie took a drink. She drank the stuff mixed with sugar and water and crept to bed even as the dizziness came on. She would not wake tonight. Tomorrow, maybe, the job would come and freedom.

The piano thumped but Pinkie did not hear; the shouts, laughter and cries did not reach her that night. Downstairs Muttsy pushed Ma into a corner.

"Looky heah, Ma. Dat girl done played me long enough. Ah pays her room rent, ah pays her boahd an' all ah gets is uh hunk of ice. Now you said you wuz gointer fix things—you tole me so las' night an' heah she done gone tuh bed on me agin."

"Deed, ah caint do nothin' wid huh. She's thinkin' sho' nuf you gon' git her uh job and she fret so cause tain't come, dat she drunk uh toddy un hits knocked her down jes lak uh log."

"Ada an' all uh them laffin—they say ah done crapped." He felt injured. "Caint ah go talk to her?"

"Lawdy, Muttsy, dat gal dead drunk an' sleepin' lak she's buried."

"Well, cain't ah go up an'—an' speak tuh her jus' the same." A yellow backed bill from Muttsy's roll found itself in Ma's hand and put her in such good humor that she let old man Turner talk all he wanted for the rest of the night.

"Yas, Muttsy, gwan in. Youse *mah* frien'."

Muttsy hurried up to the room indicated. He felt shaky inside there with Pinkie, somehow, but he approached the bed and stood for awhile looking down upon her. Her hair in confusion about her face and swinging off the bedside; the brown arms revealed and the soft lips. He blew out the match he had struck and kissed her full in the mouth, kissed her several times and passed his hand over her neck and throat and then hungrily down upon her breast. But here he drew back.

"Naw," he said sternly to himself, "ah ain't goin' ter play her wid no loaded dice." Then quickly he covered her with the blanket to her chin, kissed her again upon the lips and tipped down into the darkness of the vestibule.

"Ah reckon ah bettah git married." He soliloquized. "B'lieve me, ah will, an' go uptown wid dicties."

He lit a cigar and stood there on the steps puffing and thinking for some time. His name was called inside the sitting room several times but he pretended not to hear. At last he stole back into the room where slept the girl who unwittingly and unwillingly was making him do queer things. He tipped up to the bed again and knelt there holding her hands so fiercely that she groaned without waking. He watched her and he wanted her so that he wished to crush her in his love; crush and crush and hurt her against himself, but somehow he resisted the impulse and merely kissed her lips again, kissed her hands back and front, removed the largest diamond ring from his hand and slipped it on her engagement finger. It was much too large so he closed her hand and tucked it securely beneath the covers.

"She's *mine*!" He said triumphantly. "All mine!"

He switched off the light and softly closed the door as he went out again to the steps. He had gone up to the bed room from the sitting room boldly, caring not who knew that Muttsy Owens took what he wanted. He was stealing forth afraid that someone might *suspect* that he had been there. There is no secret love in those barrens; it is a thing to be approached boisterously and without delay or dalliance. One loves when one wills, and ceases when it palls. There is nothing sacred or hidden—all subject to coarse jokes. So Mutsy re-entered the sitting room from the steps as if he had been into the street.

"Where you been Muttsy?" whined Ada with an awkward attempt at coyness.

"What *you* wanta know for?" he asked roughly.

"Now, Muttsy you know you ain't treatin' me right, honey. How come you runnin' de hawg ovah me lak you do?"

"Git outa mah face 'oman. Keep yo' han's offa me." He clapped on his hat and strode from the house.

Pinkie awoke with a griping stomach and thumping head.

Ma bustled in. "How yuh feelin' darlin'? Youse jes lak a li'l doll baby."

"I got a headache, terrible from that ole whiskey. Thass mah first und las' drink long as I live." She felt the ring.

"Whut's this?" she asked and drew her hand out to the light.

"Dat's Muttsy' ring. Ah seen him wid it fuh two years. How'd y'al make out? He sho is one thur'bred."

"Muttsy? When? I didn't see no Muttsy."

"Dearie, you doan' hafta tell yo' bizness ef you dan wanta. Ahm a hush-mouf. Thass all right, keep yo' bizness to yo' self." Ma bleared her eyes wisely. "But ah know Muttsy wuz up heah tuh see yuh las' night. Doan' mine *me* honey, gwan wid 'im. He'll treat right. Ah *knows* he's crazy 'bout yuh. An' all de women is crazy 'bout *im*. Lawd! lookit dat ring!" Ma regarded it greedily for a long time, but she turned and walked toward the door at last. "Git up darlin'. Ah got fried chicking fuh breckfus' un mush melon."

She went on to the kitchen. Ma's revelation sunk deeper, then there was the ring. Pinkie hurled the ring across the room and leaped out of bed.

"He ain't goin' to make *me* none of his women—I'll die first! I'm goin' outa this house if I starve, lemme starve!"

She got up and plunged her face into the cold water on the washstand in the corner and hurled herself into the shabby clothes, thrust the three dollars which she had never had occasion to spend, under the pillow where Ma would be sure to find them and slipped noiselessly out of the house and fled down Fifth Avenue toward the Park that marked the beginning of the Barrens. She did not know where she was going, and cared little so long as she removed herself as far as possible from the house where the great evil threatened her.

At ten o'clock that same morning, Muttsy Owens dressed his flashiest best, drove up to Ma's door in a cab, the most luxurious that could be hired. He had gone so far as to stick two one hundred dollar notes to the inside of the windshield. Ma was overcome.

"Muttsy, dearie, what you doin' heah so soon? Pinkie sho has got you goin'. Un in a swell cab too—gee!"

"Ahm gointer git mah'reid tuh de doll baby, thass how come. An' ahm gointer treat her white too."

"Umhumh! Thass how come de ring! You oughtn't never fuh-git me, Muttsy, fuh puttin' y'all together. But ah never thought you'd mah'ry *nobody*—you allus said you wouldn't."

"An' ah wouldn't neither ef ah hadn't of seen *her*. Where she is?"

"In de room dressin'. She never tole me nothin' 'bout dis."

"She doan know. She wuz sleep when ah made up mah mind an' slipped on de ring. But ah never miss no girl ah wants, you knows me."

"Everybody in this man's town knows you gets whut you wants."

"Naw, ah come tuh take her to brek'fus' 'fo we goes tuh de cote-house."

"An' y'all stay heah and eat wid me. You go call her whilst ah set de grub on table."

Muttsy, with a lordly stride, went up to Pinkie's door and rapped and waited and rapped and waited three times. Growing impatient or thinking her still asleep, he flung open the door and entered.

The first thing that struck him was the empty bed; the next was the glitter of his diamond ring upon the floor. He stumbled out to Ma. She was gone, no doubt of that.

"She looked awful funny when ah tole her you wuz in heah, but ah thought she wuz puttin' on airs," Ma declared finally.

"She thinks ah played her wid a marked deck, but ah didn't. Ef ah could see her she'd love me. Ah know she would. 'Cause ah'd make her," Muttsy lamented.

"I don't know, Muttsy. She ain't no New Yorker, and she thinks gamblin' is awful."

"Zat all she got against me? Ah'll fix that up in a minute. You help me find her and ah'll do anything she says jus' so she marries me." He laughed ruefully. "Looks like ah crapped this time, don't it, ma?"

The next day Muttsy was foreman of two hundred stevedores. How he did make them work. But oh how cheerfully they did their best for him. The company begrudged not one cent of his pay. He searched diligently, paid money to other searchers, went every night to Ma's to see if by chance the girl had returned or if any clues had turned up.

Two weeks passed this way. Black empty days for Muttsy.

Then he found her. He was coming home from work. When crossing Seventh Avenue at 135th Street they almost collided. He seized her and began pleading before she even had time to recognize him.

He turned and followed her; took the employment office slip from her hand and destroyed it, took her arm and held it. He must have been very convincing for at 125th Street they entered a taxi that headed uptown again. Muttsy was smiling amiably upon the whole round world.

A month later, as Muttsy stood on the dock hustling his men to greater endeavor, Bluefront flashed past with his truck. "Say, Muttsy, you don't know what you missin' since you quit de game. Ah cleaned out de whole bunch las' night." He flashed a roll and laughed. "It don't seem like a month ago you wuz king uh de bones in Harlem." He vanished down the gangplank into the ship's hold.

As he raced back up the gangplank with his loaded truck Muttsy answered him. "An now, I'm King of the Boneheads—which being interpreted means stevedores. Come on over behind dis crate wid yo' roll. Mah wrist ain't got no cramp 'cause ah'm married. You'se gettin' too sassy."

"Thought you wuzn't gointer shoot no mo'!" Bluefront temporized.

"Aw Hell! Come on back heah," he said impatiently. "Ah'll shoot you any way you wants to—hard or soft roll—you'se trying to stall. You know ah don't crap neither. Come on, mah Pinkie needs a fur coat and you stevedores is got to buy it."

He was on his knees with Bluefront. There was a quick movement of Muttsy's wrist, and the cubes flew out on a piece of burlap spread for the purpose—a perfect seven.

"Hot dog!" he exulted. "Look at dem babies gallop!" His wrist quivered again. "Nine for point!" he gloated. "Hah!" There was another quick shake and nine turned up again. "Shove in, Bluefront, shove in dat roll, dese babies is crying fuh it."

Bluefront laid down two dollars grudgingly. "You said you wuzn't gointer roll no mo' dice after you got married," he grumbled.

But Muttsy had tasted blood. His flexible wrist was already in the midst of the next play.

"Come on, Bluefront, stop bellyachin'. Ah shoots huy for de roll!" He reached for his own pocket and laid down a roll of yellow bills beside Bluefront's. His hand quivered and the cubes skipped out again. "Nine!" He snapped his fingers like a trapdrum and gathered in the money.

"Doxology, Bluefront. Git back in de line wid yo' truck an' send de others roun' heah one by one. What man can't keep one li'l wife an' two li'l bones? Hurry 'em up, Blue!"

HE ALSO LOVED

Claude McKay

(from *Home to Harlem,* 1928)

IT WAS IN the winter of 1916 when I first came to New York to hunt for a job. I was broke. I was afraid I would have to pawn my clothes, and it was dreadfully cold. I didn't even know the right way to go about looking for a job. I was always timid about that. For five weeks I had not paid my rent. I was worried, and Ma Lawton, my landlady, was also worried. She had her bills to meet. She was a good-hearted old woman from South Carolina. Her face was all wrinkled and sensitive like finely-carved mahogany.

Every bed-space in the flat was rented. I was living in the small hall bedroom. Ma Lawton asked me to give it up. There were four men sleeping in the front room; two in an old, chipped-enameled brass bed, one on a davenport, and the other in a folding chair. The old lady put a little canvas cot in that same room, gave me a pillow and a heavy quilt, and said I should try and make myself comfortable there until I got work.

The cot was all right for me. Although I hate to share a room with another person and the fellows snoring disturbed my rest. Ma Lawton moved into the little room that I had had, and rented out hers—it was next to the front room—to a man and a woman.

The woman was above ordinary height, chocolate-colored. Her skin was smooth, too smooth, as if it had been pressed and fashioned out for ready sale like chocolate candy. Her hair was straightened out into an Indian Straight after the present style

113

among Negro ladies. She had a mongoose sort of a mouth, with two top front teeth showing. She wore a long mink coat.

The man was darker than the woman. His face was longish, with the right cheek somewhat caved in. It was an interesting face, an attractive, salacious mouth, with the lower lip protruding. He wore a bottle-green peg-top suit, baggy at the hips. His coat hung loose from his shoulders and it was much longer than the prevailing style. He wore also a Mexican hat, and in his breast pocket he carried an Ingersoll watch attached to a heavy gold chain. His name was Jericho Jones, and they called him Jerco for short. And she was Miss Whicher—Rosalind Whicher.

Ma Lawton introduced me to them and said I was broke, and they were both awfully nice to me. They took me to a big feed of corned beef and cabbage at Burrell's on Fifth Avenue. They gave me a good appetizing drink of gin to commence with. And we had beer with the eats; not ordinary beer, either, but real Budweiser, right off the ice.

And as good luck sometimes comes pouring down like a shower, the next day Ma Lawton got me a job in the little free-lunch saloon right under her flat. It wasn't a paying job as far as money goes in New York, but I was glad to have it. I had charge of the free-lunch counter. You know the little dry crackers that go so well with beer, and the cheese and fish and the potato salad. And I served, besides, spare-ribs and whole boiled potatoes and corned beef and cabbage for those customers who could afford to pay for a lunch. I got no wages at all, but I got my eats twice a day. And I made a few tips, also. For there were about six big black men with plenty of money who used to eat lunch with us, specially for our spare-ribs and sweet potatoes. Each one of them gave me a quarter. I made enough to pay Ma Lawton for my canvas cot.

Strange enough, too, Jerco and Rosalind took a liking to me. And sometimes they came and ate lunch perched up there at the counter, with Rosalind the only woman there, all made up and rubbing her mink coat against the men. And when they got through eating, Jerco would toss a dollar bill at me.

We got very friendly, we three. Rosalind would bring up squabs and canned stuff from the German delicatessen in One Hundred and Twenty-fifth Street, and sometimes they asked me to dinner in their room and gave me good liquor.

I thought I was pretty well fixed for such a hard winter. All I had to do as extra work was keeping the saloon clean. . . .

One afternoon Jerco came into the saloon with a man who looked pretty near white. Of course, you never can tell for sure about a person's race in Harlem, nowadays, when there are so many high-yallers floating round—colored folks that would make Italian and Spanish people look like Negroes beside them. But I figured out from his way of talking and acting that the man with Jerco belonged to the white race. They went in through the family entrance into the back room, which was unusual, for the family room of a saloon, as you know, is only for women in the business and the men they bring in there with them. Real men don't sit in a saloon here as they do at home. I suppose it would be sissified. There's a bar for them to lean on and drink and joke as long as they feel like.

The boss of the saloon was a little fidgety about Jerco and his friend sitting there in the back. The boss was a short pumpkin-bellied brown man, a little bald off the forehead. Twice he found something to attend to in the back room, although there was nothing at all there that wanted attending to. . . . I felt better, and the boss, too, I guess, when Rosalind came along and gave the family room its respectable American character. I served Rosalind a Martini cocktail extra dry, and afterward all three of them, Rosalind, Jerco, and their friend, went up to Ma Lawton's.

The two fellows that slept together were elevator operators in a department store, so they had their Sundays free. On the afternoon of the Sunday of the same week that the white-looking man had been in the saloon with Jerco, I went upstairs to change my old shoes—they'd got soaking wet behind the counter—and I found Ma Lawton talking to the two elevator fellows.

The boys had given Ma Lawton notice to quit. They said they couldn't sleep there comfortably together on account of the goings-on in Rosalind's room. The fellows were members of the Colored Y.M.C.A. and were queerly quiet and pious. One of them was studying to be a preacher. They were the sort of fellows that thought going to cabarets a sin, and that parlor socials were leading Harlem straight down to hell. They only went to church affairs themselves. They had been rooming with Ma Lawton for over a year. She called them her gentlemen lodgers.

Ma Lawton said to me: "Have you heard anything phony outa the next room, dear?"

"Why, no, Ma," I said, "nothing more unusual than you can hear all over Harlem. Besides, I work so late, I am dead tired when I turn in to bed, so I sleep heavy."

"Well, it's the truth I do like that there Jerco an' Rosaline," said Ma Lawton. "They did seem quiet as lambs, although they was always havin' company. But Ise got to speak to them, 'cause I doana wanta lose ma young mens. . . . But theyse a real nice-acting couple. Jerco him treats me like him was mah son. It's true that they doan work like all poah niggers, but they pays that rent down good and prompt ehvery week."

Jerco was always bringing in ice cream and cake or something for Ma Lawton. He had a way about him, and everybody liked him. He was a sympathetic type. He helped Ma Lawton move beds and commodes and he fixed her clotheslines. I had heard somebody talking about Jerco in the saloon, however, saying that he could swing a mean fist when he got his dander up, and that he had been mixed up in more than one razor cut-up. He did have a nasty long razor scar on the back of his right hand.

The elevator fellows had never liked Rosalind and Jerco. The one who was studying to preach Jesus said he felt pretty sure that they were an ungodly-living couple. He said that late one night he had pointed out their room to a woman that looked white. He said the woman looked suspicious. She was perfumed and all powdered up and it appeared as if she didn't belong among colored people.

"There's no sure telling white from high-yaller these days," I said. "There are so many swell-looking quadroons and octoroons of the race."

But the other elevator fellow said that one day in the tenderloin section he had run up against Rosalind and Jerco together with a petty officer of marines. And that just put the lid on anything favorable that could be said about them.

But Ma Lawton said: "Well, Ise got to run mah flat right an' try mah utmost to please youall, but I ain't wanta dip mah nose too deep in a lodger's affairs."

Late that night, toward one o'clock, Jerco dropped in at the saloon and told me that Rosalind was feeling badly. She hadn't eaten a bite all day and he had come to get a pail of beer, because she had asked specially for draught beer. Jerco was worried, too.

"I hopes she don't get bad," he said. "For we ain't got a cent o' money. Wese just in on a streak o' bad luck."

"I guess she'll soon be all right," I said.

The next day after lunch I stole a little time and went up to see Rosalind. Ma Lawton was just going to attend to her when I let myself in, and she said to me: "Now the poor woman is sick, poor chile, ahm so glad mah conscience is free and that I hadn't a said nothing evil t' her."

Rosalind was pretty sick. Ma Lawton said it was the grippe. She gave Rosalind hot whisky drinks and hot milk, and she kept her feet warm with a hot-water bottle. Rosalind's legs were lead-heavy. She had a pain that pinched her side like a pair of pincers. And she cried out for thirst and begged for draught beer.

Ma Lawton said Rosalind ought to have a doctor. "You'd better go an' scares up a white one," she said to Jerco. "Ise nevah had no faith in these heah nigger doctors."

"I don't know how we'll make out without money," Jerco whined. He was sitting in the old Morris chair with his head heavy on his left hand.

"You kain pawn my coat," said Rosalind. "Old man Greenbaum will give you two hundred down without looking at it."

"I won't put a handk'chief o' yourn in the hock shop," said Jerco. "You'll need you' stuff soon as you get better. Specially you' coat. You kain't go anywheres without it."

"S'posin' I don't get up again," Rosalind smiled. But her countenance changed suddenly as she held her side and moaned. Ma Lawton bent over and adjusted the pillows.

Jerco pawned his watch chain and his own overcoat, and called in a Jewish doctor from the upper Eighth Avenue fringe of the Belt. But Rosalind did not improve under medical treatment. She lay there with a sad, tired look, as if she didn't really care what happened to her. Her lower limbs were apparently paralyzed. Jerco told the doctor that she had been sick unto death like that before. The doctor shot a lot of stuff into her system. But Rosalind lay there heavy and fading like a felled tree.

The elevator operators looked in on her. The student one gave her a Bible with a little red ribbon marking the chapter in St. John's Gospel about the woman taken in adultery. He also wanted to pray for her recovery. Jerco wanted the prayer, but Rosalind said no. Her refusal shocked Ma Lawton, who believed in God's word.

The doctor stopped Rosalind from drinking beer. But Jerco slipped it in to her when Ma Lawton was not around. He said he couldn't refuse it to her when beer was the only thing she cared for. He had an expensive sweater. He pawned it. He also pawned their large suitcase. It was real leather and worth a bit of money.

One afternoon Jerco sat alone in the back room of the saloon and began to cry.

"I'll do anything. There ain't anything too low I wouldn't do to raise a little money," he said.

"Why don't you hock Rosalind's fur coat?" I suggested. "That'll give you enough money for a while."

"Gawd, no! I wouldn't touch none o' Rosalind's clothes. I jes kain't," he said. "She'll need them as soon as she's better."

"Well, you might try and find some sort of a job, then," I said.

"Me find a job? What kain I do? I ain't no good foh no job. I kain't work. I don't know how to ask for no job. I wouldn't know how. I wish I was a woman."

"Good God! Jerco," I said, "I don't see any way out for you but some sort of a job."

"What kain I do? What kain I do?" he whined. "I kain't do nothing. That's why I don't wanna hock Rosalind's fur coat. She'll need it soon as she's better. Rosalind's so wise about picking up good money. Just like that!" He snapped his fingers.

I left Jerco sitting there and went into the saloon to serve a customer a plate of corned beef and cabbage.

After lunch I thought I'd go up to see how Rosalind was making out. The door was slightly open, so I slipped in without knocking. I saw Jerco kneeling down by the open wardrobe and kissing the toe of one of her brown shoes. He started as he saw me, and looked queer kneeling there. It was a high, old-fashioned wardrobe that Ma Lawton must have picked up at some sale. Rosalind's coat was hanging there, and it gave me a spooky feeling, for it looked so much more like the real Rosalind than the woman that was dozing there on the bed.

Her other clothes were hanging there, too. There were three gowns—a black silk, a glossy green satin, and a flimsy chiffon-like yellow thing. In a corner of the lowest shelf was a bundle of soiled champagne-colored silk stockings and in the other four pairs of shoes—one black velvet, one white kid, and another gold-finished. Jerco regarded the lot with dog-like affection.

"I wouldn't touch not one of her things until she's better," he said. "I'd sooner hock the shirt off mah back."

Which he was preparing to do. He had three expensive striped silk shirts, presents from Rosalind. He had just taken two out of the wardrobe and the other off his back, and made a parcel of them for old Greenbaum. . . . Rosalind woke up and murmured that she wanted some beer. . . .

A little later Jerco came to the saloon with the pail. He was shivering. His coat collar was turned up and fastened with a safety pin, for he only had an undershirt on.

"I don't know what I'd do if anything happens to Rosalind," he said. "I kain't live without her."

"Oh yes, you can," I said in a not very sympathetic tone. Jerco gave me such a reproachful pathetic look that I was sorry I said it.

The tall big fellow had turned into a scared, trembling baby. "You ought to buck up and hold yourself together," I told him. "Why, you ought to be game if you like Rosalind, and don't let her know you're down in the dumps."

"I'll try," he said. "She don't know how miserable I am. When I hooks up with a woman I treat her right, but I never let her know everything about me. Rosalind is an awful good woman. The straightest woman I ever had, honest."

I gave him a big glass of strong whisky.

Ma Lawton came in the saloon about nine o'clock that evening and said that Rosalind was dead. "I told Jerco we'd have to sell that theah coat to give the poah woman a decent fun'ral, an' he jes brokes down crying like a baby."

That night Ma Lawton slept in the kitchen and put Jerco in her little hall bedroom. He was all broken up. I took him up a pint of whisky.

"I'll nevah find another one like Rosalind," he said, "nevah!" He sat on an old black-framed chair in which a new yellow-varnished bottom had just been put. I put my hand on his shoulder and tried to cheer him up: "Buck up, old man. Never mind, you'll find somebody else." He shook his head. "Perhaps you didn't like the way me and Rosalind was living. But she was one naturally good woman, all good inside her."

I felt foolish and uncomfortable. "I always liked Rosalind, Jerco," I said, "and you, too. You were both awfully good scouts to me. I have nothing against her. I am nothing myself."

Jerco held my hand and whimpered: "Thank you, old top. Youse all right. Youse always been a regular fellar."

It was late, after two a.m. I went to bed. And, as usual, I slept soundly.

Ma Lawton was an early riser. She made excellent coffee and she gave the two elevator runners and another lodger, a porter who worked on Ellis Island, coffee and hot home-made biscuits every morning. The next morning she shook me abruptly out of my sleep.

"Ahm scared to death. Thar's moah tur'ble trouble. I kain't git in the barfroom and the hallway's all messy."

I jumped up, hauled on my pants, and went to the bathroom. A sickening purplish liquid coming from under the door had trickled down the hall toward the kitchen. I took Ma Lawton's rolling-pin and broke through the door.

Jerco had cut his throat and was lying against the bowl of the water-closet. Some empty coke papers were on the floor. And he sprawled there like a great black boar in a mess of blood.

PRODIGAL

Laura D. Nichols

(from *Opportunity: Journal of Negro Life,* 8.2, December 1930)

A SUDDEN HUSH fell on the congregation, and the faces of the listeners assumed the leaden stillness of masks. Only the startled black eyes that stared out from the vari-colored wall of faces told the earnest, young preacher that his people were listening as never before. A child cried, and its mother dropped a full, golden breast into its mouth, not once moving her eyes from the preacher's face.

Unperturbed by this unwonted stillness that held a people usually so ready to respond with "Amen" and "Tell the truth, brother," the minister went on in his cool, even voice, "And God holds us to this commandment as it is written, 'Thou shalt not commit adultery.' Inquire into your own lives, my brothers, my sisters. Too many of you are living in a way to shame your church and your profession as Christians."

"Do that young fool know what he's sayin'? Don't he know he's hittin' some of the best givers in the church? Who he hittin' at anyhow?" Deacon Jones shook his head and sighed. He knew what this sermon would mean to the collection. And the responsibility of raising the preacher's salary rested heavily upon the shoulders of Deacon Jones.

"Thang God it don't hit me." Mama Jane shifted her snuff to the other side of her mouth, and managed a muffled "Amen." Mama Jane did not know her age, but she was "a good-sized gal in time of Abraham Lincoln's war." She had come north with her children and grand-children during the industrial boom that had

121

followed the World War, and had aided in establishing this little church. The migrant Negro did not often find the established churches of the North to his liking, and so began his own. Mama Jane continued to mutter to herself, "Old as I is, do', and many preachers as I'se heard in my time, I ain't never hear one ain't got no mo' sense dan to badaciously insult de people wha' he got to git his bread and butter f'om."

Her mumbling did not stop the preacher. Indeed, he must have taken it for sanction, for sharper, more trenchant words fell from his lips, and hung like small, glittering blades in the air. His voice rang out once more, "The wages of sin is death, but the gift of God is eternal life."

The service was over, and the people swarmed out to the lawn surrounding the pretty little church, to give vent to feeling that this morning had not found the usual emotional outlet. An odd picture they made, these transplanted human beings, pulled up from their rural homes in the Southland and dropped in the heart of an eastern industrial city. The problems of adjustment were often disconcerting, but they had kept their religious life entirely apart from the changes. There was to be a lodge funeral this afternoon, and many of these people must "turn out." While they waited, they fell into groups on the ill-kept green to discuss the sermon.

"Ef I had only known that was wha' he was goin' to talk about, I'd a' sho' stayed home and baked my rolls dis mornin'. Spec dey riz all out de pan by now." Sister Mary was plainly peeved. She had on a good-as-new black straw hat her "Tuesday Lady" had given her. And not the least excuse to shout. Sister Mary was an expert shouter. She always circled the church before the 'spirit' departed from her. She sometimes embraced happy fellow Christians, but she never committed the blunder of hugging comely Anna Brown. Not since Big Lige Pierce had taken up with Anna over a year ago.

Partly hidden by the fragrant, feathery beauty of a lilac in full bloom, a group of men, strong, black and young, passed a bottle from hand to hand, and shakily condemned the sermon and the preacher. "Better learn to tend to his own business ef he wants to stay here."—"How come you so touchy, big boy? Eve'y body know Anna Brown' husband ain't dead. Wouldn' I love to see him walk up someday when you 'busin some o' his children! Preacher sho' have one mo' sermon to preach. Fesser Brown plumb crazy 'bout his lil yaller children." Big Lige made no answer to this.

On the steps a group of deacons and other officers of the church smoked and spat and studied. Deacon Jones grumbled, "Collection was powerful small this mornin.' That man 'go' ruin hisself yet. Better be studyin' bout them hongry children o' his'n, stead o' insultin' some o' his best payin' members." The old man spat viciously into space.

Apart from these various groups, Anna Brown and her three attractive children laughed and talked happily together. The sermon was not mentioned. Anna was by far the best-looking woman in the congregation and by the same token, one of the least popular. Though rather given to plumpness, she was both neatly and becomingly dressed. Her small bright eyes twinkled in a yellowish brown face, like stars peeping thru a sunset sky and laughing because they shouldn't be there. She was the sort of woman who says little soft, kind things to people when she might just as well say nothing at all. Mama Jane, who took care of the children while Anna went out to sew by the day, often said of her, "Poor chile, she don' do nobody no harm, only wha' she do to herself." Though for the life of her, Mama Jane couldn't see what Anna wanted of that big, rough Lige Pierce hanging around, and her husband a school teacher in the South, and as nice a boy as ever drew breath. She could never understand why Anna and Hal had separated, for Anna was a close-mouthed woman, for all her gentle, smiling ways. Her lips could close in a hard, straight line, and the warm twinkle in her eyes change to the cold gleam of burnished steel.

The people began to move quietly toward the church door, as the funeral cars approached. From hidden recesses in bags and purses, quaint little black and purple bonnets appeared, along with big, bright badges. Hands slipped awkwardly into white gloves, and the order formed in solemn procession behind the bier and followed it into the church.

Lige Pierce sauntered over toward the little group that remained outside, for Anna did not belong to the order, and had only tarried because the children wanted to see the order turn out. Lige's hungry eyes rested, not on the familiar form of the woman, but on the slim, brown girl at her side. Esther, still unconscious of the charm of youth's first rounding out, felt his look, and flinched. Anna saw it with her smiling eyes, and the glint of steel veiled the smile. The words of the preacher fell again on her heart and cut like small, sharp blades. "The wages of sin is death." Death, yes; but that caressing look at her girl meant hell itself.

All the sorry memories of these past three years came to her as she walked slowly to the car line with her children. Lige was a few paces behind, and her heavy heart told her where his eyes rested now and again. Hal's voice rose in her ears as on the day he left to go back South to his schoolroom: "I cannot do the rough railroad yard work which is all our men find to do here now that the boom is over. We can make it at home on my salary, and send the children away to school later on." And her own voice, "Never. I'd rather wash and iron and be free than to have my children grow up on the South." Hal had gone, and Lige had drifted into her life. Hal's letters always begged her to return, but without avail. She could think of no reason why she should.

Until today.

When the little party stopped in town to transfer, Anna slipped around the corner and sent Hal the following terse message: "Home next Sunday." She would need a few days to get the children ready.

And on the next Sunday, all the pent-up emotion of the worshippers burst forth when the earnest young minister thanked God that his words had borne fruit in one heart. Sister Mary gave two or three quick, frog-like jumps, and let the 'spirit' have full sway. She circled the church three times and fell exhausted in her seat. Mama Jane, too old for active shouting, fanned her vigorously and murmured, "God do move in a musterious way. Bless his name."

In a little southern city, Hal Brown welcomed his loved family home, and thanked God piously that his prayers had at last been answered.

And Anna held her peace and smiled her quiet smile.

CONDEMNED HOUSE

Lucille Boehm

(from *Opportunity: Journal of Negro Life*, 7.6, June 1939)

DUSK WAS FALLING across the Harlem River like a blanket of cold mud. The sky was dirty with fog. You slipped on the freezing carpet of slush once or twice, but you didn't notice. You were too tired. A big ache filled your thoughts. You saw the street ahead of you, but it looked small—dingy—like it was far away. You stared at the kids teasing bonfires along the curb. Running their fingers through the flames. Chasing each other, dashing into the streets between great groaning trucks. Your nostrils widened, sucking in familiar odors—the oily smell of the fish store on the corner, cooking grease, cheap gasoline, "King Kong," garbage. The stale smells of poverty. On a nearby stoop a gang of boys and girls, giggling, yawning. Nothing to do. Not enough change among them for a tune on the piccolo. Somewhere a radio beat out the rhythm of Count Basie's "One O'Clock Jump." Music that throbbed at the pit of your stomach. Men lolled outside the candy store—no work, nothing to do. The thought of it burned fiercely in your brain.

You walked as far as your own stoop, down toward the end of the street. Across the way were the condemned houses. Half a block of them. They stood there sagging against each other like tired women in a subway jam—ready to collapse. Some of the windows were gaping black holes, where the boards had been chopped away for fire wood. An iron girder held two of the walls apart over a dark alley-way that looked like a missing tooth in the long row. In the end house was a big, jagged opening where the stoop used to be. Ruins of brick and plaster cluttered the floor. An ugly black seam scarred the face of the house from the ground almost to the roof. You couldn't make out if it was a crack in the wall or only a heavy dirt stain.

They, too, were out of a job—these rotten shells of houses. They were mean-looking, like people who get old and sick and useless.

Out of a job! You shivered. There were four dollars in your pocketbook. You'd been saving up for weeks, stretching the relief check like a worn rubber band over the rent and the food and the unpaid debts. It was like hanging onto a tuft of grass with a flood raging around you, but you had managed to get those four dollars together. You had hoped maybe you'd find a job in one of the Sixth Avenue agencies if you had money enough for the fee. But. . . .

Something seethed in your brain. It had happened at that last agency, where you had gone after three hours of steady searching. You were too tired to stretch your eyes over the mob around the door reading the cards. You went straight in, climbed two long flights of stairs and asked for a house job, part-time, sleep-in—anything. The man behind the dark wood partition was sweaty in rolled-up blue shirt sleeves. He looked fagged out—stared at you with dead grey eyes.

"Now see here, girlie," he said in a tired voice, "You're just wasting your time and mine. If I *wanted* black girls I'd have said so on the cards, wouldn't I? Why don't you take the trouble to . . ."

You didn't hear the rest. There was hot acid boiling inside you, from your stomach to the nape of your neck. You rushed downstairs, hurried along the avenue, too mad to cry.

The four dollars were still in your pocketbook. You opened the change purse, took them out and counted them slowly. Then you rolled them into a tight little sausage and tucked them back. The rent agent would grasp at them like a hungry tiger. You couldn't hold him off any longer.

You stared through the boarded-up house across the way. It sulked there in the surly gloom of dusk. It wavered before your eyes like it was under water, with bright sun spots dancing around it. You backed up and leaned weakly against the stoop railing.

"Watch out!" bleated a shrill voice behind you, and you jumped. A square-faced little boy pushed you out of his way and scooted across the street like he was on wheels. . . .

"Clarence!" you yelled, startled.

Clarence disappeared in the big black maw of the condemned house.

"Clarence, hey!" you shouted. "Didn't I tell you not to go in that there house? You stay away from there."

"Gramma sent me for wood!" was the reply from the yawning mouth of the old tenement. "She says if I see you to tell you she wants you upstairs."

You looked after him. A sick, worried feeling jumped in your throat. Kids shouldn't go into those houses, even for chopping up the rotten old boards. You wanted to call him back again but it was no use. He was your sister's kid and if she didn't mind—

You shrugged and turned for the door of our house. Your heels dragged at you. You hated to go upstairs, to face the hungry family without a job without food for supper. Hated to warm over yesterday's boiled rice while six pairs of eyes drilled through your back. . . .

Suddenly something stunned you.

You had been glaring at that big-mouthed skeleton of a house across the way. At the evil-looking scar like a knife-slash up its face. Now you stiffened with a shock like a bolt of lightning. Your jaw fell open and you forgot to breathe. You saw that the dark seam in the wall of the old tenement was widening straining apart into a jagged crack between the bricks. The wall was quivering, crumbling. The house was going to collapse!

You felt like you were having a nightmare. Blinked. Didn't know if you should believe it. But there was the crack opening black and wide like in a movie earthquake. And Clarence was inside!

Your heart pounded hot blood into your throat. Your knees sagged and sweat prickled your skin. You thought you would drop before you could move. Then you wrenched yourself from the stoop and sprinted wildly across the street.

"Clarence!" you shrieked, "Clarence!"

The wide toothless mouth closed around you. Cans and broken bottles jabbed at your ankles. You stumbled through a chalky rug of fallen plaster and naily boards. In the back, under the rotten steps, Clarence looked up at you, scared.

"The house is falling!" you screamed, and grabbed him by the arms. Junk tripped you, held you back like in a terrible dream. You fought it—dragged yourself and Clarence across the floor. Out toward the dim light of the front opening. Into the slush of the street, splashing it on your legs as the two of you raced through puddles to our own stoop. You held Clarence tight against you.

He hung on to your coat, whimpering with fright. You watched the old house, shuddered, waited for it to collapse.

The street lamp on the corner lighted, feeble against the evening fog. A truck rumbled up the block. The piccolo in the candy store rocked with Fats Waller's piano. The condemned house still stood in the darkness, like a naked old woman. Its wood and plaster guts lay in ruins on the floor. The ugly scar was slashed up its face like it had been ever since you could remember. You squinted at it but couldn't make out in the dark if it was really a crack or only a heavy dirt stain. You frowned, open-mouthed, and shook your head in wonder. Your arms slacked around Clarence's shoulders.

He had stopped whimpering. Was calm—had already forgotten the scare. He looked up at you, puzzled. Then he looked at the house.

"It ain't falling!" he exclaimed. He thought you had played a joke on him. "Aaa! You ain't so funny," he growled sullenly. With the sudden impulse of a child he slipped out of your grasp like an eel and dashed across the street, mocking you with laughter and yelling, "House is falling! House is falling! House is. . . ."

His voice and his body were swallowed up in the greedy black mouth of the tenement. Worried, you watched again. The house was still there, crumbling, rotting, biding its time. Not today; perhaps tomorrow it might go. Maybe next day. Maybe next year.

Suddenly you hated the old house as you would loathe a person who slowly, coolly plotted murder. You wanted to claw it to pieces. You wanted to dig your nails into the cement and tear it brick from brick.

A heavy sigh rose and fell in your chest. Your throat made a flat sound, like a chuckle, and you shook your head and smiled. Why in the world should you have thought it was going to fall in when there it was—still standing big as life!

"I must be going nuts!" you told yourself.

You turned and pushed open the door leading to the hallway of your house. You climbed upstairs, wondering at yourself. What had put such a crazy notion into your head? Scaring the kid like that! What on earth made you do it? The useless old tenement had been there all your life. Why were you suddenly so sure that it must come down? What was it that made you feel deep inside that somewhere, somehow, you must some day help build decent houses where poor people like yourself could live?

GEORGE SAMPSON BRITE

Anne Scott

(from *George Sampson Brite,* 1939)

"Miz Smith, Miz Herman sent George Sampson outa Music 'cause when we was singin' 'Th Ole Time Religun' he kept on pattin' his feet."

After dutifully delivering this message, Marjorie Moore, a trim little brown-skinned miss of nine years, looked up into the teacher's face to note the effect. Seeing from the manner in which Miss Smith was glaring down at George Sampson that the message had carried, Majorie raised up on her tip-toes, placed one arm around the teacher's neck and whispered, with one eye on George Sampson, "An' he said his mother was comin' over Thursdee and beat you up."

"I ain't said nuthin'," ejaculated George Sampson, "an' my mutha did say that, too."

Miss Smith, a tall slender, light brown-skinned young woman with well groomed black hair, had no toleration for foolishness. She drew herself up to her full height, folded her arms, looked sternly down on George Sampson Brite and demanded, "Boy! What do you mean by patting your feet!"

"That's d'way they does in church," grumbled George Sampson sulkily.

"Church! You're a good one to be talking about church. You were reported every day last week for poor conduct. Even Miss Ross, the apprentice teacher, reported you Friday for sliding down the bannisters an' here you are starting off again, Monday, first

129

day in the week, with the same thing. Tell your mother I wish to see her."

"My mutha's at th' horspital," whimpered George Sampson.

"It's no wonder she's in the hospital having to be bothered with you," said Miss Smith.

"She ain't *in* th' horspital, she jis work there an' she gits off on Thursdee aftanoon," grumbled George Sampson.

"Um–hum, just write your name on the board an' stay in the cloakroom until recess," ordered the teacher.

So George Sampson shuffled to the board grumbling and muttering to himself and scribbled his name, George Sampson Brite, in large illegible script across the entire front blackboard. The children looked at the board and at each other and kind of giggled and looked to see what the teacher was going to say. Miss Smith came in, paid no attention whatever to George Sampson, took her seat and went on with the lesson.

The children were so interested in their work that they soon forgot about George Sampson. They were making designs to put on the baskets which they would eventually make for Christmas. The designs were in the first stages. The children had drawn a number of flower forms on a sheet of paper. From these they were working out various designs. Eventually each would select the best design and work it out to fit the shape of his basket. Each row in turn took the designs up to the teacher. The teacher corrected them and the children returned to their seats and continued with the work.

George Sampson was still messing around at the front board thinking with satisfaction that his mother was coming over "Thursdee" and beat the teacher up.

Miss Smith's room was located at the end of the second floor next to the stairway. The school was made up of three floors. On the first floor were five class rooms, the principal's office and the kindergarten, on the second floor were five class rooms, a teacher's rest room and a store room, on the third floor were six class rooms.

The school year comprised forty weeks and was divided into four quarters. Each grade comprised four quarters of ten weeks each. The quarters were designated as a, b, c, d; that is the children in the first quarter of the first grade were I-d, the second quarter I-c, the third quarter I-b, and the fourth quarter I-a. At the end of each ten weeks the quarter changed and those children who had passed in the previous quarter's work were promoted to the next quarter. Those who had not passed in the quarter's work were not promoted to the next quarter but repeated the work of the quarter in which they had failed. Each room had two quarters of a grade. Report cards were given out every five weeks or half quarter. The important promotions from room to room were made twice a year, in January or February and September as the graduation exercises were held twice a year. Often in June a whole room was graduated. Usually in the mid-year only one class.

On the third floor the rooms were divided into two departmental units with three rooms in each unit. On the second floor the three highest rooms, 7, 8, and 9, were arranged into a departmental unit. The schedule was carefully made out so that each subject received its allotted time. Miss Smith's room was No. 8, Grade 5-c and 5-d. Marjorie and George Sampson were both in the B. Class in Miss Smith's room—5-d. Miss Green's room was No. 9, Grade 4-a and 4-b, Miss Herman's room was No. 7, Grade 5-a and 5-b. Miss Hodges in No. 10 and the other rooms below operated on the all-day plan, that is, the teacher taught all the subjects to one room of children.

Miss Smith taught Arithmetic and Drawing. Miss Herman taught Music and English. Miss Green taught Physical Training and Geography. Each teacher also taught Health and Science to her own home room group. The children stayed in their home rooms one hour in the morning, from 9 to 10, and one hour in the afternoon from 1:00 to 2:00.

However the district superintendent had been changed and the present one did not believe in the departmental plan for the children of the fourth and fifth grades. He thought that the younger children had difficulty in adjusting themselves to the different personalities and also that the younger children profited more by staying in one room where the teacher could correlate the subjects and give individual instruction where needed. So it was understood that the next quarter the three rooms on the second floor would go back to the all-day plan and the departmental plan would be used only on the third floor.

Miss Smith's room was a light, airy one with a large cloakroom in front. The cloakroom was in reality a little ante-room with a large window. In the center of the cloakroom were a small table and four small chairs. The entrance to Miss Smith's room was on the

left side at the front. The door was a large square-like one with a
square glass panel in it Three large windows on the opposite side
of the room faced the door. Across the front and back of the room
and on the left side with the door were blackboards. Between the
windows also were small blackboard panels. Each child had a number over his coat hook in the cloakroom so he would know just
where to place his wraps. On the wall were vivid pictures and in
the window was a box of artificial flowers which looked almost
real. Miss Smith was exceedingly fond of pictures and flowers.

The children worked diligently on their designs while George
Sampson wrote his name in large letters across the front board.
Miss Smith went on with the work. After a while she turned
around to see what George Sampson was doing and seeing what
she saw ordered George Sampson to, "Erase that—whatever it is,
write smaller and write so it can be read, and simply write
George *Brite*."

The children smiled to themselves. George Sampson proceeded
to stick his mouth out. He stood and looked sullen for a few minutes but no one paid any attention to him so he began to write and
rewrite and erase and rewrite until he finally succeeded in improv-
ing matters a little. Miss Smith went on correcting designs and paid
no attention to him. Finally she turned around and contemplated
the board for a few seconds, then finally said, "Um-hum—now
march yourself into that cloakroom an' there stay until recess an'
perhaps you'll know how to act in Music hereafter—an' at recess
I'll see more about you."

George Sampson shuffled into the cloakroom, wormed and
squirmed, sat down on the table, played with the buttons on the
children's coats and every now and then meowed like a cat. Finally
he came to the door, stuck his head out, stated that he was tired and
made a face. The teacher paid no attention whatever to him.

The recess bell rang. The class that was in Miss Smith's room
passed to Miss Herman's room and Miss Smith's home room children returned to her room, got their wraps and lined up for recess.
Miss Smith watched George Sampson with an eagle eye to see that
he did not slip out. After the lines had gone out George Sampson
sidled up to the door and peeped out to see what his chances were
for slipping out. Just then Miss Smith came in and ordered him to
"sit down." George Sampson went reluctantly to his seat, mumbled
and grumbled and turned and twisted.

The bell rang for the children to come in from recess. The children went to their home rooms and put up their wraps. Miss Smith watched them as they passed in. The teachers stood on duty at the door whenever the lines came in or went out. Each teacher went out into the yard once a week at recess and noon to supervise the children. This was Miss Herman's day in the yard so Miss Smith was keeping an eye on Miss Herman's children until she came in.

The bell rang for the children to pass to their proper departmental rooms. As the children lined up, George Sampson, seeing that the teacher was not looking so closely, started pushing ahead of a boy in the line and so a kind of fight, not exactly a fight, but a pushing back and forth started and the teacher told George Sampson to go back into the cloakroom and stay until noon. George Sampson straggled reluctantly into the cloakroom; sat down on the little table, looked out of the window, got up and sat down again, discovered a book of funny paper characters, took out his pencil and some paper which he found in his pocket and began to draw pictures from the "funny paper book," as the children called it. After a while he became tired of drawing, stuck his head out of the door several times and shuffled around and around in the cloakroom. Finally the noon bell rang.

As George Sampson shuffled out of the cloakroom and got in the back of the line Miss Smith reminded him positively that she wished to see his mother.

"You gonna see hu all right 'nough," muttered George Sampson as he sauntered out.

He gave a loud whoop as the air struck his lungs, hopped a truck which conveyed him a part of the way home, kicked a tin can the rest of the way and went through the side gate and into the back door.

George Sampson lived about five blocks from the school, in a little three room house with a large yard around it, front, back and side. Each room, the front room, the kitchen and the middle room had a door of its own. A plank walk extended from the front gate all around the house to the kitchen door and back to the coal shed. On one side of the house was a large vacant lot full of trees and sunflowers and wild clover where June bugs, grasshoppers and butterflies reveled in the summer time. The front yard was enclosed by a picket fence with a picket gate which swung open and shut. George Sampson and his little sister, Lottie, loved to swing back and forth on the gate. The side fence, a strong board fence which separated the yard from the vacant lot, had a gate in it about midway. This gate was on a line with the kitchen door. Across the street was another large vacant lot opposite the lot next door to George Sampson's house. When going to school it was more convenient for George Sampson and Lottie to go out of the front gate and cut across the lot across the street. When coming home they usually came through both lots and through the side gate into the kitchen door. When the lot was muddy they came in the front gate. George Sampson often made a shorter cut still by cutting through both lots and hopping the fence. In good weather George Sampson and Lottie went home to lunch, in bad weather they took their lunches to school or bought them.

George Sampson began getting a pitiful look on his face as he went in the kitchen door. Granny, a dark, thin, white-haired personage was fixing the lunch at the kitchen sink in the corner. His little sister, Lottie, was standing looking on. Lottie had not gone to school that day because she had a cold. Lottie was 3-d and in Miss Wray's room on the first floor.

"How'd Granny's boy git 'long t'day?" inquired his grand-mother. "Did'y tell Lottie's teecha that she had a cold an' couldn't come to school t'day?"

George Sampson did not answer but stuck out his mouth, attempted to squeeze out a tear and whined, "That ole Miz Smith's still pickin' on me, come makin' me stay in the cloakroom till noon cause that ole Margee what's hu pet come tellin' hu a lotta stuff 'bout me what warn't so an she's alays makin' fun a my clothes an' callin' my writin' hen scratchin' an' things lak that an' said I warn't no count an' didn't hab no home trainin' an' said my mutha didn't teech me no mannas.—An' she say I ain't got good sense."

"You got jis as much sense as she's got," sympathized Granny.— "Well jis git 'long th' best you can an' whin y'come home this evenin' tell y'ma bout it and I bitchu she'll go ova there an' beat hu head in."

Mrs. Brite, a widow, stout, dark brown and capable looking, worked in a hospital and was the breadwinner of the family. She supported her two children and her mother. Granny stayed home and kept house and did quilting when she could get it to do. She always had the supper ready and "saw" to the children as Mrs.

Brite went early and stayed late. On Thursday Mrs. Brite got off at 12 o'clock and had the afternoon off.

George Sampson followed Granny's advice and got along the best he could. He was able to get through the afternoon without any serious mishap. He kept his mind on his lessons a little longer than usual and managed not to get into mischief but he was still peeved at what he termed being "picked on."

About six-thirty Mrs. Brite arrived home and placed her groceries and bundle of working clothes on the table and inquired of Granny, "Well, Ma, how's things been goin' t'day?"

"O tol'able—tol'able," replied Granny, "but that ole teecha's still apickin' on George Sampson."

"Yessum, she jis treated me awful t'day," complained George Sampson coming in from the middle room, "come makin' me stay in the cloak room 'cause hu pet tol hu a lotta stuff on me what warn't so and said she was gonna smack my head off—an' said I ain't got no sense."

"I'm sick an' tired a hu foolishness," declared Mrs. Brite indignantly—"always apickin' on my chile—my chile's jis as good as inybody else's chile an' got jis as much sense, too.—Now George Sampson, jis try t'git along till Thursdee when I gits off. Then I'm goin' ova there an beat hu head in."

Things went fairly well the next day. George Sampson was on his "P's and Q's" in order to get out at recess to play ball. One of his classmates and bosom friends, Thomas Brown, had brought a brand new ball and bat to school.

The following day was the last Wednesday of the month, the day on which Miss Herman, the Music and English teacher, always had a program consisting of solos, speeches and dances. The children marched single file to Miss Herman's room, took seats and the program started. The pupils always marched single file from one departmental room to another. When they were passing into and out of the yard they went in twos.

Helen Jenkins played a piano solo with many runs and trills, after which some of the children applauded too loudly and one boy whistled.

Miss Herman explained to them that it was perfectly all right to applaud but applause must be given in a refined manner. To make the point perfectly clear she had Helen Jenkins play the last section of the solo again, after which she illustrated to the children the proper manner in which to applaud. The children applauded in the manner indicated by Miss Herman.

The program continued. Samuel Jones played a violin solo and three children dramatized Dunbar's poem, "In the Morning." The class applauded in the manner prescribed by the teacher. The next number was a Spanish dance by Thelma Wells, a plump little miss, with black eyes and hair, dressed in a red and yellow Spanish costume. She danced, turned, whirled around and beat the tambourines in real Spanish fashion. Marjorie played for Thelma to dance.

The children gave hearty but refined applause. George Sampson, however, was so elated that he could not contain himself. Instead of applauding in the manner approved by the teacher, he raised up in his seat and whooped, "Hot dog!"

The little girls looked from Miss Herman to George Sampson in duly horrified fashion. The boys wanted to do their duty by appearing shocked but they could not refrain from chuckling. Miss Herman looked severely at George Sampson and ordered, "Go to your home room an' don't come back."

George Sampson sauntered down the steps looking glum and grumbling to himself, "Nobodee can't neva hab no fun."

After a few minutes Miss Herman turned to Marjorie and said, "See if George Sampson has gone to Miss Smith's room an' tell Miss Smith I simply can't have that boy in my room. He's a disgrace.—Every time he comes in here there's trouble."

Marjorie was pleased to take the message and tripped to Miss Smith's room with nimble feet. George Sampson straggled to the home room, stood outside but did not venture in. He stood there toying with the Indian clubs which hung on the wall outside the door. Some time previously Indian clubs had been used for the Physical Training exercises. The use of Indian clubs in Physical Training had been discontinued. The "setting up" exercises were all "free hand." But the Indian clubs still hung around the walls and were sometimes used for games.

After a minute or so Marjorie came to bring the message from Miss Herman. George Sampson was toying with an Indian club as Marjorie passed by. Marjorie made a face at George Sampson as she passed by him. George Sampson shook the Indian club at her. Marjorie tossed her head scornfully into the air signifying that she knew he dare not bother her because she had a brother twice his size.

She tipped to the teacher's desk and whispered airily, "George Sampson's outside the door. He got sent outa Music for hollering 'Hot dog' when Thelma did her Spanish dance."

Miss Smith's face clouded. Miss Herman's children who were in Miss Smith's room doing their design work looked up casually. They were used to hearing about George Sampson and did not wish to take up time from their designs to interest themselves in his performances.

Miss Smith began severely, "Sent out of Music again. I'm so sick an' tired of that boy I don't know what to do. Every time I turn around he's into one thing or another."

She went to the door and opened it with a sharp push. George Sampson stood guiltily toying with the Indian club and turning and twisting uneasily. "What do you mean by getting sent out of Music again?" demanded Miss Smith. "Every time I turn around I'm hearing about you.—What is the matter with you anyhow?— Put that Indian club up an' fix up that trouser leg.—You look like some I don't know what—all disconnected."

Miss Smith looked through the glass to see what the children were doing. The children were busy with their work. They were anxious to finish the designs so they could start the construction of the baskets. The construction work consisted of making the basket from strawboard and colored paper. After the basket was constructed the design was traced on it and painted. This kind of work was more or less individualized. Some children naturally worked faster than others and Miss Smith allowed each to progress at his own rate.

Mrs. Hopson, the matron, passed by, broom in hand, and looked amusedly at George Sampson.

"What is the matter with you?" continued Miss Smith.

"You ain't got no bizness makin' fun a'peeple's clothes," mumbled George Sampson.

"Shut your mouth!—What do you mean by whooping an' yelling, 'Hot dog?'"

"Nuthin'."

"What!"

"I don mean nuthin'," mumbled George Sampson.

"Um-hum, well stay in here at recess an' learn how to act," commanded Miss Smith.

The children returned to their home rooms and passed out to recess.

Miss Smith took pains to see that George Sampson did not slip out during the recess period. George Sampson sat in his seat and twisted and turned and mumbled and grumbled. Finally the bell rang for the children to come in from recess.

George Sampson's class was scheduled to go to Miss Green's room after recess. This was the Physical Training day and as the weather was good the children expected to go out doors and play ball. George Sampson was a good ball player and captain of his team. The captains were elected by democratic vote. George Sampson was very anxious to go out and play with his team so he got over to one side where Miss Smith could not see him and be reminded of his conduct and attempted to go to the next room with the other children. Miss Smith spied him however and thinking that perhaps he would get into more mischief told him to go to his seat and stay in the room. "I'll write Miss Green a note," she said, "and tell her I'm keeping you. I'm sure she won't grieve over the matter."

"I don see why I can't play ball sometime lak otha peeple," grumbled George Sampson.

"Shut your mouth—I don't see why you can't do right like other people either. You'll get out in that yard an' the first thing I know you'll be starting up something else. Now just get out that geography book an' study that lesson that you don't know!" instructed Miss Smith.

George Sampson went reluctantly back to his seat and took out his geography book and pretended to be studying.

The class that came into Miss Smith's room paid no attention to George Sampson. They were too much interested in their arithmetic work. They were solving orally problems without numbers and this always proved fascinating to them. Time hung heavily on George Sampson's hands. He fumbled and fiddled with his geography book, listened to the children working arithmetic problems and tried to fathom out what they were doing.

Then thoughts of vengeance filled his mind. He rejoiced to think that his mother was coming over to beat the teacher up. It seemed to him years before the bell rang for noon. At last the first bell rang and the children passed to their home rooms to get their wraps and pass out for the noon intermission.

As the children came into the home room to get their wraps Thomas told George Sampson that Sam Smith made the team lose. George Sampson punched Sam Smith slyly, so he thought, but it happened that Miss Smith was looking in his direction and ordered him to stay in at noon.

The children lined up. Miss Smith cautioned them to be back on time and come in with the lines. The lines came in at one o'clock but the children were not marked tardy until one-fifteen. The lines passed out for the noon intermission. As the lines were passing a boy handed Miss Smith a notice to read and sign. George Sampson seeing Miss Smith's attention diverted crouched down behind Thomas, Robert and Jesse Redd, another member of his team, ran home top speed and told his grandmother amid many crocodile tears, "That ole teecha's still pickin' on me. Made me stay in at recess for nuthin' an' wouldn't lemme play ball or nuthin' an' come tellin' me t'stay in at noon 'cause anotha boy hit me—but I come on home 'cause I was hongree."

"Y'done right," answered Granny sympathetically. "Thim teechas makes me sick pickin' on peeple's chillun. All they thinks 'bout is dressin' theyself up an' struttin' 'round with they nose stuck up puttin' on airs. Jis wait till t'morra whin yo Ma gits off—I bitchu she'll go ova there an' beat hu head in. Now jis stay home wid Granny an rest yo'self."

So George Sampson remained at home that afternoon and threw rocks and played ball and shot marbles to his heart's delight.

The next morning George Sampson reached school at ninethirty and sauntered sheepishly into the room. He would have stayed home but he feared the truant officer, who had been after him several times on previous occasions. The children were busy with their arithmetic when he walked in.

Miss Smith looked up, saw George Sampson and ordered him to, "Stand outside the door," adding—"the idea of you having the nerve to cross this threshold after your actions of yesterday."

Miss Smith assigned the lesson in arithmetic. The children were finishing up the subject of addition of fractions. Miss Smith had placed eight examples in addition of fractions on the board. Each child had a large sheet of paper which he tore into eight pieces. On each piece of paper he placed one of the examples. When he had finished the first example he laid it aside and went on with the next one. Miss Smith marked the examples in order and handed them back. The children strove to see how many examples they could get right. The teacher jotted down the names of the children who did not seem to understand the examples so that she could come back to these children later and give them individual instruction.

The children began their work and Miss Smith stepped outside of the door to "see about" George Sampson.

George Sampson was shifting uneasily from one foot to another.

"Where were you at noon yesterday?" demanded Miss Smith, "I told you to stay in!"

"I was hongree," muttered George Sampson, "an' I had t'go home an' eat, an' my mutha said she's comin' ova here t'day all right 'nough."

"Well she won't get here a minute too soon," observed the teacher, "an' if she isn't here this week I'm gonna know the reason why. March yourself into this room an' don't let me hear one word from you."

George Sampson stuck his mouth out about three inches, shuffled down the aisle to his seat, flopped down heavily, all the time mumbling to himself something to the effect that, "his mutha was coming over an' beat that ole hard-boiled teecha up." Some of the children who heard the remark looked wide-eyed at George Sampson and then at the teacher to see if she had heard the remark. According to the look on the teacher's face she evidently had heard nothing.

Sophie Campbell, a plump energetic little girl, seated near enough to overhear the remark got out of her seat and tip-toed conscientiously up to the teacher, and whispered in her ear repeating what George Sampson had said.

"Um-hum is that so?" inquired Miss Smith with a dark look at George Sampson, and then went on with the lesson. The children passed up Example No. 1. The teacher marked and returned it and followed the same procedure with the rest of the examples. Those children who got all of the examples right were highly elated and piled them up in a neat pile to take home.

The bell rang for the classes to change. Miss Smith's room passed to Miss Green for Geography while Miss Green's room came to Miss Smith for Arithmetic. Miss Smith, as usual, cautioned the children to have good lessons and conduct and no bad reports.

The geography class had just completed the topic, "Why New England is a great manufacturing center." Miss Green had planned a test upon the topic just finished. The paper was passed and the children began eagerly to answer the questions because Miss Green had an honor roll on the wall upon which she would place the names of those who had a good mark on the test.

George Sampson sat for a full ten minutes making figures on the desk. Finally he condescended to consume one-half of the paper with his full name, George Sampson Brite. He looked at the questions on the board and seeing none to his liking took out his page from the funny paper and drew a picture of a cowboy.

Miss Green, suspecting George Sampson of irregularities, went to the window, adjusted the shade, came casually around by George Sampson's seat, took hold of his paper and examined it.

"Where is your work?" she asked.

"I ain't got none," grumbled George Sampson, "I done f'got all that stuff an' b'sides I warn't here."

"You were here," asserted Miss Green, "an' in the first place why do you write your name all over the paper an' what has this picture to do with the test? There's Miss Smith passing the door now. Thelma, ask her to step inside a minute please."

Miss Smith came in looking inquiringly at the children and said, "Good morning, Miss Green."

"Good morning, Miss Smith," answered Miss Green. "I wish you would look at this boy's paper. This is what he's done in twenty minutes—name all over the paper—no room for anything else an' look at that picture."

"What is this?" exclaimed Miss Smith taking hold of the paper and reading it.

George Sampson grumbled something.

"Just keep your mouth shut," ordered Miss Smith, "an' stay in at noon until you learn how to act."

Miss Smith returned to her room. Shortly the bell rang for the children to pass back to their home rooms preparatory to the noon intermission. George Sampson attempted to slip out down behind some members of his team, but Marjorie saw him and immediately informed Miss Smith. Miss Smith spotted him and ordered him back to his seat. So George Sampson stayed in his seat until 12:30 looking glum at what he termed being picked on, but with a feeling of satisfaction in knowing that his mother would soon be over to settle the score.

At 12:30 he set out for home pondering upon his wrongs that would soon be avenged. He cut across the lot, burst in through the side gate and on in through the kitchen door. As it was Thursday his mother was off for the afternoon. As soon as he got into the kitchen he began shedding crocodile tears.

"What's d'matta wid you, boy?" demanded Mrs. Brite in alarm.

"Well what on earth!" exclaimed Granny as she looked up from where she was sitting by the kitchen sink peeling potatoes.

"That ole mean, hard-boiled teecha's still pickin' on me," wept George Sampson. "Come makin' fun a me an said I don know nuthin' an' ain't got no sense. An' she wouldn't lemme go out an' play ball an' she let all th' otha children go out an' play ball an' they acted worsin' me. An' a lil' ole gal name Margee what's hu pet, she b'lieves everythin' she says an' she's alays makin' up things 'bout me an' tellin' hu. An she tol hu I was cheatin' in gography an' she came fussin' at me an' made me stay in at noon."

"Well you got jis as much sense as she is," retorted his mother.

"Sho is," piped up Granny from where she sat in the corner. "Sho is."

"I'm sick an' tired a hu pickin' on my chile," went on Mrs. Brite, "an' this here is th' day I said I was goin' after hu an' I'm a goin', too."

Granny nodded her head approvingly.

"She lits thim otha peeple's chil'rin do as they pleases an' picks on my George Sampson," raved Mrs. Brite. "I ain't gonna stand f'it no longer. I'm goin' ova there an' bust hu in hu mouth."

Granny continued to nod approval.

The one o'clock bell had just rung. Miss Smith was standing just outside of her door supervising the passing in of lines. In a few minutes the lines were all in and Miss Smith was preparing to go into the room when George Sampson and his mother appeared on the scene.

"That's hu," whispered George Sampson indicating Miss Smith, as they came up the steps.

Mrs. Brite swaggered forward and demanded in loud tones, "Is you Miss Smith?"

"Good afternoon, Madam," answered the teacher as she pushed the door of her room shut. "Yes, I'm Miss Smith. I presume that you're George Sampson's mother. Well, I'm sorry to say that George Sampson's conduct has been very poor."

"His connuck ain't been no poorer'n nobody else's," contradicted Mrs. Brite in loud tones, "you jis got a pick on my chile—my chile's jis as good as inybody else's chile an' b'sides he's got jis as much sense too, an' you an' nobody else ain't got no bizness makin' fun a him an' callin' him crazy."

"Madam, I think you had better see the principal," advised Miss Smith coldly.

"I ain't studin' th' principal," yelled Mrs. Brite, "my bizness is wid you an' I come ova here to show you how to quit pickin' on my George Sampson." So saying she made a threatening launch toward the teacher and raised her right arm in a menacing manner.

The children, hearing the loud tones, crowded to the door and peered through the glass. Miss Green and Miss Herman stepped to their doors to see what was going on. Mrs. Hopson, the matron, stepped up, broom in hand, to see what the trouble was.

George Sampson stepped up briskly behind his mother when she launched forward.

Miss Smith stepped agilely to one side and coldly taking hold of one of the Indian clubs from the wall stood in readiness to meet further advances from the enemy.

She took one step back and Mrs. Brite's eyes grew large. George Sampson's eyes bulged and his mouth hung open. Mrs. Brite waved her hand to one side saying, "Now, Miz Smith, I didn't come here t'start up no fussin' an' fightin' wid no teechas. I'm a peacable woman, I am. I sends George Sampson t'school t'do what y'all tells him an' ef he don do it I wants t'know. Look here, George Sampson, git outa my sight be'fo I lands on you right now! Well, I'll see you some mo, Miz Smith. Good-bye."

"Good-bye, Mrs. Brite."

AFTERNOON

Ralph Ellison

(from *American Writing,* 1940)

THE TWO BOYS stood at the rear of a vacant lot looking up at a telephone pole. The wires strung from one pole to the next gleamed bright copper in the summer sun. Glints of green light shot from the pole's glass insulators as the boys stared.

"Funny ain't no birds on them wires, huh?"

"They got too much 'lectricity in 'em. You can even hear 'em hum they got so much."

Riley cocked his head, listening:

"That what's making that noise?" he said.

"Sho, man. Jus like if you put your ear against a streetcar-line pole you can tell when the car's coming. You don't even have to see it," Buster said.

"Thass right, I knowed about that."

"Wonder why they have them glass things up there?"

"To keep them guys what climbs up there from gitting shocked, I guess."

Riley caught the creosote smell of the black paint on the pole as his eyes traveled over its rough surface.

"High as a bitch!" he said.

"It ain't so high I bet I caint hit that glass on the end there."

"Buster, you fulla brown. You caint hit *that* glass, it's too high."

"Shucks!! Gimme a rock."

They looked slowly over the dry ground for a rock.

"Here's a good one," Riley called. "An egg rock."

"Throw it here, and watch how ole Lou Gehrig snags 'em on first base."

Riley pitched. The rock came high and swift. Buster stretched his arm to catch it and kicked out his right leg behind him, touching base.

"And he's out on first!" he cried.

"You got 'im all right," Riley said.

"You jus watch this."

Riley watched as Buster wound up his arm and pointed to the insulator with his left hand. His body gave a twist and the rock flew upward.

Crack!

Pieces of green glass sprinkled down.

They stood with hands on hips, looking about them. A bird twittered. A rooster crowed. No one shouted to them and they laughed nervously.

"What'd I tell you?"

"Damn! I never thought you could do it."

"We better get away from here in case somebody saw that."

Riley looked around: "Come on."

They walked out to the alley.

Chickens crouched in the cool earth beneath a shade tree. The two boys hurried out of sight of a woman piling rubbish in the next yard. A row of fence stretched up the alley, past garages and outhouses. They walked carefully, avoiding burrs and pieces of glass, over ground hot to their bare feet. The alley smelled of dust and the dry pungence of burning leaves.

Buster picked up a stick and stirred in the weeds behind an unpainted garage. It raised dust, causing him to sneeze.

"Buster, what the hell you doing?"

"Looking for liquor, man."

"Looking for *liquor*?"

"Sho, man." He stopped, pointing: "See that house down on the corner?"

Riley saw the back of a small green house with a row of zinc tubs on the rail of its porch.

"Yeah, I see it," he said.

"Bootleggers live down there. They hid it all along here in these weeds. Boy, one night the cops raided and they was carrying it outa there in slop jars and everything."

"In *slop* jars?"

"Hell yes!"

"Gee, the cops catch 'em?"

"Hell naw, they poured it all down the toilet. Man, I bet all the fish in the Canadian River was drunk."

They laughed noisily.

Buster dug in the weeds again, then stopped:

"Guess ain't nothing in here."

He looked at Riley. Riley was grinning to himself.

"Boy, what's the matter with you?"

"Buster, I'm still thinking about 'em throwing that liquor down the toilet. You know one thing? When I was little and they would set me on the seat, I useta think the devil was down there gitting him some cigars. I was scaired to sit down. Man, one time my ole lady like to beat the hell outa me 'cause I wouldn't sit down."

"You crazy, man," Buster said. "Didn't I tell you, you was crazy?"

"Honest," Riley said. "I useta believe that."

They laughed. Buster dragged his stick through the weed tops. A hen cackled in the yard beyond the fence they were moving past. The sound of someone practicing scales on a piano drifted to them. They walked slowly.

The narrow road through the alley was cut with dried ruts of wagon wheels, the center embedded with pieces of broken glass. "Where we going?" Buster asked. Riley began to chant:

> *"Well I met Mister Rabbit*
> *down by the pea vine . . ."*

Buster joined in:

> *"An' I asked him where's he gwine*
> *Well, he said, Just kiss my behind*
> *And he skipped on down the pea vine."*

Buster suddenly stopped and grabbed his nose.

"Look at that ole dead cat!"

"Ain't on my mama's table."

"Mine neither!"

"You better spit on it, else you'll have it for supper," Buster said.

They spat upon the maggot-ridden body, and moved on.

"Always lots a dead cats in the alley. Wonder why?"

"Dogs get 'em, I guess."

"My dog ate so many dead cats once, he went crazy and died," said Riley.

"I don't like cats. They too sly."

"Sho stinks!"

"I'm holding my breath."

"Me too!"

Soon they passed the smell. Buster stopped, pointing.

"Look at the apples on that tree."

"Gittin' big as hell!"

"Sho is, let's git some."

"Naw, they'll give you the flux. They too green."

"I'm taking a chance," Buster said.

"Think anybody's home?"

"Hell, we don't have to go inside the fence. See, some of 'em's hanging over the alley."

They walked over to the fence and looked into the yard. The earth beneath the trees was bare and moist. Up near the house the grass was short and neat. Flagstones leading out of the garage made a pattern in the grass.

"White folks live here?"

"Naw, colored. White folks moved out when we moved in the block," Buster said.

They looked up into the tree: the sun broke through the leaves and apples hung bright green from dull black branches. A snake-doctor hummed by in long, curving flight. It was quiet and they could hear the thump, thump, thump of oil wells pumping away to the south. Buster stepped back from the fence, and held his stick ready.

"Look out now," Buster said. "They might fall in the weeds."

The stick ripped the leaves. An apple rattled through the branches, thumping to the ground inside the fence.

"Damn!"

He picked up the stick and threw again. The leaves rustled; Riley caught an apple. Another fell near Buster's toes. He looked at Riley's apple.

"I git the biggest! You scaired to eat 'em anyway."

Riley watched him an instant, rolling the apple between his palms. There was a spot of red on the green of the apple.

"I don't care," he said finally. "You can have it."

He pitched the apple to Buster. Buster caught it and touched first base with his toe.

"He's out on first!"

"Let's go," Riley said.

They walked close to the fence, the weeds whipping their thin legs. A woodpecker drummed on a telephone pole.

"I'm gonna remember that tree. Won't be long before them apples is ripe."

"Yeah, but this *here'n* sho ain't ripe," Riley said. Buster laughed as he saw Riley's face twist into a wry frown.

"We need some salt," he said.

"Man, damn! Hot springs water won't help this apple none."

Buster laughed and batted a tin can against a fence with his stick. A dog growled and sniffed on the other side. Buster growled back and the dog went barking along the fence as they moved past.

"Sic 'im, Rin Tin Tin, sic 'im," Riley called.

Buster barked. They went past the fence, the dog still barking behind them.

Buster dropped his stick and fitted his apple carefully into his fingers. Riley watched him.

"See, here's the way you hold it to pitch a curve," Buster said.

"How?"

"Like this: these two fingers this here way; you put your thumb this here way, and you let it roll off your fingers this a way."

Riley gripped his apple as Buster showed him; then wound up and threw. The apple flew up the alley in a straight line and suddenly broke sharply to the right.

"See there! You see it break? That's the way you do it, man. You put that one right up around the batter's neck."

Riley was surprised. A grin broke over his face and his eyes fell upon Buster with admiration. Buster ran and picked up the apple.

"See, here's the way you do it."

He wound up and pitched, the apple humming as it whipped through the air. Riley saw it coming at him and curving suddenly, sharply away. It fell behind him. He shook his head, smiling:

"Buster?"

"What?"

"Boy, you 'bout the throwin'est nigguh I ever seen. Less see you hit that post yonder, that one over there by the fence."

"Hell, man! You must think I'm Schoolboy Rowe or somebody."

"Go on, Buster, you can hit it."

Buster took a bite out of the apple and chewed as he wound up his arm. Then suddenly he bent double and snapped erect, his left foot leaving the ground and his right arm whipping forward.

Clunk!

The apple smashed against the post and burst into flying pieces.

"What'd I tell you? Damn, that ole apple come apart like when you hit a quail solid with a shotgun."

"Thass what you call control," Buster said.

"I don't know what you call it, but I'd sho hate to have you throwin' bricks at me," said Riley.

"Shucks, you ain't seen nothin'. You want to see some throwin' you jus wait till we pass through the fairgrounds to go swimming in Goggleye Lake. Man, the nigguhs out there can throw Coca-Cola bottles so hard that they bust in the air!"

Riley doubled himself up, laughing.

"Buster, you better quit lying so much!"

"I ain't lying, man. You can ask anybody."

"Boy, boy!" Riley laughed. The saliva bubbled at the corners of his mouth.

"Come on over to my house and sit in the cool," Buster said.

They turned a corner and walked into a short stretch of grassy yard before a gray cottage. A breeze blew across the porch; it smelled clean and fresh to Riley. The wooden boards of the porch had been washed white. Buster remembered seeing his mother scrubbing the porch with the suds after she had finished the clothes. He tried to forget those clothes.

A fly buzzed at the door screen. Riley dropped down on the porch, his bare feet dangling.

"Wait a minute while I see what's here to eat," Buster said.

Riley lay back and covered his eyes with his arm. "All right," he said.

Buster went inside, fanning flies away from the door. He could hear his mother busy in the kitchen as he walked through the little house. She was standing before the window, ironing. When he stepped down into the kitchen she turned her head.

"Buster, where you been, you lazy rascal! You knowed I wanted you here to help me with them tubs!"

"I was over to Riley's, Ma. I didn't know you wanted me."

"You didn't know! Lawd, I don't know why I had to have a chile like you. I work my fingers to the bone to keep you looking decent and that's the way you 'preciates it. You didn't know!"

Buster was silent. It was always this way. He had meant to help; he always meant to do the right thing, but something always got in the way.

"Well what you standing there looking like a dying calf for? I'm through now. Go on out and play."

"Yessum."

He turned and walked slowly out of the back door.

The cat arched its back against his leg as he went off the porch, stepping gingerly over the sun-heated boards. The ground around the steps was still moist and white where Ma had poured the suds. A stream of water trickled rapidly from the hydrant, sparkling silver in the sunlight. Suddenly he remembered why he had gone into the house. He stopped and called:

"Maaa . . ."

"What you want?"

"Ma, what we gonna have for supper?"

"Lawd, all you think about is your gut. I don't know. Come on back in here and fix you some eggs if you hongery. I'm too busy to stop—and for the Lawd's sake leave me alone!"

Buster hesitated. He was hungry but he could not stay around Ma when she was like this. She was like this whenever something went wrong with her and the white folks. Her voice had been like a slap in the face. He started slowly around to the front of the house. The dust was thick and warm to his feet. Looking down, he broke a sprig of milk-weed between his bare toes and watched the green stem slowly bleeding white sap upon the brown earth. A tiny globe of milk glistened on his toe, and as he walked to the front of the house he dug his foot into the dry dust, leaving the sap a small spot of mud.

He dropped down beside Riley.

"You eat so quick?" asked Riley.

"Naw, Ma's mad at me."

"Don't pay that no mind, man. My folks is always after me. They think all a man wants to do is what they want him to. You oughta be glad you ain't got no ole man like I got."

"Is he very mean?"

"My ole man's so mean he hates hisself!"

"Ma's bad enough. Let them white folks make her mad where she works and I catch hell."

"My ole man's the same way. Boy, and can he beat you! One night he come home from work and was gonna beat my ass with a piece of 'lectricity wire. But my ole lady stopped 'im. Told 'im he bet' not."

"Wonder why they so mean," Buster said.

"Damn if I know. My ole man says we don't git enough beatings these days. He said Gramma useta tie 'em up in a gunny sack and smoke 'em, like they do hams. He was gonna do that to me. But Ma stopped 'im. She said, 'Don't you come treating no chile of mine like no slave. Your Ma mighta raised you like a slave, but I ain't raising him like that and you bet' not harm a hair of his head!' And he didn't do it neither. Man, was I glad!"

"Damn! I'm glad I don't have no ole man," Buster said.

"You just wait till I get big. Boy, I'm gonna beat the hell outa my ole man. I'm gonna learn to box like Jack Johnson, just so I can beat his ass."

"Jack Johnson, first colored heavyweight champion of the whole wide world!" Buster said. "Wonder where he is now?"

"I don't know, up north in New York, I guess. But I bet *wherever* he is, ain't nobody messing with him."

"You mighty right! I heard my Uncle Luke say Jack Johnson was a better fighter than Joe Louis. Said he was fast as a cat on his feet. Fast as a cat! Gee, you can throw a cat off the top a house and he'll land on his feet. Why by golly, I bet you could throw a cat down from heaven and the son-of-a-bitch would land right side up!"

"My ole man's always singing:

> *'If it hadn't a been*
> *for the referee*
> *Jack Johnson woulda killed*
> *Jim Jefferie,'"*

Riley said.

The afternoon was growing old. The sun hung low in a cloudless sky and soon would be lost behind the fringe of trees across the street. A faint wind blew and the leaves on the trees trembled in the sun. They were silent now. A black-and-yellow wasp flew beneath the eaves, droning. Buster watched it disappear inside its gray honeycomblike nest, then rested back on his elbows and crossed his legs, thinking of Jack Johnson. A screen slammed loudly somewhere down the street. Riley lay beside him, whistling a tune between his teeth.

THE WOMAN IN THE WINDOW

Ramona Lowe

(from *Opportunity: Journal of Negro Life,* 18.1, January 1940)

THE EMPLOYMENT AGENCY sent her to a place that wanted a cook. Fifteen a week, they paid. Twelve hours a day, but after all fifteen's good wages.

When the proprietor, Mr. Parsons, saw her he was delighted. He rubbed his hands and showed her the kitchen. There was no need for a prolonged interview. He could see that she was just the thing. And the rest of the establishment was invited to take a peep to see what a treasure had been found.

Mrs. Jackson went right to work frying chicken with a lofty unconcern for the curious faces peeping in at the door and the proprietor's nervously evident pleasure. The tenth time the proprietor appeared in the kitchen he was accompanied by a stout man with an appraising eye, apparently a partner in the restaurant.

"Mr. Kraft," Parsons said loudly by way of introduction, "this is our new cook."

Mrs. Jackson turned her broad back indifferently on the two men. This was not the expected reaction. Parsons cleared his throat for attention. "I didn't get your name."

"You never asked it," Mrs. Jackson corrected him brusquely. "My name's Mrs. Jackson."

"What's your first name?" asked Kraft, surveying her with the brazen air of a master.

"Where I works," Mrs. Jackson replied with finality, "I'm known as Mrs. Jackson."

Kraft, trying to overlook this show of dignity, simply remarked, "She'll be a beaut in the window, Mike. A beaut!"

The proprietor rubbed his hands and addressed Mrs. Jackson. "You look straight from the South," he said.

Mrs. Jackson, suspicious of the compliment, was non-committal.

"I'll bet your home's in Georgia," continued Parsons chaffingly. Without waiting for this conjecture to be confirmed, he turned to his partner. "How soon can you get the equipment up?"

"Couple of weeks for everything," Kraft replied.

"Good. Good. Mrs. Jackson, we're going to make a few alterations, but business will go on just the same. When the alterations are complete, you will be cooking in the window!"

Shock ran through Mrs. Jackson. Her mind had not followed the trend of their remarks to this conclusion.

"Yes, ma'm," Kraft rocked on his heels. "You'll be displayed just like the pancakes and the waffles."

Mrs. Jackson was verbally not quite equal to the unexpected. She knew where she stood, but she didn't know how to express it. "The 'ployment agency jus' tol me cookin'," she floundered.

"That's all it is," said Kraft. "Cookin'.""

"What you talkin' 'bout a winda?" she wanted to know.

"We're gonna let you do your cookin' in the winda," Kraft explained.

"I doan like nobody watchin' me cook," she protested.

The proprietor sensed the need of tact. "It should be a privilege," he assured her, clipping his words and using his hands for emphasis.

"Humph!" was Mrs. Jackson's wordless comment. Signs of anger were becoming evident.

Kraft selected a piece of chicken from the freshly cooked pile.

"I ain' one for a show, Mr. Parsons," Mrs. Jackson explained; "so if it's a show you want I reckon you'll have t' get somebody else."

But the proprietor's zeal could not recognize lack of enthusiasm in anyone else. "We're gonna have all new equipment," he announced. "Everything new. You can see everything that's going on in the street. Our customers will see how clean and tempting everything is. We'll run the frauds that advertise Southern cooking out of business."

Mrs. Jackson was not interested.

But Kraft, eating his piece of chicken, knew a formula for compulsion to his will. "We'll make it eighteen a week—give you a vegetable preparer and a dishwasher," he offered.

Mrs. Jackson did not take long to consider. A family that had to be supported, when jobs were scarce and poor-paying, made duty triumph over pride.

Parsons beamed. "Then it's eighteen a week. All settled."

Kraft wiped his greasy fingers on a dish towel with the satisfied and confident air of a man who always knows how to settle all things. "Anybody who can cook chicken like that is worth a million," he said.

When the alterations were complete, Mrs. Jackson was moved into the window. She was wearing her neat blue cover-all apron. But she hadn't reckoned with enterprise.

Parsons hovered about, rubbing his hands.

"Mrs. Jackson, that's fine. Now. I wonder if you have a skirt. Green or purple. And a big white apron. Then we'll have to have a bandanna."

Mrs. Jackson was appalled. She drew herself up indignantly. "No, sir!" she said. "I ain' got none of them things."

Parsons was not discouraged. "Well, we'll have to get them, Mrs. Jackson. We'll have to get them."

And he did. . . . He got a voluminous dark purple skirt, a big white apron, a loose snowy blouse, a green shawl and a red bandanna. "Now," he cautioned, "no corsets, Mrs. Jackson, and we're made."

Mrs. Jackson, who had always minimized her bulk with the soberest of colors, was stubborn. "I'm cookin' in this here winda, but I ain' gonna look like no circus freak."

"This is Southern," said Parsons brightly.

"The South ain' never had nothin' looked like that," averred Mrs. Jackson.

Parsons, convinced of his infallibility, was heedless of criticism. "Now I'm just going to make you a present of this," he said.

But Mrs. Jackson would have none of his generosity. "What I want with that stuff?" she snapped.

Parsons, baffled by this ingratitude, was reduced to one word, "Please."

"Why, folks'd laugh," argued the offended woman.

Parson was exultant again. "That's just it! That's just what we want! We want people to laugh."

Mrs. Jackson put down her cooking fork with a look that predicted resignation from a distasteful occupation.

"Twenty dollars a week," offered the resolute Parsons, remembering how Kraft had achieved his success.

Mrs. Jackson had a conscience quickened by four little children who had to be clothed and fed and who belonged to her. She grumbled, "Ain' *nobody* ever wore no such foolishness!" But she accepted.

Parsons was jubilant. There was his bright spot to attract, his mass of color to display, his invitation to new volumes of business. He arranged the bandanna-ends to stand up like two impudent ears. His caricature lacked but one detail.

"Now if you could just smile, Mrs. Jackson."

But Mrs. Jackson couldn't. "I spose you think smiles is put on like cloes," she said. "I ain' no actress, Mr. Parsons."

So she set to work in the window. Children trooped past, just out of school. One of the white youngsters, sighting her, cried out gleefully, "Oooh lookee, Aunt Jemima!"

"That Aunt Jemima?" queried another.

"Sure that's Aunt Jemima. Hey you, Aunt Jemima!"

One of the colored youngsters, flattening his dusky face against the pane, saw his mother.

The blood ran molten from her throat to the pit of her stomach.

"Oh black mammy! Oh Aunt Jemima!" shouted the white children. And one broke out in song,

> "Nigger, nigger in the pot.
> Stew him till his bones all rot."

The dark youngster ran on, his companions following with their tormenting ditty.

Mrs. Jackson wondered if her other children would pass by. The perspiration stood out on her forehead. She had no strength to wipe it away. She leaned against the table and looked out, and the world looked in curiously at the embodiment of a fiction it had created. But then three round, dark faces appeared at the pane who had never imagined this fantasy before them. They gazed with wonder. With an almost imperceptible movement of her head, she ordered them away. They started to run, but the youngest looked back and asked, "What's Mama doing there?"

Coming out of the alley-way, her day's work done, Mrs. Jackson was confronted by a huge new neon sign in front of the restaurant. It bore the legend: *Mammy's.*

What could she say to the children? Should she take advantage of her superior position and force them to an unquestioning subservience to the indignities of human life, or should she make them comrades in her battle for a livelihood? When she reached the door of her flat, she paused. She was so ashamed. Four pairs of eyes were wide open as she tiptoed into the room. "You wake?" she asked.

"Yes'm," replied the eldest.

Mrs. Jackson took off her coat and hat busily, wishing vaguely that they had been asleep and she might defer explanation till morning at least. But her young son allowed her no leeway. "Mama, that wasn't you in the winda, was it?" He asked the question with a downward inflection, as though convinced that it couldn't have been she.

"Yes, honey, that was me. Why ain' you children sleep?" There was silence for a moment. Then another question.

"What you in the winda for?"

"I got t' work. Tha's my job."

"I thought you did cookin', Mama," remarked one of the girls. "Tha's cookin.'"

Her son thought. Then he spoke. "I don't like that kind of cookin'."

"Now you children jus' lissen t' me. There's some things you got t' unnerstan'. Some work's dignified 'n' some ain' so dignified. But it all got t' be done. My work's cookin' 'n' there ain' nothin' wrong with that. If I didn' cook you wouln' have no shoes 'n' I wound' have no shoes 'n' we wouldn' have nothin' t' eat 'n' I 'speck we'd jus' lay up here 'n' die." She paused for breath, then went on:

"The owner man where I works thinks he gonna dress me up t' look like a ol' Southern mammy 'n' get a lotta business—"

"What's a ol' Southern mammy, Mama?"

"A Southern mammy's a ol' colored woman who had the nursin' of all the little white children t' do in the South doin slavery times. Sometimes you hears folks talkin' big 'bout their ol' mammy 'n' how powerful much they loved her 'n' all."

"Is that good, Mama?" asked her son, doubting that a mammy was to be approved.

"Well, when you hears such talk you jus' say, 'uh huh,' 'n' let whoever's talkin' talk on."

"Then what happened after you was a Southern mammy, Mama?" The little girls were impatient.

"Then I had t' do my cookin' in the winda. 'N' when you go pas', you can speak, but doan you linger. 'N' if your little fren's asks questions, you tell'm, that's your mama all right. She's got t' work for a livin.'" She paused. *"N' son, doan you never let me see you run no more when a body say nigger. You turn roun' 'n' give'm such a thrashin' they woan never forget. Unnerstan'?"*

The youngster remonstrated. "They said in Sunday school we wasn't to fight—"

"You got t' use a little horse sense bout some things, son," his mother replied tersely. "Now you all go t' sleep."

The little boy went back to his cot and the little girls snuggled against each other under the thin blanket. Mrs. Jackson was about to lift her weary self from the edge of the bed when the smallest girl, as if divining the trouble stirring in her mother's soul, crept up to her and whispered, "Mama, I thought you looked pretty in the winda. Real pretty."

MAMMY

Dorothy West

(from *Opportunity: Journal of Negro Life,* 18.10, October 1940)

THE YOUNG NEGRO welfare investigator, carrying her briefcase, entered the ornate foyer of the Central Park West apartment house. She was making a collateral call. Earlier in the day she had visited an aging colored woman in a rented room in Harlem. Investigation had proved that the woman was not quite old enough for Old Age Assistance, and yet no longer young enough to be classified as employable. Nothing, therefore, stood in the way of her eligibility for relief. Here was a clear case of need. This collateral call on her last employer was merely routine.

The investigator walked toward the elevator, close on the heels of a well-dressed woman with a dog. She felt shy. Most of her collaterals were to housewives in the Bronx or supervisors of maintenance workers in office buildings. Such calls were never embarrassing. A moment ago as she neared the doorway, the door-man had regarded her intently. The service entrance was plainly to her left, and she was walking past it. He had been on the point of approaching when a tenant emerged and dispatched him for a taxi. He had stood for a moment torn between his immediate duty and his sense of outrage. Then he had gone away dolefully, blowing his whistle.

The woman with the dog reached the elevator just as the doors slid open. The dog bounded in, and the elevator boy bent and rough-housed with him. The boy's agreeable face was black, and the investigator felt a flood of relief.

The woman entered the elevator and smilingly faced front. Instantly the smile left her face, and her eyes hardened. The boy straightened, faced front, too, and gaped in surprise. Quickly he glanced at the set face of his passenger.

"Service entrance's outside," he said sullenly.

The investigator said steadily, "I am not employed here. I am here to see Mrs. Coleman on business."

"If you're here on an errand or somethin' like that," he argued doggedly, "you still got to use the service entrance."

She stared at him with open hate, despising him for humiliating her before and because of a woman of an alien race.

"I am here as a representative of the Department of Welfare. If you refuse me the use of this elevator, my office will take it up with the management."

She did not know if this was true, but the elevator boy would not know either.

"Get in then," he said rudely, and rolled his eyes at his white passenger as if to convey his regret at the discomfort he was causing her.

The doors shut and the three shot upward, without speaking to or looking at each other. The woman with the dog, in a far corner, very pointedly held the small harmless animal on a tight leash.

The car stopped at the fourth floor, and the doors slid open. No one moved. There was a ten-second wait.

"You getting out or not?" the boy asked savagely.

There was no need to ask who he was addressing.

"Is this my floor?" asked the investigator.

His sarcasm rippled. "You want Mrs. Coleman, don't you?"

"Which is her apartment?" she asked thickly.

"Ten-A. You're holding up my passenger."

When the door closed, she leaned against it, feeling sick, and trying to control her trembling. She was young and vulnerable. Her contact with Negroes was confined to frightened relief folks who did everything possible to stay in her good graces, and the members of her own set, among whom she was a favorite because of her two degrees and her civil service appointment. She had almost never run into Negroes who did not treat her with respect.

In a moment or two she walked down the hall to Ten-A. She rang, and after a little wait a handsome middle-aged woman opened the door.

"How do you do?" the woman said in a soft drawl. She smiled. "You're from the relief office, aren't you? Do come in."

"Thank you," said the investigator, smiling, too, relievedly.

"Right this way," said Mrs. Coleman leading the way into a charming living-room. She indicated an upholstered chair. "Please sit down."

The investigator, who never sat in overstuffed chairs in the homes of her relief clients, plumped down and smiled again at Mrs. Coleman. Such a pleasant woman, such a pleasant room. It was going to be a quick and easy interview. She let her briefcase slide to the floor beside her.

Mrs. Coleman sat down in a straight chair and looked searchingly at the investigator. Then she said somewhat breathlessly, "You gave me to understand that Mammy has applied for relief."

The odious title sent a little flicker of dislike across the investigator's face. She answered stiffly, "I had just left Mrs. Mason when I telephoned you for this appointment."

Mrs. Coleman smiled disarmingly, though she colored a little.

"She has been with us ever since I can remember. I call her Mammy, and so does my daughter."

"That's a sort of nurse, isn't it?" the investigator asked coldly. "I had thought Mrs. Mason was a general maid."

"Is that what she said?"

"Why, I understood she was discharged because she was no longer physically able to perform her duties."

"She wasn't discharged."

The investigator look dismayed. She had not anticipated complications. She felt for her briefcase.

"I'm very confused, Mrs. Coleman. Will you tell me just exactly what happened then? I had no idea Mrs. Mason was—was misstating the situation." She opened her briefcase.

Mrs. Coleman eyed her severely. "There's nothing to write down. Do you have to write down things? It makes me feel as if I were being investigated."

"I'm sorry," the investigator said quickly, snapping shut her briefcase. "If it would be distasteful—. I apologize again. Please go on."

"Thank you! Mammy was happy here, believe me. She had nothing to do but a little dusting. We are a small family, myself, my daughter, and her husband. I have a girl who comes every day to do the hard work. She preferred to sleep in, but I wanted Mammy to have the maid's room. It's a lovely room with a private bath. It's next to the kitchen, which is nice for Mammy. Old people potter about so. I've lost girl after girl who felt she was meddlesome. But I've always thought of Mammy's comfort first."

"I'm sure you have," said the investigator politely, wanting to end the interview. She made a move toward departure. "Thank you again for being so cooperative."

Mrs. Coleman rose and crossed to the doorway.

"I must get my purse. Will you wait a moment?"

Shortly she reappeared. She opened her purse.

"It's been ten days. Please give that landlady this twenty dollars. No, it isn't too much. And here is a dollar from Mammy's cab fare. Please put her in the cab yourself."

"I'll do what I can." The investigator smiled candidly. "It must be nearly four, and my working day ends at five."

"Yes, of course," Mrs. Coleman said distractedly. "And now I just want you to peep in at my daughter. Mammy will want to know how she is. She's far from well, poor lambie."

The investigator followed Mrs. Coleman down the hall. At an open door they paused. A pale young girl lay on the edge of a big tossed bed. One hand was in her tangled hair, the other clutched an empty bassinet. The wheels rolled down and back, down and back. The girl glanced briefly and without interest at her mother and the investigator, then turned her face away.

"It tears my heart," Mrs. Coleman whispered in a choked voice. "Her baby, and then Mammy. She has lost all desire to live. But she is young and she will have other children. If she would only let me take away that bassinet! I am not the nurse that Mammy is. You can see how much Mammy is needed here."

They turned away and walked in silence to the outer door. The investigator was genuinely touched, and eager to be off on her errand of mercy.

Mrs. Coleman opened the door, and for a moment seemed at a loss as to how to say good-bye. Then she said quickly, "Thank you for coming," and shut the door.

The investigator stood in indecision at the elevator, half persuaded to walk down three flights of stairs. But this, she felt, was turning tail, and pressed the elevator button.

The door opened. The boy looked at her sheepishly. He swallowed and said ingratiatingly, "Step in, miss. Find your party all right?"

She faced front, staring stonily ahead of her, and felt herself trembling with indignation at this new insolence.

He went on whiningly, "That woman was in my car is mean as hell. I was just puttin' on to please her. She hates niggers 'cept when they're bowin' and scraping. She was the one had the old doorman fired. You see for yourself they got a white one now. With white folks needin' jobs, us niggers got to eat dirt to hang on."

The investigator's face was expressionless except for a barely perceptible wincing at his careless use of a hated word.

He pleaded, "You're colored like me. You ought to understand. I was only doing my job. I got to eat same as white folks, same as you."

They rode the rest of the way in a silence interrupted only by his heavy sighs. When they reached the ground floor, and the door slid open, he said sorrowfully, "Good-bye, miss."

She walked down the hall and out into the street, past the glowering doorman, with her face stern and her stomach slightly sick.

The investigator rode uptown on a north-bound bus. At One Hundred and Eighteenth Street she alighted and walked east. Presently she entered a well-kept apartment house. The elevator operator deferentially greeted her and whisked her upwards.

She rang the bell of number fifty-four, and visited briefly with the land lady, who was quite overcome by the unexpected payment of twenty dollars. When she could escape her profuse thanks, the investigator went to knock at Mrs. Mason's door.

"Come in," called Mrs. Mason. The investigator entered the small, square room. "Oh, it's you, dear," said Mrs. Mason, her lined brown face lighting up.

She was sitting by the window in a wide rocker. In her black, with a clean white apron tied about her waist, and a white bandanna bound around her head, she looked ageless and full of remembering.

Mrs. Mason grasped her rocker by the arms and twisted around until she faced the investigator.

She explained shyly, "I just sit here for hours lookin' out at the people. I ain' seen so many colored folks at one time since I left down home. Sit down, child, on the side of the bed. Hit's softer than that straight chair yonder."

The investigator sat down on the straight chair, not because the bedspread was not scrupulously clean, but because what she had come to say needed stiff decorum.

"I'm all right here, Mrs. Mason. I won't be long."

"I was hopin' you could set awhile. My landlady's good, but she's got this big flat. Don't give her time for much settin'."

The investigator, seeing an opening, nodded understandingly.

"Yes, it must be pretty lonely for you here after being so long an intimate part of the Coleman family."

The old woman's face darkened. "Shut back in that bedroom behin' the kitchen? This here's what I like. My own kind and color. I'm too old a dog to be learnin' new tricks."

"Your duties with Mrs. Coleman were very slight. I know you are getting on in years, but you are not too feeble for light employment. You were not entirely truthful with me. I was led to believe you did all the housework."

The old woman looked furtively at the investigator. "How come you know diff'rent now?"

"I've just left Mrs. Coleman."

Bafflement veiled the old woman's eyes. "You didn' believe what all I tol' you?"

"We always visit former employers. It's part of our job Mrs. Mason. Sometimes an employer will re-hire our applicants. Mrs. Coleman is good enough to want you back. Isn't that preferable to being a public charge?"

"I ain't a-goin back," said the old woman vehemently.

The investigator was very exasperated. "Why, Mrs. Mason?" she asked gently.

"That's an ungodly woman," the old lady snapped. "And I'm god-fearin'. 'Tain't no room in one house for God and the devil. I'm too near the grave to be servin' two masters."

To the young investigator this was evasion by superstitious mutterings.

"You don't make yourself very clear, Mrs. Mason. Surely Mrs. Coleman didn't interfere with your religious convictions. You left her home the night after her daughter's child was born dead. Until then, apparently, you had no religious scruples."

The old woman looked at the investigator wearily. Then her head sank forward on her breast.

"That child warn't born dead."

The investigator said impatiently, "But surely the hospital—?"

" 'T'warnt born in no hospital."

"But the doctor—?"

"Little sly man. Looked like he'd cut his own throat for a dollar."

"Was the child deformed?" the investigator asked helplessly.

"Hit was a beautiful baby," said the old woman bitterly.

"Why, no one would destroy a healthy child," the investigator cried indignantly. "Mrs. Coleman hopes her daughter will have more children." She paused, then asked anxiously, "Her daughter is really married, isn't she? I mean, the baby wasn't—illegitimate?"

"Its ma and pa were married down home. A church weddin'. They went to school together. They was all right till they come up N'th. Then *she* started workin' on 'em. Old ways wasn't good enough for her."

The investigator looked at her watch. It was nearly five. This last speech had been rambling gossip. Here was an old woman clearly unoriented in her northern transplanting. Her position as mammy made her part of the family. Evidently she felt that gave her a matriarchal right to arbitrate its destinies. Her small grievances against Mrs. Coleman had magnified themselves in her mind until she could make this illogical accusation of infanticide as compensation for her homesickness for the folkways of the South. Her move to Harlem bore this out. To explain her reason for establishing a separate residence, she had told a fantastic story that could not be checked, and would not be recorded, unless the welfare office was prepared to face a libel suit.

"Mrs. Mason," said the investigator, "please listen carefully. Mrs. Coleman has told me that you are not only wanted but very much needed in her home. There you will be given food and shelter in return for small services. Please understand that I sympathize with your—imaginings, but you cannot remain here without public assistance, and I cannot recommend to my superiors that public assistance be given you."

The old woman, who had listened worriedly, now said blankly, "You mean I ain't a-gonna get it?"

"No, Mrs. Mason, I'm sorry. And now it's ten to five. I'll be glad to help you pack your things, and put you in a taxi."

The old woman looked helplessly around the room as if seeking a hiding place. Then she looked back at the investigator, her mouth trembling.

"You're my own people, child. Can' you fix up a story for them white folks at the relief, so's I could get to stay here where it's nice?"

"That would be collusion, Mrs. Mason. And that would cost me my job."

The investigator rose. She was going to pack the old woman's things herself. She was heartily sick of her contrariness, and determined to see her settled once and for all.

"Now where is your bag?" she asked with forced cheeriness. "First I'll empty these bureau drawers." She began to do so, laying things neatly on the bed. "Mrs. Coleman's daughter will be so glad to see you. She's very ill, and needs your nursing."

The old woman showed no interest. Her head had sunk forward on her breast again. She said listlessly, "Let her ma finish what she started. I won't have no time for nursin'. I'll be down on my knees rasslin' with the devil. I done tol' you the devil's done eased out God in that house."

The investigator nodded indulgently, and picked up a framed photograph that was lying face down in the drawer. She turned it over and involuntarily smiled at the smiling child in old-fashioned dress.

"This little girl," she said, "it's Mrs. Coleman, isn't it?"

The old woman did not look up. Her voice was still listless.

"That *was* my daughter."

The investigator dropped the photograph on the bed as if it were a hot coal. Blindly she went back to the bureau, gathered up the rest of the things, and dumped them over the photograph.

She was a young investigator, and it was two minutes to five. Her job was to give or withhold relief. That was all.

"Mrs. Mason," she said, "please, please understand. This is my job."

The old woman gave no sign of having heard.

THE BONES OF LOUELLA BROWN

Ann Petry

(from *Opportunity: Journal of Negro Life,* 25.4, April 1947)

OLD PEABODY AND Young Whiffle, partners in the firm of Whiffle and Peabody, Incorporated, read with mild interest the first article about Bedford Abbey which appeared in the Boston papers. But each day thereafter the papers printed one or two items about this fabulous project. And as they learned more about it, Old Peabody and Young Whiffle became quite excited.

For Bedford Abbey was a private chapel, a chapel which would be used solely for the weddings and funerals of the Bedford family—the most distinguished family in Massachusetts.

What was more important, the Abbey was to become the final resting place for all the Bedfords who had passed on to greater glory, and been buried in the family plot in Yew Tree Cemetery. These long-dead Bedfords were to be exhumed and reburied in the crypt under the marble floor of the chapel. Thus Bedford Abbey would be officially opened with the most costly and the most elaborate funeral service ever held in Boston.

As work on the Abbey progressed, Young Whiffle (who was seventy-five) and Old Peabody (who was seventy-nine), frowned and fumed while they searched the morning papers for some indication of the date of this service.

Whiffle and Peabody were well aware that they owned the oldest and the most exclusive undertaking firm in the city; and, having handled the funerals of most of the Bedfords, they felt that, in all logic, this stupendous funeral ceremony should be managed by their firm. But they were uneasy. For Governor Bedford (he was still called Governor though it had been some thirty years since he held office) was unpredictable. And, most unfortunately, the choice of undertakers would be left to the Governor, for the Abbey was his brain-child.

A month dragged by, during which Young Whiffle and Old Peabody set an all-time record for nervous tension. They snapped at each other, and nibbled their fingernails, and cleared their throats, with the most appalling regularity.

It was well into June before the Governor's secretary finally telephoned. He informed Old Peabody, who quivered with delight, that Governor Bedford had named Whiffle and Peabody as the undertakers for the service which would be held at the Abbey on the twenty-first of June.

When the Bedford exhumation order was received Old Peabody produced an exhumation order for the late Louella Brown. It had occurred to him that his business of exhuming the Bedfords offered an excellent opportunity for exhuming Louella, with a very little additional expense. Thus he could rectify a truly terrible error in judgment made by his father, years ago.

"We can pick 'em all up at once," Old Peabody said, handing the Brown exhumation order to Young Whiffle. "I want to move Louella Brown out of Yew Tree Cemetery. We can put her in one of the less well-known burying places on the outskirts of the city. That's where she should have been put in the first place. But we will, of course, check up on her as usual."

"Who was Louella Brown?" asked Young Whiffle.

"Oh, she was once our laundress. Nobody of importance," Old Peabody said carelessly. Though as he said it he wondered why he remembered Louella with such vividness.

Later in the week, the remains of all the deceased Bedfords, and of the late Louella Brown, arrived at the handsome establishment of Whiffle and Peabody. Though Young Whiffle and Old Peabody were well along in years their research methods were completely modern. Whenever possible they checked on the condition of their former clients and kept exact records of their findings.

The presence of so many former clients at one time—a large number of Bedfords, and Louella Brown—necessitated the calling in of Stuart Reynolds. He was a Harvard medical student who did large-scale research jobs for the firm, did them well and displayed a most satisfying enthusiasm for his work.

It was near closing time when Reynolds arrived at the imposing brick structure which housed Whiffle and Peabody, Incorporated.

Old Peabody handed Reynolds a sheaf of papers and tried to explain about Louella Brown, as tactfully as possible.

"She used to be our laundress," he said. "My mother was very fond of Louella, and insisted that she be buried in Yew Tree Cemetery." His father had consented, grudgingly, yes, but his father should never have agreed to it. It had taken the careful discriminatory practices of generations of Peabodies, undertakers like himself, to make Yew Tree Cemetery what it was today—the final home of Boston's wealthiest and most aristocratic families. Louella's grave had been at the very top edge of the cemetery in 1902, in a very undesirable place. But just last month he had noticed, with dismay, that due to the enlargement of the cemetery, over the years, she now lay in one of the choicest spots—in the exact center.

Before Old Peabody spoke again he was a little disconcerted. For he suddenly saw Louella Brown with an amazing sharpness. It was just as though she had entered the room—a quick-moving little woman, brown of skin and black of hair, and with very erect posture.

He hesitated a moment and then he said, "She was—uh—uh—a colored woman. But in spite of that we will do the usual research."

"Colored?" said Young Whiffle sharply. "Did you say 'colored'? You mean a black woman? And buried in Yew Tree Cemetery?" His voice rose in pitch.

"Yes," Old Peabody said. He lifted his shaggy eyebrows at Young Whiffle as an indication that he was not to discuss the matter further. "Now, Reynolds, be sure and lock up when you leave."

Reynolds, accepted the papers from Old Peabody and said, "Yes, sir. I'll lock up." And in his haste to get at the job he left the room so fast that he stumbled over his own feet and very nearly fell. He hurried because he was making a private study of bone structure in the Caucasian female as against the bone structure in the female of the darker race, and Louella Brown was an unexpected research plum.

Old Peabody winced as the door slammed. "The terrible enthusiasm of the young," he said to Young Whiffle.

"He comes cheap," Young Whiffle said gravely. "And he's polite enough."

They considered Reynolds in silence for a moment.

"Yes, of course," Old Peabody said. "You're quite right. He is an invaluable young man and his wages are adequate for his services." He hoped Young Whiffle noticed how neatly he had avoided repeating the phrase 'he comes cheap.'

"'Adequate,'" murmured Young Whiffle. "Yes, yes, 'adequate.' Certainly. And invaluable." He was still murmuring both words, as he accompanied Old Peabody out of the building.

Fortunately for their peace of mind neither Young Whiffle nor Old Peabody knew what went on in their workroom that night. Though they found out the next morning to their very great regret.

It so happened that the nearest approach to royalty in the Bedford family had been the Countess of Castro (nee Elizabeth Bedford). Though neither Old Peabody or Young Whiffle knew it, the Countess and Louella Brown had resembled each other in many ways. They both had thick glossy black hair. Neither woman had any children. They had both died in 1902, when in their early seventies, and been buried in Yew Tree Cemetery within two weeks of each other.

Stuart Reynolds did not know this either, or he would not have worked in so orderly a fashion. As it was, once he entered the big underground workroom of Whiffle and Peabody, he began taking notes on the condition of each Bedford, and then carefully answered the questions on the blanks provided by Old Peabody.

He finished all the lesser Bedfords, then turned his attention to the Countess.

When he opened the coffin of the Countess, he gave a little murmur of pleasure. "A very neat set of bones," he said. "A small woman, about seventy. How interesting! All of her own teeth, no repairs."

Having checked the Countess, he set to work on Louella Brown. As he studied Louella's bones he said, "Why how extremely interesting!" For here was another small-boned woman, about seventy, who had all of her own teeth. As far as he could determine from a hasty examination, there was no way of telling the Countess from Louella.

"But the hair! How stupid of me. I can tell them apart by the hair. The colored woman's will be——." But it wasn't. Both women had the same type of hair.

He placed the skeleton of the Countess of Castro on a long table, and right next to it he drew up another long table, and placed on it the skeleton of the late Louella Brown. He measured both of them.

"Why, it's sensational!" he said aloud. And as he talked to himself he grew more and more excited. "It's a front page story. I bet they never even knew each other and yet they were the same height, had the same bone structure. One white, one black, and they meet here at Whiffle and Peabody after all these years—the laundress and the countess! It's more than front page news, why, it's the biggest story of the year—"

Without a second's thought Reynolds ran upstairs to Old Peabody's office and called the *Boston Record*. He talked to the night city editor. The man sounded bored but he listened. Finally he said, "You got the bones of both these ladies out on tables, and you say they're just alike. Okay, be right over—"

Thus two photographers and the night city editor of the *Boston Record* invaded the sacred premises of Whiffle and Peabody, Incorporated. The night city editor was a tall, lank individual, and very hard to please. He no sooner asked Reynolds to pose in one position then he had him moved, in front of the tables, behind them, at the foot, at the head. Then he wanted the tables moved. The photographers cursed audibly as they dragged the tables back and forth, turned them around, sideways, lengthways. And still the night city editor wasn't satisfied.

Reynolds shifted position so often that he might have been on a merry-go-round. He registered surprise, amazement, pleasure. Each time the night city editor objected.

It was midnight before the newspaperman said, "Okay, boys, this is it." The photographers took their pictures quickly and then stared picking up their equipment.

The newspaperman watched the photographers for a moment, then he strolled over to Reynolds and said, "Now—uh—Sonnie, which one of these ladies is the Countess?"

Reynolds started to point at one of the tables, stopped, let out a frightened exclamation. "Why—" his mouth stayed open. "Why—I don't know!" His voice was suddenly frantic. "You've mixed them up! You've moved them around so many times I can't tell which is which—nobody could tell—"

The night city editor smiled sweetly and started for the door.

Reynolds followed him, clutched at his coat sleeve. "You've got to help me. You can't go now," he said. "Who moved the tables first? Which one of you—" The photographers stared and then started to grin. The night city editor smiled again. His smile was even sweeter than before.

"I wouldn't know, Sonnie," he said. He gently disengaged Reynolds' hand from his coat sleeve. "I really wouldn't know—"

It was, of course, a front page story. But not the kind that Reynolds had anticipated. There were photographs of that marble masterpiece, Bedford Abbey, and the caption under it asked the question that was later to seize the imagination of the whole country: "Who will be buried under the marble floor of Bedford Abbey on the twenty-first of June—the Countess or the colored laundress?"

There were photographs of Reynolds, standing near the long tables, pointing at the bones of both ladies. He was quoted as saying: "You've moved them around so many times I can't tell which is which—nobody could tell—"

When Governor Bedford read the *Boston Record*, he promptly called Whiffle and Peabody, on the telephone, and cursed them with such violence that Young Whiffle and Old Peabody grew visibly older and grayer as they listened to him.

Shortly after the Governor's call, Stuart Reynolds came to offer an explanation to Whiffle and Peabody. Old Peabody turned his back and refused to speak to, or look at, Reynolds. Young Whiffle did the talking. His eyes were so icy cold, his face so frozen, that he seemed to emit a freezing vapor as he spoke.

Toward the end of his speech, Young Whiffle was breathing hard. "This house," he said, "the honor of this house, years of working, of building a reputation, all destroyed. We're ruined, ruined—" he choked on the word. "Ah," he said, waving his hands, "Get out, get out, get out, before I kill you—"

The next day the Associated Press picked up the story of this dreadful mix-up and wired it throughout the country. It was a particularly dull period for news, between wars so to speak, and every paper in the United States carried the story on its front page.

In three days' time Louella Brown and Elizabeth, Countess of Castro, were as famous as movie stars. Crowds gathered outside the mansion in which Governor Bedford lived; still larger and noisier crowds milled in the street in front of the offices of Whiffle and Peabody.

As the twenty-first of June approached, people in New York and London and Paris and Moscow asked each other the same question, Who would be buried in Bedford Abbey, the countess or the laundress?

Meanwhile Young Whiffle and Old Peabody talked, desperately seeking something, anything, to save the reputation of Boston's oldest and most expensive undertaking establishment. Their talk went around and around, in circles.

"Nobody knows which set of bones belong to Louella and which to the Countess. Why do you keep saying that it's Louella Brown who will be buried in the Abbey?" snapped Old Peabody.

"Because the public likes the idea," Young Whiffle snapped back. "A hundred years from now they'll say it's the colored laundress who lies in the crypt at Bedford Abbey. And that we put her there. We're ruined—ruined—ruined—" he muttered. "A black washerwoman!" he said, wringing his hands. "If only she had been white—"

"She might have been Irish," said Old Peabody coldly. He was annoyed to find how very clearly he could see Louella. With each passing day her presence became sharper, more strongly felt. "And a Catholic. That would have been equally as bad. No, it would have been worse. Because the Catholics would have insisted on a mass, in Bedford Abbey, of all places! Or she might have been a foreigner—a—a—Russian. Or, God forbid, a Jew!"

"Nonsense," said Young Whiffle pettishly. "A black washer-woman is infinitely worse than anything you've mentioned. People are saying it's some kind of trick, that we're proving there's no difference between the races. Oh, we're ruined—ruined—ruined—" Young Whiffle moaned.

As a last resort, Old Peabody and Young Whiffle went to see Stuart Reynolds. They found him in the shabby rooming house where he lived.

"You did this to us," Old Peabody said to Reynolds. "Now you figure out a way, an acceptable way, to determine which of those women is which or I'll—"

"We will wait while you think," said Young Whiffle, looking out of the window.

"I have thought," Reynolds said wildly. "I've thought until I'm nearly crazy."

"Think some more," snapped Old Peabody, glaring.

Peabody and Whiffle seated themselves on opposite sides of the small room. Young Whiffle glared out of the window and Old Peabody glared at Reynolds. And Reynolds couldn't decide which was worse.

"You knew her, knew Louella, I mean," said Reynolds. "Can't you just say, this one's Louella Brown, pick either one, because, the body, I mean, Whiffle and Peabody, they, she was embalmed there—"

"Don't be a fool!" said Young Whiffle, his eyes on the window sill, glaring at the window sill, annihilating the window sill. "Whiffle and Peabody would be ruined by such a statement, more ruined than they are at present."

"How?" demanded Reynolds. Ordinarily he wouldn't have argued but being shut up in the room with this pair of bony-fingered old men had turned him desperate. "Why? After all who could dispute it? You could get the embalmer, Mr. Ludastone, to say he remembered the neck bone, or the position of the foot—." His voice grew louder. "If you identify the colored woman first nobody'll question it—"

"Lower your voice," said Old Peabody.

Young Whiffle stood up and pounded on the dusty window sill. "Because colored people, bodies, I mean the colored dead—"

He took a deep breath. Old Peabody said, "Now relax, Mr. Whiffle, relax. Remember your blood pressure."

"There's such a thing as a color line," shrieked Young Whiffle. "You braying idiot, you, we're not supposed to handle colored bodies, the colored dead, I mean the dead colored people, in our establishment. We'd never live down a statement like that. We're fortunate that so far no one has asked how the corpse of Louella Brown, a colored laundress, got on the premises in 1902. Louella was a special case but they'd say that we—"

"But she's already there!" Reynolds shouted. "You've got a colored body or bones, I mean there now. She *was* embalmed there. She *was* buried in Yew Tree Cemetery. Nobody's said any-thing about it."

Old Peabody held up his hand for silence. "Wait," he said. "There is a bare chance—" He thought for a moment. He found that his thinking was quite confused, he felt he ought to object to Reynolds' suggestion but he didn't know why. Vivid images of Louella Brown, wearing a dark dress with white collars and cuffs, added to his confusion.

Finally he said, "We'll do it, Mr. Whiffle. It's the only way. And we'll explain it with dignity. Speak of Louella's long service, true she did laundry for others, too, but we won't mention that, talk about her cheerfulness and devotion, emphasize the devotion, bury-ing her in Yew Tree Cemetery was a kind of reward for service, payment for a debt of gratitude, remember that phrase 'debt of gratitude.' And call in—" he swallowed hard, "the press. Especially that animal from the *Boston Record*, who wrote the story up the first time. We might serve some of the old brandy and cigars. Then Mr. Ludastone can make his statement. About the position of the foot, he remembers it—" He paused and glared at Reynolds. "And as for you! You needn't think we'll ever permit you inside our doors again, dead or alive."

Gray-haired, gray-skinned Clarence Ludastone, head embalmer for Whiffle and Peabody, dutifully identified one set of bones as being those of the late Louella Brown. Thus the identity of the Countess was firmly established. Half the newspapermen in the country were present at the time. They partook generously of Old Peabody's best brandy and enthusiastically smoked his finest cigars. The last individual to leave was the weary gentleman who represented the *Boston Record*.

He leaned against the doorway as he spoke to Old Peabody. "Wonderful yarn," he said. "Never heard a better one. Congratulations—" And he drifted down the hall.

Because of all the stories about Louella Brown and the Countess of Castro, most of the residents of Boston turned out to watch the funeral cortege of the Bedfords on the twenty-first of June. The ceremony that took place at Bedford Abbey was broadcast over a national hook-up, and the news services wired it around the world, complete with pictures.

Young Whiffle and Old Peabody agreed that the publicity accorded the occasion was disgraceful. But their satisfaction over the successful ending of what had been an extremely embarrassing situation was immense. They had great difficulty preserving the solemn mien required of them during the funeral service.

Young Whiffle and Old Peabody both suffered slight heart attacks when they saw the next morning's edition of the *Boston Record*. For there on the front page was a photograph of Mr. Ludastone, and over it in bold, black type were the words "child embalmer." The article which accompanied the picture, said, in part:

"Who is buried in the crypt at Bedford Abbey? The Countess, or Louella, the laundress? We ask because Mr. Clarence Ludastone, the suave gentleman who is head embalmer for Whiffle and Peabody, could not possibly identify the bones of Louella Brown, despite his look of great age. Mr. Ludastone, according to his birth certificate (which is reproduced on this page) was only two years old at the time of Louella's death. This reporter has questioned many of Boston's oldest residents but he has, as yet, been unable to locate anyone who remembers a time when Whiffle and Peabody employed a two-year-old child as embalmer—"

Eighty-year-old Governor Bedford very nearly had apoplexy when he saw the *Boston Record*. He hastily called a press conference. He said that he would personally, publicly (in front of the press), identify the Countess, if it was the Countess. He remembered her well for he was only thirty-five when she died. He would know instantly if it were she.

Two days later the Governor stalked down the center aisle of that marble gem—Bedford Abbey. He was followed by a veritable hive of newsmen and photographers. Old Peabody and Young Whiffle were waiting for them just inside the crypt.

The Governor peered at the interior of the opened casket and drew back. He forgot the eager-eared newsmen, who surrounded him, pressed against him. When he spoke he reverted to the simple speech of his early ancestors.

"Why they be nothing but bones here!" he said. "Nothing but bones! Nobody could tell who this be."

He turned his head, unable to take a second look. He, too, some day, not too far off, how did a man buy immortality, he didn't want to die, bones rattling inside a casket—ah, no! He reached for his pocket handkerchief, and Young Whiffle thrust a freshly laundered one into his hand.

Governor Bedford wiped his face, his forehead. But not me, he thought. I'm alive. I can't die. It won't happen to me. And inside his head a voice kept saying over and over, like the ticking of a clock, It will, It can, It will, It can, It will.

"You were saying, Governor," prompted the tall thin newsman from the *Boston Record*.

"I don't know!" Governor Bedford shouted angrily. "I don't know! Nobody could tell which be the black laundress and which the white countess from looking at their bones."

"Governor, Governor," protested Old Peabody. "Governor, ah—calm yourself, great strain—" And leaning forward, he hissed in the Governor's reddening ear, "Remember the press, don't say that, don't make a statement, don't commit yourself—"

"Stop spitting in my ear!" roared the Governor. "Get away! And take your blasted handkerchief with you." He thrust Young Whiffle's handkerchief inside Old Peabody's coat, up near the shoulder. "It stinks, it stinks of death." Then he strode out of Bedford Abbey, muttering under his breath as he went.

The Governor's statement went around the world, in direct quotes. So did the photographs of him, peering inside the casket, his mouth open, his eyes staring. There were still other photographs that showed him charging down the center aisle of Bedford Abbey, head down, shoulders thrust forward, even the back of his neck somehow indicative of his fury. Cartoonists showed him, in retreat, words issuing from his shoulder blades, "Nobody could tell who this be—the black laundress or the white countess—"

Sermons were preached about the Governor's statement, editorials were written about it, and Congressmen made long-winded speeches over the radio. The Mississippi Legislature threatened to declare war on the sovereign State of Massachusetts because Governor Bedford's remarks were an unforgivable insult to believers in white supremacy.

Many radio listeners became completely confused and, believing that both ladies were still alive, sent presents to them, sometimes addressed in care of Governor Bedford, and sometimes addressed in care of Whiffle and Peabody.

Whiffle and Peabody kept the shades drawn in their establishment. They scuttled through the streets each morning, hats pulled low over their eyes, en route to their offices. They would have preferred to stay at home (with the shades drawn) but they agreed it was better to act as though nothing had happened. So they spent ten hours a day on the premises as was their custom, though there was absolutely no business.

Young Whiffle paced the floor, hours at a time, wringing his hands, and muttering, "A black washerwoman! We're ruined—ruined—ruined—"

Old Peabody found himself wishing that Young Whiffle would not speak of Louella with such contempt. In spite of himself he kept dreaming about her. In the dream, she came quite close to him, a small, brown woman with merry eyes. And after one quick look at him, she put her hands on her hips, threw her head back and laughed and laughed.

He was quite unaccustomed to being laughed at, even in a dream; and the memory of Louella's laughter lingered with him for hours after he woke up. He could not forget the smallest detail of her appearance: how her shoulders shook as she laughed, and that her teeth were very white and evenly spaced.

He thought to avoid this recurrent visitation by sitting up all night, by drinking hot milk, by taking lukewarm baths. Then he tried the exact opposite—he went to bed early, drank cold milk, took scalding hot baths. To no avail. Louella Brown still visited him, each and every night.

Thus it came about that one morning when Young Whiffle began his ritual muttering: "A black washerwoman—we're ruined—ruined—ruined—," Old Peabody shouted: "Will you stop that caterwauling? One would think the Lock Ness monster lay in the crypt at Bedford Abbey." He could see Louella Brown standing in front of him, laughing, laughing. And he said, "Louella Brown was a neatly built little woman, a fine woman, full of laughter. I remember her well. She was a gentlewoman. Her bones will do no injury to the governor's damned funeral chapel."

It was a week before Young Whiffle actually heard what Old Peabody was saying, though Peabody made this same outrageous statement, over and over again.

When Young Whiffle finally heard it, there was a quarrel, a violent quarrel, caused by the bones of Louella Brown—that quick-moving, merry, little woman.

By the end of the day, the partnership was dissolved, and the ancient and exclusive firm of Whiffle and Peabody, Incorporated, went out of business.

Old Peabody, retired, after all there was no firm he would consider associating with. Young Whiffle retired, too, but he moved all the way to California, and changed his name to Smith; in the hope that no man would ever discover he had once been a member of the blackguardly firm of Whiffle and Peabody, Incorporated.

Despite his retirement, Old Peabody found that Louella Brown still haunted his dreams. What was worse, she took to appearing before him during his waking moments. After a month of this, he went to see Governor Bedford. He had to wait an hour before the Governor came down stairs, walking slowly, leaning on a cane.

Old Peabody wasted no time being courteous. He went straight to the reason for his visit. "I have come," he said stiffly, "to suggest to you that you put the names of both those women on the marble slab in Bedford Abbey."

"Never," said the Governor. "Never, never, never!"

He is afraid to die, Old Peabody thought, eyeing the Governor. You can always tell by the look on their faces. He shrugged his shoulders. "Every man dies alone, Governor," he said brutally.

"And so it is always best to be at peace with his world and any other world that follows it, when one dies."

Old Peabody waited a moment. The Governor's hands were shaking. Fear or palsy, he wondered. Fear, he decided. Fear beyond the question of a doubt.

"Louella Brown visits me every night, and frequently during the day," Peabody said softly. "I am certain that unless you follow my suggestion she will also visit you." A muscle in the Governor's face started to twitch. Peabody said, "When your bones finally lie in the crypt in your marble chapel, I doubt that you want to hear the sound of Louella's laughter ringing in your ears—toll doomsday."

"Get out!" said the Governor, shuddering. "You're crazy as a loon."

"No," Old Peabody said, firmly. "Between us, all of us, we have managed to summon Louella's spirit." And he proceeded to tell the Governor how every night, in his dreams, and sometimes during the day when he was awake, Louella came to stand beside him, and look up at him and laugh.

He told it very well, so well in fact that for a moment he thought he saw Louella standing in the room, right near Governor Bedford's left shoulder.

The Governor turned, looked over his shoulder. And then he said, slowly, and reluctantly, and with the uneasy feeling that he could already hear Louella's laughter, "All right." He paused, took a deep unsteady breath, "What do you suggest I put on the marble slab in the crypt?"

After much discussion, and much writing, and much tearing up of what had been written, they achieved a satisfactory epitaph. If you ever go to Boston and visit Bedford Abbey you will see for yourself how Old Peabody propitiated the bones of the late Louella Brown. For after these words were carved on the marble slab, Louella ceased to haunt Old Peabody:

Here lies
Elizabeth, Countess of Castro
or
Louella Brown, Gentlewoman
1830–1902
Reburied in Bedford Abbey June 21, 1947
"They both wore the breastplate of faith and love;
And for an helmet, the hope of salvation."

FEET LIVE THEIR OWN LIFE

Langston Hughes

(from *The Best of Simple,* 1961)

"IF YOU WANT to know about my life," said Simple as he blew the foam from the top of the newly filled glass the bartender put before him, "don't look at my face, don't look at my hands. Look at my feet and see if you can tell how long I been standing on them."

"I cannot see your feet through your shoes," I said.

"You do not need to see through my shoes," said Simple. "Can't you tell by the shoes I wear—not pointed, not rocking-chair, not French-toed, not nothing but big, long, broad, and flat—that I been standing on these feet a long time and carrying some heavy burdens? They ain't flat from standing at no bar, nei-ther, because I always sets at a bar. Can't you tell that? You know I do not hang out in a bar unless it has stools, don't you?"

"That I have observed," I said, "but I did not connect it with your past life."

"Everything I do is connected up with my past life," said Simple. "From Virginia to Joyce, from my wife to Zarita, from my mother's milk to this glass of beer, everything is connected up."

"I trust you will connect up with that dollar I just loaned you when you get paid," I said. "And who is Virginia? You never told me about her."

"Virginia is where I was borned," said Simple. "I *would* be borned in a state named after a woman. From that day on, women never give me no peace."

179

"You, I fear, are boasting. If the women were running after you as much as you run after them, you would not be able to sit here on this bar stool in peace. I don't see any women coming to call you out to go home, as some of these fellows' wives do around here."

"Joyce better not come in no bar looking for me," said Simple. "That is why me and my wife busted up—one reason. I do not like to be called out of no bar by a female. It's a man's perogative to just set and drink sometimes."

"How do you connect that prerogative with your past?" I asked.

"When I was a wee small child," said Simple, "I had no place to set and think in, being as how I was raised up with three brothers, two sisters, seven cousins, one married aunt, a common-law uncle, and the minister's grandchild—and the house only had four rooms. I never had no place just to set and think. Neither to set and drink—not even much my milk before some hongry child snatched it out of my hand. I were not the youngest, neither a girl, nor the cutest. I don't know why, but I don't think nobody liked me much. Which is why I was afraid to like anybody for a long time myself. When I did like somebody, I was full-grown and then I picked out the wrong woman because I had no practice in liking anybody before that. We did not get along."

"Is that when you took to drink?"

"Drink took to me," said Simple. "Whiskey just naturally likes me but beer likes me better. By the time I got married I had got to the point where a cold bottle was almost as good as a warm bed, especially when the bottle could not talk and the bed-warmer could. I do not like a woman to talk to me too much—I mean about me. Which is why I like Joyce. Joyce most in generally talks about herself."

"I am still looking at your feet," I said, "and I swear they do not reveal your life to me. Your feet are no open book."

"You have eyes but you see not," said Simple. "These feet have stood on every rock from the Rock of Ages to 135th and Lenox. These feet have supported everything from a cotton bale to a hongry woman. These feet have walked ten thousand miles working for white folks and another ten thousand keeping up with colored. These feet have stood at altars, crap tables, free lunches, bars, graves, kitchen doors, betting windows, hospital clinics, WPA desks, social security railings, and in all kinds of lines from soup lines to the draft. If I just had four feet, I could have stood in more places longer. As it is, I done wore out seven hundred pairs of shoes, eighty-nine tennis shoes, twelve summer sandals, also six loafers. The socks that these feet have bought could build a knitting mill. The corns I've cut away would dull a German razor. The bunions I forgot would make you ache from now till Judgment Day. If anybody was to write the history of my life, they should start with my feet."

"Your feet are not all that extraordinary," I said. "Besides, everything you are saying is general. Tell me specifically some one thing your feet have done that makes them different from any other feet in the world, just one."

"Do you see that window in that white man's store across the street?" asked Simple. "Well, this right foot of mine broke out that window in the Harlem riots right smack in the middle. Didn't no other foot in the world break that window but mine. And this left foot carried me off running as soon as my right foot came down. Nobody else's feet saved me from the cops that night but these *two* feet right here. Don't tell me these feet ain't had a life of their own."

"For shame," I said, "going around kicking out windows. Why?"

"Why?" said Simple. "You have to ask my great-great-grandpa why. He must of been simple—else why did he let them capture him in Africa and sell him for a slave to breed my great-grandpa in slavery to breed my grandpa in slavery to breed my pa to breed me to look at that window and say, 'It ain't mine! Bam-mmm-mm-m!' and kick it out?"

"This bar glass is not yours either," I said. "Why don't you smash it?"

"It's got my beer in it," said Simple.

Just then Zarita came in wearing her Thursday-night rabbit-skin coat. She didn't stop at the bar, being dressed up, but went straight back to a booth. Simple's hand went up, his beer went down, and the glass back to its wet spot on the bar.

"Excuse me a minute," he said, sliding off the stool.

Just to give him pause, the dozens, that old verbal game of maligning a friend's female relatives, came to mind. "Wait," I said. "You have told me about what to ask your great-great-grandpa. But I want to know what to ask your great-great-grand*ma*."

"I don't play the dozens that far back," said Simple, following Zarita into the smoky juke-box blue of the back room.

EVERYDAY USE

Alice Walker

(from *In Love and Trouble: Stories of Black Women*, 1973)

for your grandmama

I WILL WAIT for her in the yard that Maggie and I made so clean and wavy yesterday afternoon. A yard like this is more comfortable than most people know. It is not just a yard. It is like an extended living room. When the hard clay is swept clean as a floor and the fine sand around the edges lined with tiny, irregular grooves, anyone can come and sit and look up into the elm tree and wait for the breezes that never come inside the house.

Maggie will be nervous until after her sister goes: she will stand hopelessly in corners, homely and ashamed of the burn scars down her arms and legs, eying her sister with a mixture of envy and awe. She thinks her sister has held life always in the palm of one hand, that "no" is a word the world never learned to say to her.

You've no doubt seen those TV shows where the child who has "made it" is confronted, as a surprise, by her own mother and father, tottering in weakly from backstage. (A pleasant surprise, of course: What would they do if parent and child came on the show only to curse out and insult each other?) On TV mother and child embrace and smile into each other's faces. Sometimes the mother and father weep, the child wraps them in her arms and leans across the table to tell how she would not have made it without their help. I have seen these programs.

Sometimes I dream a dream in which Dee and I are suddenly brought together on a TV program of this sort. Out of a dark and soft-seated limousine I am ushered into a bright room filled with many people. There I meet a smiling, gray, sporty man like Johnny Carson who shakes my hand and tells me what a fine girl I have. Then we are on the stage and Dee is embracing me with tears in her eyes. She pins on my dress a large orchid, even though she has told me once that she thinks orchids are tacky flowers.

In real life I am a large, big-boned woman with rough, man-working hands. In the winter I wear flannel nightgowns to bed and overalls during the day. I can kill and clean a hog as mercilessly as a man. My fat keeps me hot in zero weather. I can work outside all day, breaking ice to get water for washing; I can eat pork liver cooked over the open fire minutes after it comes steaming from the hog. One winter I knocked a bull calf straight in the brain between the eyes with a sledge hammer and had the meat hung up to chill before nightfall. But of course all this does not show on television. I am the way my daughter would want me to be: a hundred pounds lighter, my skin like an uncooked barley pancake. My hair glistens in the hot bright lights. Johnny Carson has much to do to keep up with my quick and witty tongue.

But that is a mistake. I know even before I wake up. Who ever knew a Johnson with a quick tongue? Who can even imagine me looking a strange white man in the eye? It seems to me I have talked to them always with one foot raised in flight, with my head turned in whichever way is farthest from them. Dee, though. She would always look anyone in the eye. Hesitation was no part of her nature.

"How do I look, Mama?" Maggie says, showing just enough of her thin body enveloped in a pink skirt and red blouse for me to know she's there, almost hidden by the door.

"Come out into the yard," I say.

Have you ever seen a lame animal, perhaps a dog run over by some careless person rich enough to own a car, sidle up to someone who is ignorant enough to be kind to him? That is the way my Maggie walks. She has been like this, chin on chest, eyes on ground, feet in shuffle, ever since the fire that burned the other house to the ground.

Dee is lighter than Maggie, with nicer hair and a fuller figure. She's a woman now, though sometimes I forget. How long ago

was it that the other house burned? Ten, twelve years? Sometimes
I can still hear the flames and feel Maggie's arms sticking to me,
her hair smoking and her dress falling off her in little black papery
flakes. Her eyes seem stretched open, blazed open by the flames
reflected in them. And Dee. I see her standing off under the sweet
gum tree she used to dig gum out of; a look of concentration on
her face as she watched the last dingy gray board of the house fall
in toward the red-hot brick chimney. Why don't you do a dance
around the ashes? I'd wanted to ask her. She had hated the house
that much.

I used to think she hated Maggie, too. But that was before we
raised the money, the church and me, to send her to Augusta to
school. She used to read to us without pity; forcing words, lies,
other folks' habits, whole lives upon us two, sitting trapped and
ignorant underneath her voice. She washed us in a river of make-
believe, burned us with a lot of knowledge we didn't necessarily
need to know. Pressed us to her with the serious way she read, to
shove us away at just the moment, like dimwits, we seemed about
to understand.

Dee wanted nice things. A yellow organdy dress to wear to her
graduation from high school; black pumps to match a green suit
she'd made from an old suit somebody gave me. She was determined to stare down any disaster in her efforts. Her eyelids would
not flicker for minutes at a time. Often I fought off the temptation
to shake her. At sixteen she had a style of her own: and knew what
style was.

I never had an education myself. After second grade the school
was closed down. Don't ask my why: in 1927 colored asked fewer
questions than they do now. Sometimes Maggie reads to me. She
stumbles along good-naturedly but can't see well. She knows she
is not bright. Like good looks and money, quickness passed her
by. She will marry John Thomas (who has mossy teeth in an earnest face) and then I'll be free to sit here and I guess just sing
church songs to myself. Although I never was a good singer.
Never could carry a tune. I was always better at a man's job. I used
to love to milk till I was hooked in the side in '49. Cows are
soothing and slow and don't bother you, unless you try to milk
them the wrong way.

I have deliberately turned my back on the house. It is three
rooms, just like the one that burned, except the roof is tin; they

don't make shingle roofs any more. There are no real windows, just some holes cut in the sides, like the portholes in a ship, but not round and not square, with rawhide holding the shutters up on the outside. This house is in a pasture, too, like the other one. No doubt when Dee sees it she will want to tear it down. She wrote me once that no matter where we "choose" to live, she will manage to come see us. But she will never bring her friends. Maggie and I thought about this and Maggie asked me, "Mama, when did Dee ever *have* any friends?"

She had a few. Furtive boys in pink shirts hanging about on washday after school. Nervous girls who never laughed. Impressed with her they worshiped the well-turned phrase, the cute shape, the scalding humor that erupted like bubbles in lye. She read to them.

When she was courting Jimmy T she didn't have much time to pay to us, but turned all her faultfinding power on him. He *flew* to marry a cheap city girl from a family of ignorant flashy people. She hardly had time to recompose herself.

When she comes I will meet—but there they are!

Maggie attempts to make a dash for the house, in her shuffling way, but I stay her with my hand. "Come back here," I say. And she stops and tries to dig a well in the sand with her toe.

It is hard to see them clearly through the strong sun. But even the first glimpse of leg out of the car tells me it is Dee. Her feet were always neat-looking, as if God himself had shaped them with a certain style. From the other side of the car comes a short, stocky man. Hair is all over his head a foot long and hanging from his chin like a kinky mule tail. I hear Maggie suck in her breath. "Uhnnnh," is what it sounds like. Like when you see the wriggling end of a snake just in front of your foot on the road. "Uhnnnh."

Dee next. A dress down to the ground, in this hot weather. A dress so loud it hurts my eyes. There are yellows and oranges enough to throw back the light of the sun. I feel my whole face warming from the heat waves it throws out. Earrings gold, too, and hanging down to her shoulders. Bracelets dangling and making noises when she moves her arm up to shake the folds of the dress out of her armpits. The dress is loose and flows, and as she walks closer, I like it. I hear Maggie go "Uhnnnh" again. It is her sister's hair. It stands straight up like wool on a sheep. It is black as night and around the edges are two long pigtails that rope about like small lizards disappearing behind her ears.

"Wa-su-zo-Tean-o!" she says, coming on in that gliding way the dress makes her move. The short stocky fellow with the hair to his navel is all grinning and he follows up with "Asalamalakim, my mother and sister!" He moves to hug Maggie but she falls back, right up against the back of my chair. I feel her trembling there and when I look up I see the perspiration falling off her chin.

"Don't get up," says Dee. Since I am stout it takes something of a push. You can see me trying to move a second or two before I make it. She turns, showing white heels through her sandals, and goes back to the car. Out she peeks next with a Polaroid. She stoops down quickly and lines up picture after picture of me sitting there in front of the house with Maggie cowering behind me. She never takes a shot without making sure the house is included. When a cow comes nibbling around the edges of the yard she snaps it and me and Maggie *and* the house. Then she puts the Polaroid in the back seat of the car, and comes up and kisses me on the forehead.

Meanwhile Asalamalakim is going through the motions with Maggie's hand. Maggie's hand is as limp as a fish, and probably as cold, despite the sweat, and she keeps trying to pull it back. It looks like Asalamalakim wants to shake hands but wants to do it fancy. Or maybe he don't know how people shake hands. Anyhow, he soon gives up on Maggie.

"Well," I say. "Dee."

"No, Mama," she says. "Not 'Dee,' Wangero Leewanika Kemanjo!"

"What happened to 'Dee'?" I wanted to know.

"She's dead," Wangero said. "I couldn't bear it any longer, being named after the people who oppress me."

"You know as well as me you was named after your aunt Dicie," I said. Dicie is my sister. She named Dee. We called her "Big Dee" after Dee was born.

"But who was *she* named after?" asked Wangero.

"I guess after Grandma Dee," I said.

"And who was she named after?" asked Wangero.

"Her mother," I said, and saw Wangero was getting tired. "That's about as far back as I can trace it," I said. Though, in fact, I probably could have carried it back beyond the Civil War through the branches.

"Well," said Asalamalakim, "there you are."

"Uhnnnh," I heard Maggie say.

"There I was not," I said, "before 'Dicie' cropped up in our family, so why should I try to trace it that far back?"

He just stood there grinning, looking down on me like somebody inspecting a Model A car. Every once in a while he and Wangero sent eye signals over my head.

"How do you pronounce this name?" I asked.

"You don't have to call me by it if you won't want to," said Wangero.

"Why shouldn't I?" I asked. "If that's what you want us to call you, we'll call you."

"I know it might sound awkward at first," said Wangero.

"I'll get used to it," I said. "Ream it out again,"

Well, soon we got the name out of the way. Asalamalakim had a name twice as long and three times as hard. After I tripped over it two or three times he told me to just call him Hakim-a-barber. I wanted to ask him was he a barber, but I didn't really think he was, so I didn't ask.

"You must belong to those beef-cattle peoples down the road," I said. They said "Asalamalakim" when they met you, too, but they didn't shake hands. Always too busy: feeding the cattle, fixing the fences, putting up salt-lick shelters, throwing down hay. When the white folks poisoned some of the herd the men stayed up all night with rifles in their hands. I walked a mile and a half just to see the sight.

Hakim-a-barber said, "I accept some of their doctrines, but farming and raising cattle is not my style." (They didn't tell me, and I didn't ask, whether Wangero (Dee) had really gone and married him.)

We sat down to eat and right away he said he didn't eat collards and pork was unclean. Wangero, though, went on through the chitlins and corn bread, the greens and everything else. She talked a blue streak over the sweet potatoes. Everything delighted her. Even the fact that we still used the benches her daddy made for the table when we couldn't afford to buy chairs.

"Oh, Mama!" she cried. Then turned to Hakim-a-barber. "I never knew how lovely these benches are. You can feel the rump prints," she said, running her hands underneath her and along the bench. Then she gave a sigh and her hand closed over Grandma Dee's butter dish. "That's it!" she said. "I knew there was something I wanted to ask you if I could have." She jumped up from the table and went over in the corner where the churn stood, the milk in it clabber by now. She looked at the churn and looked at it.

"This churn top is what I need," she said. "Didn't Uncle Buddy whittle it out of a tree you all used to have?"

"Yes," I said.

"Uh huh," she said happily. "And I want the dasher, too."

"Uncle Buddy whittle that, too?" asked the barber.

Dee (Wangero) looked up at me. "Aunt Dee's first husband whittled the dash," said Maggie so low you almost couldn't hear her. "His name was Henry, but they called him Stash."

"Maggie's brain is like an elephant's," Wangero said, laughing. "I can use the churn top as a centerpiece for the alcove table," she said, sliding a plate over the churn, "and I'll think of something artistic to do with the dasher."

When she finished wrapping the dasher the handle stuck out. I took it for a moment in my hands. You didn't even have to look close to see where hands pushing the dasher up and down to make butter had left a kind of sink in the wood. In fact, there were a lot of small sinks; you could see where thumbs and fingers had sunk into the wood. It was beautiful light yellow wood, from a tree that grew in the yard where Big Dee and Stash had lived.

After dinner Dee (Wangero) went to the trunk at the foot of my bed and started rifling through it. Maggie hung back in the kitchen over the dishpan. Out came Wangero with two quilts. They had been pieced by Grandma Dee and then Big Dee and me had hung them on the quilt frames on the front porch and quilted them. One was in the Lone Star pattern. The other was Walk Around the Mountain. In both of them were scraps of dresses Grandma Dee had worn fifty and more years ago. Bits and pieces of Grandpa Jarrell's Paisley shirts. And one teeny faded blue piece, about the size of a penny matchbox, that was from Great Grandpa Ezra's uniform that he wore in the Civil War.

"Mama," Wangero said sweet as a bird. "Can I have these old quilts?"

I heard something fall in the kitchen, and a minute later the kitchen door slammed.

"Why don't you take one or two of the others?" I asked. "These old things was just done by me and Big Dee from some tops your grandma pieced before she died."

"No," said Wangero. "I don't want those. They are stitched around the borders by machine."

"That'll make them last better," I said.

"That's not the point," said Wangero. "These are all pieces of dresses Grandma used to wear. She did all this stitching by hand. Imagine!" She held the quilts securely in her arms, stroking them.

"Some of the pieces, like those lavender ones, come from old clothes her mother handed down to her," I said, moving up to touch the quilts. Dee (Wangero) moved back just enough so that I couldn't reach the quilts. They already belonged to her.

"Imagine!" she breathed again, clutching them closely to her bosom.

"The truth is," I said, "I promised to give them quilts to Maggie, for when she marries John Thomas."

She gasped like a bee had stung her.

"Maggie can't appreciate these quilts!" she said. "She'd probably be backward enough to put them to everyday use."

"I reckon she would," I said. "God knows I been saving 'em for long enough with nobody using 'em. I hope she will!" I didn't want to bring up how I had offered Dee (Wangero) a quilt when she went away to college. Then she had told me they were old-fashioned, out of style.

"But they're *priceless!*" she was saying now, furiously; for she has a temper. "Maggie would put them on the bed and in five years they'd be in rags. Less than that!"

"She can always make some more," I said. "Maggie knows how to quilt."

Dee (Wangero) looked at me with hatred. "You just will not understand. The point is these quilts, *these* quilts!"

"Well," I said, stumped. "What would *you* do with them?"

"Hang them," she said. As if that was the only thing you *could* do with quilts.

Maggie by now was standing in the door. I could almost hear the sound her feet made as they scraped over each other.

"She can have them, Mama," she said, like somebody used to never winning anything, or having anything reserved for her. "I can 'member Grandma Dee without the quilts."

I looked at her hard. She had filled her bottom lip with checker-berry snuff and it gave her face a kind of dopey, hangdog look. It was Grandma Dee and Big Dee who taught her how to quilt herself. She stood there with her scarred hands hidden in the folds of her skirt. She looked at her sister with something like fear but she wasn't mad at her. This was Maggie's portion. This was the way she knew God to work.

When I looked at her like that something hit me in the top of my head and ran down to the soles of my feet. Just like when I'm in church and the spirit of God touches me and I get happy and shout. I did something I never had done before: hugged Maggie to me, then dragged her on into the room, snatched the quilts out of Miss Wangero's hands and dumped them into Maggie's lap. Maggie just sat there on my bed with her mouth open.

"Take one or two of the others," I said to Dee.

But she turned without a word and went out to Hakim-a-barber.

"You just don't understand," she said, as Maggie and I came out to the car.

"What don't I understand?" I wanted to know.

"Your heritage," she said. And then she turned to Maggie, kissed her, and said, "You ought to try to make something of yourself, too, Maggie. It's really a new day for us. But from the way you and Mama still live you'd never know it."

She put on some sunglasses that hid everything above the tip of her nose and her chin.

Maggie smiled; maybe at the sunglasses. But a real smile, not scared. After we watched the car dust settle I asked Maggie to bring me a dip of snuff. And then the two of us sat there just enjoying, until it was time to go in the house and go to bed.

THE GIFT

Kia Penso

(from *Spectrum*, 1979)

Miss Gladys' married daughter Annetta had been living in Miami almost four years. Since they had left Jamaica, Annetta and her husband and three children had not been back, and Miss Gladys had not been able to go and visit them until now.

The trip was in the middle of July, the mango season. This had been very important to Miss Gladys, because if she carried nothing else for her daughter, she had to take a St. Julian mango from the big tree in the back yard. As it was, she had spent half the night before her departure cooking up ackee and saltfish, roasting a breadfruit, and making up two quarts of rum punch, and a few other things to take for Annetta and the family. She was convinced that they had to be suffering for the lack of them.

Bright and early the next morning, her young son Errol climbed the big Julie mango tree and picked the mango. It was one that Miss Gladys had been watching for weeks. Every day she went outside to check and make sure that neither the birds nor the neighborhood children had got to it. It was finally in her possession, perfect. It was big, and smooth and green with a pale hint of yellow on one of the cheeks. It weighed about a pound and a half, and the flesh under the skin was firm but not hard, under the tight skin. She noticed that the stem had not bled when the mango was picked, which meant that it was very ripe indeed. It was elegantly shaped, like a teardrop, but round at the top. And the smell! If anyone wanted to know what a mango was and could be, they had only to smell this one. The smell almost made Miss Gladys weep for joy with the beauty of it.

The mango was king. Oh, yes, there were oranges and tangerines and bananas, water coconuts and star apples and rose apples and naseberries and guavas. There were countless other fruits, but the mango was King, and the St. Julian mango was King of the mangoes. It wasn't too sweet or too cloying, or too stringy, like some commoner types. It was a high class mango, a whole meal of a mango.

Miss Gladys wrapped up the mango with tenderest care, first in a plastic bag, then in a hand towel, and packed it firmly in the shopping bag with the other foodstuffs.

She walked heavily through the corridors of Miami airport, loaded down with two shopping bags. One was filled with gifts from the Victoria Crafts Market, and the other was filled with the food, and the mango. She felt pleasure in the presence of it, and thought of Annetta.

The customs man saw her coming. He saw her with her two big shopping bags and the enormous suitcase she had brought from the baggage claim area. He thought she had probably never travelled before. Miss Gladys put the shopping bags on the conveyor belt at the customs desk. There was a low, sudden murmur of machinery, and the belt leaped forward, carrying the bags. The customs man smiled at the surprise on Miss Gladys' face.

"Okay, let's see, what have we got here?" he grinned, and looked inside one of the shopping bags.

"Is just some little presents I bringing for me daughter children, sir." She said this politely, covering her resentment at the invasion of her privacy.

"And what's in here?" He had moved to the other shopping bag, the one with the food in it.

"Just some food I cook up for me daughter, sir. She can't buy it here, so I did bring it for her. Is long time now she don't eat none."

He took the roast breadfruit out of the bag, and unwrapped it. It was a big, black, charred thing the size of a bowling ball, and it left soot all over his hands. Obviously cooked, no problem there. He examined the pot of ackee and saltfish, and saw that that was cooked. The same procedure for the curried goat, the rum punch (which he did not open), the escoveitch fish. He took one whiff of the fish and his eyes started to water. He saw in the bottom of the bag a little round bundle in a hand towel. He took it out.

Miss Gladys was furious. Her jaw was set, but she spoke politely when he asked her what it was.

"Nothing, sir." He frowned and unwrapped the mango. The smell hit the air, and lust suddenly shone in the eyes of the customs man.

"You know that it is not permitted to bring fresh fruit into the United States?"

"No, I never know, sir. Is just the one so-so mango I did was bringing for me married daughter, four year now I don't see her. You going take it weh from me, sir?"

"I'm sorry, but we will have to confiscate this." He caressed the mango.

Miss Gladys' eyes grew moist, and her lower lip trembled. "All right, sir, I beg you just to please let me hold it one time. Just for me daughter, sir?"

The man handed it to her reluctantly. "It's not really allowed, but . . ."

He didn't get to finish his sentence, because Miss Gladys had sunk her teeth into the top of the mango. The smell rose when the golden meat of the mango was exposed. Miss Gladys peeled the skin off in strips with her teeth. It came off smoothly, and she held the strips in her hand. She bit into the firm meat and juice poured down her chin, but she couldn't stop now to clean it up. The juice ran down her arm and dripped to the floor where her elbow was bent. Miss Gladys ate that mango with a vengeance. She ate it for love of Annetta, she ate it for hatred of the greedy little man watching her. She saw her young son Errol up in the mango tree, climbing down, handing her the mango, smiling at her over the mango. The juice was everywhere; on her nose, her cheeks, her chin, the front of her dress, her arm. It shined up in little golden drops on the floor. And the smell spoke for all the enjoyment that was in it. When Miss Gladys was finished, there was no juice left on the mango; the seed was white. She handed the skin and the big, flat seed to the customs man, and with her clean hand reached into the sleeve of her dress and pulled out a dainty handkerchief. She mopped her face delicately, and moistened one corner of the handkerchief in her mouth and rubbed at the spots on the front of her dress. She wiped her arm and her hand, and called a porter. She packed the other food carefully in the shopping bag, and made the porter carry the suitcase and the bag from the crafts market. She could see Annetta waiting worriedly at the exit to the customs

area. She walked towards her, and then turned and spoke to the
customs man, loudly, for everyone to hear.

"You wicked brute, you. You think I never know sey dat did
want eat it you'self. Eh? You think I never know when you damn
ol' eye dem was a shine like when mawga dag deh in a butcher
shop? If it wasn't das me married daughter was here me woulda dis
tun round same time go home a mi yard. Damn likkle red boy like
you, though."

Miss Gladys turned and proudly took the arm of her married
daughter.

GIRL

Jamaica Kincaid

(from *At the Bottom of the River,* 1983)

WASH THE WHITE clothes on Monday and put them on the stone heap; wash the color clothes on Tuesday and put them on the clothesline to dry; don't walk barehead in the hot sun; cook pumpkin fritters in very hot sweet oil; soak your little cloths right after you take them off; when buying cotton to make yourself a nice blouse, be sure that it doesn't have gum on it, because that way it won't hold up well after a wash; soak salt fish overnight before you cook it; is it true that you sing benna in Sunday school?; always eat your food in such a way that it won't turn someone else's stomach; on Sundays try to walk like a lady and not like the slut you are so bent on becoming; don't sing benna in Sunday school; you mustn't speak to wharf-rat boys, not even to give directions; don't eat fruits on the street—flies will follow you; *but I don't sing benna on Sundays at all and never in Sunday school*; this is how to sew on a button; this is how to make a buttonhole for the button you have just sewed on; this is how to hem a dress when you see the hem coming down and so to prevent yourself from looking like the slut I know you are so bent on becoming; this is how you iron your father's khaki shirt so that it doesn't have a crease; this is how you iron your father's khaki pants so that they don't have a crease; this is how you grow okra—far from the house, because okra tree harbors red ants; when you are growing dasheen, make sure it gets plenty of water or else it makes your throat itch when you are eating it; this is how you sweep a corner;

this is how you sweep a whole house; this is how you sweep a yard; this is how you smile to someone you don't like too much; this is how you smile to someone you don't like at all; this is how you smile to someone you like completely; this is how you set a table for tea; this is how you set a table for dinner; this is how you set a table for dinner with an important guest; this is how you set a table for lunch; this is how you set a table for breakfast; this is how to behave in the presence of men who don't know you very well, and this way they won't recognize immediately the slut I have warned you against becoming; be sure to wash every day, even if it is with your own spit; don't squat down to play marbles—you are not a boy, you know; don't pick people's flowers—you might catch something; don't throw stones at blackbirds, because it might not be a blackbird at all; this is how to make a bread pudding; this is how to make doukona; this is how to make pepper pot; this is how to make a good medicine for a cold; this is how to make a good medicine to throw away a child before it even becomes a child; this is how to catch a fish; this is how to throw back a fish you don't like, and that way something bad won't fall on you; this is how to bully a man; this is how a man bullies you; this is how to love a man, and if this doesn't work there are other ways, and if they don't work don't feel too bad about giving up; this is how to spit up in the air if you feel like it, and this is how to move quick so that it doesn't fall on you; this is how to make ends meet; always squeeze bread to make sure it's fresh; *but what if the baker won't let me feel the bread?*; you mean to say that after all you are really going to be the kind of woman who the baker won't let near the bread?

PICTURE THIS

Jervey Tervalon

(from *Spectrum*, 1984)

THERE WAS A knock at the screen door of the tiny shotgun house. August's grandmother put down her rosary and hurried to answer it. Jody and little Josh were at the door. They watched her fumble to unlock the screen and run to the bed where August was lying. She touched his shoulder to wake him but he wasn't asleep. He sat up slowly and without opening his eyes asked Jody and Josh to come into the room.

"I'm glad you guys could come. I'm scaring my grumma bad."

His grandmother took him by the hand and led him to Jody.

"Oh, he's not scaring me but I can't get him to the doctor. His daddy is out fishing and I can't stand to see him suffering."

Jody smiled awkwardly as he took his cousin's hand and led him down the stairs to the car. After little Josh slid into the front seat, Jody helped August in.

"You can't open your eyes?" Jody said as he started the car and drove away.

"No, they hurt too much."

"You blind?" Josh asked.

"I hope not."

It became obvious to Jody and Josh that August was in a lot of pain. A few times he sighed loudly, trembling.

"You're really hurtin'?" Jody asked.

"Yeah, it's pretty bad. My eye is killing me."

"You cut it at the picnic?"

"Yeah, but I can't talk right now. It makes my eye hurt more."

Josh slid closer to his brother but watched his cousin even more intently. Soon, Jody arrived at the hospital; he opened the car door for August and took his hand and led him carefully through the busy parking lot. Josh trailed behind them, counting August's stumbles. At the window of the hospital register they waited patiently for the nurse to finish registering the man ahead of them. August struggled to keep himself from crying out loud; tears forced their way out of his tightly clenched eye lids. Little Josh hopped up and grabbed hold of the counter ledge of the register booth. He pulled himself up and looked inside to see what the nurse was doing. The nurse ignored him and continued to stamp and sign papers. Jody grabbed his brother and carried him to a seat and came back to speak to the nurse.

"Nurse, my cousin got glass in his eye."

"Glass?" She put her pen down. "You've got glass in your eye?"

August heard the alarm in her voice; he didn't think nurses got alarmed. It made him feel worse.

"Yes. It happened at the beach."

"We'll have a doctor right with you. But first I'll need your name and your address."

He spelled the information out for her.

"You're from L.A.? Here you are on your vacation and you had to get glass in your eye. That's a shame."

She pointed to Jody, then to a waiting room. "Take him over there. We'll have a doctor with you right away."

After twenty minutes or so, Josh was in a deep sleep and Jody was dozing. August was leaning over, head in hands, trying to keep perfectly still. He listened to the noisy Friday night emergency room crowd. Every now and then he could make out the cough of a child or hear the worried conversation of the people sitting behind him; but he couldn't concentrate on what they were discussing; the throbbing in his eye was growing strong. It felt a whole lot like having elephants running around in his head. He heard footsteps coming toward him.

"We've been looking all over for you. You're sitting in the wrong area."

It was the nurse. She led them to another waiting room that was less noisy.

"I'm gonna wait with you but I gotta take Josh out of here. You can't have little kids here," Jody said.

August heard Jody lifting Josh from the chair and carrying him out of the waiting room. Alone, he held his head in his hands and waited for the doctor. Jody returned before the doctor came.

"You asleep?" he asked August so as not to wake him if he were sleeping. August shook his head but was unable to say anything. Finally, the doctor arrived and squatted down in front of him.

"You're the one who has glass in his eye?"

August nodded. When the doctor reached out to touch his face, Jody leaned close to watch him work. The doctor glared at him.

"You shouldn't be in here."

"I'm leaving."

Jody smiled and shifted in his chair but he didn't leave. The doctor ignored him and took August's face in his hands.

"Open your eyes."

"I don't know if I can."

"I can't examine them if you don't."

"Okay, I'll try."

Before he lost his resolve, he forced his eye lids apart. As quickly as he opened his eyes they squeezed shut again. Hot pokers! Hot pokers! He was sick enough to faint.

"I can't get a look in. We'll have to use an anesthetic." Through the noise of the pain, he heard the doctor walk away. Jody patted him on the shoulder.

"God, Jody, the doctor almost killed me."

"Yeah, I thought you were going to faint."

The throbbing diminished enough for him to sit up and stretch. Jody whispered to August.

"You should see this. This big niggah just came in here and he's fucked up. His eye is busted up big. It's big and red like a fat tomato."

The doctor led the new patient into the room. He pulled away from the doctor and sat down across from them. After lighting a cigarette he stared hard at them with his good eye.

"What happened to you?" Jody asked.

"Nothing."

The man paused from glaring at Jody long enough to take a puff off his cigarette.

"Nothing happened to me that I can't handle. Jessie gonna give me that money. Hitting me in the eye ain't gonna stop that."

"He punched you in the eye?"

"Naw, he hit me with a pipe, but I'm alright. And Jessie is gonna give me the money, hitting me when I wasn't looking ain't nothing. . . . What's wrong with your brother? He looks a whole lot worse than me."

"He's alright."

August straightened up and held the position for a second and then sank back down.

"Your eye hurt?" Jody asked the busted eye man.

"Naw, I wasn't even gonna come to the hospital but Jessie's brother drug me here. I ain't paying, though."

The conversation stopped when the doctor returned to the waiting room. He examined the busted eye man's eye and asked him a few questions. August hoped the doctor would leave soon. Listening to that guy talk made him almost forget that he was hurting. Jody nudged him.

"Man! The doctor brought this white lady into the room and she's got blood all over her."

August sat up and tilted his head in the direction of the conversation between the doctor and the woman.

"Okay, lady, what happened?"

"I don't know! I don't know! Where am I?"

"Lady, you're in the hospital."

"The hospital? How did I get here? The last thing I remember was seeing Bill come out of the restaurant with that woman he works with. I took my gun out of my purse and pointed it at him and then everything went blank. Where am I!"

The doctor pushed the woman into a seat and left her. She was seated right next to them. There was silence for a while, then the guy with the busted eye started talking to her.

"So, what happened to you?"

"Me? What happened to me? I don't know what happened to me."

"You got blood all over you; something happened!"

The woman shook her head violently until her hair was wild about her head.

"You know something happened," the guy said sliding forward in his chair.

The woman stopped shaking her head and looked at him, a big crazy look.

"He was with her, taking her to dinner. He never takes me to dinner but I caught him taking her out. Well, he never takes me anywhere and what I can't understand is why he likes such a big bottom girl like that. But I don't know what happened so you can stop asking me."

"Well, why he takes her out and not you, you look pretty good."

"I don't know. She has a job."

"She has a job, shit, I'd go out with her too."

"Who hit you in the eye, smart ass?"

"You oughta get a job," the guy said.

Jody started laughing and so did August and the guy. The white lady started shaking her head again. The nurse hurried from behind the desk and led the woman away. Another nurse took August, who was feeling a little better, into a tiny waiting room; a doctor was waiting there to have a look at him.

"Let's have a look at that eye."

"I can't open it."

"Hold on. I've got a spray for the pain."

August heard him reach into his desk for something.

"Go ahead and open it."

August forced his eye open and the doctor sprayed something cool into it. The pain stopped immediately. It was like somebody had turned off a gigantic radio.

The doctor cleaned and dressed his eye and wrapped half his head with a bandage. August was relieved to find out that there wasn't too much wrong with him. He wondered what would happen when the anesthetic wore off. He walked into the hallway and saw the hospital for the first time. It was cluttered and dirty and drab, nothing like the antiseptically perfect world that he had imagined. Without Jody he was lost. It seemed he should know the building but he didn't. A short time later he found the right waiting room, and Jody, who was sleeping in a chair, with little Josh asleep in his lap. He tapped Jody. He wakened and smiled at him.

"Got you bandaged up like a mummy."

"Yep, they do."

Jody stood and lifted his brother to lug him to the car. August took Josh out of his arms and carried him outside for Jody.

"Man, since he sprayed my eye with a pain killer I feel great! I'm even hungry. Wanna get some donuts?"

"Sure, sleeping makes me hungry."

In the parking lot, walking next to Jody, carting his little cousin to the car, he looked through his unbandaged eye at the colorful street lights, feeling happy and relieved. Then he felt the distant faint throbbing: The elephants were coming home again.

THE DRILL

Breena Clarke

(from *Streetlights: Illuminating Tales of the Black Urban Experience,* 1996)

"TAKE THE BUS out Forty-second Street—the cross-town bus, the M42—and get off at Seventh Avenue. Then take the Number One train. Get off at 157th Street. Don't get off at 168th Street. Okay? When you're riding the Number One and you get off at 168th Street, you have to ride the elevator and the elevator is nasty. Also, there are too many homeless people on the platform at 168th Street. Anything can happen in that station. Don't get off at 168th Street. Take the Number One at Times Square and get off at 157th Street. Okay? I'll wait in the station at 157th Street. But if you don't see me, don't wait for me. Start walking up on the east side of the street, and I'll walk down on the east side and I'll see you. So walk on the east side of the street."

She starts off a good ten minutes earlier than the earliest time he could have gotten to the station at 157th Street unless they got let out early. It's the middle of winter and has been dark for hours. She turns over in her mind the color of the cap he wore that morning and recalls what color the coat was. As if she needed clues to recognize him! She is absolutely certain that blindfolded and unable to hear or touch him, she'd be able to distinguish her son in a stadium full of fourteen-year-olds. She knows him in every cell of her body. But when you love someone, you memorize their clothes.

It's ten P.M. and she wishes she were reclining in front of the TV. She is playing and replaying in her head the tape of his itinerary from the deck of the docked aircraft carrier *Intrepid*, through the midtown streets, north on the subway, to the subway station where she'll meet him. "He can do it. I mean, there's no reason to think he'll get lost or anything."

They'd struck a bargain. He wanted so badly to be independent and out after dark that he agreed to all her prerequisites. If she would agree not to go over there with him—after the first time—and stand around waiting for him to be finished and walk him home, he promised to follow the one and only agreed-upon itinerary and not make any unauthorized stops. She agreed he should have money for a slice and a Coke or a hot dog and a Coke and some candy probably. He agreed to travel quickly and prudently in the company of his new friend, Derrick. He would sit in the subway car with the conductor in it—only.

His smile when she was finally won over was triumphant. He exchanged a victory glance with his stepfather over her head as if they'd been together on a strategy against her. They thought she didn't catch it, but she could smell the testosterone in the air. She detected a difference in the house lately. Those two sharing a certain odor of complicity. Their hormones lined up against hers.

She is letting the kite out a little farther every day. She's giving it more string, exposing it to the wind, but holding her end tighter and tighter. The city closes in around kids nowadays, and walking through the streets is like passing through a gauntlet. Her husband thinks it's queer the way she leaps into the gutter to put her arms out like a crossing guard when the three of them approach a street corner. "Look at all these people," he says sarcastically. "Most of them born and raised in New York City, and somehow they've survived as pedestrians without your help." This is not amusing to someone who regularly tests her own reflexes to be sure she's alert enough to charge in front of a raging bull of a car, driven by Lucifer's own taxi driver, careening directly toward her child.

Her letting him go by himself to the cadet practice way across town, his walking in a part of the city that's dark, his having to move through the gaudy neon swirl of Times Square, his traveling by himself on the subway at a dicey hour—this is all new.

He's had to memorize four different combinations for four different locks this year: his locker for coat and books, his locker for gym stuff, his swimming locker at the Y, and the lock for the chain on his bike. She bought him a bicycle, but they both know he better not take his hand off it unless he puts on the fifty-dollar lock with the money-back guarantee. When he had to replace a defective part on the bicycle, she put on jeans and a sweatshirt and rode with him and the bike on the subway. They're both glad he prefers his skateboard. It's easier to defend and cheaper to replace.

He's not a street child, but he's got pluck. He's not a fighter, but he's scrappy. He's tall, brown, with a sweet face, and she ruminates about what the cops will think if he reaches into his pocket for his gloves.

His wanting to join the cadet drill team is all tied up with the new friend, Derrick. They want to solidify their friendship with uniforms and syncopated walking. She disapproves of mumbling, but likes this boy who mumbles shyly and respectfully. He's got home training.

"Better to exit up this stairway than that because you'll be facing the right direction. Best to stand directly under the streetlamp so the bus driver will see you. Remember how we decided that standing well back from the edge of the platform is the best protection against an insane person pushing you onto the tracks in front of an arriving train? Keep your eyes and ears open, your mouth shut. Don't spend the transportation money on junk snacks and then try to get away with using your school pass after seven P.M. Don't jump the turnstile no matter what except in a case of being utterly stranded and having exhausted all other alternatives, including pleading with the token clerk."

Per the agreement, on the first night of the cadet program she went with him. She traced the route and discussed the idiosyncrasies in detail. She rolled her head from left to right and back again, surveying the street ahead—a walking defense mechanism picked up in the city. You let your eyes sweep the street broadly as far in front of you as possible. This way, you see certain crazies and drunks and friends you're not in the mood for before they see you. Leaving the *Intrepid*, standing with the two boys in the full bloom of a streetlamp, she was quietly annoyed with Derrick's people for not sending someone to accompany him. "He lives in the Bronx, for chrissake!" Suddenly she was not sure if she wasn't overreacting to the perceived dangers. "Don't smother the boy." Even her father chimed in. Acutely sensitive to the Daniel Patrick Moynihan school of thought on pathological black female emasculators, she checks herself.[1] "No, they should've come. These boys are still too young to scrabble around New York at ten o'clock at night."

They mounted the bus finally and the driver was cheerful. She fought the impulse to ask him if he always drove this route and if it always rounded the corner at exactly this time. When the bus crossed 42nd between Eighth Avenue and Seventh, the boys stared out the window into the nine-hundred-watt sex and sadism marquees. She saw some woman's tits and name lying across her son's cheek and *Terminator* and *Friday the Thirteenth* flickering across his blinking eyes. She really wanted to tell him not to look out the window, but realized how stupid it would sound.

Most often she believes forewarned is forearmed, but once or twice she has surrendered to an overwhelming desire to pretend that some things don't happen if you don't ever see them happening. One time she surveyed the street ahead of them as they walked together and caught sight of a man pulling down his disgusting pants and bending over and tooting his ass over a pile of garbage right on the corner of 50th Street and Eighth Avenue. She reached around and put her hand over the boy's eyes. It was a simple reflex, but he pouted a long while because he knew he'd missed seeing something interesting.

Tonight she walks down the east side of the street but sweeps the whole thoroughfare with her eyes, in case he didn't do what he was supposed to do. One of the pillars of maternal wisdom: after you've drilled into the child's head what he must do, you try to imagine what will happen if he does exactly the opposite. You've got to be prepared.

She waits at the turnstiles. She can see the platform. There is only one way to exit the station. If he's sitting in the car with the conductor, he'll be in the middle of the train. As each train enters the station, she looks at the middle first, then fans out to scout the front and back. Three trains come through and he doesn't arrive. She is sick of looking at the token clerk and annoyed that he is looking at her. She walks back toward the stairs. He's the kind of bullet-headed clerk who thinks the Transit Authority is paying

---

1. Daniel Patrick Moynihan school of thought . . . : In 1965, Moynihan published *The Negro Family: The Case for National Action*, better known as "The Moynihan Report." In it he argued that black families, and black men in particular, were damaged by black matriarchs.

him to scout fashion models rather than sell tokens. Out of his line of vision, she reads the subway map, traces grimy tiles with an index finger, and wipes her finger with a tissue.

He is not on the next train. She's getting angry and mutters to herself. She's getting scared. "Walk to the bus stop, ride across Forty-second Street, get off at Seventh Avenue, catch the uptown Number One, sit in the car with the conductor, get off at 157th Street. Simple."

Her stomach is not quiet. One hundred and thirty-eight pounds. The last time he went to the doctor's that's what he weighed, one hundred and thirty-eight pounds. I think that's accurate. Five feet eight inches tall. Half an inch taller than she. She can feel the brush of the bird's wing—the bird who brushes his wing against the mountaintop and in an eternity will have worn it to a pebble. This tiny bird of worry who brushes his wing against the soul of a mother and thus shortens her life by minutes, hours, days.

A throng of people come out of the next train and he is not among them. She sits disconsolately on the crummy station steps next to a plaque about the Jumel Mansion and silently begs whoever is listening to give her a break. "Let him be on the next train. Please!" All the while knowing that personal prayers don't alter events already in motion.

A train pulls in. She leaps to attention at the turnstile, leans over, looks anxious. She searches the windows. He bounds out of the middle of the train, poised for fussing but begging with his eyes for her to be calm. "They let us out late and the bus took forever." His voice is trembling. Words dam up behind her front teeth. She takes his hand silently and climbs the stairs behind the exiting crowd. At street level, he tactfully disengages his hand to show her the badges that have to be sewn on the sleeve of a white shirt. She stands looking at the knit cap he wears fashionably above his naked ears. Worried about the cold, she pulls it down. They walk home.

NEW YORK DAY WOMEN

Edwidge Danticat

(from *Krik? Krak!*, 1996)

TODAY, WALKING DOWN the street, I see my mother. She is strolling with a happy gait, her body thrust toward the DON'T WALK sign and the yellow taxicabs that make forty-five-degree turns on the corner of Madison and Fifty-seventh Street.

I have never seen her in this kind of neighborhood, peering into Chanel and Tiffany's and gawking at the jewels glowing in the Bulgari windows. My mother never shops outside of Brooklyn. She has never seen the advertising office where I work. She is afraid to take the subway, where you may meet those young black militant street preachers who curse black women for straightening their hair.

Yet, here she is, my mother, who I left at home that morning in her bathrobe, with pieces of newspapers twisted like rollers in her hair. My mother, who accuses me of random offenses as I dash out of the house.

Would you get up and give an old lady like me your subway seat? In this state of mind, I bet you don't even give up your seat to a pregnant lady.

My mother, who is often right about that. Sometimes I get up and give my seat. Other times, I don't. It all depends on how pregnant the woman is and whether or not she is with her boyfriend or husband and whether or not *he* is sitting down.

As my mother stands in front of Carnegie Hall, one taxi driver yells to another, "What do you think this is, a dance floor?"

My mother waits patiently for this dispute to be settled before crossing the street.

In Haiti when you get hit by a car, the owner of the car gets out and kicks you for getting blood on his bumper.

My mother who laughs when she says this and shows a large gap in her mouth where she lost three more molars to the dentist last week. My mother, who at fifty-nine, says dentures are okay.

You can take them out when they bother you. I'll like them. I'll like them fine.

Will it feel empty when Papa kisses you?

Oh no, he doesn't kiss me that way anymore.

My mother, who watches the lottery drawing every night on channel 11 without ever having played the numbers.

A third of that money is all I would need. We would pay the mortgage, and your father could stop driving that taxi-cab all over Brooklyn.

I follow my mother, mesmerized by the many possibilities of her journey. Even in a flowered dress, she is lost in a sea of pinstripes and gray suits, high heels and elegant short skirts, Reebok sneakers, dashing from building to building.

My mother, who won't go out to dinner with anyone.

If they want to eat with me, let them come to my house, even if I boil water and give it to them.

My mother, who talks to herself when she peels the skin off poultry.

Fat, you know, and cholesterol. Fat and cholesterol killed your aunt Hermine.

My mother, who makes jam with dried grapefruit peel and then puts in cinnamon bark that I always think is cockroaches in the jam. My mother, whom I have always bought household appliances for, on her birthday. A nice rice cooker, a blender.

I trail the red orchids in her dress and the heavy faux leather bag on her shoulders. Realizing the ferocious pace of my pursuit, I stop against a wall to rest. My mother keeps on walking as though she owns the sidewalk under her feet.

As she heads toward the Plaza Hotel, a bicycle messenger swings so close to her that I want to dash forward and rescue her, but she stands dead in her tracks and lets him ride around her and then goes on.

My mother stops at a corner hot-dog stand and asks for something. The vendor hands her a can of soda that she slips into her bag. She stops by another vendor selling sundresses for seven dollars each. I can tell that she is looking at an African print dress, contemplating my size. I think to myself, Please Ma, don't buy it. It would be just another thing that I would bury in the garage or give to Goodwill.

Why should we give to Goodwill when there are so many people back home who need clothes? We save our clothes for the relatives in Haiti.

Twenty years we have been saving all kinds of things for the relatives in Haiti. I need the place in the garage for an exercise bike.

You are pretty enough to be a stewardess. Only dogs like bones.

This mother of mine, she stops at another hot-dog vendor's and buys a frankfurter that she eats on the street. I never knew that she ate frankfurters. With her blood pressure, she shouldn't eat anything with sodium. She has to be careful with her heart, this day woman.

I cannot just swallow salt. Salt is heavier than a hundred bags of shame.

She is slowing her pace, and now I am too close. If she turns around, she might see me. I let her walk into the park before I start to follow again.

My mother walks toward the sandbox in the middle of the park. There a woman is waiting with a child. The woman is wearing a leotard with biker's shorts and has small weights in her hands. The woman kisses the child good-bye and surrenders him to my mother; then she bolts off, running on the cemented stretches in the park.

The child given to my mother has frizzy blond hair. His hand slips into hers easily, like he's known her for a long time. When he raises his face to look at my mother, it is as though he is looking at the sky.

My mother gives this child the soda that she bought from the vendor on the street corner. The child's face lights up as she puts in a straw in the can for him. This seems to be a conspiracy just between the two of them.

My mother and the child sit and watch the other children play in the sandbox. The child pulls out a comic book from a knapsack with Big Bird on the back. My mother peers into his comic book. My mother, who taught herself to read as a little girl in Haiti from the books that her brothers brought home from school.

My mother, who has now lost six of her seven sisters in Ville Rose and has never had the strength to return for their funerals.

Many graves to kiss when I go back. Many graves to kiss.

She throws away the empty soda can when the child is done with it. I wait and watch from a corner until the woman in the leotard and biker's shorts returns, sweaty and breathless, an hour later. My mother gives the woman back her child and strolls farther into the park.

I turn around and start to walk out of the park before my mother can see me. My lunch hour is long since gone. I have to hurry back to work. I walk through a cluster of joggers, then race to a *Sweden Tours* bus. I stand behind the bus and take a peek at my mother in the park. She is standing in a circle, chatting with a group of women who are taking other people's children on an afternoon outing. They look like a Third World Parent-Teacher Association meeting.

I quickly jump into a cab heading back to the office. Would Ma have said hello had she been the one to see me first?

As the cab races away from the park, it occurs to me that perhaps one day I would chase an old woman down a street by mistake and that old woman would be somebody else's mother, who I would have mistaken for mine.

Day women come out when nobody expects them.

Tonight on the subway, I will get up and give my seat to a pregnant woman or a lady about Ma's age.

My mother, who stuffs thimbles in her mouth and then blows up her cheeks like Dizzy Gillespie while sewing yet another Raggedy Ann doll that she names Suzette after me.

I will have all these little Suzettes in case you never have any babies, which looks more and more like it is going to happen.

My mother who had me when she was thirty-three—*l'âge du Christ*—at the age that Christ died on the cross.

That's a blessing, believe you me, even if American doctors say by that time you can make retarded babies.

My mother, who sews lace collars on my company softball T-shirts when she does my laundry.

Why, you can't you look like a lady playing softball?

My mother, who never went to any of my Parent-Teacher Association meetings when I was in school.

You're so good anyway. What are they going to tell me? I don't want to make you ashamed of this day woman. Shame is heavier than a hundred bags of salt.

BIOGRAPHICAL NOTES

Lucille Boehm (dates unknown)
Condemned House (*Opportunity: Journal of Negro Life*, June 1939)

Little is known of Lucille's Boehm's life. Her story "Condemned House," about the anxieties and terrors of everyday poverty, is set in Harlem.

Emma E. Butler (dates unknown)
Polly's Hack Ride (*The Crisis*, June 1916)

This was Emma E. Butler's sole story for *The Crisis*. No details of her life have been published. "Polly's Hack Ride" is a well-imagined tale of a young girl's casual reaction to an infant sibling's death.

Charles W. Chesnutt (1858–1932)
Uncle Wellington's Wives (*The Wife of His Youth and Other Stories of the Color Line*, 1899)

Charles Waddell Chesnutt was the first commercially successful African-American writer of fiction. Born in Cleveland, Ohio, he grew up in North Carolina, became a teacher, married, and moved to New York City before returning to live in Cleveland, where he studied law. Some of his best-known stories are essentially about reproducing the dialect of uneducated storytellers, and they were very popular in the late 1890s in national magazines. "Uncle Wellington's Wives," first published in 1898 in *The Atlantic Monthly*, is one of his fine and wry stories about "the Color Line," a line that had consequential legal and social repercussions. That is, as this miniature novella unfolds, Uncle Wellington, living in a small town in North Carolina where he grew up, in the decade after the Civil War, yearns for something else beyond his comfortable home with his impatient, hard-working wife.

Breena Clarke (b. 1951)
The Drill (*Streetlights: Illuminating Tales of the Black Urban Experience*, 1996)

Clarke grew up and lives in Washington, D.C., where she set her best-selling historical novel about the African-American community in 1925 Georgetown, *River, Cross My Heart* (an Oprah Book Club selection in 1999), and her novel of slavery and the Civil War, *Stand the Storm* (2009). "If a watchful one stands back and takes his time," she writes in *Stand the Storm*, describing a mode of imagining another era, "he can discover a lot of what is going on without actually seeing it firsthand." She administered the Editorial Diversity Program at Time Inc. in New York City, where "The Drill," about a mother's anxiety over her adolescent son, takes place.

Edwidge Danticat (b. 1969)
New York Day Women (*Krik? Krak!*, 1996)

Born on January 19, 1969, in Port-au-Prince, Haiti, Edwidge Danticat is the author of novels, essays, and collections of stories that have focused primarily on the lives and trials of Haitians and Haitian-Americans. Raised for most of her childhood by her aunt and uncle after her parents immigrated to the United States, she moved to Brooklyn to rejoin her parents when she was twelve. Already an avid reader, she learned English and, though challenged by an unfamiliar culture in America, immediately took to expressing her discoveries of her new world and herself through writing. She graduated with a degree in French literature from Barnard College in New York City and earned a master's degree in creative writing at Brown University in 1993. She won a prestigious MacArthur Foundation Award in 2009. This story, "New York Day Women," comes from her second book and first short story collection, *Krik? Krak!*

Gertrude H. Dorsey (Browne) (dates unknown)
An Equation (*Colored American Magazine*, August 1902)

Who was Gertrude H. Dorsey Browne? By the evidence of her published work between 1902 and 1907 in *Colored American Magazine*, she was a clever writer of literary short fiction at the turn of the twentieth century; the little romance "An Equation" is possibly her first published short story.

W. E. B. Du Bois (1868–1963)
Jesus Christ in Texas (*Darkwater: Voices from Within the Veil*, 1920)

The great William Edward Burghardt Du Bois (pronounced "Doo-*Boys*") was perhaps the foremost champion of black civil rights in the first half of the twentieth century. In 1909 he was one of the founders of the National Association for the Advancement of Colored People and for many years served as the editor of its journal, *The Crisis*. He was born in Great Barrington, Massachusetts, and earned a B.A. from Fisk University in Tennessee and then his B.A., M.A., and Ph.D. from Harvard University. For the rest of his long life, he applied his scholarship to publicizing African and African-American history and his analyses of them. His most famous work is a collection of digressive essays, *The Souls of Black Folk* (1903), but he wrote a variety of creative works as well, including a series of novels. His eerie "Jesus Christ in Texas" demonstrates something of his taste for the fantastical.

Paul Laurence Dunbar (1872–1906)
The Scapegoat (*The Heart of Happy Hollow*, 1904)

Dunbar grew up in Dayton, Ohio. His parents, born into slavery, moved north after the Civil War, in which his father had served as a soldier in the Union Army. The only African American in his high school, Paul Laurence Dunbar was prodigious, publishing poetry and newspaper articles in his teens. In his twenties, a young and amazing talent, he placed some of his celebrated, neatly crafted stories in national magazines, among them "The Boy and the Bayonet," "The Lynching of Jube Benson," and "Nelse Hatton's Vengeance" (later published in *The Heart of Happy Hollow*). His famous "dialect" poems amused wide audiences but also sometimes made him and later readers uneasy about their being used to mock African Americans. Dunbar married the writer Alice Ruth Moore, with whom he lived unhappily before they separated. He died of tuberculosis when he was only thirty-three. "The Scapegoat" is Dunbar's story of an ambitious and intelligent young man who sees no reason to sell himself short or accept defeat.

❧

Ralph Ellison (1913–1994)
Afternoon (*American Writing*, 1940)

Ellison was born in Oklahoma City but lived in New York City from the late 1930s. He is renowned for his novel *Invisible Man* (1952), the most influential African-American novel of the century. Ellison's first love was music, particularly jazz, and he attended Tuskegee Institute in Alabama to study music. After he reviewed a book by Richard Wright, Wright encouraged Ellison to write stories himself, and he did so, showing a real knack for it, especially with an early success, "Afternoon," a lovely and poignant evocation of boyhood and friendship. After Ellison published *Invisible Man*, he spent the next forty years uneasily putting off the completion of his second novel, which was published, in edited form, five years after his death.

❧

Jessie Fauset (1882–1961)
Mary Elizabeth (*The Crisis*, December 1919)

Jessie Redmon Fauset was born on April 26, 1882, in Camden County, New Jersey. She graduated Phi Beta Kappa from Cornell University, received an M.A. from the University of Pennsylvania, studied at the Sorbonne, and devoted much of her life to teaching French and Latin. In 1919, Fauset began her career with *The Crisis*, the periodical published by the National Association for the Advancement of Colored People. As its literary editor from 1919 to 1926, Fauset discovered and helped to promote many of the major writers of the Harlem Renaissance. She also served as the literary editor (1920) and managing editor (1921) of *The Brownies' Book*, a monthly children's magazine begun by W. E. B. Du Bois and created for "the Children of the Sun." Fauset not only identified literary talent in others, but she also penned several texts of her own. In addition to numerous poems, essays, and short stories, she wrote four novels: *There Is Confusion* (1924), *Plum Bun* (1929), *The Chinaberry Tree* (1931), and *Comedy: American Style* (1933). An important and influential figure of the Harlem Renaissance, Fauset believed that literature could educate readers and correct misconceptions about African Americans. She was also concerned about the ways racism and sexism joined to restrict black women. In "Mary Elizabeth," a story about a young couple and their housekeeper, Fauset addresses the lasting effects of slavery.

Rudolph Fisher (1897–1934)
The City of Refuge (*Atlantic Monthly*, February 1925)

Rudolph Fisher was born on May 9, 1897, in Washington, D.C., and raised in Providence, Rhode Island. He graduated Phi Beta Kappa from Brown University in 1919, earned an M.A. at Brown in 1920, received an M.D. degree from Howard University Medical School in 1924, and became a fellow of the National Research Council at Columbia University's College of Physicians and Surgeons. He went into private practice in Harlem in 1927, opened an x-ray laboratory shortly thereafter, served as superintendent of the International Hospital in Harlem from 1929-1932, and was the first lieutenant in the medical division of the 369th Infantry from 1931 to 1934. While pursuing his medical career, Fisher wrote short stories, essays, and two novels: *The Walls of Jericho* (1928) and *The Conjure-Man Dies* (1932); in addition, he arranged Negro spirituals for Paul Robeson. He won the *Crisis* short story contest for "City of Refuge" in 1925, and his short story "Miss Cynthie" (1933) appeared in Edward O'Brien's *The Best Short Stories for 1934*. That same year, Fisher died from intestinal cancer, possibly from exposure to the x-ray machines he used. Like many of Fisher's stories, "The City of Refuge" is about a Southern migrant's experience in Harlem.

Langston Hughes (1902–1967)
Feet Live Their Own Life (*The Best of Simple*, 1961)

Born in 1902 in Joplin, Missouri, Hughes moved to Cleveland as a teenager and went to high school there. He studied at Columbia University in New York City before dropping out and taking odd jobs that took him all over the country and all around the world—but he was always writing. In 1921, his poem "The Negro Speaks of Rivers" was published in *The Crisis*. Poems with jazz and blues idioms and rhythms and incorporating black vernacular were published in *The Weary Blues* (1926) and *Fine Clothes to the Jew* (1927). From the 1920s until his death in 1967, one of the most famous African-American writers of the century continually published poems, plays, novels, short stories, essays, translations, children's books, and edited anthologies. Knowing first-hand the financial difficulties and discouragement of being a writer of color, he helped numerous African Americans get noticed and published. He wrote two autobiographies, *The Big Sea* (1940) and *I Wonder as I Wander* (1956), interesting accounts of his travels and experiences, though not wholly revelatory of his private life. He created in Simple, Harlem's Jesse B. Semple, the most delightful recurring comic character in American literature. "Feet Live Their Own Life" is an expansion and revision of his first *Chicago Defender* column about Simple in 1943.

Zora Neale Hurston (1891–1960)
Muttsy (*Opportunity: Journal of Negro Life*, August 1926)

Although she gave birthdates for herself between 1898 and 1910, Zora Neale Hurston actually was born on January 15, 1891, in Notasulga, Alabama, not, as she claimed, in Eatonville, Florida. Hurston and her parents moved to the small incorporated all-black town of Eatonville in 1892, where her father became a Baptist minister and served as the town's mayor from 1912 until 1916. Hurston's mother, who instructed her to "jump at de sun," died in 1904 when Zora was thirteen. Hurston graduated from Morgan Academy (now Morgan State University) in 1918, received an associate degree from Howard University in 1920, and continued to take classes there until 1924. She published her first short story, "John Redding Goes to Sea" (1921), in *Stylus*, Howard University's literary magazine, and "Drenched in Light" three years later in *Opportunity*.

In 1925, Hurston moved to New York and became part of the Harlem Renaissance, publishing her work in various periodicals and anthologies and winning literary contests sponsored by *Opportunity*. She also continued her scholarly work, attending Barnard College and Columbia University, where she studied under the anthropologist Franz Boas. Various fellowships and money from her patron, Charlotte Osgood Mason, enabled Hurston to write and to collect data on black folklore in America and the Caribbean, and much of her research is reflected in her creative work. In the 1930s and 1940s, Hurston published several novels, including *Their Eyes Were Watching God* (1937), plays, folklore, essays, articles, and her autobiography, *Dust Tracks on a Road* (1942). In the 1950s, Hurston continued to write, but she was on the decline and worked, variously, as a maid, a librarian, a columnist, and a substitute teacher. On January 28, 1960, Hurston died in a welfare home in Florida and was buried in an unmarked grave at a segregated cemetery. In 1973, the author Alice Walker erected a gravestone to mark Hurston's life and achievements, reviving interest in a fascinating novelist, short story writer, playwright, folklorist, anthropologist, essayist, and columnist. "Muttsy" tells the story of Pinkie, a young southern migrant living in Harlem, and the effect that the title character, a smooth-talking, northern gambler, has on her life.

Jamaica Kincaid (b. 1949)
Girl (*At the Bottom of the River,* 1984)

Born Elaine Potter Richardson in Antigua, West Indies, Kincaid moved to New York City in 1966. In her twenties she decided to become a writer. In 1976, she joined the staff of *The New Yorker* magazine, where "Girl" appeared in 1978 and was republished in her book of stories. She has also published several novels, *Annie John* and *Lucy* the most popular; a collection of her unmistakably original *New Yorker* pieces; a memoir; a travel book; and a book on gardening. She lives in Vermont and has taught literature and writing at Harvard University and Claremont McKenna College.

Ramona Lowe (dates unknown)
The Woman in the Window (*Opportunity: Journal of Negro Life,* January 1940)

We know nothing of Ramona Lowe's life outside of her keen sympathy for her characters and her anger at the economic exploitation of the Aunt Jemima image and all other romanticized "mammies." "What's a ol' Southern mammy, Mama?" asks the heroine's young son. The mother answers, "A Southern mammy's a ol' colored woman who had the nursin' of all the little white children t'do in the South doin slavery times." Set during the Great Depression, the proud heroine and mother must decide how much humiliation she is willing to take for the sake of a job.

Claude McKay (1890–1948)
He Also Loved (*Home to Harlem,* 1928)

The youngest of eleven children, Festus Claudius McKay (later Claude McKay) was born on September 15, 1890, in rural Jamaica. In 1912, McKay published two volumes of poetry using Jamaican dialect: *Songs of Jamaica* and *Constab Ballads.* That year he also immigrated to the United States, attended Tuskegee Institute in

Alabama, and, shortly thereafter, transferred to Kansas State College. More interested in writing poetry than in studying agronomy and agriculture, McKay moved to Harlem in 1914, settling three years later in Greenwich Village. Here, McKay developed relationships with left-wing and revolutionary figures such as Max Eastman, the editor of *The Liberator*, an avant-garde literary and radical political journal. Eventually, McKay joined Eastman's editorial staff and, in 1921, became the journal's associate editor.

In addition to publishing a significant number of pieces in *The Liberator*, McKay also published a few poems in the avant-garde literary magazines *Pearson's* and *Seven Arts* using the pseudonym Eli Edwards. In 1922, McKay published *Harlem Shadows*, the collection that made him one of the most famous poets of the Harlem Renaissance. Over the next twelve years, McKay traveled to and lived in Russia, Europe, and North Africa, and published the novels *Home to Harlem* (1928), *Banjo: A Story without a Plot* (1929), and *Banana Bottom* (1933). *Home to Harlem* was a bestseller, but it was also at the center of arguments about whether black artists writing during the Harlem Renaissance should create art for art's sake. McKay returned to the United States in 1934, wrote the autobiographical *A Long Way from Home* (1937) and a collection of essays entitled *Harlem: Negro Metropolis* (1940), and worked with the Federal Writers' Project. In 1948, the year of his death, McKay had been working for four years as a teacher at the Catholic Youth Organization in Chicago. "He Also Loved," from *Home to Harlem*, examines the lifestyle and activities of a seemingly carefree couple living in Harlem.

Alice Ruth Moore (Dunbar-Nelson) (1875–1935)
A Carnival Jangle (*Violets and Other Tales*, 1895)

Alice Ruth Moore (Dunbar-Nelson) was born in New Orleans, Louisiana, on July 19, 1875. She attended the city's public schools and Straight College (now Dillard University) and studied at the University of Pennsylvania, Cornell University, and Philadelphia's School of Industrial Art. In 1895, while a teacher, she published her first book, *Violets and Other Tales*, and three years later, in 1898, married the poet Paul Laurence Dunbar. While married to Dunbar, and after her separation from him in 1902, Alice continued to teach and to write. In 1910, she married a young teacher about whom she was secretive and to whom she remained married for only a short time. In 1916, she married Robert John Nelson, publisher of the *Wilmington Advocate*, and became increasingly involved in political, social, and journalistic activities. The publication of her diary in 1984 reveals that Dunbar-Nelson had passionate relationships with other women, one of many indications that she rejected society's restrictions. Scholar, teacher, poet, writer, journalist, feminist, activist, and diarist, Dunbar-Nelson died on September 18, 1935, of heart disease. "A Carnival Jangle" focuses on the culture of New Orleans and its Creole characters amid a tragic event at Mardi Gras.

Laura D. Nichols (dates unknown)
Prodigal (*Opportunity: Journal of Negro Life*, December, 1930)

Laura D. Nichols is another one of the intriguing authors about whom little or nothing has been published. Her story "Prodigal" dramatizes the tension between a congregation and its new preacher, a theme as old as religion, and the voice that brings us back to ourselves.

Kia Penso (b. 1959)
The Gift (*Spectrum*, 1979)

Born in New York City, and raised in Kingston, Jamaica, Penso earned her Ph.D. in English from the University of California, Santa Barbara, and later her M.S. from Columbia University's Graduate School of Journalism. Her study of an American poet, *Wallace Stevens, Harmonium, and the Whole of Harmonium*, was published in 1991. She has worked as a writer and editor in California, the Caribbean, New York City, and Washington, D.C., where she now lives. "The Gift," written when Penso was nineteen, is about a Jamaican grandmother's first visit to her daughter in America.

Ann Petry (1908–1997)
The Bones of Louella Brown (*Opportunity: Journal of Negro Life*, 1947)

Ann Lane Petry was born on October 12, 1908 (some sources say 1911), in Old Saybrook, Connecticut. Before she began her writing career, Petry graduated from the Connecticut College of Pharmacy and, like her father, worked as a pharmacist in her hometown. She married George Petry in 1938 and moved with him to Harlem, where she worked for the newspapers *The Amsterdam News* and *The People's Voice*. In 1943, her short story "On Saturday the Siren Sounds at Noon" was published in *The Crisis*, and in 1946 her story "Like a Winding Sheet" was published in Martha Foley's *Best American Stories of 1946*. Also in 1946, Petry received a Houghton Mifflin Literary Fellowship to complete her first, and best-known, novel, *The Street*. In addition to publishing other novels and numerous short stories in periodicals such as *Opportunity*, *Phylon*, *The Crisis*, and *The New Yorker*, Petry wrote books for children. She also lectured at Berkeley and Miami University and was a visiting professor of English at the University of Hawaii. Petry's texts are often about the difficulties faced by African Americans. "The Bones of Louella Brown" explains what happens after the body of a black washerwoman is exhumed from an exclusive cemetery, "the final home of Boston's wealthiest and most aristocratic families."

Adeline Ries (dates unknown)
Mammy: A Story (*The Crisis*, January 1917)

Unfortunately, Ries's life is unknown except for her authorship of this story. The "mammy" was an image and caricature repeatedly evoked in American fiction, and here and in Dorothy West's tale "Mammy" we see the caricature transformed by the author's deeper understandings of the women who had such roles. Ries's chilling and compressed story dramatizes the suffering and restraint her heroine experienced in her long, loving life.

Anne Scott (1900–[?])
George Sampson Brite (*George Sampson Brite*, 1939)

Anne Scott published two books, one of which, *George Sampson Brite*, is a series of interconnected comic stories about a naughty and imaginative schoolboy in 1930s St. Louis. Her other book, also published by the Meador Company of Boston, was a Christmas story published in 1950. We can guess, but don't actually know, that Scott was a teacher herself—the stories are full of precise details about the particular routines and circumstances of a Southern black public school and was advertised in 1940 in *The Crisis* as a "charming story of a mischievous little colored boy" and accurately assessed on the first-edition jacket as "a delightful and unusual group of stories."

Jervey Tervalon (b. 1958)
Picture This (*Spectrum*, 1984)

Tervalon is a novelist and talented educator who has taught literature and writing at several California universities. He grew up in South Central Los Angeles and later taught at a high school there, where his first novel, *Understand This* (1994), takes place. He was born in New Orleans, the setting of two of his novels, *Lita* and *Dead above Ground*, as well as the story "Picture This." His outstanding book of short stories, *Living for the City*, was published in 1998. He earned his B.A. in Literature from the College of Creative Studies, U.C. Santa Barbara, and his M.F.A. in Creative Writing at U.C. Irvine. In 2005, Tervalon edited *The Cocaine Chronicles* with Gary Phillips; his essays and stories have appeared in several anthologies and periodicals.

Jean Toomer (1884–1967)
Becky (*Cane*, 1923)

Nathan Eugene Toomer, later Jean Toomer, was born in Washington, D.C., on December 26, 1894. Toomer, a child of racially mixed ancestry, experienced the desertion of his mother by his father less than a year after his birth; his mother, who remarried, died when he was in his early teens. Toomer spent much of his life with his maternal grandparents. When his grandfather, P. B. S. Pinchback, a mulatto who was politically active in Reconstruction Louisiana, lost his status, Toomer and his grandparents moved from a white neighborhood to a less affluent black section of Washington. He attended a number of academic institutions: the University of Wisconsin, New York University, the City College of New York, the American College of Physical Training in Chicago, and the Massachusetts College of Agriculture. A job as the temporary head of a small agricultural and industrial school for blacks in Georgia motivated Toomer to write *Cane* (1923), a book composed of poetry, sketches, stories, and a dramatic piece. Although *Cane* was met with critical acclaim, was well-received by the black community, and was a significant contribution to the literature of the Harlem Renaissance, it did not sell well at the time and marked the end of Toomer's connection to the black literary world. He stopped identifying as a member of a specific race, became increasingly attracted to mystic and spiritual teachings, and later converted to Quakerism. "Becky," which first appeared in *The Liberator* in 1922, is one of the stories recounted in *Cane*; it focuses on a community's attitude toward and treatment of a "white woman who had two Negro sons."

Alice Walker (b. 1944)
"Everyday Use" (*In Love and Trouble: Stories of Black Women*, 1973)

Alice Walker was born in Eatonton, Georgia, on February 9, 1944. She attended Spelman College, for which she received a scholarship, and earned her B.A. from Sarah Lawrence College in 1965. Walker is best known for her Pulitzer Prize-winning novel, *The Color Purple* (1982), as well as for coining the term "womanist" (an enlargement of and alternative to the term "feminist") and for recovering the works of Zora Neale Hurston. To date, she has written six other novels, four collections of short stories, seven volumes of poetry, nine collections of essays and prose, four children's books, a memoir, and a collection of interviews.

In addition to being a prolific writer, Walker has been an activist, fighting for civil rights and women's rights and against all forms of oppression and injustice; an educator, teaching and lecturing at institutions such as Wellesley College, the University of Massachusetts, and the University of California at Berkeley; and an editor for *Ms.* magazine. In 1984, she and Robert L. Allen co-founded Wild Trees Press, which publishes books by and about women. Walker often examines the effects of racism and/or sexism in her texts, and her main characters are often black women. "I am," she states, "preoccupied with the spiritual survival, the survival *whole* of my people. But beyond that, I am committed to exploring the oppressions, the insanities, the loyalties, and the triumphs of black women" ("From an Interview," *In Search of Our Mothers' Gardens*, 250). In the story "Everyday Use," first published in her short story collection *In Love and Trouble: Stories of Black Women* (1973), Walker examines conflicting ideas about identity and heritage through the lives of an African-American woman and her two daughters.

Dorothy West (1907–1998)
Mammy (*Opportunity: Journal of Negro Life*, October 1940)

A native of Boston, West was the daughter of a successful middle-class businessman who had been born a slave. She moved to New York City when she was nineteen and attended Columbia University. In 1926, she won a prize in *Opportunity*'s literary contest for her first short story, "The Typewriter." She published other stories in *Opportunity*, *Messenger*, the *Boston Post*, and the *Saturday Evening Quill*. A close friend of Zora Neale Hurston and Richard Wright, she founded a magazine, *Challenge*, in 1934, on which she worked for a short while with Wright. In the late 1930s she took a job as a welfare investigator, an experience represented in "Mammy." She joined a group of Harlem Renaissance artists, including Langston Hughes, who traveled to Russia to make *Black and White*, a film about race relations (this movie never materialized). She wrote two novels, *The Living Is Easy* (1948) and *The Wedding* (1995), and collected her stories, sketches, and reminiscences in *The Richer, the Poorer* in 1995. First Lady Hillary Clinton, at West's ninetieth birthday in Martha's Vineyard, West's home since the 1940s, called her "a real national treasure." A posthumous collection of her poems, stories, and essays, *Where the Wild Grape Grows: Selected Writings 1930–1950*, was published in 2004.

Bibliography

Ammons, Elizabeth. *Short Fiction by Black Women, 1900–1920.* New York: Oxford University Press, 1991.

Andrews, William L., ed. *Classic Fiction of the Harlem Renaissance.* New York: Oxford University Press, 1994.

———, ed. *The Oxford Companion to African American Literature.* New York: Oxford University Press, 1997.

Austin, Doris Jean, and Martin Simmons. *Streetlights: Illuminating Tales of the Black Urban Experience.* New York: Penguin, 1996.

Brown, Lois, ed. *Encyclopedia of the Harlem Literary Renaissance.* New York: Checkmark Books, 2006.

Chesnutt, Charles. *The Wife of His Youth, and Other Stories of the Color Line,* New York: Houghton, Mifflin, 1899.

Du Bois, W. E. B. *Darkwater: Voices from Within the Veil.* New York: Harcourt, Brace and Howe, 1920.

Dunbar, Paul Laurence. *The Heart of Happy Hollow.* New York: Dodd, Mead and Co., 1904.

Gates, Henry Louis, Jr. and Nellie Y. McKay, gen. eds. *The Norton Anthology of African American Literature.* New York: Norton, 1997.

Grable, Craig, ed. *Ebony Rising: Short Fiction of the Greater Harlem Renaissance Era.* Bloomington, Indiana: Indiana University Press, 2004.

Hughes, Langston. *The Best of Simple.* New York: Hill and Wang, 1961.

———, ed. *The Best Short Stories by Negro Writers.* Boston: Little, Brown and Co., 1969.

Hull, Gloria T. *Color, Sex, and Poetry: Three Women Writers of the Harlem Renaissance*. Bloomington: Indiana University Press, 1987.

Kaplan, Carla, ed. *Zora Neale Hurston: A Life in Letters*. New York: Doubleday-Random House, 2002.

Knopf, Marcy, ed. *The Sleeper Wakes: Harlem Renaissance Stories by Women*. New Brunswick: Rutgers University Press, 1993.

Lewis, David Levering, ed. *The Portable Harlem Renaissance Reader*. New York: Viking Penguin, 1994.

———. *W. E. B. Du Bois: Biography of a Race 1868–1919*. Vol. 1. New York: Henry Holt, 1993.

Musser, Judith, ed. *"Tell It to Us Easy" and Other Stories: A Complete Short Fiction Anthology of African American Women Writers in* Opportunity *Magazine (1923–1948)*. Jefferson, North Carolina: McFarland & Co. Inc., 2008.

Patton, Venetia K. and Maureen Honey, eds. *Double-Take: A Revisionist Harlem Renaissance Anthology*. New Brunswick: Rutgers University Press, 2001.

Rampersad, Arnold. *The Life of Langston Hughes, Volume 1: 1902–1941, I, Too, Sing America*. New York: Oxford University Press, 1988.

———. *The Life of Langston Hughes, Volume 2: 1941-1967, I Dream a World*. New York: Oxford University Press, 1989.

Roses, Lorraine Elena and Ruth Elizabeth Randolph, eds. *The Harlem Renaissance and Beyond: Literary Biographies of 100 Black Women Writers, 1900-1945*. Boston: G. K. Hall, 1990.

Scott, Anne. *George Sampson Brite*. Boston: Meador Publishing, 1939.

Walker, Alice, ed. *I Love Myself When I Am Laughing . . . and Then Again When I Am Looking Mean and Impressive: A Zora Neale Hurston Reader*. New York: The Feminist Press, 1979.

———. *In Search of Our Mothers' Gardens: Womanist Prose*. San Diego: Harcourt Brace Jovanovich, 1988.

Wall, Cheryl A. *Women of the Harlem Renaissance*. Bloomington: Indiana University Press, 1995.

Watson, Steven. *The Harlem Renaissance: Hub of African-American Culture, 1920–1930*. New York: Pantheon Books, 1995.

Wilson, Sondra Kathryn, ed. *The Crisis Reader: Stories, Poetry, and Essays from the N.A.A.C.P.'s Crisis Magazine*. New York: Modern Library, Random House, 1999.

————, ed. *The* Messenger *Reader: Stories, Poetry, and Essays from The* Messenger *Magazine.* New York: Modern Library, Random House, 2000.

————, ed. *The* Opportunity *Reader: Stories, Poetry, and Essays from the Urban League's* Opportunity *Magazine.* New York: Modern Library, Random House, 1999.

————, ed. *The* Crisis *Reader: Stories, Poetry, and Essays from the N.A.A.C.P.'s* Crisis *Magazine.* New York: Modern Library, Random House, 1999.

Yellin, Jean Fagan, and Cynthia D. Bond, eds. *The Pen Is Ours: A Listing of Writings by and about African-American Women before 1910 with Secondary Bibliography to the Present.* Schomburg Library of Nineteenth-Century Black Women Writers. New York: Oxford University Press, 1991.

DOVER · THRIFT · EDITIONS

POETRY

101 GREAT AMERICAN POEMS, Edited by The American Poetry & Literacy Project. (0-486-40158-8)

100 BEST-LOVED POEMS, Edited by Philip Smith. (0-486-28553-7)

ENGLISH ROMANTIC POETRY: An Anthology, Edited by Stanley Appelbaum. (0-486-29282-7)

THE INFERNO, Dante Alighieri. Translated and with notes by Henry Wadsworth Longfellow. (0-486-44288-8)

PARADISE LOST, John Milton. Introduction and Notes by John A. Himes. (0-486-44287-X)

SPOON RIVER ANTHOLOGY, Edgar Lee Masters. (0-486-27275-3)

SELECTED CANTERBURY TALES, Geoffrey Chaucer. (0-486-28241-4)

SELECTED POEMS, Emily Dickinson. (0-486-26466-1)

LEAVES OF GRASS: The Original 1855 Edition, Walt Whitman. (0-486-45676-5)

COMPLETE SONNETS, William Shakespeare. (0-486-26686-9)

THE RAVEN AND OTHER FAVORITE POEMS, Edgar Allan Poe. (0-486-26685-0)

ENGLISH VICTORIAN POETRY: An Anthology, Edited by Paul Negri. (0-486-40425-0)

SELECTED POEMS, Walt Whitman. (0-486-26878-0)

THE ROAD NOT TAKEN AND OTHER POEMS, Robert Frost. (0-486-27550-7)

AFRICAN-AMERICAN POETRY: An Anthology, 1773-1927, Edited by Joan R. Sherman. (0-486-29604-0)

GREAT SHORT POEMS, Edited by Paul Negri. (0-486-41105-2)

THE RIME OF THE ANCIENT MARINER, Samuel Taylor Coleridge. (0-486-27266-4)

THE WASTE LAND, PRUFROCK AND OTHER POEMS, T. S. Eliot. (0-486-40061-1)

SONG OF MYSELF, Walt Whitman. (0-486-41410-8)

AENEID, Vergil. (0-486-28749-1)

SONGS FOR THE OPEN ROAD: Poems of Travel and Adventure, Edited by The American Poetry & Literacy Project. (0-486-40646-6)

SONGS OF INNOCENCE AND SONGS OF EXPERIENCE, William Blake. (0-486-27051-3)

WORLD WAR ONE BRITISH POETS: Brooke, Owen, Sassoon, Rosenberg and Others, Edited by Candace Ward. (0-486-29568-0)

GREAT SONNETS, Edited by Paul Negri. (0-486-28052-7)

CHRISTMAS CAROLS: Complete Verses, Edited by Shane Weller. (0-486-27397-0)

DOVER · THRIFT · EDITIONS

POETRY

GREAT POEMS BY AMERICAN WOMEN: An Anthology, Edited by Susan L. Rattiner. (0-486-40164-2)

FAVORITE POEMS, Henry Wadsworth Longfellow. (0-486-27273-7)

BHAGAVADGITA, Translated by Sir Edwin Arnold. (0-486-27782-8)

ESSAY ON MAN AND OTHER POEMS, Alexander Pope. (0-486-28053-5)

GREAT LOVE POEMS, Edited by Shane Weller. (0-486-27284-2)

DOVER BEACH AND OTHER POEMS, Matthew Arnold. (0-486-28037-3)

THE SHOOTING OF DAN MCGREW AND OTHER POEMS, Robert Service. (0-486-27556-6)

THE BALLAD OF READING GAOL AND OTHER POEMS, Oscar Wilde. (0-486-27072-6)

SELECTED POEMS OF RUMI, Jalalu'l-Din Rumi. (0-486-41583-X)

SELECTED POEMS OF GERARD MANLEY HOPKINS, Gerard Manley Hopkins. Edited and with an Introduction by Bob Blaisdell. (0-486-47867-X)

RENASCENCE AND OTHER POEMS, Edna St. Vincent Millay. (0-486-26873-X)

THE RUBÁIYÁT OF OMAR KHAYYÁM: First and Fifth Editions, Edward FitzGerald. (0-486-26467-X)

TO MY HUSBAND AND OTHER POEMS, Anne Bradstreet. (0-486-41408-6)

LITTLE ORPHANT ANNIE AND OTHER POEMS, James Whitcomb Riley. (0-486-28260-0)

IMAGIST POETRY: AN ANTHOLOGY, Edited by Bob Blaisdell. (0-486-40875-2)

FIRST FIG AND OTHER POEMS, Edna St. Vincent Millay. (0-486-41104-4)

GREAT SHORT POEMS FROM ANTIQUITY TO THE TWENTIETH CENTURY, Edited by Dorothy Belle Pollack. (0-486-47876-9)

THE FLOWERS OF EVIL & PARIS SPLEEN: Selected Poems, Charles Baudelaire. Translated by Wallace Fowlie. (0-486-47545-X)

CIVIL WAR SHORT STORIES AND POEMS, Edited by Bob Blaisdell. (0-486-48226-X)

EARLY POEMS, Edna St. Vincent Millay. (0-486-43672-1)

JABBERWOCKY AND OTHER POEMS, Lewis Carroll. (0-486-41582-1)

THE METAMORPHOSES: Selected Stories in Verse, Ovid. (0-486-42758-7)

IDYLLS OF THE KING, Alfred, Lord Tennyson. Edited by W. J. Rolfe. (0-486-43795-7)

A BOY'S WILL AND NORTH OF BOSTON, Robert Frost. (0-486-26866-7)

100 FAVORITE ENGLISH AND IRISH POEMS, Edited by Clarence C. Strowbridge. (0-486-44429-5)

DOVER · THRIFT · EDITIONS

FICTION

FLATLAND: A ROMANCE OF MANY DIMENSIONS, Edwin A. Abbott.
  (0-486-27263-X)

PRIDE AND PREJUDICE, Jane Austen. (0-486-28473-5)

CIVIL WAR SHORT STORIES AND POEMS, Edited by Bob Blaisdell.
  (0-486-48226-X)

THE DECAMERON: Selected Tales, Giovanni Boccaccio. Edited by Bob Blaisdell. (0-486-41113-3)

JANE EYRE, Charlotte Brontë. (0-486-42449-9)

WUTHERING HEIGHTS, Emily Brontë. (0-486-29256-8)

THE THIRTY-NINE STEPS, John Buchan. (0-486-28201-5)

ALICE'S ADVENTURES IN WONDERLAND, Lewis Carroll. (0-486-27543-4)

MY ÁNTONIA, Willa Cather. (0-486-28240-6)

THE AWAKENING, Kate Chopin. (0-486-27786-0)

HEART OF DARKNESS, Joseph Conrad. (0-486-26464-5)

LORD JIM, Joseph Conrad. (0-486-40650-4)

THE RED BADGE OF COURAGE, Stephen Crane. (0-486-26465-3)

THE WORLD'S GREATEST SHORT STORIES, Edited by James Daley.
  (0-486-44716-2)

A CHRISTMAS CAROL, Charles Dickens. (0-486-26865-9)

GREAT EXPECTATIONS, Charles Dickens. (0-486-41586-4)

A TALE OF TWO CITIES, Charles Dickens. (0-486-40651-2)

CRIME AND PUNISHMENT, Fyodor Dostoyevsky. Translated by Constance
  Garnett. (0-486-41587-2)

THE ADVENTURES OF SHERLOCK HOLMES, Sir Arthur Conan Doyle.
  (0-486-47491-7)

THE HOUND OF THE BASKERVILLES, Sir Arthur Conan Doyle. (0-486-28214-7)

BLAKE: PROPHET AGAINST EMPIRE, David V. Erdman. (0-486-26719-9)

WHERE ANGELS FEAR TO TREAD, E. M. Forster. (0-486-27791-7)

BEOWULF, Translated by R. K. Gordon. (0-486-27264-8)

THE RETURN OF THE NATIVE, Thomas Hardy. (0-486-43165-7)

THE SCARLET LETTER, Nathaniel Hawthorne. (0-486-28048-9)

SIDDHARTHA, Hermann Hesse. (0-486-40653-9)

THE ODYSSEY, Homer. (0-486-40654-7)

THE TURN OF THE SCREW, Henry James. (0-486-26684-2)

DUBLINERS, James Joyce. (0-486-26870-5)

DOVER · THRIFT · EDITIONS

FICTION

THE METAMORPHOSIS AND OTHER STORIES, Franz Kafka. (0-486-29030-1)

SONS AND LOVERS, D. H. Lawrence. (0-486-42121-X)

THE CALL OF THE WILD, Jack London. (0-486-26472-6)

SHAKESPEARE ILLUSTRATED: Art by Arthur Rackham, Edmund Dulac, Charles Robinson and Others, Selected and Edited by Jeff A. Menges. (0-486-47890-4)

GREAT AMERICAN SHORT STORIES, Edited by Paul Negri. (0-486-42119-8)

THE GOLD-BUG AND OTHER TALES, Edgar Allan Poe. (0-486-26875-6)

ANTHEM, Ayn Rand. (0-486-49277-X)

FRANKENSTEIN, Mary Shelley. (0-486-28211-2)

THE JUNGLE, Upton Sinclair. (0-486-41923-1)

THREE LIVES, Gertrude Stein. (0-486-28059-4)

THE STRANGE CASE OF DR. JEKYLL AND MR. HYDE, Robert Louis Stevenson. (0-486-26688-5)

DRACULA, Bram Stoker. (0-486-41109-5)

UNCLE TOM'S CABIN, Harriet Beecher Stowe. (0-486-44028-1)

ADVENTURES OF HUCKLEBERRY FINN, Mark Twain. (0-486-28061-6)

THE ADVENTURES OF TOM SAWYER, Mark Twain. (0-486-40077-8)

CANDIDE, Voltaire. Edited by Francois-Marie Arouet. (0-486-26689-3)

THE COUNTRY OF THE BLIND: and Other Science-Fiction Stories, H. G. Wells. Edited by Martin Gardner. (0-486-48289-8)

THE WAR OF THE WORLDS, H. G. Wells. (0-486-29506-0)

ETHAN FROME, Edith Wharton. (0-486-26690-7)

THE PICTURE OF DORIAN GRAY, Oscar Wilde. (0-486-27807-7)

MONDAY OR TUESDAY: Eight Stories, Virginia Woolf. (0-486-29453-6)

DOVER·THRIFT·EDITIONS

NONFICTION

POETICS, Aristotle. (0-486-29577-X)

MEDITATIONS, Marcus Aurelius. (0-486-29823-X)

THE WAY OF PERFECTION, St. Teresa of Avila. Edited and Translated by
E. Allison Peers. (0-486-48451-3)

THE DEVIL'S DICTIONARY, Ambrose Bierce. (0-486-27542-6)

GREAT SPEECHES OF THE 20TH CENTURY, Edited by Bob Blaisdell.
(0-486-47467-4)

THE COMMUNIST MANIFESTO AND OTHER REVOLUTIONARY WRITINGS:
Marx, Marat, Paine, Mao Tse-Tung, Gandhi and Others, Edited by Bob Blaisdell.
(0-486-42465-0)

INFAMOUS SPEECHES: From Robespierre to Osama bin Laden, Edited by Bob
Blaisdell. (0-486-47849-1)

GREAT ENGLISH ESSAYS: From Bacon to Chesterton, Edited by Bob Blaisdell.
(0-486-44082-6)

GREEK AND ROMAN ORATORY, Edited by Bob Blaisdell. (0-486-49622-8)

THE UNITED STATES CONSTITUTION: The Full Text with Supplementary
Materials, Edited and with supplementary materials by Bob Blaisdell.
(0-486-47166-7)

GREAT SPEECHES BY NATIVE AMERICANS, Edited by Bob Blaisdell.
(0-486-41122-2)

GREAT SPEECHES BY AFRICAN AMERICANS: Frederick Douglass, Sojourner
Truth, Dr. Martin Luther King, Jr., Barack Obama, and Others, Edited by
James Daley. (0-486-44761-8)

GREAT SPEECHES BY AMERICAN WOMEN, Edited by James Daley.
(0-486-46141-6)

HISTORY'S GREATEST SPEECHES, Edited by James Daley. (0-486-49739-9)

GREAT INAUGURAL ADDRESSES, Edited by James Daley. (0-486-44577-1)

GREAT SPEECHES ON GAY RIGHTS, Edited by James Daley. (0-486-47512-3)

ON THE ORIGIN OF SPECIES: By Means of Natural Selection, Charles Darwin.
(0-486-45006-6)

NARRATIVE OF THE LIFE OF FREDERICK DOUGLASS, Frederick Douglass.
(0-486-28499-9)

THE SOULS OF BLACK FOLK, W. E. B. Du Bois. (0-486-28041-1)

NATURE AND OTHER ESSAYS, Ralph Waldo Emerson. (0-486-46947-6)

SELF-RELIANCE AND OTHER ESSAYS, Ralph Waldo Emerson. (0-486-27790-9)

THE LIFE OF OLAUDAH EQUIANO, Olaudah Equiano. (0-486-40661-X)

WIT AND WISDOM FROM POOR RICHARD'S ALMANACK, Benjamin Franklin.
(0-486-40891-4)

THE AUTOBIOGRAPHY OF BENJAMIN FRANKLIN, Benjamin Franklin.
(0-486-29073-5)

DOVER · THRIFT · EDITIONS

NONFICTION

DOVER·THRIFT·EDITIONS

PLAYS

THE ORESTEIA TRILOGY: Agamemnon, the Libation-Bearers and the Furies, Aeschylus. (0-486-29242-8)

EVERYMAN, Anonymous. (0-486-28726-2)

THE BIRDS, Aristophanes. (0-486-40886-8)

LYSISTRATA, Aristophanes. (0-486-28225-2)

THE CHERRY ORCHARD, Anton Chekhov. (0-486-26682-6)

THE SEA GULL, Anton Chekhov. (0-486-40656-3)

MEDEA, Euripides. (0-486-27548-5)

FAUST, PART ONE, Johann Wolfgang von Goethe. (0-486-28046-2)

THE INSPECTOR GENERAL, Nikolai Gogol. (0-486-28500-6)

SHE STOOPS TO CONQUER, Oliver Goldsmith. (0-486-26867-5)

GHOSTS, Henrik Ibsen. (0-486-29852-3)

A DOLL'S HOUSE, Henrik Ibsen. (0-486-27062-9)

HEDDA GABLER, Henrik Ibsen. (0-486-26469-6)

DR. FAUSTUS, Christopher Marlowe. (0-486-28208-2)

TARTUFFE, Molière. (0-486-41117-6)

BEYOND THE HORIZON, Eugene O'Neill. (0-486-29085-9)

THE EMPEROR JONES, Eugene O'Neill. (0-486-29268-1)

CYRANO DE BERGERAC, Edmond Rostand. (0-486-41119-2)

MEASURE FOR MEASURE: Unabridged, William Shakespeare. (0-486-40889-2)

FOUR GREAT TRAGEDIES: Hamlet, Macbeth, Othello, and Romeo and Juliet, William Shakespeare. (0-486-44083-4)

THE COMEDY OF ERRORS, William Shakespeare. (0-486-42461-8)

HENRY V, William Shakespeare. (0-486-42887-7)

MUCH ADO ABOUT NOTHING, William Shakespeare. (0-486-28272-4)

FIVE GREAT COMEDIES: Much Ado About Nothing, Twelfth Night, A Midsummer Night's Dream, As You Like It and The Merry Wives of Windsor, William Shakespeare. (0-486-44086-9)

OTHELLO, William Shakespeare. (0-486-29097-2)

AS YOU LIKE IT, William Shakespeare. (0-486-40432-3)

ROMEO AND JULIET, William Shakespeare. (0-486-27557-4)

A MIDSUMMER NIGHT'S DREAM, William Shakespeare. (0-486-27067-X)

THE MERCHANT OF VENICE, William Shakespeare. (0-486-28492-1)

HAMLET, William Shakespeare. (0-486-27278-8)

RICHARD III, William Shakespeare. (0-486-28747-5)

DOVER·THRIFT·EDITIONS

PLAYS